D1006117

THE ORPHANS
OF
MERSEA HOUSE

THE ORPHANS OF MERSEA HOUSE

A NOVEL

Marty Wingate

alcove
press

Copyright © 2022 by Marty Wingate

All rights reserved.

Published in the United States by Alcove Press, an imprint of The Quick Brown Fox & Company LLC.

Alcove Press and its logo are trademarks of The Quick Brown Fox & Company LLC.

Library of Congress Catalog-in-Publication data available upon request.

ISBN (hardcover): 978-1-63910-088-0
ISBN (ebook): 978-1-63910-089-7

Cover design by Lynn Andreozzi

Printed in the United States.

www.alcovepress.com

Alcove Press
34 West 27th St., 10th Floor
New York, NY 10001

First Edition: July 2022

10 9 8 7 6 5 4 3 2 1

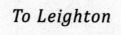

To Leighton

CHAPTER 1

Southwold, Suffolk
March 1957

Olive held the nightdress up to the sunlight that streamed through the east window in her mother's room, and admired the handiwork. Its pin-tuck pleating on the bodice had never puckered, and the scroll embroidery along the low neck and up the straps lay flat. It looked as perfect as the day, years ago, it had been wrapped in tissue and put away. Olive brushed the cotton-lawn fabric against her cheek, felt its softness, and caught a scent like dried sweet hay, acquired from the sachet deep in the drawer. The garment had been a gift to Daisy, her mother, from . . . whom? An old aunt, as Olive recalled. "You keep it for yourself, Olive," Daisy had said. "It's better suited to a young woman."

The nightdress suffered from the "too-pretty-to-wear" ailment and had been put safely away. Now, Olive, no longer young, refolded the garment, wrapped it in its tissue, and laid it in the case she was filling with a few treasures. Her other case would hold everything else she owned—practical, everyday clothes and a second pair of shoes. Anything left would be for the church's jumble sale or the rag-bag. The sum total of Olive Kersey's life. She sighed and then huffed, blowing away a cloud of useless self-pity.

A rap at the door prompted Olive to glance out the window to the doorstep below. She left her sorting and hurried downstairs to answer.

"Good morning, Miss Binny," she said.

Constance Binny adjusted her several shawls, and the pheasant tail feather that curled round her hat bobbed a greeting. "Good morning to you, Olive," she said and smiled, accentuating her sharp features. "Poor dear girl, I've been that worried about you these last two weeks since your mother's funeral. I've not heard a word and thought I'd better look in."

"That's kind of you," Olive replied, knowing that Miss Binny's appearance meant she either had town gossip to impart or needed a fresh supply of news to pass along to others about Poor Dear Olive, who had been left with nothing and no one. "Would you like coffee? I was just about to have some myself."

"Yes, that would be lovely."

They went to the kitchen, the only warm spot in the house. Olive filled the percolator and set it on the hob—Miss Binny wouldn't drink Nescafé—and put a pan of milk on to heat. Olive had bought half a seedcake at the bakery the day before against this inevitable visit and had put it away in the bread bin, hoping it wouldn't dry out too quickly.

Settled at the table, Binny started in on the news. It flowed in a continuous stream: the shortcomings of Tom, husband of Hetty Dupree who ran the tea hut at the seaside; the rumor that a chambermaid had been dismissed from The Swan Hotel under suspicious circumstances; and the sad display of altar flowers in church the previous Sunday. Olive barely listened.

Constance Binny had made a life of being in other people's lives, including the Kerseys'. As Daisy's health failed, Binny had taken it upon herself to look in regularly. Olive's mother had been bedridden, weak, and in pain, but she had been one of those women who remained pleasant and cheerful despite their circumstances, and so she had always acted happy to see her visitor. When Olive would take the coffee tray upstairs for the two women, her mother would wave her off. "Connie will catch me up on things," Daisy would say. "You go on now." And for an hour, Olive would escape, walking a wide circuit along the seafront to the mouth of the Blyth, breathing in the salt air and not caring if the north wind was pushing her along or driving her back.

In one of Daisy's less lucid moments not long before she died, she'd referred to Binny as *"that wittering witch."* It was only then the penny had dropped: all that time, Daisy had put up with the visits and never complained so that Olive could have a brief respite from the sickroom and its duties. That had been her mother's way—little kindnesses given freely throughout her life.

"I'm quite concerned about you," Miss Binny said to Olive. "If only Donald had made it through the war, he would be happily married now and could take care of you."

Olive knew that her brother, who had died at Dunkirk, would certainly have taken care of her, but she thought the possibility that he would be happily married was remote.

"It was his way, wasn't it?" Binny asked. "He was such a good boy. But now, Olive, what will you do with yourself?"

"Not to worry."

Olive didn't take her own advice. She had worried every minute of every day the last few months until the worry had woven itself into the fabric of her being. Three pounds, four and six in her post office account, and no prospects to speak of. All her worldly possessions could fit in those two cases upstairs. She, Donald, and their parents had lived in the terrace house Olive's entire life, but they had only rented, never owned. Olive couldn't even count the kettle or the dishes and saucepans as possessions. Not any longer, at least. She'd traded the lot to pay one more month's rent, and the clock was ticking.

"Have you found a position?" Miss Binny inquired.

That she must find paid work was quite clear to Olive, but what sort? She knew her limitations. At thirty-seven years old, she had experience in keeping house and looking after someone, and so she had aimed high, setting her sights on becoming companion to a young woman. Some well-to-do families believed their daughters were safer with an older woman employed to keep an eye on things. Surely Olive qualified for that. But nothing had come of the four newspaper advertisements she'd answered—one as far away as Carlisle. She then lowered her expectations. If not a young woman, Olive could be the younger companion to someone older than herself. And if not a companion, a housekeeper. If not a housekeeper . . . was she too old for factory work?

"I've received some encouragement," Olive replied as she stood and turned to the cooker to hide her red cheeks. "Would you like more coffee?"

"Yes, thank you."

Olive poured, replenished the hot milk, and sat down again.

"I do hope this will work out for you, dear, but it must be difficult, as you have no previous position and therefore no references." Miss Binny leaned over the table and in a conspiratorial tone said, "I might have a solution for you. I might just. You remember, Olive, I had a young cousin with me three years ago. She needed to be away from her family, and I was happy to offer her shelter and guidance."

Olive remembered a scared-looking girl who had lived with Binny for six or eight months. She cooked, she cleaned, she scurried after the woman round town, and at last, she had gone back to her family. Olive had said goodbye to her and wished her well. It might've been the only time she'd seen the girl smile.

"I do remember her, yes. Isn't she married now?"

"She is," Binny said, voicing a wealth of disapproval with only two words. "But you see, Olive, in only that short time, I realized how much good I could do by taking someone in who may need help. In exchange for company and the odd household chore."

A cold, creeping dread came over Olive as Binny continued to describe a scene that might've come out of a Charles Dickens story: desperate and destitute girl taken in by—in this case—an overbearing, rigid woman who seemed bent on distorting the qualities of Christian charity. Before her very eyes, Constance Binny grew in size until Olive's vision was filled with a beaky nose, a bobbing pheasant tail, and a mouth that wouldn't stop.

". . . and I feel I owe it to your mother, you know, to look after you."

Olive took a sharp breath and came to herself. She saw her hands clutching at the edge of the table, her knuckles white. She carefully let go as she said, "That's so kind of you, Miss Binny, but as I have already entered into negotiations about another post, I couldn't possibly back out now."

"Oh." The feather quivered. "So, you have had an actual offer?"

"Until the details are in order, I'd rather not say anything. I'm sure you understand." She offered a warm smile.

Miss Binny smiled in return. "There, Olive—now you look more like your cheerful self. I'm quite happy for you, my dear. But you will let me know how it turns out."

"I certainly will." After her narrow escape, Olive could breathe again. Perhaps factory work wouldn't be too bad after all.

As soon as her guest had departed, Olive pulled on her Norfolk jacket, tied a headscarf under her chin, and went out for a walk. She took her usual circuit, but counterclockwise today, making for the water tower and out to Blackshore Quay. There, she turned east, crunching on the gravel as she passed the fishing shacks. The gray skies were spitting rain, but she paid the weather no mind, heading north up Ferry Road and veering off at Gun Hill. Now, with the sea on her right and town on her left, she continued up the Parade, giving Hetty a wave as she passed the tea hut. Before she reached the pier, Olive turned one last time, up Field Stile Road and back to the house. She was pulling out her key when she heard her name called.

Olive looked over her shoulder to see a woman dressed in a rose-colored, tailored suit and no hat to cover her curly bob. She was breathing heavily and put a hand out on the low front wall to brace herself.

"I've been chasing you since you turned off North Parade," she said. "God, I'd forgotten you walk like you're running a race."

It was as if the fifteen years since they'd seen each other vanished in a second.

"Margery Paxton," Olive said with one hand on a hip, "you couldn't keep up with a snail wearing those shoes, could you?" She nodded at Margery's high heels.

Margery laughed. "I'm not made for those cobweb-clearing jaunts of yours," she said. "I never was. How are you, Olive?"

Olive nodded but didn't speak. It's a dangerous place, the junction of happiness and grief—too easy for those tears, so near the surface, to suddenly tumble out. Margery stepped forward, and the women met on the pavement and exchanged a warm embrace. Olive smiled and then laughed and brushed a hand over her wet cheek.

"I'm awfully sorry about your mum," Margery said. "And that I couldn't make it back for her funeral."

"It's all right. You'd been in town just before that, hadn't you, because of Uncle Milkey. I'm sorry he's gone."

No funeral had been held for Milkey Paxton. He had been a proud unbeliever, attending neither church nor chapel, and had specifically requested no "hocus-pocus" after he died. Instead, he'd arranged to stand his friends and associates a pint of Adnams's best bitter at the Lord Nelson when he was gone. Not only friends and associates, but also a good few hangers-on had happily taken him up on his offer.

"It was a flying visit to sort things out," Margery said, "although there's still a great deal to do."

"Well, it can't be easy to get away from your job in London, I suppose."

Margery frowned at that.

"Come in," Olive said, opening the door. "Have you had lunch? I'll put the kettle on."

In the entry, she untied her scarf, but before she could take off her coat, Margery took hold of the material and held it out and away from Olive's body. "You're swimming in this."

Olive hugged the coat round her. "It was Donald's—a good Norfolk jacket and quite warm. I couldn't let it go. All I had to do was turn up the cuffs."

Margery smiled. She said nothing about the age of the jacket or the thriftiness of its current owner. "Your brother was a good few inches taller. His jacket's turned into your coat."

When Olive had shed the coat and hung it on a peg, Margery clicked her tongue. "The coat's not the only thing too big on you."

Olive looked down at the cardigan that hung loosely over her dress, which fit about as well as a flour sack might. She crossed her arms. "I suppose I should take it in."

"I don't think that's the point," Margery said. "The point is, you haven't been eating."

Olive couldn't argue, but the reason, which she suspected Margery knew, was that there hadn't been a great deal to eat of late. But she wasn't looking for sympathy. Olive led the way into the kitchen and set the kettle on the hob. "I haven't shopped today—you wouldn't mind potted meat for a sandwich, would you?"

"Should we wrap them up and carry them down to the beach as we used to?" Margery asked, taking cups and saucers down off the shelf.

Olive laughed. "I wonder how much sand we ate growing up. We should stay here. It's raining out." She sliced the last of the loaf, opened the tin of meat, and spread a lavish amount on the bread. She would have an egg for her tea later.

"Have you had company?" Margery asked, looking at the empty coffee things.

"Constance Binny."

"Oh dear"—Margery wrinkled her nose—"Busy Binny. What news did she bring?"

"Noting of note. So, are you selling up?" Olive asked as they tucked into their sandwiches. Margery, Milkey Paxton's only living relative, had inherited not only his money, but also his shop, Paxton's Goods, and Mersea House, the large red-brick edifice with Portland stone trimming that sat on the west side of South Green. But Margery's life had been in London since the beginning of the war, and the consensus in Southwold was that house and shop would soon have new owners.

"Young Trotter asked me the same thing this morning," Margery said.

Although Uncle Milkey had stayed sharp in mind and business acumen until his end at age eighty-eight, he had grown frail in body, and Young Trotter had been his right-hand man in the shop. But

Young Trotter knew no more about the fate of the business than anyone else in town.

Margery took a large bite of her sandwich, precluding any other discussion for a few moments. When she swallowed, she asked, "What will you do now?"

If Margery wouldn't give a straight answer, then Olive didn't see why she should.

"I'm quite torn between governess to Princess Anne and house-keeping at Butlin's Holiday Camp in Skegness."

"Oh, Skegness—just up the road, then." Margery grinned, but she also narrowed her eyes at Olive, who looked away. Finished with her sandwich, Margery searched in her handbag and came up with a cigarette case and lighter. "Fag?" she asked, then shook her head. "No, you don't smoke." She lit up her own and sat back. "It's odd to think that with your mum and Uncle Milkey passing, they're all gone now. Neither of us with any family to speak of."

"Your Uncle Milkey and Auntie Von were good to you, weren't they?" Olive asked.

"The best," Margery said. "There they were fifty years old and childless, but they never thought twice about taking an orphaned baby in. I wasn't even a year old. It must've been a bit of a shock to them, but they never said."

"It's hard to believe it's been so many years since your Auntie Von died."

"And your dad at the end of the war. Uncle Milkey said he was a shattered man after Donald was killed."

Olive nodded. Her brother's death had precipitated their father's long, slow road to his own demise. "Officially, it was Dad's lungs that got him in the end—from the mustard gas in 1917."

"I'm sorry you and I didn't keep up," Margery said. "I came back so seldom, just flying visits to Uncle Milkey. I should've written."

"I should've too," Olive said. "It's just the way of things. But it's very good to see you now, even if it is a flying visit. I don't suppose there's time to catch each other up on everything." Although a summary of the past fifteen years of Olive's life wouldn't take long.

"Let's see," Margery said, "you had a beau at the start of the war."

"Stan." She hadn't said his name aloud in such a long time that it felt strange on her tongue, and without warning, a door in Olive's heart creaked open. She slammed it shut. "Just a fellow I met at the dance hall. He was killed early on." She felt Margery's eyes on her and sought a deflection. "But you—you and George."

Margery flicked ash into her plate. "George and I were finished before the war. Went our separate ways."

"And you took off for London."

"I went to London to do my bit," Margery said. "I got on as a secretary at the Ministry of Information, and the sum total of my war effort was typing leaflets about raising cabbage."

"But you stayed on. London must be exciting."

"I suppose," Margery replied. She stood. "I must dash. Look, Olive, you won't up and leave, will you? Not without telling me?"

"No, I won't," Olive said, obeying without question, just as she always had. The thought made her smile. "How will I reach you?"

"Well, I may look in again soon. Or you can leave a message with Young Trotter at the shop. All right?"

Margery left. Olive remained in the kitchen, sitting quietly and thinking of the past. She missed that boy from the dance hall, who had been more to her than she could now admit. She missed her brother, gone all these years. She missed her mother, gone a fortnight. And now, after this brief reminder, she missed Margery and their friendship.

Little good such sentimentality would do her. That's what life had taught Olive—that it was better to just get on with it.

★ ★ ★

That afternoon, Olive posted a letter to Butlin's inquiring after a housekeeping position. Skegness in Lincolnshire seemed like another world, and a holiday camp would be only seasonal work, but it would see her through September, at any rate. She dropped the letter in the pillar box, hoping it wasn't another threepenny stamp wasted. Then, she took a carton of clothes to Mrs. Tees, who ran the jumble sales at

St. Edmund's Church and who tried to press on Olive a dress from a recent generous donation.

"We'll call it an exchange, why don't we?" the woman asked, holding up a quite-reasonable day dress in a purple-and-cream plaid. It had a matching fabric belt, a full skirt, and buttons all the way down the front. Olive admired it, told Mrs. Tees she would keep an eye out for it at the next sale, and left with her head held high. She was not in need of charity. Yet.

Two nights later, she had a restless sleep as Constance Binny walked in and out of her dreams. Olive could see herself as if from a distance, scurrying after the woman across South Green and, over countless cups of coffee, listening to her litany of woes concerning the town's more wayward sorts. She awoke in the dark with a gasp, sweating, and then lay back with relief to know she was still in her own bed.

The following morning, a letter came from Butlin's, offering her a housekeeping job if she would also take on nursery duty two afternoons a week for parents who needed a holiday from their holiday. For a moment, Olive was so overwhelmed with relief that she considered going down to the phone box at the corner and ringing Butlin's to say she'd take it, housekeeping, childminding, and all. But the thought of leaving home—not just the house, but the town and everyone she had ever known—made her feel lightheaded. Instead, she folded the letter and put it in her pocket, taking it out several times during the day to read over.

Constance Binny hadn't called again—either that, or Olive had timed her walks perfectly. But her luck seemed to have run out when a rap came at the door that afternoon. Olive considered her options as she stood at the sink washing clothes, her hands in soapy hot water up to her elbows. Would Binny's visit push Olive into making a choice—holiday-camp housekeeper and childminder in some far-flung place or companion to an odious woman? Perhaps Olive could ignore the visitor and buy herself time before she had to choose between the devil and the deep blue sea. But the rapping started again—longer, insistent.

"Yes, yes," Olive muttered, heading to the entry. With wet hands, she pushed back the stray locks that had fallen onto her face, tucking them into her French braid. She dried her arms off on her pinny and pulled open the door.

Margery stood on the doorstep with her hands behind her back as if she were at school and about to recite a poem.

Olive should've been happy to see her old friend again so soon, but instead she took Margery's appearance as bad news. *She must've sold the shop already. And perhaps the house, too. She's come to say a final goodbye.*

"I'm like a bad penny," Margery said. "Even so, you'll let me in, won't you?"

"Sorry," Olive said, opening the door wide. "Yes, come in. You've found me at my best, doing the washing. Go through to the kitchen."

Olive followed Margery, who had brought with her the scent of sugar and butter. When she stopped on the far side of the table, she held out a grease-spotted paper bag.

"What have you got there?" Olive asked.

"Can't you guess?"

Olive couldn't take her eyes from the bag. "Butter buns?" she whispered.

"The very thing," Margery confirmed. "I was walking past Dawson's on the way and saw them, fresh. I can't remember the last time I had one. What do you say?"

For a moment, Olive, her mouth watering, could say nothing. She swallowed. "Oh yes."

They sat at the table, and Margery tore into the paper bag, revealing two fat buns coated in a sugar glaze. Without a word, the women each grabbed one. Olive took her first bite and sighed. Some childhood favorites, revisited as an adult, can never be as good, but she thought this butter bun might've been the best she'd ever eaten.

About halfway through, Margery licked a finger and said, "Do you remember how we'd do this every Wednesday?"

"A penny a bun," Olive said.

"That was quite dear when we were eight years old."

"Just as well, or we would've eaten them every day," Olive said. "Do you remember the time we almost lost them to the sea?"

Margery laughed. "That's right—we took them down to that place on the other side of the pier and a gull made a dive for mine, and you drove him off and almost dropped your bun doing it."

"A near tragedy narrowly averted," Olive said. "Although my mum didn't think so when she saw the state of my dress."

Olive washed her sticky fingers, put the kettle on, and passed the damp cloth to Margery, who wiped her hands and then lit a cigarette. The clothes had had a good long soak, and Olive wrung them out—a dress, a blouse, knickers, and a pair of thick stockings. The kettle boiled and she poured up the tea, set it on the table, and returned to her task, hanging the laundry on the wooden drying bars above the cooker. There was silence between the two women, the comfortable sort that comes from knowing someone for so long.

When she sat down again, Olive took the letter out of her pocket and slid it across the table. "I've had an offer of a job. I'm afraid it isn't Princess Anne," she said as she poured their tea.

"So, Skegness, is it?" Margery read over the letter as she stirred milk into her cup. "What if you could stay here"—she glanced at their surroundings—"well, not here exactly, but in Southwold. What if you could find work in town?"

"What if I could find buried treasure on the beach instead of an unexploded bomb?" Olive asked indignantly. It was obvious Margery didn't see the gravity of her situation. "That would take care of everything."

"Only if Errol Flynn came with the buried treasure," Margery said.

Olive laughed despite herself. "Oh, Captain Blood—where are you when I need you?" She grew quiet and solemn and added, "Constance Binny is looking for a companion."

"Oh, Olive, you can't."

"Well, I've got to do something," Olive said.

"Come work for me."

CHAPTER 2

Olive's brow furrowed. She stared at Margery and saw that this was no jest. "Work for you in London?"

"I'm leaving London," Margery said, as if reading a proclamation. "I'm tired of the place, if you must know. I'm coming home, and I'm going to run the shop. And what's more, I'm converting Mersea House and will take in permanent paying guests."

At first, Olive was too shocked to speak. But she sensed something in the air—something as enticing as butter buns.

"Haven't you been happy in London?" she asked.

"I couldn't let Uncle Milkey's generosity go for naught—sell everything off to a stranger. How could I do that?"

"Won't you miss it?" Olive persisted. "London. Your friends there."

Margery didn't look at her as she replied, "I daresay I'll get over it."

Olive knew better than to press when Margery was so filled with conviction. She would need to wait for the details.

"Does anyone here know of your plans?"

"One or two, but you know that's all it takes for the entire town to find out in short order. I've already been advised that it isn't my place to own a business and that I should have more common sense than to think I could."

"Oh dear." Olive swallowed a snigger. "I'd say they regretted telling you that."

"If they haven't yet, they will," Margery said with one arched eyebrow and a firm smile. "So, what do you think?"

What did she think? That she'd been thrown a lifeline, that's what. Olive felt a trembling in her breast, but she held her emotions in check because she could see Margery wasn't in the mood for that sort of response. "I think it's marvelous," she said. "What do you want from me?"

"I want you to run the boardinghouse. We'll have five rooms to let after you choose yours and I have mine. I'll move out of my old room and take Uncle Milkey's on the ground floor—once it's redecorated. Your job will be to manage the paying guests while I run the shop."

Cooking and cleaning, running a household—Olive had those skills in spades. And it wouldn't be for Constance Binny. "I'll do it."

"Right." Margery slapped a hand on the table and stood. "I'm away back to London this evening, but I'll return on Monday. We've a few things to get in order."

"Do we?" Olive asked, following her out the front door. "What?"

"Just you be ready," Margery called over her shoulder.

As Olive watched her hurry down the road, the front window next door opened and an older woman leaned out.

"'Afternoon, Olive."

"Hello, Helen."

"Was that Margery Paxton?"

"Yes, it was."

"I hear she's come back to run Milkey's shop and take in lodgers."

"That's right," Olive said. She threw her shoulders back. "And I'm going to work for her."

"I wish you luck."

★   ★   ★

The "few things" to which Margery had referred took a fortnight and a great many workers. The shop closed, and while men tore out aging shelving and rickety counters, Margery sorted through old stock and pored over catalogs of merchandise: the latest in electric steam irons, home hair dryers with plastic bonnets, and French table linens. Let suppliers balk at taking orders from a woman, and she would inform them that if they didn't want her business, she would go elsewhere.

At Mersea House, Margery had arranged and scheduled the work, but beyond that, she left decisions up to Olive, who found herself beset with questions about everything from furniture placement to paint color. She telephoned Margery so often the first few days that finally Margery said, "You choose, Olive. I trust you."

Olive was nearly immobilized by this power until one of the workers showed her a dark, dour tartan for the window covering in her own room.

"No, I want a floral, but not that one with the blue roses—whoever heard of such a thing? I want the honeysuckle."

Having thus broken the ice, Olive had no further trouble making decisions, and Margery, looking over the work when she arrived back at Mersea House, was always pleased.

Every day, Olive took two pints of milk from the doorstep and made pots and pots of tea for the workers, boiling the kettle on a spirit lamp in the lounge until the kitchen had been put back together. As rooms were refurbished, the first- and second-floor landings became populated with old lamps that needed new switches, curtains faded from the sun, rugs worn thin, and chairs with broken legs. Margery told Olive to put it all in the room across from hers on the ground floor.

"Uncle Milkey was never much of a one for a clear-out," she said. "We'll deal with it later."

As fast as Olive set aside old things, new household items arrived. One morning, she was upstairs handing out tea when she heard a call of "Mersea House?" and went down to meet a man in coveralls, standing at the open door.

"Miss Paxton?" he asked.

"No," Olive said, "I'm not Miss Paxton. Are you delivering?"

"Yes, ma'am. Twin-tub electric washer."

"You'd best go round to the kitchen door."

It was all part of Margery's idea to modernize. There was the new cooker, new fridge, a Hoover, and now this washing machine. She had stopped short of one of those flash, fitted kitchens, but still, her extravagance, as far as Olive was concerned, was breathtaking.

The electric Hoover vacuum cleaner seemed a particularly unnecessary luxury. Olive had always made do with a carpet sweeper or a brush and dustpan and would've done now, but Margery had insisted. "Housekeeping has come out of the dark ages," she had said. "You'll enjoy hoovering."

Olive was dubious, although she had put up no fuss over the washing machine. She was quite looking forward to the magic that would keep her arms out of hot, soapy water.

But electric fires in every bedroom?

"They're only one-bar heaters," Margery explained. "They'll barely take the chill off the room."

Still, Olive didn't see the point when a hot-water bottle in bed would do.

Throughout the fortnight, Olive returned to sleep at the house on Field Stile Road, but when work at Mersea House had finished, the day came for her to make the move. She took her two cases over early and then headed back to her family's home one last time. As she made her way up the North Parade, the icy north wind off the sea stung her eyes, bit her cheeks, and tugged at the headscarf knotted under her chin, but she paid no mind. When she neared the tea hut, the hatch was pushed open from the inside, revealing a round face as worn as the weather-beaten timber.

"All right there, Olive?"

"Yes, Hetty."

"Lovely weather for March."

"Good for the fish," Olive replied automatically, pausing with her hands in her coat pockets.

"Shame we don't have the herring like we used to. Shall I send my Tom to help you move?"

"No thank you, Hetty. This is my last trip, and I'll be finished."

"Ever so lucky for you, wasn't it, that old Milkey Paxton died and left the house and the shop to Margery and her needing a housekeeper, and there you were with your mum only just dying and with nothing else to do with your time?"

"Yes, lucky for me," Olive said as Hetty took a breath. "Well, I'd best push on." It was either that or be blown backward. Further up the parade, Olive turned away from the sea and wended her way, until she stopped on the pavement outside number fourteen. She dipped in her pocket and in one swift movement, marched up the walk to the door and dropped the key through the letter box. The clank as it hit the entry floor carried a note of finality to it.

As she walked away, a voice called from next door, "Be seeing you, Olive."

"Yes, Helen, be seeing you."

Olive walked back through town along the High Street and glanced across the road to Paxton's Goods. The sign in the window read "Undergoing Refurbishment," but the heavy work had finished, and Margery had started on a new window display, the first time that had happened since the war had ended twelve years earlier. She said it was to keep people interested—as if she wasn't already the talk of the town. She hadn't covered the windows, which gave anyone passing by tantalizing glimpses of the latest coffeepots and electric mixers. The grand reopening had been set for Saturday, in five days' time, and a notice had already appeared in the local advertiser.

At Market Place, Olive veered off into Queen Street and made her way to South Green and Mersea House. In the entry, she listened to the silence. She would teach herself to judge the tenor of the house just as she had always done growing up on Field Stile Road. Even as she had watched the renovation, a tiny part of her had held on to the fear that it wasn't real or it wouldn't last, but now look—here she was. She had a home and work, and that was enough. It would have to be, wouldn't it?

Olive collected the post from where it had landed on the rug, set it next to the telephone on the half-moon table, and noticed a parcel wrapped in brown paper with her name on it. She carried it to the kitchen and cut the twine with a knife. It was a book—that was obvious—but she let out a small gasp of delight when she saw the title: *The Constance Spry Cookery Book*. Olive began leafing through the pages and got quite lost among rissoles and potage and brioches. The telephone rang and she jumped. She was yet to become accustomed to a telephone in the house, and the shrill tone startled her.

"Mersea House."

"You found your parcel?" Margery asked.

"I did," Olive said. "It's lovely—thanks so much."

"You can impress us now with your skills."

"I might do a chicken curry," Olive ventured. "Do you think that's too . . . odd?"

"You do whatever you fancy," Margery said. "You were a quite enthusiastic cook as a girl, weren't you?"

"If not always successful," Olive said. "At least I bake better scones now than I did when I was twelve."

"Uncle Milkey always enjoyed your scones."

Olive laughed. "Your Uncle Milkey had a kind heart."

"He did, didn't he? Look, I've arranged for the grocery order to arrive this afternoon. After that, you'll take over with all the household affairs."

"I'll keep strict accounts," Olive promised. "I've no problem with that."

"Didn't you win an arithmetic prize at school one year?" Margery asked.

She had. Olive had kept up the skill as the years went on—her ability to do sums quickly—although she'd grown more familiar with subtracting than adding.

"Also, I wanted to tell you our first lodger arrives today," Margery said. "Hugh Hodgson. He's the new manager of the cinema. Put him on the first floor in the room at the top of the stairs. He's to pay one pound nine per week."

"For accommodations *and* meals?" Olive asked. "You won't be making much from charging that." She spoke with authority, having made a study of accommodation adverts in the newspapers and wondering where she would be able to afford to live.

"I realize it isn't enough," Margery said, "but here's the thing, Olive—in order to *be* a lodging house, we must *look* like one. And the best way to do that is to have a lodger in residence. It's the same with the shop. How will I draw customers? By having customers in the shop already."

"So, Hugh Hodgson is to prime the pump?"

"Yes," Margery said. "That's it. Now, I'll come round for tea this afternoon. You all right?"

★   ★   ★

The extensive work carried out at Mersea House had left a layer of dust over everything. Olive put aside her new cookery book and changed into dungarees—formerly her brother's and much altered. She covered her French braid with a cotton scarf, and got stuck in dusting, cleaning the bathrooms, and shaking out counterpanes from the beds.

Then she went to the cleaning cupboard off the kitchen and opened the door. There, in a dark corner, loomed the new upright Hoover like a beige-colored specter. "Come on, you," she said, and wheeled the thing through the kitchen, across the entry, and into the lounge.

After plugging it in, she reached a finger over and switched it on. The beast roared to life, lurching forward as Olive leapt back in alarm. It made straight for the spindly legs of a side table, but Olive came to herself and caught it a second before impact. With a grip that would've subdued a tiger, she took command and began running the machine back and forth across the carpet. Soon she was circling tables, running it behind the sofa, and pushing into corners as if she were an old hand. Olive didn't drive, but perhaps this was what it was like steering an automobile. She hoovered out into the entry and started on the runner.

When she'd reached the far end, she turned and caught sight of movement out the front window—someone heading her way.

"Wouldn't you know it," she muttered, switching off the machine a second before the knock came. She wheeled the Hoover back into the lounge, pulled her scarf off, and stuffed it into a deep pocket before she opened the door.

"Good morning, Miss Binny."

"Good morning, Olive. Imagine my surprise seeing you here at Mersea House. Why didn't you tell me Margery had taken you in? I've only just learned it from Hetty."

Olive didn't believe that for a minute. Binny had had two weeks to sniff out this news and was miffed because she hadn't received the proper notification. Olive would've apologized if Binny hadn't made it sound as if she were a stray dog.

"Not 'taken in,' Miss Binny. Margery has employed me to run the boardinghouse." Then, she relented. "I'm sorry I didn't let you know. There was a great deal to do. Please come in. I hope you have time for coffee." For a fleeting moment, Olive clung to the thin hope that Binny would be too busy for coffee.

"I'd love to, dear, thank you." Miss Binny stepped in, cut her eyes at the Hoover in the lounge, and looked Olive up and down. "Perhaps we'd better take it in the kitchen, don't you think?"

Olive led the way. Binny settled at the table and began her litany of news as Olive searched for two matching cups and saucers without chips and found the task not an easy one. It hadn't mattered with the workers, but Constance Binny had an eagle eye to go with her sharp nose.

". . . and I'm sure Margery has learned all manner of modern things the years she spent in London. It makes one wonder why she would come back here at all."

There was a pause, and this told Olive that an answer to this conundrum was expected. Why had Margery come back? Olive turned from the stove and smiled.

"I'm afraid there's no cake," she said. "The work has just finished on the house, and I've yet to sort out the grocery orders and weekly menus for our lodgers."

"Do you have a lodger?" Miss Binny asked.

"Yes, of course. Mr. Hodgson from the cinema is moving in."

"Mr. Hodgson, yes," Miss Binny said, as if searching her files for further details. "He's quite new, isn't he? What do you know about him?"

"Nothing," Olive said, rather pleased with herself. "He hasn't arrived yet."

"My, my," Binny said, looking about the kitchen. "I don't know what Donald would've said about you going into service." Olive set the jug of hot milk down hard, and a few drops sloshed out. Binny rushed on. "Oh, of course, not really in service. But as good as."

At the end of a cup of coffee and no cake, she saw Miss Binny out, returned to the kitchen, and made herself a sandwich, slicing the bread a bit too vehemently and shredding the second piece. She spread mustard, added cheese, and sat down to eat. There now, that was what she'd needed—she'd started her day without even a cup of tea.

Olive chewed and reflected on how quickly her life had changed. She thought about the house on Field Stile Road and wondered who would live there next after nearly forty years of the Kersey family. Do buildings retain vestiges of their former residents? In that case, was Milkey Paxton, Mersea House denizen for decades, still lurking in one of the wardrobes? Olive giggled at the thought. She popped the last bite of sandwich into her mouth at the same moment there was a knock at the door.

She looked down at her dungarees. She should've changed clothes before now. Olive was certain this wasn't the sort of image Margery wanted people to have of Mersea House. She smoothed her hair back and opened the door to two men and a wooden crate on the ground between them.

"Miss Margery Paxton?" one of them asked.

"No, Miss Paxton isn't in. May I help you?"

"Delivery for Mersea House—will you take it?"

Olive eyed the crate. "Are you certain it's for here? What is it?"

"Crockery, Miss." He glanced down at the paper in his hand. "Royal Doulton. Leighton pattern. Twelve complete place settings, plus serving dishes. You must have quite a household here."

"Or the hopes of one," Olive said. "You better bring it in."

They carried the crate into the entry and left as the phone rang. "Mersea House."

"Miss Margery Paxton?" a man's voice asked.

"No, Miss Paxton isn't in. Would you like to leave a message?"

"I've a letter here to say she's interested in our newest line of breakfast crockery—egg cups, toast plates, jam pots."

"Perhaps she wants those for the shop," Olive said, hoping that was the case. How many dishes would they need in a boardinghouse?

"Does she work in a shop?" he asked.

"She owns the shop—Paxton's Goods." She gave him the number and put down the phone.

★ ★ ★

Olive left the crate where it was and continued hoovering. She finished all the bedrooms and landings in under two hours, and her resistance to change weakened that much more. She went to her own room to unpack. Margery had tried to talk her out of living at the top of the house, but Olive had insisted, saying the rooms on the first floor should be saved for the paying guests, and after all, if she leaned out the window and looked off to the right, she could see the lighthouse and that was a lovely view.

She opened her cases and hung up her two dresses, a blouse, knitted top, and two skirts and put everything else in drawers. She took her sponge bag and had a wash in the bathroom, and returned to the ground floor to a knock at the door.

It was a boy, about eleven, seated on his bicycle with one foot on the ground. He wore a jumper with patches at both elbows and sported that backward curl to his hair called a *quiff*. His bicycle held an enormous basket of food set into the frame in front of the handlebars.

"'Afternoon, Miss Olive," he said with a toothy grin. "Fancy meeting you here."

"Billy Grunyon, whatever are you doing?"

"Can't you see—I'm making a delivery to Miss Margery's boardinghouse."

Olive put a hand on her hip. "If you're making a delivery, then you go round to the kitchen door to do it. You know better."

"I didn't go round at your house."

"No, and that was because we were on a terrace. But here at Mersea House, you do it properly. Go on now." Olive shut the front door, went through to the kitchen, and opened the door to the yard. When Billy trudged up with his bicycle, she said, "Why, look who it is—it's Billy Grunyon. Come in and bring the basket."

Billy shook his head and laughed. "You're a card, Miss Olive."

They emptied the basket on the table, and Billy, nodding to the chicken, said, "That was a stop at the butcher's as well as the grocer's."

"Was it, now?" Olive said. "Would you be interested in a slice of bread and butter and jam?"

"Yes, ma'am, thank you."

She set him up and went off in search of her purse, returning with a farthing, which she handed over.

"Thank you, Miss Olive," Billy said, mouth full. At the sight of Olive's raised eyebrows, he swallowed. "Do you have the man from the cinema here?"

"We will have. Do you go to the cinema, Billy?"

"I went once—saw John Wayne. I'd go to the cinema every day if I could, but it cost thruppence even for the front. You can learn stuff from films, you know. You can see America and cowboys and all."

"Hmm. Very instructive, I'm sure."

After Billy pocketed his farthing and left, Olive took a survey of the grocery delivery. She would cook the chicken for the evening meal, and if the lodger hadn't arrived, it would do cold for tomorrow. Cold chicken would go better with piccalilli, but when she searched the pantry shelves, all she came up with was an ancient-looking jar of chutney. It was obvious the kitchen was lacking in the staples of a good meal. She'd better start the next day's grocery order. No, first she'd write up the week's menu.

Olive put the kettle on, gathered paper and pencil, and sat down at the kitchen table, working until Margery walked in the door.

"Tea?" Olive asked.

"Oh yes," she said. "I'm gasping. I've only just got away from the fitters in the shop. They've yet to finished the new shelves, and the counter is still in pieces."

"The window looks good," Olive said.

"Well, had to give everyone something to look at. But I'll need to keep a sharp eye on what's going on inside if we're to be ready by Saturday. How's the day? You get along all right?"

Olive poured tea as she said, "Two men delivered a crate of dishes—it's out in the entry. Are they for here?"

"Look at this lot," Margery said, nodding to the kitchen dresser's plate rack. "You couldn't put three place settings together to save yourself."

"True," Olive said. "I was hard pressed to find two cups and saucers with no chips when Constance Binny stopped in."

"Oh, Binny," Margery said. "I'm sure that made your day."

"I hope it won't become a habit, but I don't feel I can chase her away." Olive, now secure with a place to live and a job, felt as if she could afford to be magnanimous.

"Has Hugh arrived?" Margery asked.

"No. Are you sure it'll be today?"

"I expect it will," Margery said. "I wonder did he nip back up to London to get the rest of his things?"

Perhaps that's how she knew Hugh Hodgson, Olive thought—not from the cinema in town, but London.

Margery stood and brushed her skirt. "Back to it. Look, we've another lodger arriving tomorrow—Mrs. Abigail Claypool. War widow."

Olive looked down at the grocery order meant for three people.

"Oh, and there's just one other thing, Olive. I've signed you up for driving lessons."

CHAPTER 3

"You what?" Olive followed Margery out the kitchen door. "Margery, I can't drive."

"Yes, I know. That's the point of lessons."

"But why do I need to know?"

Margery looked away and across the green before replying. "Well, here's how I see it. It would be quite helpful to me, if on occasion, there were someone at hand who could drive somewhere. For something. Not deliveries, mind you. General business for the shop or the house. I've no time to take the lessons myself, and so I thought you, with gaps in your day, could fill an hour a week learning to drive. Then, you can be on standby."

On standby. Olive didn't like the sound of that—it reminded her of the war and waiting in darkness and for the sirens to blare, warning of an incoming air raid. But Margery knew her business.

"All right," she said. "Where will I go?"

Margery took her lipstick from her handbag, peered at her reflection in the window next to the door, and applied a fresh coat. "You won't go to the lessons," she said. "The lessons will come to you. Starting tomorrow afternoon, Mr. Charlie Salt will be your instructor. Don't worry—you'll do fine. Now, I'd best get back to the shop. I've left Young Trotter on his own."

"Will you keep him on?"

"Unfortunately, he has developed a keen interest in drawing maps and hopes to get on with the Ramblers' Association. I'll keep him as long as he's here."

Margery hurried away down Queen Street, and Olive returned to the kitchen and prepared the chicken to roast. She reflected on how her life, dull and empty for so long, seemed to be filling with activity and people at breakneck speed. It would take a bit of getting used to.

She started on the cabbage and potatoes and then remembered the unopened crate of dishes still taking up a great deal of space in the entry. And their first lodger expected any second.

Olive dashed out into the yard and to the shed. The door caught on the flagstones, and she gave it a shove to get it unstuck. Inside it was dark and damp. She shifted an old bicycle, kicked over an empty tin marked "Paraffin," and then rifled the shelves before coming up with a crowbar, which she carried indoors in triumph.

After prying the lid off the crate, she began digging the dishes out from the packing material—mountains of long, thin wood shavings that seemed to expand once they had been set free. That's when the knock came.

There was nothing else for it. Olive answered the front door to a man about fifty, dressed in rumpled trousers and shirt, with an aged leather flight jacket that looked buttery soft with wear. He had a pleasant face, but dark circles under his eyes.

"Hello," he said, "I'm Hugh Hodgson. And you're Olive?"

"Yes, hello, Mr. Hodgson. Hugh." Olive stepped back to let him in. "Welcome to Mersea House. I hope you'll enjoy it here. Please do let me know if there's anything you need or prefer or, well, just wish for. We certainly want to make this a comfortable home for you."

Olive had thought it best to have an official greeting to the boardinghouse and had practiced those words over and over. Their effect was weakened by her attire—dungarees—and because she and Hugh were standing ankle deep in a sea of stringy wood shavings.

"I'm terribly sorry about the mess."

"Not a bit of it," Hugh said, putting down his case. "Are you unpacking? Here, let me help."

Olive put up a faint protest, but Hugh dug in, and they chatted as they worked.

"It's a fine house, isn't it?" he said, handing her a soup bowl. "A sight better than where I've been kipping."

"Have you been staying local?"

"I started the new job just last week," Hugh said.

That wasn't an answer, but Olive thought perhaps Hugh had been staying at another local boardinghouse and didn't want to say. Had Margery been pinching lodgers from other establishments?

"Mersea House is by far the best Southwold has to offer in long-term accommodations," Olive said. "A bathroom on every floor— you don't see that often, do you?"

"For a few months during the war, I had a room at the top of a house in Pimlico and had to go down four flights of steps and out to the yard every time I needed to . . ." Hugh laughed. "It was hit during the Blitz, and as no one was hurt, I wasn't terribly sorry."

"Did you work at a cinema in London?" Olive asked.

"I was a film editor," Hugh said, "so I had my fingers on the pictures before they got to the cinema. During the war, I was with the Ministry of Information."

"Is that how you know Margery?"

Hugh ran a finger along the rim of a dinner plate. "It is—we met through a mutual friend there."

When every dish had been uncovered and taken to the kitchen, Hugh stuffed as much of the packing material as he could back into the crate, carried it out to the yard, and left it next to the dustbins.

"Thanks so much," Olive said. "I promise not to put you to work again if I can help it."

"I don't mind. I've only got work Wednesday through Saturday evenings—and the Saturday matinee, of course—so I'm happy to help whenever you need me."

"Do you do everything yourself at the cinema?" Olive asked, picking a strand of packing material off the rug. "Sell tickets? Run the projector?"

"Do I wear one of those red velvet costumes and walk around peddling ices and sweets?" Hugh asked. "No, it isn't a one-man show. There are two young women on tickets and concessions. Do you like films?"

"Oh yes, I do," Olive said. It had been years since she'd been to the pictures. "Let me show you to your room—it's up on the first floor." She led the way and opened the door with a flourish. Hugh walked in, put down his case, and surveyed his surroundings. It was a comfortable room, Olive thought, with a writing desk and a reading chair near a window that faced south. "I hope this will suit you," she added.

"Suit me?" Hugh asked. He smiled—a brave smile, Olive thought. She knew the kind well. "I feel as if I've checked into the Ritz. We could hold a soiree in here and charge a shilling a head—think of the money Margery could make."

"Don't give her any ideas," Olive said. "She'll want to buy the old dance hall and start it up again."

"She would, wouldn't she? Margery's at the top of her game." Hugh took Olive's hand, pulled her in, and they did a few turns round the room as he hummed "I've Got the World on a String."

Olive hadn't danced in ages—she'd forgotten how free it made her feel. Hugh twirled, she laughed, and their dance slowed to a stop. He dropped his hands and smiled, but again, there was that touch of sadness.

"She seems well and truly pleased to be back in Southwold," Hugh said. "The place suits her. Nevertheless, we must keep our eye on her."

But Margery had been born unstoppable, and Olive, for one, didn't relish the idea of getting in her way.

"Well," she said, "I'll leave your key on the table near the front door. Please do come to the lounge whenever you like. The evening meal will be in about an hour. Margery should be back from the shop by then."

Olive ran upstairs to her own room and changed clothes, then went down to the entry and attacked the last of the wood shavings with a broom and dustpan. Hugh was a nice fellow, she thought. He reminded her of her brother somehow—it was his comfortable, friendly manner. She could only hope all the paying guests would be as easy.

Margery walked in on Olive on her hands and knees. "I'd already hoovered," Olive explained before Margery could comment. "I didn't need to get it out again. Hugh arrived while I was unpacking, and he helped."

"You see," Margery said, "he's earning his reduced weekly rate already, isn't he? Hugh?" she called up the stairs. "Drink?"

"Be right there," he called back.

"I'm done in," Margery said, going into the lounge. "Workmen underfoot, unloading new stock, everyone and his cousin trying to look in and wondering what I've done with Uncle Milkey's dartboard that sat in the window for the past fifty years. Come on, Olive. Drinks."

"I'll just lay the table first," Olive said, and went through to the kitchen.

When she came out with the dishes, Margery looked up from pouring gin. "You've only two settings there," she said.

"Yes—you and Hugh."

"Olive, you aren't a servant. There's no need to take your meals in the kitchen."

"No, I'm not a servant; I'm an employee." It was something Olive had thought about and had decided she should know her place.

"Well, then," Margery said, "as your employer, I'm saying you'll eat in the dining room. You're a part of the household, not someone to be ordered about."

"Oh really?" Olive asked, although she couldn't help but smile.

Margery laughed. "Really."

Hugh came down, and when the table had been laid for three, Olive joined them in the lounge. She thought she'd entered a new circle of society, sitting with a glass of gin and a quite small splash of tonic while the dinner kept warm and Margery and Hugh nattered on about London and how good it was to be out of it.

"Did you stay here through the war?" Hugh asked Olive.

"Yes," she replied. "The town practically emptied once they realized how vulnerable we were to German invasion. But my mum and dad wouldn't go, and I stayed on to help them. I worked with the

Women's Voluntary Services. Collecting clothes, pouring cups of tea for the wardens and ambulance workers—that sort of thing."

"That's what the Girl Guides got you ready for," Margery said.

Hugh put a hand to his chest. "Were *you* a Guide too, Margery?"

"Good God, no," she said. "I went in for dramatics."

"The summer we were fifteen," Olive said, "Margery directed a dramatics group for the children in town and put on a production of *Macbeth* just out here on South Green. I was her assistant. It was like being shepherd to a flock of balky lambs."

"*Macbeth* was quite ambitious, Margery," Hugh said.

"At that age, you think you can do anything, don't you?" she replied and clicked her tongue. "One day you're fifteen, and the next you're thirty-bloody-seven."

"Or more," Hugh replied. "Tempus fugit, ladies."

"Doesn't it just," Margery said.

★ ★ ★

The rest of the evening was quiet. Hugh switched on the wireless in the lounge, and Olive washed up and Margery dried while she talked about the latest thing in tea making: an electric kettle, which she would be carrying in the shop. "It shuts off on its own, Olive. There'll be no more boiling the kettle dry and ruining it."

"I'm quite capable of keeping an eye on the kettle," Olive replied, "so you don't need to bring one here."

"It would be a great help if I could tell customers firsthand how well it works."

"I'm sure it has its place. Why don't you use it in your office there at the shop?" Olive asked. "Customers could see how useful it is for you. 'Look here,' you could tell them. 'No more need of a spirit lamp to set your kettle on, only plug this fellow in for a quick cuppa.'"

Margery slung the tea cloth over her shoulder and leaned on the counter. "You should've gone into advertising."

"Yes, I'd be quite good at telling people what not to buy," Olive said. She took the damp cloth and draped it over the hob. "I'll lay the table for breakfast, and then I think I'll go up. I've the grocery order ready. Shall I ring them in the morning, or will you leave it on your way to the shop?"

"I'll drop it round," Margery said.

Olive went up to her room. There were two other rooms along with hers on the second floor. They were unoccupied now but wouldn't remain so forever, and Olive thought she would make the most of it by having a long soak. As the hot water poured into the tub, she leaned over and let the steam rise up in her face. Perhaps tomorrow or the next day she would pop into the chemist and buy some bath oil and hand lotion. She had the money now, didn't she? No need to feel guilty about the expense.

But thriftiness was a difficult habit to break all at once. Olive drew five inches of water in the tub, as she had done since the beginning of the war, and didn't linger. Dried and wrapped in her dressing gown, she went down to the kitchen, boiled the kettle, and filled her hot-water bottle. Clutching it to her chest with one hand, she picked up *Constance Spry* with the other and went out. She looked into the lounge, where Hugh read the newspaper and Margery had settled with a cigarette and a magazine.

"Kettle's boiled. Do you two want me to fill your bottles?"

"No, that's all right," Margery said. "Hugh?"

"No need, thanks."

"Right. Good night, then."

Margery glanced at Olive's book. "A bit of bedtime reading?"

"She might tell me what the trouble was with my scones."

"Sleep well, then."

Olive doubted she could. Her mind was too full of new things. Still, she would make a show of it. She left the book on the dresser, resolutely crawled into bed, and turned out the light. She took a deep breath, exhaled slowly, and closed her eyes. When she opened them again, she heard the gulls crying and looked out the window to see them wheeling over the housetops in the first light of day. Time to get the breakfast on.

★   ★   ★

First, she baked a seedcake, then served the breakfast, and after, cleared the table and started on her day. Once or twice she glanced out the front window in the lounge, unsure if she were looking for the new lodger or Miss Binny. She saw neither, but did notice Hugh. Across the green and between two buildings, there was a narrow view of the sea and a bench on the parade that faced the water. He was there, sitting alone, hands in the pockets of his jacket, taking in the scene.

Olive spent an hour or so gathering up the cracked and chipped dishes, dented saucepans with burned bottoms, and stained table linens that were long past remediation. She stacked everything on the kitchen table and would let Margery decide the next course of action. Now, there was the bread bin to address. It was an enormous thing and probably hadn't been cleaned out in . . . well, Olive didn't dare venture a guess, but she wouldn't've been surprised if a mouse had scurried out when she'd opened it. He'd certainly have found enough crumbs to live off. She took the bin out to the yard and, with a long, pointed knife, stabbed at its encrusted corners.

With the kitchen door open, she heard the telephone. Olive hurried in and, leaving the bread bin next to the sink, went through to the entry to answer.

"Mersea House."

"I saw the bus go by a few minutes ago," Margery said. "I looked out, and I believe I saw Mrs. Claypool get off."

"Do you know her?" Olive asked.

"Not exactly. We have a mutual friend, so she was described to me."

Was this the same mutual friend as Hugh's? Was Margery relocating all her paying guests from London?

There was a knock at the door. Olive jumped and then lowered her voice to a whisper. "I think she's here."

"Go on and answer," Margery said, and the line went dead.

Olive looked down at the knife in her hand. She dashed back into the kitchen, left it in the sink, and threw off her pinny, tossing it on a chair and smoothing down her hair as she ran back. Breathless, she opened the front door.

The woman on the doorstep was perhaps in her forties, with a thin face and high cheekbones. She wore a small saucer hat atop her head—a style popular during the war. Her coat with single buttons and a narrow outline that didn't use an excessive amount of fabric also dated from more than a decade ago. Olive had a sharp eye for such things, having mended, altered, and continued to wear as much as she could of her own wartime wardrobe.

"Hello, I'm Mrs. Claypool," the woman said, clapping a hand on her hat as a gust caught it. "Miss Margery Paxton?"

"No, I'm not Miss Paxton. She'll be along directly. I'm Olive Kersey, the housekeeper here. Welcome to Mersea House."

"Oh good, then you are expecting me?"

"Yes, of course. Please come through. We're delighted you're here, Mrs. Claypool. We have several—"

The phone rang, and Olive jumped. "Would you excuse me for a moment?" She gestured toward the lounge and said, "Please do look round," and then grabbed the receiver. "Mersea House."

"Is she there?" Margery asked.

"Yes."

"Just one thing. Don't let her take a room at the top of the house. If she does, we'll never see her again. Give her my old room. It's lovely now, all done up."

Olive glanced in the lounge, where Mrs. Claypool perused the bookshelves. "All right, but—"

"I'm on my way."

Putting the phone down, Olive said, "Let me show you to your room, Mrs. Claypool. Do you have luggage?"

"I have one case," she replied, "which I left at the butcher's, where the coach stopped. Mr. Bass, was it? I told him you would send someone to collect it."

"Yes, of course," Olive said. She'd go for it herself as soon as she could—Bass the butcher didn't run a left-luggage counter. She led the way up to the first floor and over to the corner room, opened the door, and stood back.

Mrs. Claypool remained on the landing, glancing up the stairs. "Do you have a room available on the second floor?" she asked.

"No, I'm sorry, we don't." Olive wasn't sure if she were lying or not. "But this is a lovely room with good light—windows both north and west. I hope you'll be comfortable. Our other lodger, Mr. Hodgson, has the first room at the top of the stairs."

Mrs. Claypool looked at Hugh's door. "He has a great deal of foot traffic going past, doesn't he?"

Only one pair of feet—Olive's—and now a second pair. Was that traffic?

"Hello," Margery called from below, and soon appeared, hurrying up the stairs. "Hello, I'm Margery. You're Mrs. Claypool—it's Abigail, isn't it?"

In the ensuing moment of silence, Olive seemed to hear an unspoken reply: *"No, I am not Abigail, I am Mrs. Claypool."* But then, their new paying guest smiled and said, "Yes, of course."

"And you've met Olive," Margery said. "Olive's the one who runs the place and makes this a real home for us all. She's a marvelous cook."

Olive thought that was pushing it—but she did have hopes.

"About the meals—breakfast and dinner, am I correct?" Mrs. Claypool asked. "I'd like to take them in my room."

"Oh, I am sorry," Margery said, sounding as if she really were, although Olive knew better. "We don't serve meals in the rooms. You may certainly take the odd cup of tea or coffee up with you, but breakfast and dinner will be in the dining room."

Mrs. Claypool bit her lip and looked for one second as if she might object, but then relented. "The dining room it is, then."

"Would you like coffee now?" Olive asked. "I'm happy to bring it up."

"That would be lovely."

Margery followed Olive down to the kitchen, and once they were there and the door closed, she said, "You can't mollycoddle every one of our guests. Otherwise, you'll run yourself ragged."

Olive set the percolator on the hob. "We've only two at the moment, so I'm all right. When we're full, I'll turn into a proper landlady and shout at everyone and slice the bread too thin."

"You won't," Margery said with a laugh. "Has the seedcake cooled? Shall we give Abigail a slice?"

"Who's being soft now?" Olive asked. "How has she ended up here?"

"Dolores—a woman in the office next to mine—knew Abigail. They lived in the same building, but it was about to be pulled down. Everyone was as happy as Larry to relocate, except Abigail, who practically had to be pried out of her flat. She doesn't seem the liveliest wire."

"Grieving widow?" Olive asked.

"If so, she's been at it a good while, hasn't she?" Margery said. "Dolores told me she'd lived there for years. Practically a recluse and had no family that anyone could tell. So, I offered a place here. When Dolores told her about it, she said Abigail seemed relieved to move somewhere she didn't know a soul." Margery poured out a cup of coffee. "Good for her and for us—now we have two lodgers. And I doubt if she'll be any trouble."

"That reminds me," Olive said. "She's left her case with Bass. I'll go and fetch it."

"She left her bag at the butcher's?" Margery clicked her tongue. "I'm reconsidering my statement. Don't you go for it, Olive. I'll send Young Trotter over."

Olive took Mrs. Claypool a tray and returned to find Margery had cleaned off one corner of the table and was having her own coffee and cake. Olive joined her.

"No Busy Binny today?"

Olive looked over her shoulder in case Constance Binny was lurking in the pantry. "No, she's not an everyday sort of caller. Once or twice a week is more likely. It gives her a chance to gather up enough gossip to pass along. What shall I do with all this?"

Margery considered the old dishes, pots and pans, and linens. "Put it in the box room with the rest, I suppose." She rose, picked up her handbag, and, on her way out the door, said, "Don't forget, you have a driving lesson this afternoon."

Olive had, purposely and quite successfully, put that fact out of her mind, but after Margery's reminder, could think of nothing else.

She cleaned off the kitchen table and carried things back to the box room while telling herself that she was perfectly capable of learning how to drive an automobile. Imagining herself in charge of such a large machine both excited and unnerved her, but her teacher, this Mr. Charlie Salt, would have had experience with such things. He would know how to calm her down. And she had always tried to be a good student.

Hugh had gone out after breakfast, Young Trotter had arrived with Mrs. Claypool's case in short order, and there had been no further sign of the new lodger.

Olive finished her housecleaning by lunch but wasn't terribly hungry. A half hour before her lesson, she sat in the lounge, ready and waiting, wearing her Norfolk jacket, with her headscarf tied under her chin. The letter box rattled and she leapt up, but it was only the post. She stacked the letters on the table and went back to waiting.

At last, a knock came.

The man on the front step wore a jacket and tie. He removed his hat and ran a hand over his sandy-colored hair. He couldn't be any older than Olive herself, and she was glad, having spent the most worrisome moments envisioning someone akin to gray-haired Mr. Jarvis, who had taught history in school, and had made them memorize the kings and queens of England in order, beginning with Athelstan. He had been the terror of every nine-year-old.

"Miss Margery Paxton?" the man asked.

"No, Miss Paxton is not in, but—"

He glanced down at the clipboard he held. "Miss Olive Kersey?"

"Yes, I'm Olive."

"Charlie Salt, Miss Kersey. How do you do? I'm your driving instructor. Shall we begin?" He stood aside, and there at the curb sat a pea-green car.

Olive refrained from saluting. "Ready," she said and started to close the door, but stopped. "No, wait." She dashed indoors and retrieved her handbag from the table, shutting the door firmly behind her. "Really ready." Salt strode down the walk with Olive in tow. Glancing up at the blue sky, she said, "Fine day for it."

"A good and careful driver must manage in any sort of weather," Salt replied. He circled round to the front of the car, stopped, and patted the bonnet. "Nineteen fifty-three Hillman Minx Mark Six Saloon," he said, with an approving nod. "They'd put the hand brake on the floor by then. Of course, the later models have bigger rear windows, but no matter—this is a good, reliable car. Are you familiar with automobiles, Miss Kersey?"

"Yes, Mr. Salt. I gave up the horse and cart some time ago."

Salt watched her, and in that moment of silence, Olive learned her first lesson: there was nothing funny about cars.

"Sorry," she said. "I suppose I'm a bit nervous. I've never driven an automobile."

"Just as well. It's difficult to break bad habits. Best to start fresh at the beginning." He walked round and opened the driver's door. "Climb in."

"Here? Now?" Olive's gaze darted round the green, from the Red Lion at one end toward Gun Hill at the other. She saw mothers pushing prams, old gentlemen making their way to the pub, and elderly ladies strolling along. *Dear God, was that Miss Binny?* "My first attempt to drive won't be in front of the entire town, will it?"

"No, certainly not. This first lesson is only for you to become familiar with the vehicle."

"That's all right, then." Olive sat on the bench seat and swung her legs in under the steering wheel. Her teacher shut the door and went round to the passenger side and got in.

"Well, now," he said, "how does it feel to be in the driver's seat?"

"Fine."

"Shall we go over the controls and such to get you familiar with things?"

"Yes, let's."

Salt began labeling everything, starting with the steering wheel, although Olive felt sure she could've named that on her own. Foot pedals from left to right: clutch, brake, accelerator. "You'll notice the hand brake is on your right between the seat and the door." Olive duly looked down at the hand brake. "It's pulled up and so is on. Now, your dashboard is made up of . . ."

Should she be keeping notes—did Mr. Salt expect it of her?

"Now, let's consider the gear stick," he continued. "As you can see, it's on the steering column. The Hillman Minx has four gears—and reverse, of course. The gears can be found rather in the shape of the letter H. Like this." He drew the letter on his clipboard, added numbers at each point, and held it up. "So you can think of shifting as if you were writing the letter." Salt leaned toward Olive and took hold of the stick. "As the car is switched off and the parking brake is on, I can show you this way without you worrying about the clutch."

Immediately, Olive worried about the clutch.

"First gear," Salt said, "is at the top of one of the vertical lines of the H. Second is straight down. For third gear, come up halfway, and you'll feel the stick go a bit loose in the neutral position—this is much like the line that crosses on the letter. Push the stick away from you and then up, and there's third. Straight down and you're in fourth. Shifting gears occurs only when you've depressed the clutch, so when we—"

"Mr. Salt," Olive interrupted, "isn't the letter facing the wrong way for me?"

"Sorry?"

"Well, from where you're sitting over there, it looks like the letter H, but from where I am, it's as if the two lines were one behind the other, so it isn't a letter at all."

Salt drummed his fingers on his clipboard. "If the letter H is a problem for you, Miss Kersey, don't think about it. Think of first and second gears as the line closer to you and third and fourth away from you. Would that be easier?"

"The letter H isn't the problem, it was only that . . . Wait—how do I reverse?"

"Ah," Salt said, leaning back over as Olive straightened up. "Reverse is found by pulling on the end of the gear stick like this and pushing it out, then down."

"Isn't that where fourth gear is?"

"It's further away than fourth." Salt added to the drawing by extending the horizontal bar and drawing half a vertical line. "You see?"

Olive went through changing the gears, pushing the stick up and down, then away and up and down again, and then she pulled on the end of it and pushed it out further and down.

"Well done," Salt said.

Olive pointed to the diagram. "It's an oddly shaped letter now. It's more like an Egyptian hieroglyph, isn't it?"

He didn't reply, but leaned back and looked down at his drawing. Olive thought perhaps she should just be quiet and learn to drive, because there was no point in annoying the teacher.

"Or a rune," she added against her better judgment.

Salt squinted at the paper, and Olive noticed the hint of a smile. "You know, I believe you're right," he said. "I was quite taken by runes when I was in school." Salt drew another sticklike figure. "Thought I could make a secret code with them."

"And did you?"

"Yes, I made a fine secret code. It was so good, even I couldn't figure out what I'd written."

Olive laughed, and Charlie Salt looked at her in surprise. Then, he seemed to remember what he should be doing. "Now, Miss Kersey, let's review what we've learned."

It was the only light moment in the entire lesson, but she couldn't fault him for taking his job seriously. At the end of the hour, Olive retrieved her handbag, and Charlie walked her up to the front door.

"Next week," Olive said, "will we actually start the car?"

"Patience, Miss Kersey," he replied. "Therein lies safety. Good day."

She watched him motor off toward Ferry Road and imagined herself behind the wheel and doing the same. Freedom—that's what you had when you could drive; Olive could see that now. A sudden mad desire came over her to be in the car at that moment with Charlie Salt. She laughed at herself and went indoors.

CHAPTER 4

Olive hung her jacket on a peg and stuffed the scarf in a pocket. She could do with a cup of tea.

Hugh was alone in the lounge. Without a word, he nodded her in and closed the door. "Margery is here," he said. "She's in the kitchen."

"Is she? Come round for a cuppa?"

Hugh's frown caught her attention.

"Is something wrong?" Olive asked.

"Wrong?" he repeated. "I don't know. Something is off, at any rate. I came in a while ago, and Margery was going through the post. She opened a letter, read it, and I haven't got a word out of her since. I thought you might want to start an official inquiry or something."

Hugh's frown was contagious—Olive could feel one growing on her own brow. "Yes, all right."

Margery sat smoking at the kitchen table, now cleared of debris. Her face was washed of color. A letter lay open in front of her, but she leaned back in her chair as if it wasn't safe to get any nearer to it.

"I didn't know you'd come back," Olive said. "Did you have lunch?" Margery didn't move. "Margery? Is it bad news—the letter?"

Without looking up, she said, "We'll need one of the rooms next to yours. Another lodger." She slid the letter toward Olive.

It was a proper letter written on a typewriter and from the Suffolk Children's Committee.

Dear Miss Paxton,

In our ongoing attempt to locate you, I am writing to this address, given to me at your last known residence in London (14 Bullard Square, Marylebone). I have documents that state you are the guardian of the orphan Juniper Wyckes, age 11, daughter of Mr. and Mrs. George Wyckes, born 24 February 1946. It is of paramount importance that I speak with you immediately concerning this matter so that a proper home can be found for the girl. Please expect me on Thursday morning, 21 March, at 11:00 AM, so that we can address this matter and resolve it to the benefit of all concerned, especially the girl and her particular needs. I sincerely hope this letter finds you.

Regards,

Mrs. Lucie Pagett
Children's Officer

Olive looked from the letter to Margery, who appeared transfixed on her cigarette, now mostly ash.

"Margery?"

Margery cupped the cigarette in her hand, catching the ash as it collapsed into her palm. She rose and brushed her hands off over the sink, then ran water on the burning end before dropping it into the bin.

Without looking round, she said, "You see why we need the room."

"Juniper Wyckes?" Olive asked.

Margery whipped round and braced herself against the sink. Her small, dark eyes shone hot.

"Juniper," she said. "What sort of a name is that?"

"Daughter of George Wyckes," Olive persisted, holding out the letter.

"I hope you aren't wanting details, because I have none," Margery said, her voice shaking. "Except this means he's dead."

"You didn't know?"

"How could I?" Margery cried. "I haven't laid eyes on him since 1939."

And yet Margery had been named guardian to the child of her former beau. Olive could barely hold onto these few facts, let alone suppose what it all meant.

"What will you do?"

Margery threw her shoulders back and stuck her chin out. Olive knew the look.

"Apparently, I'm going to meet with Mrs. Lucie Pagett tomorrow morning at eleven. The girl—Juniper—needs a home. And she's George's daughter. What else is there to do?"

An energetic knocking at the kitchen door to the yard broke off the discussion, and Olive answered to Billy Grunyon on his bicycle. He grinned and said, "Hiya, Miss Olive." When he saw who else was in the kitchen, he sobered up and added, "Hello, Miss Margery— good afternoon. I've your grocery order."

"Thank you, Billy," Margery said. "Does your mother allow you to wear your hair that way?"

"No, ma'am." Billy slapped at his quiff until the curl flopped over to the side.

"I must check back at the shop," Margery said. "I won't be long."

She walked out, taking the letter with her, and Olive watched her go. There would be a reckoning later. Margery must know more, and she would have to explain how this all came about.

"Do you have another lodger?" Billy asked. "You ordered four chops from Bass."

"Mr. Bass," Olive corrected him and gave a thought to Mrs. Claypool, whom she hadn't seen since the woman's arrival that morning. "Yes, a new lodger. Bring the basket in, and I'll fetch my purse."

In the entry, Olive reached in her handbag as Hugh came out of the lounge.

"Well, Olive, what news?"

"We'll be getting a new lodger. Of sorts. It's Margery's ward—an eleven-year-old girl."

Hugh cocked his head as if listening to the words again. "Is this what was in the letter?" he asked.

Olive dug a farthing out of her purse and turned it over and over in her fingers. "Yes."

"Who is she?"

"I'm not quite sure," Olive said. After all, wasn't this Margery's news to tell?

"Well, who would've thought," Hugh said.

They were quiet for a moment. Then, Billy pushed the kitchen door open, stuck his head out, and noticed the small coin in Olive's hand.

"Anything else, Miss Olive?"

Practical matters overcame speculation. "Would you like bread and butter and jam, Billy?"

"Yes, please."

"I'll be right in."

The door closed again, and Hugh asked, "Margery was a ward, wasn't she?"

"Yes. Her parents died when she was a baby, and Uncle Milkey took her in."

"Where has this girl been living?"

"I'm not sure," Olive said. "She's an orphan—the letter didn't say much more than that. But we should know more tomorrow because someone from the local authority is coming in the morning. Perhaps she has to inspect the place before allowing the girl to move in."

"Tomorrow?" Hugh asked.

"Yes, eleven o'clock," Olive replied.

"I'll be out at eleven," he said. "The cinema's records are a shambles, and I really must get them sorted. But you won't need me, will you?"

"I can't see as we would," Olive said. She looked up to the first-floor landing, and whispered, "Have you met Mrs. Claypool?"

"Not laid eyes on her yet."

A clattering came from the kitchen. "Billy," Olive reminded herself.

The boy was on the floor when she walked in, and he scrambled up, holding a few sprouts in his hands. The rest were scattered across the table, surrounded by a circle of potatoes with a tin of peaches positioned at the corner.

"The sprouts made a break for it," he said, "and the potatoes were too slow to stop them."

"What about that tin of peaches?" Olive asked as she cut a thick slice of bread and buttered it.

"It was useless as a sentry—the sprouts rolled right past. The potatoes will have to be punished, of course, and so you'll fry them up into chips."

"I will not," Olive said. "I'll turn them into mash." She set the buttered bread on the table along with the jam. "How old are you, Billy?"

"Eleven. My birthday was last month. I had a cake and all. Ma and my sister and I ate it, because Pa was working. It had those cherries on it, the ones from a jar."

"Who is your teacher at school?" The ward, Juniper Wyckes, was taking form in Olive's mind.

"Miss Browne." Billy exhaled. "She's a one, Miss Olive. You can't put a whisker out of place but she knows about it. And if you get caught, you have to stay after and do lines." He glanced up from spreading a thick layer of strawberry jam. "Or so I'm told."

Olive gathered up the sprouts, including the renegades, and began peeling them, barely listening as Billy gave her a detailed account of his comic-book hero, Dan Dare, and his latest adventure on the rings of Saturn.

★　★　★

Billy had gone, and the evening meal was nearly ready by the time Margery returned from the shop. She went straight to the lounge without a word while Olive finished laying the table. Hugh came down, likely called by the tinkling of glasses as Margery poured the gin. When Olive followed him in, it was to be handed her own drink.

"Olive, I'm sorry I forgot to ask about your driving lesson," Margery said. "How was it?"

"Good. Fine."

"And how is Mr. Salt as a teacher?" Margery asked.

"He's . . . efficient," Olive replied. "He's dedicated."

"He's going to let her start up the car's engine next week," Hugh said.

"Then, moving right along, aren't you?"

"Shall we invite Mrs. Claypool down?" Olive asked.

"Yes," Margery said, "we can at least try."

Leaving her drink behind, Olive went upstairs and knocked.

"Hello. Would you join us in the lounge? We're having a drink before dinner."

"Thank you, no," the answer came. "How long until the meal?"

"About twenty minutes."

"I'll see you then."

Olive headed for the lounge but slowed before she reached the door when she heard conversation within.

"There's no reason for you to hide," Margery said.

"I don't mind getting out of the way," Hugh replied. "It's the least I can do."

Olive continued to the kitchen instead and looked at the sprouts before returning to the lounge, where the topic had turned to the cinema.

"I can get hold of older films for pennies," Hugh said. "I'm thinking of running theme weeks, especially in summer with all the visitors. A week of Sherlock Holmes. A week of Graham Greene."

"Graham Greene?" Margery asked. "*The Third Man*, yes, but *The End of the Affair* seems a bit heavy for the holiday crowd, don't you think? What about a week of *Old Mother Riley*?"

Hugh laughed. "Margery, your taste in films is appalling."

Mrs. Claypool appeared in the doorway.

"Here we are now," Margery said. "Abigail Claypool, Hugh Hodgson."

Mrs. Claypool held out her hand, palm down. "Mr. Hodgson."

Hugh stood, and a mischievous look skittered across his face. For a moment, Olive thought he might bow and kiss the outstretched hand, but instead, he shook it and said, "Mrs. Claypool, very good to meet you."

"I'll just get the meal on the table," Olive said, hurrying off to the kitchen. "Why don't you all go through to the dining room?"

Margery helped carry the food in, and the meal began with compliments to the cook—the chops browned just the right amount, the sprouts neither mush nor crunch. But after that, the conversation faltered. Constrained by the presence of Mrs. Claypool, Olive couldn't question Margery about this newly discovered ward, and any attempt at small talk at the table dried up quickly.

Hugh made a go of it. "Were you in London before this?" he asked Mrs. Claypool.

"Yes, I was."

"The building you'd been living in was to be torn down, wasn't it, Abigail?" Margery asked. "Residual structural damage from the war? Imagine, after all these years."

"There was so much destruction," Mrs. Claypool said.

"True," Margery replied. "I had to move three times. And then again. How many times did you move, Hugh?"

"Only twice," Hugh said. "Until now."

A pause ensued, but the other Londoner did not pick up on the topic of moving house during the war.

"I didn't go anywhere," Olive offered.

"Even with bombs dropping all round you," Margery said.

"Were you hit?" Hugh asked.

"No, we weren't. But so many others were in town. Hotels, cottages. Early in '44, it practically rained incendiary bombs on the Common."

"They're still coming across land mines on the beach," Margery said. "And bombs washing up on the shore."

They were all silent until Olive added, "We had an evacuee."

"Did you?" Margery asked. "You never said."

"It's easy to forget because it was so brief," Olive said. "They brought them up in coaches from London, but they hadn't been here long before it occurred to the Ministry that Southwold was a prime spot for the Germans to hit. So, they took them all away. I think his name was Lionel."

She hoped Lionel had done all right for himself, but it was just as well he hadn't stayed with Olive's family, what with the way her father had been—spending the first part of the war angry and the rest dying. When she wasn't out with the WVS, Olive was indoors, helping her mother keep her father comfortable as he wheezed through the nights.

"Well," Olive said, standing to gather the plates, "peaches and custard should brighten us up."

Over the pudding, Mrs. Claypool spoke. "I'm having a wireless delivered on Friday."

"But we've a wireless in the lounge," Margery said. "You're welcome to listen there any time and to whatever program you like."

"I wouldn't want to put anyone out."

"You would need your own license for a wireless," Margery reminded her.

"I'll make those arrangements." Apparently, Mrs. Claypool was not to be moved.

"Well, that was a fine meal, Olive," Hugh said. "I'm off to work now. We have *20 Million Miles to Earth* through Saturday. You can't do better than space creatures."

"Unless you had Old Mother Riley," Margery said.

"You be careful what you ask for, Miss Paxton," Hugh replied. "'Evening, all."

Next, Mrs. Claypool excused herself.

"Shall I bring up a hot-water bottle for you later?" Olive asked. The woman hesitated, and Olive saw a chink in her defenses. "It's no trouble," she continued. "I'll do it when I fill my own."

"Thank you." And she was gone, leaving Olive and Margery on their own.

In the kitchen with the dishes, Olive said, "I can see what you mean about Abigail being a recluse. I can't tell if she's sad or annoyed. Do you think she lost someone in the war?"

"Didn't we all?" Margery said.

"I suppose we did. Margery, about the girl . . ."

"Please, can we leave it until tomorrow?" Margery asked, shaking the damp cloth and draping it over the hob. "Abigail will be paying four pounds a week."

That was the proper amount for accommodations and two meals a day. Hugh was paying far less. Olive thought of the state of Abigail Claypool's clothes and wondered if she could afford four pounds. Then she remembered the lodger would have her own wireless and the ensuing costs. "Yes, all right."

★ ★ ★

Lashing rain drummed against Olive's window the next morning. She served breakfast to the others and sat down with them for a cup of tea. The atmosphere round the table was heavy, and there was little talk. Margery left soon after, wearing a suit the color of a summer sky—a bold statement, Olive thought. The sort of outfit that shows the world who is in charge. Margery had a great deal to do at the shop and only two days in which to do it before the opening on Saturday. Olive started to remind her about Mrs. Pagett, but Margery cut in with "I'll be back in time."

As soon as Abigail finished her egg and toast, she vanished upstairs. Olive had washed the breakfast things and baked a pan of shortbread by the time Hugh left—getting out of the way for a reason unknown to her. Olive went up to appraise the two empty rooms on her floor and found them ready and waiting for a lodger. She imagined hearing the footsteps of an eleven-year-old running up and down the stairs— the girl might liven things up in the house.

Once Olive had dusted the lounge, set up the tray for coffee, and filled the percolator, she sat down with another cup of tea and a slice of toast, interrupting her repast once when she went to look out the front window of the lounge. She could see Hugh sitting on the bench that faced the sea. So much for spending the morning at work on the cinema's records.

It seemed as if eleven o'clock would never come, but when it did at last, the knock at the door startled her. Before going out to answer, she moved the coffee onto the hob.

The woman on the doorstep wore a suit and a pillbox hat in a deep begonia. Lucky for her the rain had stopped, because she had neither mackintosh nor umbrella. In one gloved hand she clutched the handle of a slim leather satchel; in the other, her handbag.

"Miss Margery Paxton?" she asked with a smile.

"No, I'm not Miss Paxton. She's—"

"Oh no!" the woman cried. Her shoulders drooped, and her smile evaporated. "Can you credit it? After all this time, I really thought we'd found her."

"Yes, well—" Olive began before being interrupted again.

"You wouldn't believe the trouble," the woman said, her face reddening. "Letters returned, address after address—we've looked everywhere for her. She's worse than the Scarlet Pimpernel. I had such hopes this time, though. Mersea House looked like the real thing, so I thought . . . The way people move round so much these days is astounding. And now what am I to tell the girl? She has her heart set on—"

"But Margery is here!" Olive practically had to shout it before the woman stopped talking. "At least, this is Miss Paxton's house. She'll be back any moment."

The storm clouds parted. "Really? Oh, I'm terribly sorry." She threw back her shoulders, and said, "Hello. I'm Mrs. Lucie Pagett."

"Yes, Mrs. Pagett, please come in." Olive led her to the lounge. "I'm Olive Kersey, housekeeper here at Mersea House. We take in a few paying guests."

"Oh," Mrs. Pagett said, glancing round the room. "A house-keeper."

Olive heard a clattering in the kitchen, and Margery burst out the door, across the entry, and into the lounge.

She held out her hand. "Mrs. Pagett? I'm Margery Paxton."

The woman took the offered hand and shook it vigorously. "Oh, Miss Paxton, you've no idea . . . I'm so very happy to meet you at last."

"Coffee?" Olive asked. She would serve them and then leave the room—this was not her business. Although, perhaps she could linger in the hall under the pretext of scrubbing the baseboards. Don't all housekeepers snoop?

"Yes, thank you," Mrs. Pagett said, taking one of the armchairs. "Now, Miss Paxton."

"We'll wait for Olive," Margery said. "If you don't mind. She's as much a part of the household here as I am, and so I would like her to be present."

Mrs. Pagett's hand hovered over her satchel. "Why, of course."

As Olive left, Margery sat at one end of the sofa, looking the picture of poise and calm. "Well, Mrs. Pagett, I hope you had a pleasant journey this morning."

The conversation had progressed to the weather by the time Olive returned with the tray, but as she poured out three cups and sat on the other end of the sofa, it turned to the matter at hand.

"Well," Mrs. Pagett said. She drew the papers out of the satchel and a notebook and fountain pen from her handbag. "You can't imagine my relief when I knew we'd finally found you, Miss Paxton, but we must do this the proper way. Do you affirm you are Margery Paxton of Southwold, ward of Milton Herbert Paxton known as Milkey and that you were born the fourth of September 1919?"

"Yes," Margery said. "Do you need identification?"

"We'll sort that out before I leave," Mrs. Pagett said, unscrewing the fountain pen and writing something in her notebook. Then, she held out the papers. "Here are the documents drawn up by a solicitor for Mr. George Wyckes, naming you as guardian to his daughter, Juniper."

Margery craned her neck to look but did not take them.

"Yes, I see. Shouldn't the mother have signed?"

Mrs. Pagett frowned at the document. "That wasn't possible. You see this is dated 1953, and her mother had died in 1950." There was a slight pause. "You were aware of this arrangement, weren't you?"

Margery looked at the woman, but her eyes seemed to see something far in the past.

"What do you mean?" she asked.

"It's only that, as anxious as we are to place Juniper," Mrs. Pagett said, "we understand that circumstances can change. I need to verify that you are willing to take the girl in."

"Of course I am," Margery said. "I know my responsibility."

"That's fine, then," Mrs. Pagett said. "I'm sure you can appreciate how difficult it's been. Since her father died, Juniper has told anyone who would listen, 'Miss Margery will come for me.' No one was quite sure what that meant because no one was aware of these papers. Even so, the address listed for you here is Chalk Farm Road."

Margery looked surprised. "I'd forgotten all about that flat—I wasn't there long. I suppose that makes five places I lived in London."

"Yes, well," Mrs. Pagett said, as if Margery had made the point for her. "With the girl moving from one children's home to another, her records always seemed to be a step or two behind her. She's had quite the nomadic life—not unlike you, Miss Paxton."

"She's been living in children's homes?" Margery asked.

Mrs. Pagett lifted her chin. "Yes, but they are well organized and carefully run. Since the Children's Committee was formed ten years ago, local authorities have taken over, and the entire system has been—is still being—modernized. Many of the homes are closing, as it is our goal to place children in foster care or have them adopted."

This declaration stirred something in Olive's memory. Years before, there had been a story in the newspapers about a boy in foster care who had died under the most dreadful conditions. Could that still happen?

"Yes," Margery said, "modernization. But what I meant was this: Was the girl in a home while her father was alive?"

"No," said Mrs. Pagett, "because he died in 1953, when she was seven. At that time, Juniper was spending most of her time in hospital."

A silence fell in the room like a dense, cold fog.

"In hospital?" Margery asked in a thick voice. "Why?"

Mrs. Pagett frowned. "Are you unaware of her history?"

"We . . . lost touch, I'm afraid. The war, you know."

The war had become the great excuse in the country. It covered so many faults without ever being a lie.

"Yes, of course." The woman looked down at the paperwork. "In 1950, both mother and child contracted poliomyelitis. Her mother died."

Margery squeezed her hands in her lap and didn't speak.

Olive felt as if a cold hand had touched her spine. "That's dreadful," she said. "But Juniper recovered well?" Most children did, didn't they? At least, many.

"She has recovered to some extent. I've known Juniper only these past two years, but they tell me she's come such a long way. She recalls very little of those early years. Well, who would want to remember life in an iron lung?"

Now Olive fell silent too.

"The disease left her legs quite useless, you see. She wears metal calipers on both legs, and needs sticks to help her walk." Mrs. Pagett hurried on, a bit breathless. "But that hasn't stopped her one whit. She keeps up with the other children as if she were on two good legs."

Olive glanced at Margery. Her eyes were open, but her face had gone white. She looked as if she had stopped breathing.

"I'm sure you can appreciate how difficult it can be to find the right setting for someone like Juniper, and you can see why we've put every effort into finding you, Miss Paxton. But even though we know a child's best hope is to be placed with a family, we are not beggars. We carefully choose a placement. Obviously, that can sometimes be difficult. Because of her legs, Juniper will need appropriate surroundings. Stairs, I'm afraid, are out of the question."

Mrs. Pagett's gaze darted back and forth between the two women. Olive waited for Margery to say something, but Margery was looking as if she might faint or be sick. Panic clutched at Olive's insides. This wouldn't do—the girl had no one. They dare not hesitate and cause Mrs. Pagett to think better of allowing Juniper to come to them. What would happen to her then?

"We have the perfect room," Olive said. "Isn't that right Margery?"

"Wonderful," Mrs. Pagett said, clapping her hands together. "May I see it?"

"Of course you may," Olive said. "It's down at the end of the hall here on the ground floor, just across from Margery's. The bathroom is nearby. Level the entire way. Come and I'll show you." Olive marched out of the lounge, with Mrs. Pagett behind her. Margery remained on the sofa.

Olive stopped in front of the room across from Margery's. The door was shut, and she put her hand on the knob but did not turn it. "Let me just say that it may look a bit messy at the moment, but it only needs clearing out. It's the perfect room—it really is." Mrs. Pagett raised her eyebrows. Olive opened the door and switched on the light.

The room was a sea of cartons stacked randomly on the floor and any level surface available. Castoff lamps stood like soldiers on the top of the wardrobe, one with a broken shade that hung lazily askew. Margery's childhood collection of ceramic jungle animals populated the dresser, the elephant missing his trunk. Olive had not found an empty carton for the things she'd cleared out of the kitchen, and so had piled the dented and burned pots, surplus lids, and chipped plates on the bed beside the heap of stained and worn table linens. There was a musty scent in the air.

"Oh dear," Mrs. Pagett said.

CHAPTER 5

"We didn't realize, you see," Olive explained. "About Juniper and the stairs. But there's no need to worry. I'm certain it won't take long to ready the room." She said this with conviction, because they would have at least the weekend. "When will she arrive?"

Mrs. Pagett wouldn't meet Olive's eye. "Well, and here's the thing. It has taken so very long to find Miss Paxton. The home Juniper has been living in is over near Newmarket, but it's closing, you see. We've kept her there just as long as we could. She's one of the last children. We had such hope of . . . I'm afraid it will have to be tomorrow. Otherwise, she'll be moved again to a home in Northumberland."

"You will not move her anywhere but here."

Margery had found her voice. She had come up behind them, and made her announcement so that it could've been heard across the green.

"But this is a box room," Mrs. Pagett said.

Margery pushed between them and into the room, stepping over the hurricane chimney of a paraffin lamp and glancing round at the walls. "This was my Auntie Von's sewing room, and for the last year of his life, Uncle Milkey's nurse lived in it. It's a bright and cheerful place, and it will be ready and waiting by tomorrow for the girl's arrival."

Mrs. Pagett's brow furrowed. "Well, Miss Paxton, you have put me in a pickle. I'd hate for Juniper to move again—"

"The very idea," Margery said.

"—and she is your ward." Mrs. Pagett seemed to consider her options. "Would her daily care fall to you or Miss Kersey?"

"Of course I will care for her," Margery said. "But as I own a shop in the High Street, I am away for a few hours each day. In that case, Olive will be available."

"This is a boardinghouse, isn't it? Do you have lodgers at the moment?"

"We have two," Margery said. "A war widow and a single gentleman."

"Mr. Hodgson runs the cinema in town," Olive added.

Mrs. Pagett brightened. "Really, the cinema? Imagine seeing films all the time and for free." She tapped the fountain pen against her bottom lip, then jotted something in her notebook. "All right, then, Miss Paxton, I will bring Juniper to you tomorrow. We'll give the situation to the end of summer—a trial period. I will carry out follow-up visits between now and then to check on her welfare. Still, this is a weight off my mind."

The three women stood amid boxes and broken china. Mrs. Pagett beamed. Margery looked stunned. Olive's mind was already chugging away, considering what to do with the current contents of the room.

"Now," Mrs. Pagett said, striding out of the room and back to the lounge while she talked over her shoulder. "Of course, we have a few details to work out. I must see visual proof of who you are."

"I have my old identification card from the war," Margery said as she and Olive followed. "And my passport."

"Good. There are other adjustments you may want to make so that it's easier for Juniper to take care of herself, but I don't recommend forging ahead with anything permanent until you're certain this will work out. For now, this should help." She held out a booklet titled *The Polio Child at Home*, which Margery took and set on the coffee table. Olive eyed it.

"You'll receive a weekly allowance," Mrs. Pagett said.

Margery scowled. "I don't want any money."

"It's for the girl's benefit, and it is the law. So, tomorrow, then. I'm sure we'll arrive by midmorning."

"Midmorning, yes," Margery said.

The woman departed shortly thereafter, leaving Olive and Margery with the tray of shortbread and cold coffee. Cold or not, Margery drank hers down.

"I'll take care of the room," Olive said. "You have enough to worry about."

"Yes," Margery said. "But where will we put everything—in one of the upstairs rooms?"

"No need for that. I'll have a quick sort, then I'll ring Mrs. Tees at St. Edmund's. She'll take anything that can go in the next church jumble sale, especially if I promise to help out with it." Going through donations wasn't the most sought-after task. It was odd and a bit disconcerting to see what people thought useful—one shoe, a fox stole so moth-eaten there was no fur left. "Old Trotter can take the rest away." Old Trotter was the nearest thing the town had to a rag-and-bone man.

"Thank you, Olive," Margery said, her voice breaking.

They were quiet, each lost in her own thoughts.

"Did George not have any relations?" Olive asked.

Margery roused herself as from a dream. "No—neither of us did. We used to talk about children and how we wanted a houseful of them."

"That must be why he—"

Margery sniffed and rose, brushing off her skirt. "Silly dreams. Come on, we'd better get to it."

★ ★ ★

Olive made the arrangements over the telephone. When she went back to the box room—Juniper's room—Margery came in after her and said, "I wonder if we should put up new wallpaper."

"In twenty-four hours?" Olive asked. "We'll be doing well to find the bed. And anyway, I rather like the wallpaper." What she could see of it. "Colorful, floral, but not too busy."

"I need to get back to the shop," Margery said, "but I can't leave you with this."

The front door opened and closed, and Olive looked out to see Hugh had returned.

"Just the man," she said. "Are you busy this afternoon?"

"I'm not. What do you need?"

"Help with a bit of clearing out," Olive replied and turned to Margery. "There, now, you don't need to worry."

"I won't," Margery said as she came out of the room. "Not with you two in charge." She headed for the kitchen and, without breaking her stride, added, "Thanks, Hugh. Olive will explain. I'll check back later."

Olive drew Hugh back to the box room but waited until she'd heard the door close before she said, "You wouldn't know it to look at her now, but she was that shaken earlier. It was quite a shock."

"Is it the girl—her ward?"

"Yes. She's arriving tomorrow, and this is her room," Olive said.

Hugh peered over Olive's shoulder at the clutter. "Why here and not upstairs?"

"I'll explain while we work. We need to separate the wheat from the chaff and take it all out the kitchen door into the yard for collection."

Olive put her pinny on, and they got started on dividing and repacking cartons while she told Hugh about the visit from Mrs. Pagett.

"Polio," he said. "The poor kid. But Margery hasn't filled in any of the blanks for you?"

"She swears she doesn't know anything," Olive said. "Margery seemed as shocked by the whole affair as we are. More so. Her name—the girl's—is Juniper Wyckes."

"Juniper," Hugh repeated and smiled. "That shows a bit of spirit, doesn't it?"

"Just how well do you know Margery?" Olive asked.

"We met through—"

"Yes, through a mutual friend," Olive said. "Where?"

"We both worked at the Ministry during the war. A group of us would meet up after work and stay out far too late. You know what it's like— aware that a bomb could drop at any moment, but pretending you didn't care."

"Were you and Margery ever . . . you know." Olive turned away, folding a tablecloth to hide her blush. "Am I prying?"

Hugh laughed. "Pry all you like, Olive. No, we weren't."

"Did you leave someone behind in London?" she persisted, looking back at him.

"I suppose I did."

Olive went back to her sorting, embarrassed that she'd even asked. Eventually, she said, "Margery had a fellow here, before she left for London. I'm not sure of the details because it was the time when the two of us were busy with our own lives." Olive stuck her hands in the pockets of her pinny and watched Hugh as she said, "His name was George Wyckes."

Hugh looked up from an open carton. "Wyckes? As in Juniper Wyckes?"

"Yes," Olive said, "the girl's father. Margery and George broke up before the war. She went off, and apparently George married someone else. What about Margery? Did she have a fellow in London? She won't tell me anything about her life there."

Hugh's gaze dropped back to the contents of the box. "You know Margery—Churchill could've used her on those posters about loose lips sinking ships."

"You're right there," Olive said. "She's never been one to tell you what you want to know until she's ready. And I must say, you're quite good at keeping mum yourself."

He grinned and lifted the carton to show her the contents. "Looks as if Milkey was fond of a boater."

The box held at least a dozen old straw hats. Some of the brims were moldy, and there were holes in the crowns. "It was definitely his signature hat in the summer," Olive said. "I can remember him walking round town wearing one. Looks like the damp got to those."

Olive gave up trying to learn anything else about Margery's life in London—or Hugh's, for that matter—and they continued to work, their only topic of conversation to rate the quality of the used goods.

It took less time than she thought, and when they'd cleared out the room, she and Hugh sat down to lunch in the kitchen. Just as they finished their sandwiches, Old Trotter came round in his van.

"Hoya, Olive. Yawright?"

"Good, Reg. Thanks for this," she said. They all three helped to load, and then away everything went—the best to church, and the rest to where only Old Trotter could say.

"Thanks, Hugh," Olive said. "You're off duty now." She glanced up the stairs. "I wonder how Mrs. Claypool is doing."

"She's gone out," Hugh said.

"I didn't see."

"She slipped off while we were working," he said. "She's a secret one, this Abigail Claypool."

"She is that."

Hugh went upstairs, and Olive back to the nearly empty room. She felt as if they'd missed something, but there wasn't a moldy boater or broken lampshade left. It wasn't large, but the room seemed spacious now that all it held was a bed, dresser, wardrobe, and chair. She crossed to the corner, threw back the curtains, and flung open the window. A gust of wind blew in fresh sea air as she turned back to give the space a critical eye. She had been right about the wallpaper—in good condition and quite cheerful. The bed linens needed washing, and she'd have to get out the Hoover for the rug. Olive might know little of Margery's time in London and nothing about the girl, but she did know about keeping house, and so that's what she would do.

It made her a bit late starting the evening meal, and when Margery arrived back and Hugh came down, Olive didn't have time to join them for a drink. She heard the wireless—dance music and then the shipping forecast—but no conversation. When Olive came out of the kitchen, Hugh was there to help her carry out the food. The elusive Mrs. Claypool appeared at the appropriate time and not a minute before, and they sat down to sliced ham accompanied by bubble and squeak. Olive told herself she'd get creative with the meals once she had more time to study her cookery book.

They began in silence, but eventually Margery told Mrs. Claypool about the new arrival.

"A child?" Abigail asked, her voice shrill. "You never said there would be children."

"I never said there wouldn't," Margery said. Hugh coughed. "And you can be sure she'll be no trouble to you, Abigail. I only thought it best to let you know."

Margery said nothing about polio or calipers or walking sticks. In fact, she said nothing else at all, and the four of them continued to eat.

At last, Olive couldn't stand the silence. "Who was the band on the wireless?" she asked.

"The Northern Dance Orchestra," Hugh said.

"They're quite good, aren't they?"

"Smashing," Hugh replied.

Olive eyed the other two women. Margery was pushing a bit of potato about her plate, and Mrs. Claypool ate her food as if it were something she had to get through. Olive carried on. "I enjoy the music, but I believe my favorite program on the wireless is *A Book at Bedtime*. Though I can easily fall asleep before the installment is finished. It makes for interesting dreams."

She lifted her eyebrows at Hugh, who took the plunge. "And you, Mrs. Claypool, what do you like to listen to on the wireless?"

The woman looked up, her eyes wide. "Oh. That is, I generally listen to whatever is on."

He didn't even bother to ask Margery.

★　★　★

After dinner, Margery and Olive went to Juniper's room. The fresh scent of clean bed linens and curtains had banished the musty smell.

"You've done a splendid job," Margery said, and then looked at her shoes. "I'm sorry I was such a lump at dinner."

"Were you?" Olive asked. "I hadn't noticed." She nodded to the bedside table. "I took a few books from the shelves in the lounge and left them for her. What do you think?"

Margery crossed and bent over to read the spines. "Look at this— here's my collection of *Just William*."

"I thought it would be nice for her to have a story to read. You loved those books."

"I did," Margery said in almost a whisper. She chose one, stroked its cover, and ran a finger over the worn corners. "It's a bit ragged now, isn't it?"

"No matter. Are you nervous to meet her?"

"Are you?" Margery asked.

"A bit, I suppose. You're very good to take her in."

"She deserves a chance, doesn't she?" Margery said. "For a normal life. Whatever that is."

"What about school?"

"Mrs. Pagett said she should be able to go straight into the class for her age. We'll have to sort that out." Margery rubbed her forehead.

"You have enough to do between now and Saturday," Olive said. "School will keep until next week."

★ ★ ★

Olive had her first cup of tea sitting in the kitchen at six o'clock the next morning. Margery soon joined her. They talked little, but every few minutes one or the other of them would go back to Juniper's room under the excuse of making sure the window was open or the lamp plugged in.

"I read through this," Margery said, nodding to *The Polio Child at Home*, which had made it to the kitchen table. "She may need help with her bath and such."

"We can sort it out," Olive replied. "Accommodations can be made. The important thing is to make her feel at home."

At breakfast, Hugh kept up a one-man monologue as now all three women were unresponsive. Soon after, he donned his jacket and said something about going to Lowestoft for the morning and returning in the afternoon.

Margery left to look in on Young Trotter at the shop. "He's no eye for a display," she said, "and I do so want things to look their best tomorrow."

Olive cleared the breakfast dishes, cleaned downstairs, and then baked a pan of shortbread, after which she walked over to the bakery for an extra loaf. By the time she returned, it was nearly ten thirty. Midmorning. Where was Margery?

She arrived five minutes later, and the two of them stood in the lounge, Olive hovering over the electric fire that wasn't switched on and Margery at the window, watching as people outside went about their business. Olive laughed. "You'd think we were waiting for the Queen."

At last, a car pulled up to the curb. Margery parted the curtains with a finger, then backed away and took a deep breath. Olive dashed to the kitchen and set the percolator on the hob. When the knock came, the two of them met at the door, and Olive opened it.

Mrs. Pagett had a large brown envelope under one arm and clasped a small case and her handbag in her other hand. Her smile emitted an aura of victory. Next to her stood a girl who wore a thin brown coat over a yellow dress with daisies stitched along the neckline. She had a bag sewn from a solid blue fabric slung across her shoulder. Her straight, thick brown hair was neatly combed and held back with two slides, one at each ear. Her eyes, a rich chestnut brown, were wide, and her face looked a bit pale for her coloring.

What had Olive expected? True, the girl had walking sticks that wrapped round each forearm and metal calipers that went right down into her shoes and made her legs look as if they were in cages. Barely noticeable, really.

"Well, ladies," Mrs. Pagett said, "here is Juniper Wyckes." Gesturing to the two women, she continued. "Juniper, this is Miss Margery Paxton and Miss Olive Kersey."

Margery swayed slightly and Olive put a hand on her back. The girl gave them a tentative smile and, a bit breathless, said, "Hello. I'm very pleased to meet you."

Olive's heart melted.

CHAPTER 6

"Well, let's get you in here, then," Margery said, her voice as breathless as Juniper's. She stepped aside, but held out her hands to the girl. "Are you all right there?"

"Yes, Miss Margery," Juniper said. They watched as she placed her sticks across the threshold and then swung both legs over at the same time. She continued into the entry, where she stopped and took in her surroundings.

"Right, here we are," Mrs. Pagett said, following. "I'll set your case just here, Juniper. Now, shall I leave you to it?"

"What?" Margery shot Olive a panicked look.

"Won't you stay for coffee?" Olive asked.

The woman pushed back her sleeve at the wrist and tapped her watch face with a fingernail. "Yes, I believe I do have a bit of time. That would be lovely, thank you."

"The lounge, then," Margery said.

Mrs. Pagett led the way, taking one of the upholstered chairs across from the sofa. The girl, Margery, and Olive followed but stood clustered just inside.

"What sort of chair is best, do you think?" Margery asked.

Mrs. Pagett surveyed the possibilities and then said, "Why don't we let Juniper decide?"

"I can sit over there," the girl said, nodding to a chair with a rush seat a few inches lower than the others.

"Here, I'll bring it over so you can join us," Olive said.

"Thank you, Miss Olive," Juniper said. "You'd best give me room in front so I don't knock anything over."

Olive saw what she meant. When Juniper sat on the edge of the seat, her legs stuck straight out in front of her, the heels of her shoes resting on the floor. She leaned her sticks against the end of the sofa and manipulated the metal calipers at her knees. That released locks, so that her knees bent, and she was able to put her feet flat on the floor.

During the process, Margery's gaze darted from Juniper's legs, away, and back again, and her hands twitched as if she wanted to reach out and help. It was obvious Juniper needed no help in the matter, and the process lasted only a few seconds.

Olive had leaned forward to watch carefully. "That's quite marvelous, isn't it?" she asked.

"It's nice that you've a chair the right size for me," Juniper said.

"That was mine when I was young," Margery said, sinking onto the sofa.

"There you are, then." Mrs. Pagett said. Her hand slipped into her bag and brought out the notebook and fountain pen. She unscrewed the top and wrote something down, which Olive tried to read upside down but couldn't.

"I'll bring the coffee in," Olive said. "Juniper, would you like Ribena or a glass of milk?"

The girl hesitated for a moment as if perplexed at the choice. "Ribena, please."

In the kitchen, Olive had taken the coffee off the heat and reached for the china pot on the warming shelf above the cooker, when Margery appeared.

"Is everything all right?" Olive asked.

"Yes, just fine," Margery said. "I thought I'd give you a hand."

"You pour up the coffee." Olive measured the blackcurrant concentrate into a glass, added water, and stirred. "She's lovely, isn't she?"

Margery frowned. "Do you think I scare her?"

"I don't think you've had the chance to scare her yet," Olive said. "She's only just arrived. Give it time."

Something halfway between a laugh and a sob caught in Margery's throat. "I've worked myself up a bit about her arrival. I want her to feel welcome, of course, but I don't want to overwhelm her. What should I do?"

"You should take the shortbread in."

The three women drank coffee and chatted about the remarkable spring weather—a chance warm, still day—while Juniper gazed at Margery, crunched on shortbread, and drank her Ribena, which turned her lips purple.

Eventually, Mrs. Pagett had to be on her way. She stood, gathered her gloves and bag, and said, "I can see you're all going to get along famously."

Margery shot off the sofa. "Must you go?"

Mrs. Pagett reached over to pat Margery's arm. "It'll be fine. Juniper is well able to tell you what she needs. Aren't you?"

"Yes, ma'am."

"And I'll be back in touch," Mrs. Pagett said. "You'll register Juniper with the local surgery as soon as ever you can, won't you? That way her records can be sent on to the local doctor."

"Of course," Margery said. "Our local. Our local is—" She looked at Olive.

"Dr. Atterbury," Olive said.

"Yes, he's the one," Margery said. "Of course, the doctor I knew growing up has long since retired, but Dr. Atterbury took care of my Uncle Milkey."

"He's a good man," Olive added, watching Mrs. Pagett write in her notebook.

"You'll like him," Margery said to Juniper.

Juniper smiled, looking unconcerned. She had probably encountered more doctors in her short life than Olive would ever do.

Mrs. Pagett drew up her shoulders as she inhaled, and let her breath out with a flourish. "Here's a happy ending for everyone. Of course the court will finalize the arrangement after a trial period. Miss Paxton, if you'll sign on that top paper to say you've had receipt of the allowance." She gave Margery a lumpy brown envelope.

Margery scowled. The girl paid no attention to this as she was leaning forward to set her empty glass on the coffee table, which was just out of her reach. Olive took it from her.

"Well, Juniper," Mrs. Pagett said. "I know you'll do your very best for Miss Margery and Miss Olive, won't you?"

"Yes, ma'am."

Margery and Olive followed the woman to the door, bade her goodbye, and returned to find Juniper leaning over to look out the front window as Mrs. Pagett drove off.

"Is that the sea?" the girl asked.

"It is," Margery said. "Have you been to the seaside before?"

"Yes. I was in a home in Norfolk, and they took us for a day's outing," Juniper said. "But I wasn't allowed on the beach, so I stayed with the coach driver, and we had our tea together."

That she was kept from the sea bothered Olive—what was the point of taking her otherwise?—but what bothered her more was that Juniper didn't seem to mind. Had she been left behind so often while the rest of the children ran and played that she'd become inured to such treatment?

"We could walk down to the seafront this afternoon, if you like," Olive said.

"Could we? Will you come, too, Miss Margery?"

Margery swallowed. "I'd love to, I really would, it's just that—"

"Did Mrs. Pagett tell you that Miss Margery owns a shop in town?" Olive asked. Juniper nodded. "Well, the shop's been closed for work—to make it new and fresh—and it's opening again tomorrow. It's going to be grand—like a party, I'd say. So, Miss Margery will need to go back to the shop this afternoon and see after things."

"I will," Margery said, throwing Olive a smile. "Tomorrow, Olive can bring you round to see the place, what do you think?"

"What sort of a shop is it?" Juniper asked.

"Well, it isn't a sweets shop, if that's what you were hoping." Juniper blushed, and Margery winked and added, "More's the pity. Olive, will you be all right?"

"We'll be fine," Olive said, not terribly sure of it.

Juniper watched Margery's retreating figure.

"Shall I give you a tour of your new home?" Olive asked.

"Yes, please." Juniper locked her calipers straight and took up her sticks, which she used to heave herself out of her chair.

They stopped in the entry, and Olive pointed up the stairs. "We have two other people who live here—they're lodgers. Mr. Hodgson and Mrs. Claypool. You'll meet them at dinner. My room is on the floor above theirs. The kitchen is through here, and that door is to the dining room." Olive picked up Juniper's case—it was made of cardboard, and a few of the metal caps designed to protect the corners were missing. It wasn't terribly heavy. "Your room is here at the back and just across from Miss Margery's. You've the bathroom between you."

"Oh," the girl said. "May I use the toilet?"

"Of course you may. This is your house now—you do whatever you like whenever you like. Within reason." Olive pushed open the bathroom door and hesitated. "Do you need help?"

Juniper looked in. It was a large bathroom with Victorian half-tiled walls and light from a high window. The facilities were spread out: the footed tub sat against the far wall; the sink on the wall to the left; and on the right was the toilet, with the chain hanging from the cistern above.

Juniper studied the scene for a moment and then said, "Yes, I will need help."

"Of course you will," Olive replied. The toilet was an island with nothing useful nearby to rest against or take hold of. "Do you take off your calipers first?"

"No, I don't need to. Here, I'll show you." She leaned back against the doorpost and lifted her dress. Olive saw the metal calipers that held her thin legs in place extended to midthigh, ending in leather bands with buckles. From there, straps continued up over her under-pants to her waist, where a broad leather belt with more buckles held everything fast.

With great effort Olive fought the tears that sprang to her eyes. "Well, now," she said enthusiastically, "that's quite something, isn't it? What can I do to help?"

"You can be a tree," Juniper said. "A bendable one. I'll hold onto you to sit down and stand back up again."

Olive did as she was told, and when it was finished and Juniper was washing her hands, she said, "You have a good way of explaining what you need."

"Sister Freddie taught me that I must be clear, or I could end up with my knickers caught in my—" Juniper, a mortified look on her face, glanced in the mirror at Olive's reflection.

Olive smiled, and then she laughed. Juniper giggled.

"Who is this wise Sister Freddie?" Olive asked.

"She's a nurse at the hospital where I've gone for my operations. She was my favorite, but she was always in trouble with matron for her language." Juniper gave the toilet an appraising look. "At the hospital, I didn't need anyone to help me because there was a rail to hold on to."

Although Olive hadn't studied the booklet Mrs. Pagett left, she felt certain there must be useful information in it on the subject of bathrooms. "Margery will have someone come round and sort it out for you. Do you think you could explain what you need?"

"I could draw a picture," Juniper said.

Olive left the girl at the kitchen table with paper and pencil and rang Margery.

"She needs a railing. Juniper says she can be on her own with that," Olive said. "We should sort this out now, don't you think?"

"Yes, yes, of course," Margery said. "I'll ring Casper. No, you ring him, why don't you—tell him it's urgent. Now I must run— Young Trotter needs help out front."

Olive made the call, pleading their case to Casper, who had worked at Mersea House refitting the bathrooms, replacing the coke burner in the kitchen with piped-in gas, and installing electric-bar heaters—he was a jack-of-all-trades and quite an expert at any of them.

"Oh yes," Casper said when she had explained. "My wife heard tell about this girl coming to Margery. Right, Olive, I'll be round just before teatime."

While Juniper was busy at the kitchen table, Olive took the girl's case into the bedroom, where she saw the menagerie of ceramic jungle animals arranged on the dresser—even the trunkless elephant. Margery must've carried out a last-minute rescue of the collection before everything in the room had been packed up and carried off.

Juniper's small case held a wooden cigar box with a sliding lid that had a crack in it. Suspecting it contained personal items, she set it on the nightstand and attended to the clothes: one dress, one cardigan that looked too small, three pairs of underpants and socks, plus two vests and her night things. The state of the girl's wardrobe was even worse than her own. Olive's mind flew to Mrs. Tees and the growing collection of clothes for the next jumble sale. Children's clothes were always popular—both to donate and to buy—and so surely there would be things to fit Juniper. Olive could wait until the next sale for the day dress that had caught her own eye, but she wouldn't mind jumping the queue for the girl.

Olive put her head into the kitchen where Juniper was still at work. "I need to get on with my cleaning. You can stay here or go out to the lounge—doesn't matter. Mr. Casper will come by this afternoon about the bathroom. You all right?"

"Yes, Miss Olive. Thank you."

Upstairs, Olive knocked on Mrs. Claypool's door.

"I'm running a bit late today, but shall I clean your room now?" she said.

"No thank you, Olive," came the voice on the other side of the door. "The room is fine."

"Wouldn't you like to come downstairs to the lounge and have coffee? It won't take me a minute to clean. It's awfully quiet down there."

The promise of solitude must've done the trick, because she agreed. Olive hurried down, cleared away remnants of the earlier coffee, and had a fresh pot and plate of shortbread ready when the lodger walked in.

Mrs. Claypool took her coffee to a chair on the far side of the room, with a view out the window. Olive dragged the Hoover upstairs, and when she finished, toted it back down and put it away. When she looked in the lounge, she found Mrs. Claypool where she'd left her, sitting at the front window. Back in her low rush seat, Juniper was reading *Just William*.

"Keeping an eye out for your wireless?" Olive asked the lodger.

The woman leapt out of the chair and made straight for the door. "Oh, you've finished cleaning upstairs? Thank you for the coffee, Olive."

Olive stood in the doorway blocking her escape. "You two have most likely already spoken, but let me introduce you properly. Mrs. Claypool, this is Juniper Wyckes, Margery's ward, who has come to live with us. Juniper, Mrs. Claypool." *Such a mouthful of a name.* "Mrs. C.?" Olive asked with raised eyebrows.

"Yes, of course." Mrs. Claypool turned her head vaguely in the girl's direction. "I believe I'll go back to my room now, but I will listen out for the delivery. I don't want to be any trouble."

And like a scared rabbit, she shot back to her hole.

Olive followed. She reached Abigail's door as it was being closed in her face.

"Sorry," Olive said, "it's only that I did want to say one other thing. I'm sure you noticed Juniper's calipers and her walking sticks."

A troubled look drifted across the woman's face. "I didn't want to say anything."

"It's all right to say something," Olive said. "No one will mind, least of all Juniper."

"Is she a polio?" Mrs. Claypool whispered.

"Yes," Olive replied at a normal volume. "She contracted polio when she was four. But she survived—and isn't it remarkable how well she does?" She didn't wait for a reply. "There, that's all. I only wanted to tell you so you wouldn't wonder."

*   *   *

Olive and Juniper ate lunch in the kitchen and, afterward, walked the Parade with the beach on their right and the row of seafront houses across the road on their left. Juniper stared out at the horizon, a gauzy line separating sea from sky. She gazed at the foamy waves rushing up onto the beach, and put her nose up and sniffed the salty air. Her delight made Olive see and hear and smell the sea as she hadn't in ages.

"We've the wind in our faces this afternoon," she told Juniper. "It can be fierce—it's practically knocked me over once or twice, so do be careful."

"I will," Juniper promised, her cheeks ruddy and her smile wide. "Could we go onto the beach one day?"

There were steps to the beach—steep ones. And the beach itself was a mix of shingle and sand. Olive thought about Juniper's calipers and shoes and wondered how she would manage. Perhaps the day out to the seaside when the girl stayed back with the coach driver wasn't meant to exclude, but to protect. Still.

"Yes, we'll get all that sorted so you can put your feet in the sea," Olive said. "But this is only your first day."

They got as far as Hetty Dupree's tea hut, and that meant stopping to say hello. Olive introduced the girl, and Hetty leaned her arms on the hutch opening and smiled down at her, showing a gap where she was missing an eyetooth.

"Oh yes, you're Margery's ward," Hetty said.

"Yes, Mrs. Dupree," Juniper said. "I'm pleased to meet you."

That both Casper and Hetty already knew of Juniper's existence was no surprise to Olive: the lines of communication round the town spread far, wide, and unseen, like the roots of a tree.

"I've been watching you and Olive coming up the Parade," Hetty said. "I'd say you're quicker on those sticks of yours than ever I would be on my own feet or even a bicycle or in a cart or any old way. Won't it be lovely for Margery to have a child about the place now she's back from London and settling down right and proper—or not actually right and proper, of course, her running a business and all."

"Yes, ma'am," Juniper replied and looked to Olive.

"This is Juniper's first time out since she arrived this morning," Olive said, "so I'd say we'd best be getting back now. See you, Hetty."

"I'll be looking in at Paxton's Goods tomorrow," Hetty called after them. "See what Margery's got herself into. I suppose if any woman can do it, she's the one. At least Milkey thought so, but of course he was always a bit of a free thinker."

Uncle Milkey's confidence in his niece had been a constant in Margery's life, imbuing her with the idea that she could do anything she wanted if she worked at it. That spirit was probably what took her off to London. At the beginning of the war, that had seemed the epitome of glamour.

It had never occurred to Olive to go anywhere, because she had been in love. The love—or the fading memory of it—had lasted longer than Stan. He'd died in Norway. More death followed—her brother, Donald, at Dunkirk; her father at the end of the war. With each succeeding loss, Olive settled for a smaller and smaller life.

But perhaps it hadn't been easier for Margery in London, because she had returned all these years later. It could be Milkey's generosity that brought her back, and she saw her uncle's bequest as a lifeline in rather the same way Olive regarded Margery's offer of a job and a home.

Olive thought on those things as she and Juniper made their way. They turned on East Street, and just before they went down Pinkney's Lane, Olive looked further up the road and spotted Billy Grunyon, sitting on his bicycle, one foot on the ground, watching them.

They arrived at Mersea House at the same time as Casper. He wore his usual work coveralls, the pockets overflowing with stubby pencils, notebooks, measuring tapes, and small tools he liked to have near to hand. He was a gentle man with a perpetually bewildered look about him, possibly because he and his wife had six children between them—three of hers, two of his, and one together—with ages ranging from seventeen down to three.

In the entry, Olive made the introductions and explained the situation.

"It's this ground-floor bathroom, is it?" Casper asked and led the way there. "Yes," he answered his own question as he contemplated the toilet, "I can see as how you might need a hand. Now, Missy, can you tell me about what sort of setup the hospital had?"

"I drew a picture," Juniper said. She pulled a paper out of the fabric bag, unfolded it, and handed it over.

Casper looked down his nose and through his glasses and studied the paper. And then he studied the girl.

"You drew this?"

"Yes, sir."

"Well, my, my."

Olive looked over his shoulder and saw that Juniper had drawn several pictures: one looking at the toilet straight on and one looking from the side. On either side of the seat were short railings. In the corner of the drawing, she had written her name.

"An artist who signs her work," Casper said. He tapped the paper with the only two fingers he had on his left hand, the other two having been lost in a sawmill accident when he was young. "These railings here bring to mind one of those walking frames."

"Yes," Juniper said, "except the railings need to stay put. If they slide away, I would slide away with them."

Casper guffawed. "I do like a person who knows what she wants. You just stand up there, and we'll take a few measurements." Casper and Juniper continued to discuss what was needed, and when he'd finished jotting in his notebook, he closed it up and said to Olive, "I'll need to drill into the tile floor—fix the railings permanently, you know."

Without a thought, Olive replied, "Yes, that's fine."

"Well, ladies," Casper said, "I'll be back as soon as ever I can. Perhaps even Monday."

"Thank you, Mr. Casper," Juniper said.

"Tea?" Olive asked.

★   ★   ★

She set Casper up with tea and the last of the shortbread, and went back to find Juniper in her own room, sitting on the bench at the dressing table, examining the ceramic jungle animals.

"Those were Margery's when she was a girl," Olive said. "I suppose she thought you might like them."

"Oh, I do," Juniper said, picking up the elephant. "Too bad about this fellow."

"Perhaps we could fashion him a new trunk?" Olive saw the girl stifle a yawn. "Would you like to lie down for a bit? You've had quite a day."

"I would, but I shouldn't put my shoes on the bed, and my calipers and shoes are all of a piece, you see. I usually don't take them off until bedtime."

"Easily sorted," Olive said. She got a towel from the cupboard and put it over the counterpane. Juniper sat on the edge of the bed and Olive lifted the girl's legs and moved her into position. Juniper scooted herself up so that she had her head propped against a pillow. Olive left her with *Just William* and went back to the kitchen, where Casper was ready to leave. When he opened the door to the yard, there was Billy.

"Hiya, Mr. Casper," Billy said.

"Hard at work, Billy," Casper said as he left. "Good to see that."

"Yes, sir," Billy called and then turned. "Hiya, Miss Olive." He looked past her into the kitchen. "I've your groceries."

"Right, come in. Was there any rhubarb?"

"Yes," Billy said as he set the basket on the table and they unpacked. "Mr. Farnham said it's the first week. Came all the way from Kent, he said."

Billy shot a glance at the door to the entry, which Olive had left open in case Juniper needed something.

"I see the cod, but where's the smoked haddock?" Olive asked. "Oh, here it is." Fish-and-potato pie for the evening meal, and sponge with stewed rhubarb and custard for afters.

"Do you have a new lodger, Miss Olive?"

"No, Billy, only the two you know about. Why do you ask?"

"I saw you this afternoon, and I thought . . . well, who was that, then?"

"You saw me with Juniper," Olive explained. "She's Miss Margery's ward, and she's come to live here."

"Juniper?" Billy asked in a scoffing tone. "Why's she called that?"

"She's called Juniper because that's her name," Olive said, and her tone put an end to the topic. "Billy, I didn't order this tin of celery. Why would I do that when I'm quite capable of cooking celery myself?"

"Sorry, Miss Olive," Billy said. "That belongs to my last delivery. I'll take it."

He hung his head, appearing well and truly chastised, and Olive relented.

"Will you stay for bread and butter and jam?"

Billy gave the errant tin a hard look and huffed. "I'd best not— old Mrs. Norris'll have my head if she doesn't get her celery."

"Wait a minute, then," Olive said, "and I'll fetch my purse."

She returned with a farthing and sent Billy on his way.

CHAPTER 7

Somewhere between Billy's leaving and time for the evening meal, Olive made the fish pie, stewed the rhubarb, let in the man who delivered Abigail's wireless, and fretted about Margery's being late on Juniper's first day. Her worry was unfounded. Margery was in time for Olive to give her an account of Casper's visit over a quick drink in the lounge with Hugh. "You should see how she can draw," Olive told them.

Juniper came to dinner with combed hair and clean hands.

"Why don't you sit here?" Olive asked, indicating a place next to Margery's. The girl, holding onto the back of the chair with one hand, rested her sticks against the wall. She turned and moved sideways, rocking from side to side to lift each foot off the floor until she was in position to sit. Knees unlocked, Olive scooted her up to the table only a moment before Abigail appeared.

It was a large dining table, well able to seat ten or twelve people without knocking elbows, but Olive set the five places at one end. The evening before, Abigail had looked longingly at the empty end of the table, as if she would prefer to be just that much further away from the rest of them. This second night, Olive had pushed the extra chairs against the wall.

"Now," Margery said, "introductions before we eat. Abigail, Hugh, this is Juniper Wyckes, who has come to live here at Mersea House. Juniper, here are Mrs. Claypool and Mr. Hodgson."

"Mrs. C. and I met this morning, didn't we?" Juniper asked.

Abigail smiled at her plate.

Hugh put his hand out across the table. "Happy to meet you, Juniper. I'm Hugh."

"There," Margery said. "Shall we begin?"

The fish pie was too hot to pass, and so the adults served themselves. Olive caught Margery's eye and nodded toward Juniper, who couldn't reach the dish.

"Here," Margery said, taking the girl's plate, "let me do this for you. Have you had fish pie before?"

"Oh yes," Juniper said. "Often."

"Olive is a wonderful cook. I know you'll enjoy it."

The bowl of peas went round, and everyone began. Juniper took up her fork and gingerly poked a piece of fish, at last stabbing it along with a bit of potato. She opened her mouth wide with a look of grim determination not unlike Mrs. Claypool getting through her meal. The girl chewed slowly once, twice, and then plunged her fork back in with enthusiasm.

"Miss Olive, this is the best fish pie I've ever eaten in my life."

"Thank you," Olive said, wondering to what her dish was being compared.

"Did you know Mr. Hugh runs the cinema?" Margery asked.

"I've never been to the pictures," Juniper said in awe.

"We'll have to remedy that, won't we?" Margery asked. "We'll let Hugh tell us when he's showing something you might like. Davy Crockett? Or one of the Walt Disney cartoons?"

"Yes, please," Juniper said. "Do you go to the pictures, Mrs. C.?"

Abigail flinched. She glanced up at Juniper's big chestnut-colored eyes, and it was as if she couldn't look away. "Oh," she replied, "it's been years. The last film I saw was *English Without Tears*."

"Was it sad?" Juniper asked.

Mrs. Claypool dropped her gaze, and Hugh jumped in. "Michael Wilding, 1944, wasn't it? That was a comedy."

It didn't look as if Abigail Claypool had found it so.

"How was your afternoon?" Margery asked Juniper.

"Miss Olive took me along the seafront," the girl said, "and promised we could go onto the beach soon. Will you come too?"

"I wouldn't miss it," Margery said. "We'll have sandwiches, and we'll buy ice cream from Hetty's tea hut."

"And I can put my feet in the water?" Juniper asked.

Margery hesitated. "Yes, of course. Yes. Will that be all right?" she asked Olive.

How would Olive know? "We'll sort it out."

"Well, Margery," Hugh said, "ready for tomorrow?"

"I'd better be," Margery said. "The door will open at ten o'clock regardless. I do hope Young Trotter remembers to wear a clean shirt."

Over pudding, Hugh said, "Juniper, you've quite an interesting name—it's lovely. How did you come by it?"

"I'm named for a tree," Juniper said. "Because my mum was named for a tree."

"Was she?" Hugh asked. "Was she called . . . Box?"

Juniper giggled. "No, not Box."

"Was she called Hornbeam?" Olive offered, and the girl laughed again.

"No." She looked to the head of the table. "Miss Margery knows what her name was, don't you?"

Margery stared at Juniper, her look softening and her voice low. "Yes, I saw it on Mrs. Pagett's papers. Your mum's name was Holly."

Juniper nodded with vigor. "Yes. And my grandmother's name was Cherry. You see, we are all trees. When I get married and have a baby, I'm going to name her Hazel."

"Willow would be a lovely name too," Olive said.

"As would Walnut," Hugh offered.

Juniper grinned at him. "That would be silly."

★ ★ ★

Hugh left for the cinema, Abigail for her enclave, and it was Juniper's bedtime. Olive set the kettle on to boil, came out of the kitchen, and saw Margery standing outside the bathroom door. She gestured Olive over.

"She's getting herself ready for bed," Margery whispered. "Do you think she needs any help?"

"With the toilet, yes," Olive replied. "Juniper, shall I come in?"

There was a garbled reply, followed by a spitting sound and the tap at the sink running. In a moment the door opened to Juniper wearing a short dressing gown over a longer nightie. She bared her teeth at them.

"Well done," Olive said and followed her back in. "Margery, you'll want to see how Juniper will manage until Casper fits the railings in."

"I tell you what," Margery said, "why don't I get your hot-water bottle ready? You two carry on, and I'll meet you back." She dashed off.

Olive helped Juniper out of her calipers, and once she was settled in bed, the girl reached for the wooden cigar box that Olive had unpacked earlier and left on the nightstand. Juniper slid the top open. All that was inside were two photos.

"Who's this now?" Olive asked.

Juniper took out the snapshots and held them up for Olive. "This one is my mum and this is my dad."

There he was, George, sitting for a portrait photograph, wearing his uniform and a smile, looking confident in life. Olive hadn't known him long and would've been hard-pressed to give a full description, but she recognized him. The other photo was an equally happy young woman, with blond hair framing her face and wearing a soft dark hat like a beret.

Margery returned with the bottle.

"Here now, this'll keep you warm," she said, and slid it between the covers, smoothing the blanket and patting it down.

Olive held out the photos. "See what Juniper has."

Margery took one and cocked her head as she studied it. She smiled. "Ah, George, look at you now. Your dad was a fine-looking man, wasn't he?"

"Yes," Juniper said. "And there's my mum."

Margery turned a more discerning eye on the other photo. "Isn't she's lovely? I see where you got your smile."

"That's what my dad said." The girl returned the photos to the cigar box and scooted down in the bed.

"Good night, Juniper." Olive leaned over and kissed the top of her head. "We're awfully glad you're here."

Olive went to the door, but Margery hesitated.

"I tell you what," she said to Juniper, "why don't I stay until you're asleep. I'll sit over here." Margery went to the chair and picked up the extra blanket Olive had left. "You just close your eyes."

Juniper reached over and switched off the lamp. "Good night."

Olive left them that way, the room dark and the door ajar, and went to her own bed.

★   ★   ★

Olive awoke the next morning at six o'clock, wondering what an eleven-year-old girl did with her Saturdays. What had she done at that age? She found it difficult to trace back the years but finally realized that would've been 1930, during her field-hockey craze. She had played hockey until she grew tired of banged-up shins and then had moved onto . . . boys. Quite a string of them for a few years until the war took them away.

She went downstairs to a quiet house and first put the kettle on, then looked in on Juniper. The girl was still asleep—and so was Margery, in the chair. She was dressed in yesterday's clothes, although she'd kicked off her shoes at some point and thrown the blanket over herself. She had it clasped under her chin, and her head rested at an awkward angle against the wing. She snored slightly.

Olive went over to her and bent down. "Margery," she whispered, touching her arm lightly. "Margery?"

Margery's eyes opened. Then she shut them tightly and opened them wider still. She looked round her, sat up, and grabbed her neck.

"Ah!" she whispered. "What time is it?"

"Just gone six. Have you been here all night?"

Margery shrugged and winced. Rolling her shoulders, she glanced at Juniper. "I was afraid she'd wake, not know where she was, and be frightened."

Olive smiled. "That was very good of you."

Margery ignored the sentiment. "I'd best get myself in order."

"I'll have tea ready," Olive said, and crept out.

Margery lost no time. She had tea and toast in the kitchen and was pulling on her coat over a lovely mint-green suit, ready to leave, while Olive started the porridge. Breakfast was still an hour away.

"Don't you look nice," Olive said. "You must have a suit for every day of the week."

Margery glanced down at her clothes. "It's what comes of working in an office, isn't it? I should give them up and turn Bohemian." She put a coin on the kitchen table. "That's for Juniper."

Olive couldn't believe her eyes. "A half-crown?"

"They're giving me money for her, and I don't want it," Margery said, whipping her lipstick out of her handbag.

"That doesn't mean you should hand over great gobs of it to her. You could put it in a post-office account for her." Olive knew the value of saving against what might come.

Margery paused with one lip done. "Yes, that's good. But I'll give her something for pocket money, don't you think? But perhaps a half-crown is a bit much. A shilling?"

"Sixpence," Olive said. "At that, she'll think she's the richest girl in town."

Margery switched out the coins and buttoned her coat. "I'll see you later. Wish me luck."

She didn't wait for it, and was out the door before Olive said, half to herself, "Luck."

★ ★ ★

The reopening of Paxton's Goods was the talk of the breakfast table at Mersea House. "We're going to Miss Margery's shop today," Juniper told the lodgers. "Miss Margery gave me sixpence, and I'm going to buy something. Will you be there, Mr. Hugh?"

"Wouldn't miss it," Hugh replied. "What will you spend your sixpence on?"

"I don't know," Juniper said. "I could buy just about anything."

"Oh, for the days when sixpence would buy you the world," Hugh said.

"Will you be going to Miss Margery's shop, Mrs. C.?" Juniper asked.

Abigail roused herself from buttering a slice of toast. "I don't believe I need anything today."

After breakfast, Olive cleaned upstairs. Hugh obligingly had gone out to give her free rein, but Abigail had remained. This time, Olive decided on a different tack.

"You don't need to leave," she said when Abigail answered the knock at her door. "I won't be a minute."

"If I'm not in your way," Abigail said. She put her knitting bag away in the wardrobe and turned down the volume on the wireless until it was a murmur of voices, then she moved to the window.

It didn't take Olive long. It was three days since Abigail had arrived at Mersea House, and her room still looked as if no one lived there—no photos of loved ones on the dressing table to dust round, no postcards of holidays gone by tucked into the mirror frame. Perhaps she wasn't the sentimental sort. Their lodgers were both mysteries, but at least Hugh entered into conversations. Abigail acted as though she worried about staying too long in other people's company, as if she might accidentally let something slip. What was she holding in? The days were long gone when you could suspect a person of being a German spy.

"I hope you feel comfortable here at Mersea House." Olive straightened the bedcovers and kept her back to Abigail. "It must've been difficult leaving London and your old life behind. All those memories. Not that we don't carry memories wherever we go."

"Yes," Abigail replied.

Olive moved to the dresser and dusted. "My brother died at Dunkirk, and I still think of him every day." She glanced in the mirror at Abigail. "Your husband . . . was he RAF? Navy?"

"Army," Abigail whispered. "North Africa."

"I am sorry," Olive said.

Abigail stared out the window and didn't answer.

Downstairs again, Olive met Juniper coming out of her room.

"I see you've made your own bed," she said to the girl. "That's quite helpful to me."

"Will you or Miss Margery give me my work assignments?" Juniper asked. "We had them in the home. Also, I'm quite good with the beds and dusting, but not so much with carrying dishes, although I did try it once."

Olive had an immediate picture of Juniper as Oliver Twist, struggling to carry her bowl of porridge. Her heart burned with anger.

"Let's have a think about your chores," Olive said. "After all, you'll have school lessons as well. What sort of work did you do in the home?"

"The girls learned how to run a knitting machine there, and we made a great many socks," Juniper said. "But one of the teachers taught me proper knitting, and I made myself a sleeveless jumper. When I outgrew it, I gave it to one of the little girls."

"Would you like to knit something new?" Olive asked. "We could shop for wool while we're out."

Juniper hesitated.

"You don't have to knit if you don't want to," Olive said.

"I liked it. It's only . . . would I spend my sixpence to buy the wool?"

"Certainly not," Olive said. "We'll let Margery take care of it. That sixpence is for you to buy whatever you want. As long as you don't spend it entirely on fruit gums."

Juniper grinned. "Then, I'd like to knit."

Late morning, they set off for the High Street. The north wind had blown the morning's heavy mist away, and blue sky reigned. As they walked along Queen Street, Juniper said, "I woke up in the night."

"Did you?" Olive asked. "You weren't frightened, were you?"

"Oh no," the girl replied. "My curtains were open, and the moonlight came in, and I saw Miss Margery in the chair. She looked like an angel."

"Did she now?" There's a first.

When they reached Market Place, they met Mr. Bass, who was tying on his butcher's apron for the day. Olive introduced Juniper, and he replied, "Aren't you the brave girl, now? And you, Olive— always thinking of others." He gave Olive a sympathetic nod.

They started up East Street to the bakery. Juniper stopped to admire the racks of buns and cakes in the window, and Mr. Dawson poked his head out. Olive made the introductions.

"Margery's ward, is that right?" the baker asked. "And you've walked all this way from Mersea House?"

A journey of two minutes, not counting the stop to meet Mr. Bass.

"I'll have a large loaf, Mr. Dawson," Olive said. "We're a growing household."

"Right you are," the baker said and nipped back into the shop.

Olive had her coins ready when he came back with the bread, but he also carried a small grease-spotted bag.

"And for you, little miss," he said to Juniper, "a butter bun."

The girl looked to Olive, who caught a whiff of the bag's contents.

"Well, yes, of course you should have it," Olive said. She dug back into her purse.

"No charge for the bun, Olive."

"Thank you, Mr. Dawson," Juniper said. "That's very kind of you."

He patted the girl on the head.

Olive sighed inwardly. She wanted to tell them that Juniper was just a girl and should be treated as such, but she knew Bass and Dawson meant well and so said nothing. She tucked her purse, the loaf, and the bun into her string bag. "We'd best be off now," she told the baker. "We're on our way to Paxton's Goods."

"Best of luck to Margery," Mr. Dawson said, and followed a customer back into his shop.

"Well," Olive said as they continued up the street. "You've met the butcher and the baker."

"Now we need the candlestick maker," Juniper said.

Olive laughed, but the sound died on her lips when she looked up and saw Constance Binny coming toward them.

"Olive," Binny said with a quick glance at Juniper. "Hasn't Margery done a fine job on Milkey's shop? I've just had a look-see. It's quite odd to be able to walk round and look at things instead of asking for what I want at the counter."

That may not have been a new concept in London, but it was a shake-up in Southwold.

"Good morning, Miss Binny. We're heading for the shop now. This is Juniper, Margery's ward. You might have heard she's come to live at Mersea House."

"Yes," Binny murmured, "I daresay I have, although not from you." She turned to Juniper and raised her voice, enunciating each word with too much care. "Hello, Juniper. Aren't you a fine girl?"

"Yes, Miss Binny, thank you. I'm very pleased to meet you."

They were nearly even with Paxton's Goods and had a view of it across the road. The pavement was fairly bustling, and Juniper was watching people going in and coming out of the shop.

"Do you want to go on over and look in the window?" Olive asked. "I won't be a minute." She hoped.

Juniper went to the curb and waited for the traffic on the road— one car—to pass.

Binny whispered to Olive, "Is that wise, to let her go off on her own like that?"

"She's eleven years old, Miss Binny," Olive said. "I wouldn't dare admit to what Margery and I were up to at her age. I'm sure Juniper can manage crossing the road."

"They say it's polio," Binny continued in a low voice colored with doom. Olive whipped round, and she saw a dark look cross the woman's face and then vanish.

"Yes. When she was four."

"Olive, you poor dear," Binny said, shaking her head slowly. "You've just finished years of tending to the needs of one invalid after another, and here you are tethered once again."

Olive clenched her teeth to keep from letting words out she would regret later.

"Juniper isn't an invalid. She isn't sick and getting worse. This is a condition that she lives with."

"If you say so," Binny said. "Still, more work for you than for Margery, I'd say."

She must escape. "I don't want to be the last one to see the shop, so I'll be on my way. Good day, Miss Binny."

"I'll look in next week, Olive," Binny called after her, "just to see how you're faring. I know your mother and Donald would want me to keep an eye on you."

★   ★   ★

Juniper had stopped on the pavement outside the shop and was gazing through the window at the array of spiffing new merchandise. Through the open door, Olive could see across to the counter, where Margery chatted with a customer and Young Trotter wrapped brown paper around a parcel. They each wore a crisp green apron with "Paxton's Goods" embroidered across the chest—the work of Mrs. Pinkerton, the seamstress in town.

"Shall we?" Olive asked Juniper, and gestured for her to go first.

Would anyone recognize this as Milkey's shop? New counters ran along each wall, with shelves above, and rectangular display tables sat in the middle of the open spaces. Customers seemed to be fascinated with the array of goods. Margery had added many new products for the home and kitchen—there were cake tins, sieves, rolling pins, and rows of thermos flasks, neatly set out.

But Margery had saved something of the shop they'd grown up with. Beyond the electric toasters, matching pudding bowls, egg cups shaped like hens, and kitchen linens in the latest colors and prints— in fact, in the far back of the shop—was a sign that read "Uncle Milkey's Corner." Olive saw the old dartboard, so full of holes there was more cork showing than black or white. On the counter, in wooden trays, were the sorts of items Milkey had sold—door hinges, crystal knobs, dibbers, horse brasses. He'd made his money dealing goods for hotels and the like, but Milkey had always had time and space for the little things his cronies liked to fuss over. Even now, the corner was crowded with old men.

Juniper made her way up to the till.

"Hello, Malc," Olive said, "how are you?"

Young Trotter—who did have a first name after all, even if no one in the town used it—pushed his glasses further up the bridge of his nose. "Fine, Olive. It's a good crowd."

"This is Juniper, Margery's ward," Olive said. "And this is Mr. Malcolm Trotter."

"Pleased to meet you, sir," Juniper replied as her head swiveled round to take in the scene.

"You did a smashing job on the signs," Olive said. Young Trotter had channeled his love of cartography, using his careful lettering skills to paint the hanging sign above the door as well as the gold lettering on the window.

Margery finished up with a customer, turned to them, and drew the back of her hand across her forehead. "Well, now."

"Looks a success," Olive said.

"It's going all right," Margery said. "You've met Mr. Malc, have you?"

"Yes," Juniper replied. "May I look round?"

"Of course," Margery said. "I've brought in a line of ladies' hair accessories over on that wall. You might fancy a new hair slide or something."

Margery stayed behind the counter but watched as Juniper made her way through the crowd.

"I've just learned that Juniper knits," Olive said. "Why don't you bring home some wool and needles and . . . we'll need a pattern for her, won't we? No, wait—there's something in *Woman's Weekly*. I saw it in the lounge."

"Right, wool," Margery said as the counter became congested with customers.

"I'll get out of the way and wait up at the front," Olive said. She stationed herself near the window display. Outside, people on the pavement stopped to look and then moved on or went in. But one person stayed put. She looked up and saw Charlie Salt watching her. He gave a nod and came inside.

"Mr. Salt," Olive said, "out for a day of shopping?"

Salt took off his hat. "Not as such, Miss Kersey. I've been sent out for a particular purpose."

"I'm sure you'll find whatever you need in here."

"I'm certain I will." He took a step away, but Margery swept up to them, and he stopped.

"Mr. Salt," she said, "good to see you. Are you only looking about, or is there something you're after?"

"Washing tongs," he declared.

"Washing tongs, of course," Margery said. "For your wife?"

"No, Miss Paxton. I'm unmarried," he replied.

"Oh," Margery said. "I see."

"The tongs are for my cousin's wife."

"At the garage?" Margery asked.

What garage was this, Olive wondered, and thought her confusion might've shown on her face, because Salt addressed her. "My cousin owns a garage just up the road in Reydon, you see. I work there and live on the premises."

Margery stuck her hands in the large apron pockets. "Washing tongs coming up." When Salt made to follow, she added, "Why don't you stay here and keep Olive company? We'll have the tongs for you at the till whenever you're ready. There's no hurry."

But when Margery left, conversation dried up. Olive busied herself by inspecting the sign for a toaster that promised never to burn a slice while Salt gazed at a tea trolley set up on top of the highest shelf. At last he said, "I'll have a copy of the highway code for you on Wednesday. You'll need to study the rules of the road before you receive your license."

"Yes," Olive said, thinking this sounded more like school than she'd first thought. "I will. Thank you."

Billy Grunyon slipped in the door and mumbled, "'Morning, Miss Olive," as he made for a display of seed packets, where he planted himself and then scanned the shop.

"'Morning, Billy," she called after him. "So, Mr. Salt, are you from Reydon?"

"No, I'm not," he said. "I moved here three years ago when my cousin opened his garage. I'm from the south."

Juniper came up to them, stopped, and took a bright-pink plastic comb from her fabric bag. "Miss Olive," she said, "see what I've found. It has a handle. And it's only four pence. That would leave me with tuppence, and I could save that for another time."

"There's a canny shopper," Salt said, looking down at Juniper.

Olive introduced the girl, and then said, "This is Mr. Charlie Salt, who is teaching me to drive."

"Pleased to meet you, sir," Juniper said.

"How do you do, Miss Juniper."

"May I buy it?" the girl asked Olive.

"It's a lovely comb," Olive said. "But it's your money and so your decision."

Juniper considered the comb for about a second. "Right. I'll go up and pay."

Charlie's eyes followed the girl swinging through the crowd, and Olive sighed. *Here we go.*

"Polio," she said. "When she was four."

"Is that so?" he replied. "But you hardly notice, do you? I mean, it isn't the first thing you see."

Olive smiled at him, and Salt looked startled. His lips twitched—not quite a smile in return, but nearly.

"You're exactly right, Mr. Salt," she said. "She's Juniper first—an eleven-year-old girl. I've discovered that, and she's been with us only a day."

Olive watched as Juniper handed her sixpence over to Young Trotter at the till and received a tuppence in change. Next to him, Margery was wrapping the washing tongs—for a moment, she looked over at Olive and then back down at her work. She was smiling.

When Juniper returned from paying for her comb, Salt left to collect his washing tongs. "Until Wednesday, Miss Kersey."

"Goodbye, Mr. Charlie," Juniper called.

The moment they stepped out, they were hit with the acrid smell of stale sweat and roasted barley from a large man almost blocking the door.

"Oi!" he yelled, pointing into the shop. Olive took a step back and put an arm in front of Juniper.

"Oi!" he shouted again. "You come out of that shop, Billy! Grunyons are banned in this establishment!"

People continued to come and go from the shop, glancing up and then away, but they parted when Margery marched out. She went straight up to the man, who towered over her.

"Your son is perfectly welcome in this shop, Pauley," Margery said, her voice even and calm.

The man rubbed his stubbly chin on the sleeve of his jacket. "Milkey told me—"

"Billy said he's buying flower seeds for his mother," Margery cut in. "I'm happy to keep an eye on him, so there's no need for you to stay."

Pauley huffed once and then jerked his head. "Yeah, well." He nodded to the women. "Margery. Olive."

"'Morning, Pauley," Olive said.

They watched as he made his way up the road with his slight limp, courtesy of a German shell. After a moment Margery said, "Uncle Milkey did ban a Grunyon from the shop, but it wasn't Billy."

CHAPTER 8

Margery returned to the shop, and Olive looked down at Juniper.

"I don't know about you, but I'm done in. I've some soup for our lunch, and then how about a rest?"

"Was that man angry at Miss Margery?" Juniper asked as they made their way home.

"Pauley? Not especially. He's one of those people who seem to be angry all the time—he's always been that way. It can't make for a terribly pleasant home atmosphere." Olive thought she should remember that next time Billy tried her patience.

Over lunch, Juniper said, "If I had a pinny with really large pockets, I could lay the table for you at dinner. Not the dishes, but the cutlery."

"You mean pockets as big as Miss Margery's on her apron for Paxton's Goods?" Olive said, throwing a look over her shoulder.

"It would be fun to work in a shop," Juniper said.

It would be fun, Olive thought, until Pauley Grunyon came shouting, or customers demanded to buy what you didn't carry, or some lout tried to walk off with a set of egg cups without paying. It seems with a shop you had to please everyone all the time. That wasn't quite how Olive would define Margery's personality.

Juniper went back to her room after lunch, and Olive looked through several issues of *Woman's Weekly* until she found what might be a suitable knitting pattern for Juniper. She hoped Margery would remember the yarn and needles. Olive had never taken to knitting, and neither had Margery, but perhaps Juniper wouldn't need guidance.

The girl came out to the lounge, went to the front window, and looked across the green and between the buildings to the sea sparkling in the afternoon sun. "I see a bench," she said. "May I walk out and sit there?"

"On your own?" Olive asked.

And with that, she was aware how easily she could become one of those well-meaning but annoying people who see calipers before they see the girl. *Go on, Olive—have the courage of your convictions.* After all, the bench was in plain sight.

"Of course," Olive said. "What a fine idea. But, as you still don't know your way round town yet"—there, that was a good excuse—"you'll need to stay just there where I can see you. Is that all right?"

"Yes," Juniper said. "And I'll wear my coat buttoned up too."

Olive smiled at the old ploy. Do many of the things grown-ups say, and then maybe you can do something you want.

"You can have your bun when you come in again. I've put it on the warming shelf above the hob."

A deal was struck. Olive stood at the window and watched Juniper cross the green and make her way to the bench, where she turned and waved toward the house and then sat down. Olive wondered if she would be able to move or if she would stand there until Juniper returned. Then the telephone rang, giving her the answer.

"Mersea House."

As soon as she said the words, she heard a click and a clank as money dropped, and then a man's voice came on the line.

"'Afternoon," he said. "Is Hugh Hodgson in?"

"He isn't here at the moment. Would you like to leave a message for him?" Olive reached for the paper and pad.

"Is this Olive?" the man asked.

"Yes. How did you know that?"

"Well, you aren't Margery," he said, and then laughed. "I mean, I would know her voice, and so it must be you."

Did that answer her question? "And what's your name?"

"Sid."

"What message would you like to leave for Hugh?"

"Oh, nothing really. Tell him I rang, that's all."

"Sid rang," Olive said as she wrote the words. She could hear the roar of traffic behind him. "Are you ringing from London, Sid?"

He raised his voice. "Yes, I'm in a call box near the Vauxhall Bridge. Am I difficult to hear?"

"No, but a call from London—it's quite expensive, isn't it?"

"No matter, I've paid my one and six, and I've got my three minutes. How are things going there?"

Was Sid the mutual friend of Margery and Hugh? Regardless, he sounded amiable, and perhaps if Olive kept talking, Hugh would arrive. It would be a pity for Sid to waste his money.

"Quite well," Olive replied. "Margery's shop opened today."

"Are the crowds thronging?"

Olive laughed. "Yes, as much as they can in our town. Hugh had a matinee this afternoon, you know."

"Yes, of course. How is it at the seaside?"

And for the next couple of minutes, Olive had a conversation about the weather with someone who could've told her so much about Margery and Hugh and their London lives. Or would questioning Sid be the act of a nosey-parker housekeeper?

Pip-pip-pip sounded on the line.

"Right, that's my time up," Sid said. "'Bye, Olive."

"I'll give Hugh your message," Olive called out a second before the line was cut.

She'd tell Margery too. Sid was a piece of the London puzzle.

The front door opened, and Hugh and Juniper were blown in by a gust of wind.

"I was taking the long way home from the matinee," Hugh said, "and came across this young lady by the sea."

"Not too close to the sea, I hope," Olive said, guilty that she had taken her eyes off Juniper.

"I was sitting on the bench," Juniper said. "I promise."

"Good," Olive replied. "Now, that butter bun is waiting for you. And Hugh—cup of tea?"

Hugh checked his watch. "No, thanks. But, it'll soon be time for a drink. You?"

"Why not? I hope Margery doesn't stay too long after the shop closes." Olive pushed the swing door open for Juniper and, over her shoulder, nodded to the pad of paper. "You've had a telephone call from Sid."

"Oh, right. Thanks," Hugh replied, his face and voice neutral in the extreme. He turned and went up the stairs.

Juniper sat at the kitchen table, eating, while Olive had a cup of tea and told her the story of the gull's attempted bun robbery. It was received with peals of laughter.

"You ask Margery," Olive said, "and she'll show you the very spot it happened—on the beach the other side of the pier."

"Do gulls really like butter buns?" Juniper asked.

"Gulls like just about anything." Olive finished her tea and began preparing the evening meal—chicken-and-ham pie, which would use up leftovers. "Tomorrow, we'll have a proper Sunday dinner with beef and roast potatoes. I hope you'll like it."

"I like everything you cook," Juniper said. "I've never had such fine food."

Juniper hadn't been with them more than a day, but Olive took the compliment as meant. "Thank you. In the morning, I'll put the beef in to cook before I go to church."

"Do you always go to church?"

"Most Sundays I do. You can come along if you like." Olive turned round. "But it isn't required."

"Will Miss Margery go to church?"

"No," Olive said, "she won't."

Juniper looked thoughtful. "Perhaps I won't go tomorrow, but I might go another time."

"That's fine, then. Now, you'd better wash up those sticky fingers."

Juniper had no more gone out of the kitchen than a knock came at the door to the yard.

"Is that you, Billy?" Olive called, her hands covered in flour as she rolled out a pastry. "Come in."

He entered and looked round the kitchen. "Hello, Miss Olive. I've your Sunday joint, the potatoes, two tins of peas, and four onions. What will you do with four onions?"

"I was thinking of stirring them into tomorrow's porridge," Olive said, wiping her hands off. "What do you think?"

Billy's eyes popped open. "What do I think?" And then he laughed.

"What flower seeds did you buy your mum at Paxton's Goods?"

"Marigolds," Billy said, pulling the penny packet out of his trouser pocket and holding it out. "Yellow ones. Ma likes yellow, says it makes her happy."

"How is your mother?" Olive asked.

"She's good. Dr. Atterbury took her on cleaning the surgery."

Olive rarely saw Lorna Grunyon, but knew she took any work she could find to supplement her husband's income, which was spotty at best.

"And little Sammie?"

"She's all over the place and into everything," Billy said about his little sister, but he said it with a grin.

Olive said nothing about Billy's father shouting in the door of the shop. Pauley's behavior was one of those things that was just accepted. School had looked into the matter and so had Father Carrington, with the conclusion that there was no harm being done, only a raised voice. Not that shouting couldn't still do damage to the spirit, as Olive well knew. Her father's voice echoed in her mind as if it were yesterday. *"You're a disgrace to the uniform!"* His words hadn't been aimed at her, but they'd still hurt.

With the evening meal under control, Olive crossed the entry and joined Hugh in the lounge, where he had a gin and tonic waiting. She sat on the edge of the sofa, took a drink, and then flumped back into the cushions.

"Sid and I had a lovely chat about the weather," she said, marveling at how one sip of gin could boost her courage. Hugh didn't answer, and so she added, "He was ringing all the way from London—I hope it wasn't with bad news."

"No, I'm sure it wasn't," Hugh said. "What did you think of the shop? I went early, and everyone seemed to be in good spirits."

Olive let out an exasperated sigh at Hugh changing the subject, but he took no notice, and so she said, "The shop looks to be a success. I'm happy for Margery, but not surprised. When she decides something, she does it."

"The town won't mind a powerful businesswoman in their midst?"

"Perhaps if it were someone else," Olive said. "And I daresay there'll be one or two naysayers. But the thing is, people expect Margery to be Margery."

"And what do people expect of Olive?" Hugh asked.

"They expect Olive to be good."

Margery called out from the kitchen, and in only a moment she walked into the lounge, waving the note from the telephone table, which she handed to Hugh in exchange for a drink. "Sid rang," she said.

"Yes, I know," Hugh said, his response clipped.

Margery watched Hugh over the rim of her glass. "Give him my love when you ring him back."

Hugh inclined his head—it was almost a nod—and a smile played on his lips.

A light thump-thump in the hall announced Juniper's approach. Funny how quickly the sound had become familiar, Olive thought. The girl stopped in the doorway.

"Shall I go into the dining room?" she asked.

"Not a bit of it," Margery said. "Come and talk with us. Tell me what you did this afternoon?"

Juniper went to her chair and adjusted her calipers, all the while talking. "I walked out to the bench and Mr. Hugh came along, and I ate a butter bun, and I've combed my hair."

"Very good choice on your purchase," Margery said, and Juniper beamed.

Without making a sound, Abigail appeared in the doorway and stopped, looking as surprised at being there as Olive felt at seeing her.

"Hello, Mrs. C.," Juniper said.

The woman slipped just inside the lounge. Hugh stood. Margery said, "Would you like a drink?"

"No, thank you," Abigail said. "I . . . that is . . . Your shop opening went well, did it?"

"The shop—yes, very well." Margery leapt up. "I've brought wool for you, Juniper, and something else. Won't be a tick." Out she went, and returned with her handbag, from which she drew a small packet wrapped in brown paper. She handed it to Juniper.

"Go on—open it," Margery said.

Juniper took the paper off with care. Inside were two small picture frames.

"They should be the right size for those photos of your mum and dad, don't you think?"

Juniper lifted her face in adoration.

"Thank you, Miss Margery."

★   ★   ★

Abigail's exchange had been stilted and brief, but it still had felt like a victory, and so it didn't matter that she fell silent again over dinner. Hugh and Margery nattered on about films, wandering their way through their favorites.

"You can't go wrong with a ghost story," Margery said, "even if you don't believe in them. *The Ghost and Mrs. Muir* was lovely."

"I saw my mother after she died," Juniper said.

The girl didn't seem to notice the silence.

"It was when I was still in the iron lung," she continued. "I don't remember very much about then, except the world was upside down unless I looked in the mirror above my head. But one day I saw my mother outside, walking past the window, wearing her brown felt hat. And another time, when a crowd of doctors came in, she was there, standing at the back. She was wearing her hat again." The girl looked round the table. Margery's eyes were dark, and Hugh frowned. A look of pain crossed Abigail's face before she dropped her head. Juniper shrugged. "I don't think she was a ghost. It's just what I saw."

She had told her story in such a simple way, as if relating her walk out to the bench, it took Olive's breath away, and she fought against telling Juniper what a brave girl she was.

"I'm sorry about your mum," Olive said, "but we're so glad you're here with us."

"My dad was right," Juniper said. "He told me I'd be happy when I came to live with Miss Margery. Is there pudding?"

Only semolina pudding with sauce made from the remnants of a jar of raspberry jam, but no one complained.

After the meal, Hugh headed for the cinema, and Mrs. Claypool withdrew upstairs. In the kitchen, Olive and Margery washed up, and Juniper sat at the table, drying dishes and listening to stories of the past.

". . . and we were only seven at the time," Olive said, ending a tale.

"I was about to turn eight," Margery pointed out.

"Yes, but that held no sway with the man rowing the boat, did it?" Olive asked. "All we wanted was to be ferried across the river, and we had the money and all, but it took some doing to persuade him."

"It was the weather, you see," Margery explained to Juniper. "A high tide was expected. Still, we got over and back and home before anyone was the wiser. Not like the surge tide here in '53. Uncle Milkey told me about it."

Olive shuddered. "That was dreadful. We were in town and far enough away from the river, but those poor people along Blackshore Quay. You can see the flood mark on the wall outside the Harbour Inn."

"Can I go and see it?" Juniper asked.

"Of course you can," Margery said. "Now, time for bed. Will you be all right if I'm in my own room tonight? It's just across the way."

"Oh yes," Juniper said. "I feel quite at home now." She swung her way out of the kitchen.

"Why don't you help her in the lav?" Olive asked.

"You go on," Margery said, "and I'll finish up here."

She turned her back on Olive and set about putting the dishes away. After waiting for a moment, Olive left, and by the time she and Juniper came out of the bathroom, they met Margery emerging from the kitchen.

"Now, isn't that good timing—you can show Miss Margery how your calipers come off." Juniper led the way, and Olive nudged Margery ahead of her into the bedroom.

The girl braced herself against the bed and pulled up her nightie. "This is how they go on and off," she said, and went through her routine as if demonstrating how the new washing machine worked. She lay back on the bed, and Olive pulled off the apparatus. Juniper's thin legs dangled above the floor.

"Here," Margery said, "shall we tuck you up?"

Juniper shifted round, but it was Olive who moved the girl's legs under the covers.

"I'll just go and get your hot-water bottle filled, shall I?" Margery asked, and dashed out.

With Margery out of the room, Olive sat at the end of the bed. "It's lovely that you remember your mother. And that you had your dad for so many more years." In truth, not so many. "Did you live with him at all before he died?"

"No," Juniper said. "He wasn't able to do it himself. And then, I was always going back into hospital for something. He said he missed me and it made him sad. But he visited on Sundays if I wasn't too far away. Then, he started getting sick. That's when he told me about Miss Margery and that if anything happened to him, she would come for me."

As it turned out, the authorities had had to come for Margery, but that didn't seem to matter to Juniper. Olive folded the girl's dressing gown and finally she said, "I'll just go check how it's going with your bottle, shall I?"

In the kitchen, the kettle was set off the fire, a ribbon of steam rising from its spout. The door to the yard was open, and there, near the rotary washing line, Olive saw Margery, hunched over, her body shaking.

"Margery?" Olive said. She went out to her and touched her shoulder.

Margery spun round, holding herself tightly. Her face was a misery, and her tears so profuse, they dripped off her chin.

"Look at me," Margery said, "I'm afraid it's all caught up to me at once."

That Margery would admit such a weakness made Olive smile. She put an arm round Margery's shoulders and said, "C'mon, let's go inside."

Olive led her to a chair in the kitchen, pulled her handkerchief out, and handed it over, then put the kettle back on the hob and waited as it came to a boil. Behind her, Margery blew her nose and sighed heavily.

Olive took the kettle off just as its whistle began, low and mournful. She filled Juniper's bottle and screwed the rubber stopper in. "It's heartbreaking that she can't do things other girls can do, but it doesn't make her less. Anyway, I suppose we'll get used to it. Juniper certainly has."

She looked over her shoulder as Margery straightened up and said, "I don't want her to hate me."

Olive laughed. "You silly goose—you're her savior." Alarm registered on Margery's face, and Olive quickly added, "But even better than that, you're the one who is giving her sixpence a week."

Margery wiped her nose and stuffed the hankie in her own pocket. "What will Mrs. Pagett think of us?"

"I can't see as how that will really matter," Olive said without quite believing it.

"She'll be coming on these welfare visits," Margery said. "What if she decides to take Juniper away?"

Olive had the kettle in her hand, and she banged it down on the cooker with such force the lid flew off. "Just let her try!"

CHAPTER 9

Margery looked stunned at the declaration, and Olive hurried on.

"That is, we—you won't let her, will you?" Olive asked. This worry—would Mrs. Pagett see them as a proper family for Juniper and not a crazy patchwork quilt?—had started only the day before. How had the seed taken root so quickly?

"There now," Margery said, turning into the consoler. "We'll be fine. We'll manage. I couldn't do this without you, Olive. You're the steady one."

Olive's mood lightened. "You say that now—that I'm the steady one," she replied, "but just you wait. I may run off to join the girls in the chorus line at the Windmill Theatre."

Margery laughed and reached for the bottle. "We'd best get this into her bed." As they walked out of the kitchen, she said, "I've been to the Windmill. Nonstop show, even during the Blitz. It's good fun."

In bed, Juniper had pulled the covers up to her chin but was wide awake.

"Here I am, the slowcoach," Margery said. She lifted the covers and slid the bottle in. "How's that?"

Juniper shivered. "It's lovely and warm."

Margery leaned over the girl and smoothed her hair. "'Night, now."

Olive watched as Juniper took her arms out from under the covers, put them round Margery's neck, and pulled her close enough to kiss her cheek. "Good night."

Margery straightened, nodded Olive out, and pulled Juniper's door almost closed behind them. Without a word, they headed to the lounge.

"Brandy?" Margery asked, lighting a cigarette with a shaky hand.

"Yes," Olive said, "but you'd better let me pour."

*   ★   ★

Olive's first Sunday morning running the boardinghouse was a rushed affair. She cooked, served, and then washed up after breakfast, followed by preparing as much as she could of the midday dinner. When she came down ready for church, she put the beef joint in the oven and walked out the door, leaving Margery, Juniper, and the lodgers to their own devices.

After church, she returned through the kitchen door, checked on the beef, added the potatoes to the pan, set the percolator on the hob, and went out to the entry. There she stood and listened to the house. All was quiet, serene almost. She opened the door to the lounge, where Hugh sat on his own, anchoring one end of the sofa.

"Where is everyone?" Olive asked.

"Not at home at present."

"Not even Abigail?"

"Ah, now there you have me," Hugh said. "She could be. I went out for the papers, and when I returned, Margery and Juniper were setting off for destinations unknown. You aren't worried, are you?"

"No," Olive said with a bit too much force. "I'm glad they're together."

"Margery seems to have taken to the girl," Hugh said, "and Juniper thinks Margery hung the moon."

"I believe you're right there. Well, good." Olive looked out the front window and could see the bench facing the sea was empty. Margery would know not to take the girl too far, wouldn't she? "Coffee?" she asked Hugh.

"I'd love some."

Abigail returned as the coffee came ready and took her own cup upstairs. Olive settled on the other end of the sofa from Hugh, with newspapers between, and their own coffee on the table in front of them.

"How was church?" Hugh asked.

"Good," Olive said. *Wearisome,* she thought as she stared at the newspaper in front of her without reading. After the service, it had been made clear to her that people now considered her not only the face of Mersea House but also dispenser of information about Margery. Many people offered opinions and comments about the shop: "Didn't the place look fine!" "I hope Margery isn't getting above herself," and "Mind you, I'm ever so pleased with the new toaster."

Then, there were observations on Juniper. "Sweet girl, poor dear" was the overriding sentiment, followed close on by "It's just like Margery, isn't it? You would think she had enough to do, and then she goes and takes in an orphan. A cripple, at that. Good thing you're there, Olive."

Constance Binny, wearing her Sunday hat ringed with violets in place of her pheasant tail feather, had sidled up to her and said, "People are wondering, of course, where this girl has come from. You know what I mean—just what is she to Margery?"

Nearby conversations had ceased, and Olive could've sworn a few people leaned in to hear her response. She had smiled at Binny and said, "Margery stepped in to help an old friend," and then Olive immediately took her leave. She couldn't know for sure but didn't think anyone would know the name Wyckes or remember George, who had been from West Suffolk. It was another world over there.

Olive heard Margery and Juniper come in the front door; she snapped the newspaper closed and rose to lay the table.

"We walked past the pier," Juniper called out as she unbuttoned her coat. "Miss Margery showed me where the gull tried to take your butter buns and where she liked to sit and think."

"Where she liked to hide and smoke so her Uncle Milkey wouldn't see," Olive murmured to Margery as she crossed to the kitchen.

Margery followed her, laughing. "I believe he knew all along." She took a deep breath and exhaled in a rush. "Juniper's got more energy than this old body—I'm that knackered. Is there any coffee left?"

"You go on, and I'll bring it out," Olive said.

The rest of the day was as a Sunday should be—a good dinner, followed by an easy afternoon. Margery presented the wool and needles to Juniper, and Olive set out on her walk, the first proper walk she'd had in almost a week. She started at the north end of town and headed south, with the water on her left and the road of seafront houses across the road on her right. A short shower of rain caught her on Ferry Road, but it had stopped by the time she passed the water tower and came back into town.

As she neared the top end of the town, she heard a burst of laughter from the call box at Victoria Street. It was Hugh. He turned toward her, phone receiver to his ear, looking truly happy, not the mixture of happy and sad Olive had seen since he'd arrived. He noticed her and lifted his chin in acknowledgment. She returned a smile.

At Mersea House, she hung her Norfolk jacket on the drying rail above the cooker and put the kettle on. Margery came in, popped the lid off the biscuit tin, and stuck one in her mouth, then put others on a plate.

"How's the knitting?" Olive asked.

Margery shook her head, mouth full of biscuit. When she could talk, she said, "I don't remember enough to do any good, and Juniper hadn't followed written directions before. We're stuck. You don't want to have a look?"

"I don't imagine I'll be any better," Olive said as she counted the spoonfuls of tea into the pot.

"I'll visit school in the morning," Margery said. "Do you want to come along?"

Olive would have liked to, but as she reached for cups and saucers and set them on the tray, she said, "No need for me to be there. You'll be fine."

"Of course I'll be fine."

"Mrs. Tees caught me on my way out from church this morning," Olive said. "She's offered to give us a look at the girl's dresses and things tomorrow afternoon. That was good of her—we won't have another jumble sale until after Easter, and Juniper is in great need of clothes."

"She is that," Margery said. "Which reminds me, I have a couple of dresses I'm not wearing, and I wonder if you'd be interested."

"You don't need to supply me with a wardrobe," Olive said as she thought of that plaid day dress awaiting the next jumble sale and how far away that seemed.

"Then consider it sharing," Margery said. "Remember we did that all the time? There was that pink cardigan with the roses embroidered down the front. We passed that back and forth for ages."

"Until the embroidery became unpicked," Olive said, "and you repaired it as best you could. But ever after we thought the biggest rose looked like Miss Adelstrop in the school office, and we giggled if one of us was wearing it and we saw her."

"Miss Adelstrop," Margery said with a shudder. "She's long gone from the school, I hope." She reached for another biscuit and broke it into pieces. "Juniper will need to see the doctor too, to get on his rolls. I'll ring the surgery and make an appointment. You'll go along to that one, won't you?"

"Yes, all right. Here, carry the tea out to the lounge, and I'll take a cup upstairs to Abigail."

*   *   *

Monday was washing day, and, twin-tub washer or no, Olive had her hands full of bed linens. The machine may do the washing, but she still had to put things through the mangle and then hang them to dry. She began her Monday damp, the same way she had ended her Sunday. That thought made her smile.

Sunday evening was bath time, and Margery had gone in early to put on the one-bar electric fire, which had just about taken the chill out of the air. The three of them—Olive, Margery, and Juniper—then gathered to contemplate the tub.

"What did they do at the homes?" Olive had asked.

"Two of the lady workers would pick me up and put me in and then take me out again when I finished," Juniper had told them. "But if I was the only one that needed help, they sometimes forgot me for a while." The girl said this without rancor, and added, "If I sat on the edge, couldn't I do it myself?"

That seemed unlikely—the tub had no ledge to speak of and a steep slope. In the end, Olive and Margery had picked her up and put her in and then taken her out again. It may have started with only an errant splash, but they all three finished drenched and overcome with giggles. After, they'd had cocoa, sitting in the girl's bedroom, with the electric fire on to help dry her hair.

"Good thing bath night is only once a week," Margery had said.

Refitting the bath—another job for Casper, Olive thought as she pegged one set of linens out on the rotary washing line and took the almost-dry set in to hang on the wooden bars above the cooker.

When the wash was under control, she went out of the kitchen, looking into the dining room, where Hugh and Juniper sat working on a jigsaw puzzle of the *Queen Mary.*

"Found it in that chest in the lounge," Hugh explained, "and I thought it would keep both of us out of your way for a while."

"There's an awful lot of water," Juniper said, holding up a piece and gazing at the finished picture on the box, which showed the ocean liner in a literal sea of blue.

Olive left them to it and dragged the Hoover upstairs, switching on the machine but keeping an ear out in case Margery telephoned with news about school. But instead of the shrill ring, there was a knock at the door.

"Don't hurry, Olive," Hugh called up as he came out of the dining room. "I'll see to it."

But when he opened the door, and Olive caught sight of a bobbing pheasant tail feather, she did hurry.

"Good morning, Miss Binny," she said, pushing loose hair back from her face. "Lovely to see you. Won't you come in?"

"Thank you, Olive, dear."

Olive and Hugh fell back as she stepped in.

"Miss Constance Binny, this is Hugh Hodgson."

"How do you do, Miss Binny," Hugh said. "Pleased to meet you."

"Coffee?" Olive asked.

"That would be lovely," Binny said. "I do hope Mr. Hodgson and little Juniper can join us?"

"Oh, well," Olive said, unable to come up with a reasonable excuse in time.

"I'd love to," Hugh said, "and I'm sure Juniper needs saving from the *Queen Mary*. I'll fetch her—Juniper, that is."

"Yes, of course," Olive said. She gestured to the lounge. She returned with the coffee tray a few minutes later as Binny interrogated Hugh.

"Do you have family in the area, Mr. Hodgson?"

"No, I don't. I'm originally from Bedfordshire, but I've been living in London."

"Bedfordshire," Binny said, as if it were the ends of the earth. "And you have family there?"

"I have a brother," Hugh replied.

"I'm sure you keep up with him."

"I certainly try," Hugh said obligingly.

"Olive had a brother," Binny said, shaking her head. "Donald. Perhaps she's told you about him? He was a fine, upstanding young man, greatly loved by his parents and terribly missed by all in town. Isn't that right, Olive? He died at Dunkirk, you see. Such a terrible loss. Didn't I see you in a call box yesterday, Mr. Hodgson? Were you speaking to your brother?"

One of Binny's tactics of eliciting information from unwary people was rabbiting on about something and then producing a surprise jab. Many people would answer automatically, but Olive knew her technique and intercepted.

"How is your nephew, Miss Binny? Is he still in London at the *Daily Sketch*?"

"He is," Binny replied, and turned to Hugh. "Norman, my nephew, is a newspaperman. Olive remembers him from his visits, although I do wish I could see a bit more of him. He, too, is a fine, upstanding man, and I'm quite proud of him. Now, Olive dear, don't you have another lodger? Wouldn't she like to join us?"

"Perhaps another day," Olive replied.

"What did you say her name is?"

"She's Mrs. C.," Juniper replied.

Until that moment, the girl had sat quietly with her Ribena and seedcake. Olive recalled doing much the same thing when she was young—sitting unobtrusively while Daisy and her friends drank their coffee and chatted about nothing that interested Olive in the least.

"Yes," Olive said. "Abigail Claypool."

"And from which far corner of the world has Margery brought this lady?" Binny asked.

"Mrs. C. lived in London," Juniper said.

"Did she now? Remarkable that Margery has found her first two lodgers from the vast population of London, isn't it? Did you answer an advertisement, Mr. Hodgson? Is there some secret society that is stealing away to Suffolk to escape their nefarious London doings?" Binny chuckled.

Hugh kept the pleasant smile on his face, but Olive saw his guard go up. "You underestimate the allure of the seaside, Miss Binny," he said.

"Yes, I suppose I do." She turned her gaze back to Juniper. "Well, now, how are you, Juniper? In a new town and a new home—what a difficult time you've had, I'm sure. You poor dear thing, you must miss your mummy and daddy dreadfully. I suppose Margery will give you work to do here at Mersea House."

Olive clenched her fists. "Juniper will be starting school tomorrow."

"Will you now?" Binny asked Juniper. "I wonder what class they will put you in."

"She'll be in the class for her age, of course," Olive said.

Binny clicked her tongue. "I hope it won't be too difficult."

"I like school," Juniper said. "Reading is my best subject."

"Do you have a favorite book?" Hugh asked.

Juniper thought. "I read *Ivanhoe* last year—that was quite good."

"*Ivanhoe*?" Binny's eyes widened. "To the very end?"

"Yes, ma'am."

They finished coffee in relative peace. When Binny left, Juniper went back to the jigsaw, and Hugh carried the coffee tray into the kitchen. Olive followed him, and as she pulled the dry bed linens off the rods, she asked, "Is Sid your brother?"

"No, he isn't. Sid is just . . . he's a friend."

Olive watched Hugh, who didn't meet her gaze. "You're reminding me very much of Abigail Claypool at this moment," she said. "Perhaps I'm prying, but as I recall, you did invite me to do so."

"Sorry, Olive, it's only that . . ." Hugh picked up the sugar bowl and put it down again. "Sid is a good friend, but Miss Binny wasn't far wrong when she talked about escaping London. When Margery told me a manager was needed at the cinema here, I saw my chance. It's better I left, and I'm happy I did. Although, I'm rather sad about it too." He shook his head. "That doesn't make much sense."

"It makes perfect sense to me," she said, confident in her supposition, although she couldn't've said why. "You didn't want to leave Sid."

A wave of emotions crossed Hugh's face before he got himself in hand, leaving only red cheeks.

"Olive, I don't want you to—"

"My brother was a homosexual."

Hugh opened his mouth as if to speak but closed it again, and so Olive added, "Not that Binny ever knew."

"That was Donald? I'm sorry you lost him." Hugh took her hand briefly. "Thank you, Olive. Thank you for telling me. But then you must understand how . . . difficult things can be."

"Yes, I do. Don't worry."

Hugh left, and Olive stood, clasping a bed sheet to her chest. *My brother was a homosexual.* How odd to say those words. She'd never said them to anyone, and she realized now what a disservice that had been to Donald—like a denial of who he was as a person. Not that the entire world needed to know, of course, not when a man could be jailed for it. Olive remembered how tentative Donald had been when he'd tried to explain to her that it didn't matter how many girls their mother introduced to him, it just wouldn't work. She hadn't

completely understood, but she'd loved her brother and been happy
for him, because he'd been happy. For a time.

★   ★   ★

In the afternoon, Olive and Juniper visited Mrs. Tees in the church
hall. She led them to a chilly storage room, where she switched on
the light and closed the door. They surveyed her domain—tables and
boxes and shelves of clothes and household goods, all well organized
and quite tidy, unlike Mrs. Tees herself, whose gray hair escaped its
French roll in wisps like scraps of fog, and whose seemingly bottom-
less cardigan pockets held bits and bobs such as pencil stubs, stray buttons, and—always—a bag of peppermint humbugs. She was known
for pulling the bag out just before the Sunday sermon began and
offering a sweet to those in the nearest pews.

The woman now stood in front of Juniper and looked her up and
down. Olive knew the calipers made no difference to Mrs. Tees—
after all, wasn't her husband in a wheelchair?—and that the woman
was merely sizing the girl up.

"Right, young lady, let's see what we have." She made straight for
a particular corner, where she selected a dress, shook it out, and held
it up to Juniper's shoulders. It was blue and sleeveless with a square
neck and buttons down the back. "Now, what do you think of this
one?"

"I like it very much," Juniper said.

"You'll need a blouse under it or perhaps a jersey, won't you—not
just a vest? Let's see what we can find." As Mrs. Tees dug through
a stack of clothes, she added, "Olive, I've pulled out that day dress.
Why don't you give it a try?"

Olive had seen the purple plaid frock when they'd walked in, and
it was even nicer than she recalled. It was weeks until the jumble sale,
and her wardrobe was as skint as Juniper's. What a luxury it would
be to have a new dress. Newish.

They left the church hall each sucking on a peppermint humbug
and having paid shillings for their bounty: three dresses and two
jumpers for Juniper and the day dress for Olive.

Casper arrived shortly after they returned to Mersea House. He'd taken his Saturday afternoon and gone to Ipswich and bought a walking frame, which he had cut into pieces and now carried under his arm with his toolbox in hand.

"Ready, Missy?" he asked.

"Ready, sir," Juniper said, and off they went to the bathroom. Olive watched from the entry as Juniper settled on a stool. Casper stuck the girl's drawing up on the wall, and they proceeded to discuss the installation. When the telephone rang beside her, Olive didn't even flinch.

"Mersea House."

"Casper stopped on his way," Margery said. "Is he there now?"

"He is," Olive replied, "and Juniper is consulting."

"Look, Olive, about school tomorrow. As it turns out, I've a salesman coming in before the shop opens, so will you walk her over in the morning?"

★   ★   ★

"Hello, Miss Browne. I'm Olive Kersey, the housekeeper at Mersea House. And this is Juniper Wyckes."

Tuesday morning, they stood in front of the teacher's desk as Miss Browne looked at them over the rim of her glasses. Olive could see that Billy's description of his teacher as "a one" had been spot on—firm mouth, thin lips, hair scraped back into a low bun and a rolled fringe that looked as if she'd glued a sausage high on her forehead.

"Good morning, Miss Kersey," Miss Browne boomed. "Good morning, Juniper, and welcome to my class."

"Good morning, Miss Browne," Juniper said.

The girl was pale and her eyes large. Olive hadn't been able to calm her own butterflies, and Juniper had been quiet at breakfast and uninterested in her food. She wore one of her new dresses and had a proper school bag slung across her body—Margery had thought of that.

"Well, now," Miss Browne continued, "we have a great deal to discover about each other, don't we? It won't be easy dropping into school this late in the year, and so, as I told Miss Paxton, you will need to apply yourself to the task of catching up."

"Miss Paxton is sorry she was unable to be here herself this morning," Olive said, and smiled. Miss Browne responded with a lessening of her hard look.

"I also explained that we are not entirely set up for a child with Juniper's needs," Miss Browne said. Olive bit her tongue, because she knew the woman wasn't complaining, only pointing out the situation. "But Miss Voss from the infants class has agreed to lend a hand, and the two of us will assist Juniper at the dinner break."

When the interview finished, Olive and Juniper walked out to the schoolyard because the bell had yet to ring. The yard was chockfull of children—the younger ones tearing round with a great deal of energy and the older ones standing about in groups, trying to look older still.

"Was this your school, Miss Olive?" Juniper asked.

"No, this school was built after the war. They've knocked down the school building Margery and I attended, and built a terrace on it. Well," Olive said, reluctant to leave. "I'll be round to collect you at the end of the day."

"Yes," Juniper said, eyeing a few girls about her age who were standing near the gate, eyeing her back.

Olive looked at them, too, and smiled. One girl returned the smile, and the others switched their focus to their shoes. Olive scanned the yard and noticed Billy Grunyon loitering near the railing under a beech tree. How was Olive to abandon Juniper to this lot?

The bell rang.

★ ★ ★

Olive returned to Mersea House the long way, shaking off a few of her nerves, and once in the door, she rang Casper.

"The school lav?" he said. "Oh, don't you worry, Olive. Haven't I kept their boiler going for these many years and replaced windows and repaired desks and laid the lino in the teachers' room? They won't tell me 'no.'"

"And they'll let you bolt the railings down?"

"I don't see as I need to ask permission," Casper replied. "Let them send me to the headmaster if they like."

His good-natured challenge reminded Olive that Casper's wife was related to the headmaster—he was a cousin or brother-in-law or something.

Olive kept herself busy dusting and hoovering and baking the day away, the end of school like the light at the end of a tunnel. When at last it came time, she stood outside the gate with a smattering of other women, greeting many with a nod.

"Waiting for Margery's ward, are you?" one of them asked.

"Yes," Olive replied. "Her first day, you know."

The bell rang, and a second later children tumbled out the door, the youngest ones making straight for their mothers, and the rest dashing across the yard, out the gate, and to the four winds. A moment later, when Juniper emerged with Miss Browne, Olive hurried up to them.

The girl offered Olive a wan smile, looking as if she'd had every last ounce of energy wrung out of her.

"She did very well today," the teacher reported. "First days can be difficult, I know, but it will become easier. I will see you tomorrow, Juniper."

"Goodbye, Miss Browne. Thank you."

When Juniper moved toward the gate, Miss Browne put a hand on Olive's arm. "I'll need to talk with Miss Paxton after school on Friday. Just a few things to discuss."

"I'll let Margery know. Is there a problem?"

"No, no, no, no," Miss Browne said.

But that was too many *nos* for there not to be.

Olive followed Juniper out the school gate, where they paused.

"Good day?" Olive asked.

"Yes," Juniper replied.

Were the lessons difficult? Was the school dinner dreadful? Did you make any friends?

"You wouldn't fancy some chips, would you?" Olive asked.

A bit of color returned to the girl's face. "Chips? Really?"

"Come on."

They stopped at the chippy at the end of the road, and Olive carried two hot newspaper cones, their contents redolent of vinegar and grease, to a bench along the Parade. There was no talk at first—they only ate and gazed out to sea—but in a few minutes, Juniper pointed to a gull pacing back and forth in front of them as if it were on sentry duty.

"Does he want a chip?" Juniper asked.

"I'm sure he does, but we won't give him one. It's no good encouraging them—they'd never leave you alone. Remember those butter buns."

Juniper held her chips close to her chest and, keeping an eye on the gull, pointed in a different direction. "Can we walk out on the pier?"

"Best not to, I think. The pier is an old thing, built about 1900. To begin with, it had a crosspiece at the end where steamships would dock. That part was swept away in a storm in the '30s. Then, it was damaged during the war. It was repaired after, but a couple of years ago another storm hit and washed away the end of it." After a quiet moment, Olive took a chance. "Did you talk with any of the other girls in your class?"

"Linda sat with me at the dinner break."

"Linda," Olive repeated. "Did you like her?"

Juniper nodded. "She's nice. Mr. Casper is her stepfather."

Of course—the girl who had smiled in the schoolyard that morning. She had looked a bit familiar. Casper might have told Linda to be nice to Juniper, but what if he had? Great friendships probably started the same way.

"And I met Patsy. She's in my class too."

Two friends on the first day. Olive breathed a sigh of relief.

"I see a ship," Juniper said, squinting at the horizon.

Olive shaded her eyes. "Yes, a big one. I wonder where it's going."

"My friend Minnie went to Canada on a ship."

"Did she?" Olive asked. "With a family?"

"No. Last year, they took a group of them from the home to live there. They'll have jobs and get married and all. I couldn't go."

Olive looked down at Juniper. "I'm sorry Minnie went to Canada, but I'd have been terribly sad if you'd gone too."

Juniper turned to her with a puzzled look in her brown eyes. "But Miss Olive, you didn't know me then."

"It sounds a bit daft, doesn't it?" Olive admitted. "But somehow I feel it's true."

The girl smiled and shifted her attention back to the horizon. "I like the sea."

CHAPTER 10

They made their way home, and Juniper went back to her room. Soon after, Billy arrived with the groceries. He stood in the kitchen expectantly while Olive checked the order and went to fetch his farthing.

"Ice cream, Miss Olive," he observed. "Is it someone's birthday?"

"No, Billy," Olive replied as she tried to insert the block of ice cream into the rectangular freezer space of the fridge. It looked as if it should fit, but there was a buildup of ice on the inside of the small compartment, and Olive had to chip away at it. She didn't notice that Juniper had come in until the girl spoke.

"Hello," she said.

"Yeah, hiya," Billy said.

Olive closed the fridge. "So, you two are in the same class, aren't you?" They agreed with nods. "Billy, would you like bread and butter and jam?"

The boy pulled himself up to his full height. "Sorry, I can't stay, Miss Olive. I've two other grocery deliveries. People count on me, you know."

"Yes, Billy, we certainly count on you. All right, see you tomorrow."

"Yeah, see ya," Billy said to Juniper.

"'Bye," the girl replied. When he'd gone, she said, "I sit behind him at the end of a row."

"Miss Browne put you in the back of the class?" Olive asked, indignation at the ready.

"Yes, because there's no other desk beside me, so I have room to swing my legs round, you see."

"Oh, well, that's all right, then."

★   ★   ★

The evening meal began with Margery quizzing Juniper—How was Miss Browne? What subjects did you cover? What did you learn today?

Juniper reported that the class was memorizing Wordsworth's "I Wandered Lonely as a Cloud" and that she'd made a start of it during the afternoon break. That sounded admirable, but to Olive it meant that she'd been left alone. *It's only her first day,* Olive reminded herself. *Give it time.*

"Well, let's hear it then," Margery said. "The lines you've learned."

"We stand up to recite," Juniper said.

"You're at home now," Olive said, "so that isn't necessary."

Juniper straightened up in her chair and began.

> "'I wandered lonely as a cloud
> That floats on high o'er vales and hills,
> When all at once I saw a crowd,
> A host of golden daffodils;
> Be . . . beneath . . .'"

She faltered, and Olive frantically searched her mind for the next words, but the prompt came from elsewhere.

"'Beside the lake, beneath the trees,'" Abigail said.

"'Fluttering and dancing in the breeze!'" Juniper finished. "Thank you, Mrs. C. Did you learn that for school too?"

The woman's face flamed scarlet. "I . . . that is . . ."

"We had to recite 'Gunga Din' one year," Olive said. "Do you remember that, Margery?"

"Right," Hugh said. "Let's hear it."

Margery leaned over the table and in a low, gravelly voice, said, "'You may talk o' gin and beer, when you're quartered way out 'ere.'" She sat back. "That's all I can remember."

Olive smiled at Juniper. "She took in her uncle Milkey's rusty old rifle from the Great War to use as a prop."

"It helped me get into character," Margery said.

The conversation then turned to more adult matters—Margery talked about the shop, and Hugh spoke of repairs on the spare projector. Left to herself, Juniper nearly fell asleep but brightened considerably when the pudding arrived: ice cream and squares of strawberry jelly in celebration of her first day of school.

Abigail spent the remainder of the meal in her usual silent mode, but Olive saw her cast Juniper the occasional wistful look. That the girl had a way of drawing Abigail out of her hiding place was clear. Whether Abigail wanted to be drawn out was something entirely different.

★ ★ ★

At the school gate Wednesday morning, Juniper paused.

"Miss Olive, now that I know where the school is, you won't have to walk me over and come back to collect me in the afternoons, will you?"

In Olive's mind, the journey—barely a ten-minute walk—was suddenly fraught with danger.

"I am old enough, aren't I?" Juniper asked. "And I could always look in at Miss Margery's shop on the way back in the afternoon, and she could see I was all right."

This was sound logic and a good plan, and Olive did not like it one bit. Then, her mind flashed to a time when she and Margery were about Juniper's age. They'd become fascinated with stories about a mythical beast in the guise of an enormous black dog that haunted the church at Blythburgh. The two of them had spent several weeks traipsing over after school—a journey of more than an hour—to sit in the churchyard and wait for its appearance, with no luck. And they had often been late back to their tea. Olive looked down at Juniper and sighed.

"You're right, you are old enough. Why don't I collect you this afternoon, but starting tomorrow morning, you're on your own."

"Thanks, Miss Olive. See you later."

Olive watched Juniper make her way to the door of the school. The bell had yet to ring, and so the girl stopped and waited, a lone figure amid a sea of children. Then, in a moment, Linda appeared at Juniper's side, and the two girls started chatting. Olive turned toward home with a happy heart.

The morning passed with organizing menus, writing grocery lists, and doing the accounts. An idea had floated into Olive's head, and so, after she set a pan of shortbread on the kitchen table to cool, she took a dust cloth out to the entry. Whisking it over the telephone table, she then took the stairs, running the cloth up the banister until she reached the first floor. She heard a low, melodious tune from Abigail's wireless.

Olive knocked at the door. "All right if I come in?"

"Yes," Abigail replied. When Olive entered, the woman set her knitting aside, rose, and stood near the window.

"I walked Juniper to school again this morning," Olive said as she made a show of dusting. "Her second day, so not quite so many nerves—for her or for me."

"A new school is a big step."

"Abigail, I wonder if I might ask a favor of you?"

The woman turned a wary eye on Olive. "Oh?"

"Juniper has asked if she could walk to and from school on her own. She's right, really—she's far too old to be met at the gate every afternoon. It's occurred to me that occasionally I may be out when she arrives home."

Olive had been keeping Abigail in her peripheral vision and saw the woman shoot her a look of . . . what? Olive hurried on. "If you wouldn't mind, when that happens, I was hoping you could keep an eye out for her."

"Oh no," Abigail whispered—more a plea than a rejection. She took a step back into the corner. "You can't. You mustn't."

Olive approached. Beads of sweat had broken out on Abigail's upper lip, and her face had lost all color.

"You won't have to do anything," Olive said. "It's only for her to know someone was about."

"You don't understand," Abigail said, choking on the last word. Her breathing was shallow, and she reached out and took hold of Olive's arm, her grip like a vise. "I can't be responsible. I can't. Please don't—"

"No, of course not." Olive guided her to the chair. "Here, sit down. It's all right, really it is. We'll say no more about it. Would you like coffee?"

★ ★ ★

After lunch, Olive sat in the lounge, Norfolk coat on, handbag in her lap, and scarf tied under her chin, when Hugh walked in.

"Ah, driving lesson this afternoon," he said.

She glanced out the window. "Yes."

"And you'll actually drive today?"

She exhaled a laugh. "I hope so."

Hugh sat on the sofa, picked up a newspaper and, in a casual voice, asked, "Do you need to wear the scarf?"

Olive's hand flew to her head. "It might be windy."

"Will he put the top down?"

She dropped her hand. "No, it isn't that sort of car."

"Look at the time you put into that braid. And your hair is a lovely shade of brown—it gleams in the sun. It's a shame to cover it."

Olive sobered up. "That isn't what this is about!"

"All right, all right." He went back to the paper.

Olive took a forefinger and scratched at the knot under her chin, loosening it enough to whip off the scarf just as Charlie Salt pulled up out front. Hugh smiled, and she threw the scarf at him as she went to the door.

"Miss Kersey," Salt said, standing on the doorstep. He took his hat off. "Good afternoon."

"Good afternoon, Mr. Salt."

"Well, shall we?"

They walked together to the curb and stopped.

"Today," Salt said, "you will learn the feel of the automobile and become competent in changing gears."

Olive didn't move. "But doesn't that seem a bit ambitious for only my second lesson?"

Salt turned to her and, as if he'd read her mind, said, "Never fear, Miss Kersey; your first excursion will not be in public."

With great relief, Olive followed him round to the passenger side, where he opened the door for her.

As they motored off, she watched Salt work the pedals, steering wheel, and gearshift with coordinated ease. He would, wouldn't he? After all, he was the teacher—but how was she to manage it? But such thoughts drifted away as Salt drove them down the road alongside the Common. It was seldom she was in a vehicle that wasn't a bus, so she should enjoy herself.

When they were passing by Reydon, Olive said, "Was that your cousin's garage just off the road back there?"

"Yes, Stanton Motors, that's Harold's," Salt said. "He and his wife live next door, and I have a cottage in back."

"We both live quite close to our work, don't we?" Olive said. As buildings gave way to woodland and field, she spoke her thoughts aloud. "Juniper started school yesterday."

"I hope it went well for her," Salt said.

"It's a difficult time, so late in the school year," Olive said. "She doesn't know anyone. The class is well into their studies."

"She's a bright girl, though. I could see that as soon as I met her." He glanced over at Olive. "You aren't worried, are you?"

"No," she said, and then added, "well, maybe a bit."

It wasn't long before Salt turned off the road and stopped in front of a five-bar gate where beyond, Olive could see fields of barley.

"This farm was a base during the war," Salt told her. "Not RAF— the Yanks had it. Afterward, it was turned back to farming, but they kept most of the roads and runways and use them as farm tracks. You can see a few Nissen huts too. The family that owns the place has given me leave to conduct driving lessons here where we won't be bothered by road traffic."

"What about tractors?"

"If there are any about, we'll see them in plenty of time."

Olive got out and opened the gate. Salt drove through, and Olive closed it again, but instead of getting back in the car, she stood beside it, closed her eyes, and turned her face to the sun, smelling the green growth and listening to the call of birds in the hedgerow. Olive heard Salt get out of the car and walk round. She opened her eyes, and he stood beside her.

"It's so peaceful now," she said. "It's hard to imagine how busy it was during the war years—on the ground and in the sky."

Salt looked out over the fields. "Yes. There were many bases in Suffolk, weren't there? It must've made for a lively atmosphere in the town."

Olive's eyes darted to him and away. "I suppose. I wasn't in a position to take advantage of it."

She had spent the beginning of the war oblivious to others. Stan had left early in '40, and Olive had lived quietly with the happy hope of his return. That is, until a letter came from Stan's sister in Gloucester with the news that he'd been killed. The sister wrote that he had spoken of Olive, and so the family wanted her to know of their loss.

After that, like a row of dominoes, the people in Olive's life fell. Stan was gone. Donald was killed. It seemed only the day after word came of her brother's death, her father could no longer walk up the stairs unaided.

"Were you in the forces, Mr. Salt?"

"Navy," he said. "I spent the war below deck in the engine room of first one ship, then another."

Olive detected a note of dismissal in his voice. "You did your bit," she said.

"Did I?" Salt squinted out into the sunshine. "Some would say working the engine room was hardly the actions of a brave man. Coming through the war without a scratch while so many others were so . . . heroic."

"That's nonsense," Olive said. "You were in danger every minute, and yet there you were making the ship safe for others."

Salt studied her face for a moment and then looked away.

"Well, Miss Kersey, shall we begin?"

Olive sat in the driver's seat while Salt checked his clipboard.

"You'll switch the engine on in gear, and so you'll need to be ready. First, depress the clutch with your left foot and, at the same time, the brake pedal with your right foot. Put the gear stick into first, and only then turn the key."

It seemed a great deal to remember—each of her four limbs with its own assignment—but Olive made a stab at it, and soon found herself behind the wheel of a car with its engine running.

"Next, release the hand brake at the floor on your right. There you go. Now, take your foot off the brake and move it to the accelerator. Begin to depress the pedal at the same time as you let up on the clutch."

Olive did as she was told, but as she let up on the clutch, the car lurched forward so violently, she jerked her feet away from the pedals and took her hands off the wheel. The engine died with a shudder. She clasped her hands at her breast, panting.

"That didn't go well, did it?" she asked.

"Ah, but now you have a sense of the controls," Salt said with perfect calm. "Try again."

The second, third, fourth, and fifth attempts were a repeat of the first, but on the sixth try, the car took off, sailing along the farm track. Olive swelled with pride until Salt said, "And now, shift into second gear."

More bucking and lurching as the engine sputtered. Olive shoved the gear stick down into second, and this time, the car made a horrible sound like the gnashing of metal teeth before it shuddered and died.

Salt didn't blink. "Start again," he said.

She did as she was told and felt herself close to achieving the impossible—shifting from first to second—when came the horrible sound and the lurching stop. Olive cried out in exasperation, threw open the car door, and stalked off. She stood at the edge of the field, wondering how she had never known she was so uncoordinated.

Once calm, she returned to the car and climbed back in. Salt, still in the passenger seat, asked, "Better?"

"Yes, thank you. I'm sorry about that."

"No need to apologize. But do remember to pull the hand brake on before you exit the car."

Her shoulders slumped. "Am I a poor student, Mr. Salt?"

"You are not, Miss Kersey," he said emphatically. "You're doing fine."

"The engine made that dreadful sound."

"Grinding the gears—it happens when the clutch is not fully engaged. It's a common mistake. Learning to drive is not easy. Why, there was one fellow who was so slow to learn this shifting business that he stripped all the gears, and the entire gearbox had to be changed out."

"Really?" Olive asked. "You aren't just saying that to make me feel better?"

"It's a true story."

"And, I'm not as bad as that, am I?" She smiled at the thought.

Salt smiled in return—a quick grin that banished all vestiges of his serious manner and made him look even a bit playful. It must've surprised him as much as it did Olive, because he looked down at his clipboard and then out the window before he got himself in hand.

"No, Miss Kersey, you are not as bad as that."

By the end of the session, the magic moment had arrived—the intersection of comprehension and muscle movement: Olive could shift gears and turn a corner with at least some confidence. Once, she even got the car into third.

"Well, Miss Kersey, are you game for reversing?" Salt said.

Olive checked her watch. "Oh, the time. I should meet Juniper, and it's getting near the end of the school day."

"Righto," Salt replied. "School it is. May I drop the two of you back at Mersea House?"

They pulled up as children were shooting out the door of the school, and Olive walked up to the gate only a moment before Miss Browne emerged with Juniper. The girl looked no less wan than she had the day before.

"See Mr. Charlie there at the curb—he's going to take us back in his car," Olive told Juniper. "You go on, and I'll have a quick word with Miss Browne."

"All right," Juniper said. "Goodbye, Miss Browne."

"Until tomorrow," the teacher replied.

Olive watched as Juniper went out the gate. "I hope her second day went well," she said to the teacher.

"She's a lovely child," Miss Browne replied. "However, her attention does seem to wander. During arithmetic, I found her drawing a picture in her lesson book."

"Oh, but I'm sure she didn't mean to—"

"I don't believe she was misbehaving," Miss Browne said. "It's the subject. I'll go into this further with Miss Paxton. We must always look to the future, you know, Miss Kersey."

"Yes, of course."

Miss Browne returned to the school building, and Olive thought about the teacher's remarks. That Juniper needed extra help in school couldn't be a surprise—her learning had been disrupted by hospital visits and moves. There would be a remedy, wouldn't there?

"How was your lesson, Miss Olive?" Juniper asked from the back seat as they motored off.

Olive looked over her shoulder. "I'm not the best driving student."

"Miss Olive is a fine driving student," Salt corrected her. "She's learning quickly."

"Mr. Charlie told me I could drive," the girl said.

Olive looked at Salt, whose face reddened.

"Mr. Charlie is mistaken," Olive said. "You cannot drive."

"Yes, I can," the girl insisted. "There are cars with hand controls, so it doesn't matter that my legs don't work."

"That may be," Olive said, turning to her, "but you cannot drive because you're too young. When you're sixteen years old, then you can drive."

Charlie glanced in the rearview mirror. "Well, she has us there, doesn't she?"

"Yes," Juniper said and sighed. "I suppose I'll have to wait."

At Mersea House, Salt walked Olive and Juniper up to the door. The girl went in, and Olive spoke before she lost her nerve.

"Would you care to come in for a cup of tea, Mr. Salt?"

"Oh, er, thank you, but no, I won't." His gaze fell down to his feet as if he were working out an escape route.

Well, what did she care if he had a cup of tea or not? Olive put her chin in the air. "Thank you for the lesson." And with that, she shut the door and stalked off to the kitchen, where she turned the tap on full blast to fill the kettle and sprayed her face with water.

Both Hugh and Juniper appeared in the doorway.

"All right there?" Hugh asked.

"Yes, fine," Olive said, spooning tea furiously into the pot and catching a drip off her chin with her shoulder. "Why wouldn't I be?" She paused. "Oh dear, I've lost count. Was that three or four spoonfuls?"

A knock came at the front door, and Juniper said, "I'll answer." Olive waited, and Hugh stayed where he was.

In a moment, Juniper returned and whispered loudly, "It's Mr. Charlie."

Olive dropped the spoon, patted her wet face with the tea cloth, and went to the front door, where Charlie Salt, looking chagrined, held out a booklet.

"Your copy of the highway code, Miss Kersey. You'll need to study it."

Olive snatched the booklet from him. "Thank you, Mr. Salt. See you next week." She closed the door, returned to the kitchen, and waited for the kettle to boil.

★ ★ ★

Margery downed tea and toast at the kitchen table the next morning, readying to make her usual early exit. But Olive had a mental list of items to discuss with her, and so stood at the hob with her hands in the pockets of her pinny. She began by relating her exchange with Abigail Claypool the previous morning.

"She was frantic when I asked her if she could occasionally look out for Juniper. Why? Do you think she lost a child?"

"All I know is what I told you at first," Margery said, "that she's a widow and keeps herself to herself."

"I asked too much of her to start with," Olive said. "Perhaps she could help Juniper memorize her poems."

"Maybe she wants nothing to do with Juniper," Margery replied.

"No," Olive said, "that isn't it. It's something else."

Margery stood and reached for her coat she'd flung over a chair, but Olive hadn't finished yet.

"Juniper will be walking to school on her own starting today—she asked if she could."

"Yes, right," Margery replied, searching her coat pockets and coming up with her cigarettes.

"And you remember Miss Browne wants to talk with you tomorrow afternoon?"

"Tomorrow is Friday," Margery said, as if reminding herself. "Wait, now. I made the appointment with Dr. Atterbury. That's for his afternoon surgery tomorrow. That's an hour or more I'd be away from the shop. Could you take her—or could you see the teacher?"

"I am not her guardian," Olive snapped.

"I never said you were," Margery said. "It's just that you seem to know what to say."

"If you like," Olive said, "I'll go along with you."

CHAPTER 11

"You're sure you're all right?" Olive asked Juniper as they stood at the door, the girl ready to set out.

She looked confident, although a bit nervous as she adjusted her school bag. "Yes, I think it's for the best. I'll be fine, really I will, because now no one can . . ."

"Can what?" Olive asked.

"Oh, nothing. It's that I'll be like the others in my class, won't I? Not like the children in the classes under me."

Olive's blood began to simmer. "Has someone said something to you?" she asked.

"No," Juniper said, shaking her head vehemently. "No one."

Was it Linda, Casper's stepdaughter? Or her friend Patsy? What about Billy Grunyon and his rough ways—had he bothered her during class? Olive swallowed hard lest she renege on her promise to let Juniper walk to school on her own.

"Right, well," Olive said. "Remember, wave to Miss Margery as you pass the shop, and she'll ring to let me know."

But it was Young Trotter who telephoned to say the girl had made sure she was seen. Olive's mind was eased. She started her day with a walk and after that had coffee while she read a few recipes in *Constance Spry*.

In the afternoon, the school bell, although far out of hearing, rang in Olive's mind. She walked out onto the green and searched the foot traffic on Queen Street, hoping to spot the girl. Instead, she caught sight of Binny and so retreated indoors, waiting until she thought the coast was clear before making another recce. Unsuccessful, she forced herself to go in and put the kettle on, after which Juniper came in the kitchen door from the yard, looking both pale and happy.

"Good day?" Olive asked.

"Yes," she replied with a weak smile.

"Wash up," Olive said, "and come back."

Juniper continued through to her room, leaving Olive to wonder if school might be too much for the girl. Perhaps she would ask Dr. Atterbury about it. No—Olive corrected herself—Margery could ask.

Awhile later, Olive looked in on Juniper. The girl was in her room, sitting in the chair Margery had spent the night in, and drawing in one of her lesson books.

Olive looked over her shoulder. "Is that your school desk?" The sketch was quite good—Juniper had used shading to bring a three-dimensional quality out.

"Yes. I was thinking with my pencil." She tapped the page. "If the seat swiveled, it would be easier for me to turn and set the locks at my knees and reach my sticks and stand up."

Olive noticed she'd used a page full of multiplication problems on which to draw her picture.

"That would be a fine idea. Why don't you talk with Mr. Casper about it?"

Juniper nodded. "I will do."

Olive heard a distant knock from the kitchen. "That'll be Billy with the groceries. You carry on."

Her time with *The Constance Spry Cookery Book* had led to changes and additions to the grocery order, and this had not gone unnoticed by Billy Grunyon. As he brought the basket in, he said, "Mince from Bass—Mr. Bass. And this bit of cheese. It's hard as a rock, Miss Olive. You sure you don't want to send it back?"

"It's Parmesan cheese, Billy." Good thing Bass was not only the butcher, but also the cheesemonger. "I'm cooking spaghetti à la Bolognese for the evening meal."

Billy gave her a narrow look. "Is that French or something?"

"It's Italian."

"Blimey, Miss Olive, we fought them during the war."

"It wasn't their food we objected to," Olive said. "Bread and butter and jam?"

"Yes, ma'am, thank you."

Olive cut two slices of bread, buttered them both, and handed one plate over to Billy. Then ever so casually, she added, "How was school today?"

This prompted a cautious look. "'S all right."

"How many are in your class?"

"I dunno. We're full up, I guess. Let me see, six rows of desks across and one-two-three . . . six down."

"Except for the short row," Juniper said. She had pushed open the door from the entry and stuck her head in. "There are only five desks there. So, that's . . ." She frowned in concentration.

"Six sixes is thirty-six, take away one is thirty-five," Billy said. "That's easy arithmetic."

Olive shot him a look, and Billy busied himself with the jar of jam.

"Have a seat," Olive said to Juniper.

The girl sat at the far corner from Billy. Neither talked until the boy finished eating, wiping his hands on his trousers. "Spelling test tomorrow."

"Miss Browne gave me the list to copy out," Juniper said. "Fifty words."

"Fifty words?" Olive asked, looking up from her recipe. "How could you possibly learn fifty words so quickly?"

"The test is only ten words," Billy said in a hard-done-by tone, "but Miss Browne won't say which ten, so we have to learn them all."

* * *

Friday after lunch, Margery telephoned. Olive had intended to go out for a walk, but instead found herself sitting in the lounge and skimming *Picturegoer*, a magazine Hugh had brought in. Only later did she realize she must've been expecting the call.

"Look, Olive," Margery said, "I'm in a bit of a bind here. Could you go over to school and start up with Miss Browne, and I'll follow along quick as I can."

And so, Olive went to school and explained, ending with, "But Miss Paxton did say to please begin without her."

"Well, then, we shall," Miss Browne said. "Please sit." Juniper adjusted her calipers and rested her sticks against the chair, and Olive sat, holding her handbag in her lap, while the teacher fetched a third chair from the room across the hall. Olive had the niggling suspicion it wouldn't be needed.

The teacher sat, rested her forearms on top of the attendance ledger, and leaned forward.

"I wanted to wait a few days before I brought this up so that I could see how well Juniper did in a variety of subjects."

"She's an exceptional reader," Olive said.

"I got all the spelling words correct," Juniper added.

"Yes, and well done," Miss Browne said. "But it's the arithmetic, isn't it? Not only sums but reasoning with numbers."

"Juniper's had a great amount of upheaval in her schooling," Olive said.

"Of course she has," Miss Browne said, "and none of it was your fault, Juniper."

"Yes, ma'am," the girl said.

"But here we are April and next comes summer term, and before you know it, autumn term will begin."

The way the teacher spoke, Olive thought they'd be Christmas shopping by next week.

"Autumn term in the final year of primary school means the eleven-plus exam," Miss Browne continued, "which tests on general comprehension, reading, and arithmetic. A student must pass all sections of the exam in order to go on to a grammar school. Failing the exam would mean a trade school."

Although Olive was aware of the eleven-plus, it had started after she'd finished school. But she knew with all her heart that although trade schools were quite suitable for many young people, Juniper needed a proper education, eventually receiving her higher education certificate—no wait, that was called A-levels these days—and after that, go to university. But only if she passed the eleven-plus. At once, a clear and present danger arose in Olive's mind.

"And so," Olive said, "Juniper must pay close attention in arithmetic so she'll be ready."

Miss Brown shook her head. "The exams are cumulative, Miss Kersey, and based on knowledge gained throughout the child's schooling. I'm afraid Juniper has large gaps in her arithmetic learning, and it will take more than a quick review. I believe it would be best for her to be moved back a year immediately, in order to give her a full school year to catch up."

Neither Olive nor Juniper spoke. The teacher glanced at the empty chair. "Will you explain this to Miss Paxton? She can let me know of her decision, but I must say, the sooner the better."

With that dismissal, Olive stood and said, "Thank you." She gave Juniper an encouraging smile. "We'd best be off."

They left Miss Browne at her desk, and when they'd crossed the schoolyard and gone out the gate, both of them paused.

"All right there?" Olive asked.

Juniper hung her head, looking very much like a rag doll propped up on two sticks. "I don't want to be left behind," she said, her voice wobbly with tears.

"Ah, now." She reached out, and Juniper threw her arms round Olive's waist. The dangling walking sticks knocked gently against her calves, and the girl's sobs reverberated in Olive's chest. They stood like that, Olive stroking her hair, until Juniper sniffed, sighed deeply, and was still. Olive kissed the top of her head and offered her a handkerchief. Juniper took it and blew her nose.

"Linda's sister is in the class behind us," she said. "She's a very little girl—she's practically in the infants class."

"We aren't going to worry about this now," Olive said decisively. "We're going to have a think about it. I'll tell Miss Margery and . . . well, we'll have a think. All right?"

Juniper gave her a watery smile. That such an empty promise could so easily brighten the girl's countenance steeled Olive's will.

The doctor was next. Olive knew everyone at the surgery—the receptionist, Mrs. Wilkins; the nurse, who was Dr. Atterbury's wife; and the doctor himself—because they'd seen Daisy through her last years and done it with great compassion. The first thing that happened upon their arrival was that Mrs. Wilkins informed Olive that Margery had telephoned to say she was unable to attend Juniper's appointment and would let Olive carry on.

Olive and Juniper settled themselves in chairs set against the wall.

Mrs. Wilkins paused in sorting patient cards and looked over the rim of her glasses. "I hope Southwold will be a good home for you, Juniper."

"Thank you, Mrs. Wilkins," Juniper said. "I like it very much."

"How are you, Olive?" Mrs. Wilkins asked.

"Good, thanks. And you?"

"Staying out of trouble or making the right kind, as the Major often said." Olive smiled at this—Mrs. Wilkins, just short of matronly, didn't look as if she'd ever made trouble in her life. "I must say," the woman continued, "that we all miss your mother, but wouldn't she be pleased to know you've done well for yourself. You're getting along at the boardinghouse?"

"Yes," Olive replied. "We've only two paying guests at the moment."

"The gentleman from the cinema and a war widow," Mrs. Wilkins said, and at Olive's look, added, "Constance Binny was in earlier in the week."

"Oh, of course."

"I know she can be tiresome, but I must always remind myself to give Connie leeway," Mrs. Wilkins said. "She is alone and lonely. The two don't always go together, you know, but in her case, they are inseparable."

Should Olive be so charitable? Daisy had said much the same thing, but Olive had conveniently forgot that and mostly remembered her mother's *wittering witch* remark.

"How is your garden, Mrs. Wilkins?"

"Oh!" The receptionist threw her hands up in surrender. "Things are starting to get away from me at Beech View—first the daffs, then the tulips, the wallflowers, and the lawn is about to become a meadow." She sighed. "It's a jungle. And then there's the veg. It's a pity Thompson retired."

Two years earlier, Thompson, age eighty-nine, had given up gardening for other people and currently worked only his own plot. Olive could see how this would affect Mrs. Wilkins—who lived alone but never seeming lonely—because she grew enough veg to feed "half the town," as Daisy had said. She said it with gratitude, of course, as Olive and her mother had been among the recipients of the bounty.

"He didn't do for you full-time, did he?" Olive asked.

"No, only a day or two a week. Mind you, it seemed to make all the difference, and Thompson took direction well. I don't know where I'll find anyone to replace him—the boys nowadays don't seem to care for the work as much as they care for their motorbikes and such."

"I may know someone," Olive said. "One of our lodgers—the cinema manager. He works only Wednesday to Saturday."

"Does Mr. Hugh like gardening?" Juniper asked.

"Who wouldn't like gardening?" Mrs. Wilkins said. "Mondays and Tuesdays would suit me. Tell him I'll provide lunch as well as his wages. Oh, Olive, I do hope he'll say yes. The broad beans must go in forthwith if I'm to enter them in this summer's show. Also, the pea trellis needs a fair bit of repair and the ramblers will take over if they aren't tied in. I wonder how he feels about—"

Before Hugh's work schedule filled for a job he had yet to take, the nurse called Olive and Juniper back to the doctor.

"Leave it with me, Mrs. Wilkins," Olive said.

Dr. Atterbury had received the girl's records from the children's authority, and, after an examination of the patient and her calipers, he chatted with Juniper about her hospital stays and various surgeries. After, Juniper went out and was talking with Mrs. Wilkins, but Olive held back.

"Dr. Atterbury, Juniper was only four when she contracted polio, and she spent time in an iron lung. You saw that in her records, of course. She was quite young and doesn't recall much, except this—she says that she saw her mother. Twice. She knows her mother had already died, but those sightings seemed quite real to her."

Dr. Atterbury nodded. "Hallucinations. It's been reported as a common side effect during the initial phase of the disease. She's a wise girl to be able to say she knows it isn't true and yet hold to the knowledge it was so real. Look, Olive, anything you need or want to know about her condition, you just ask."

Olive didn't bother to say it would be Margery who should ask.

★   ★   ★

Clouds swelled up on the horizon late Friday afternoon, and by evening it was bucketing rain. In the kitchen, Olive had just put the potatoes on, and Juniper sat at the table counting out the cutlery, when Margery came in, shaking the raindrops from her shoulders and running a hand through her hair.

"Is it raining?" Olive asked as Margery dripped on the spot. "Here, give me your coat."

Margery shrugged out of it and then took a brown-paper parcel from her handbag and gave it to Juniper. "There you are, now."

Juniper unwrapped the parcel and gazed at its contents. A true artist's sketchbook with a spiral binding so that pages would lie flat, and along with it, a pencil box decorated with drawings of seabirds.

"Oh, thank you," Juniper exclaimed, clasping the pad and box to her chest.

"Artists need proper equipment just the same as anyone else," Margery said.

"Now you can save your lesson books for actual lessons," Olive said.

"Lesson books are good for tracing," Juniper said. "Sister Freddie gave me one when I was in hospital time before last, and I traced the pictures from a catalog. That's how I learned to draw."

"What sort of catalog?" Olive asked.

"Hospital equipment—wheelchairs, splints, artificial hands, breathing tubes, surgery equipment. That sort of thing."

She spoke as if she were reciting a shopping list, her attention claimed by her pencil box, but Olive and Margery exchanged looks over the girl's head.

"I'm sorry I missed your doctor's appointment," Margery said.

"And Miss Browne," Olive added.

At this reminder, Juniper looked up. But Olive wanted to talk with Margery alone about school and so diverted the conversation.

"Shop was busy?" Olive asked.

"I was waiting by the telephone in my back office for a call from the Chamber of Commerce," Margery explained. "I'm one of the first women to join the Suffolk chapter."

Hugh popped his head in. "Drinks?" And with that, the evening drifted away.

★ ★ ★

Sunday afternoon the rain let up, but the clouds closed in and it was so dark indoors, they had to switch on lamps. Olive came in from cleaning the kitchen after the midday dinner to find Hugh working the *Times* crossword puzzle and Juniper at the window, drawing. Margery, wearing capris for her day off, dozed on the sofa. Olive spotted Juniper's abandoned knitting project in a basket near the fireplace.

"Margery." Olive shook the foot that hung off the cushion. "Margery?"

"Mmm. Is it tea?"

"No, not yet. Look, why don't you and Juniper have another go at the knitting?" She looked over at the girl. "What do you think?"

Juniper looked from Olive to Margery and back. "All right," she said.

"But I'm no good at it," Margery said.

"Go on," Olive said. "At least try."

Olive waited until Margery and Juniper had settled at the front window with their heads together over the magazine instructions, and then she strolled out and headed up the stairs.

"Abigail?" Olive tapped lightly at the door. "It's Olive." As if it would be anyone else.

"Yes?"

"Isn't it dark this afternoon?" Olive said in a conversational tone through the closed door. "I've put the kettle on—won't you come down for tea? It's just that bit brighter in the lounge, what with the big window. Knocks a bit of gloom off the afternoon."

Abigail emerged from her room. *There's the first battle won,* Olive thought. They went downstairs to the lounge, where the woman stopped inside the door.

"Margery," Olive said. "Come help me with the tea, please."

Margery frowned. "You've just told me to get this knitting pattern sorted."

"Well, it doesn't look as if you're doing much good, so you may as well leave Juniper to forge on by herself."

Juniper looked up from the needles, appearing lost at this announcement, but Olive held firm. "C'mon," she said, nodding Margery out the door. As they left, Olive saw Hugh's raised eyebrows.

The swing door to the kitchen closed behind them, and Margery said, "What was all that about?"

"Nothing," Olive said, "it's only that I thought you'd do more good in here than in there. Why don't you set the tray up?"

"Shall I take the plates and cups and saucers in?" Margery asked.

"No, don't," Olive said, glancing at the door. "Leave them a few minutes."

"Them?"

Olive sighed with exasperation. "Abigail knits."

Margery frowned, and then Olive could see the penny drop.

"Oh, this is a setup, is it? Try to get Abigail to talk to Juniper?"

"She wants to be near Juniper, but she's afraid," Olive said, summing up her beliefs. "I thought if they shared an activity, it might make it easier."

"Trying to arrange other people's lives?"

"If I am," Olive said, "I wonder where did I learn it?"

Margery laughed.

They took their time with the tea and about twenty minutes later walked into the lounge. Hugh continued to work the crossword. Juniper and Abigail were in the front window, wool in their laps and needles in the girl's hands.

"Did I drop a stitch, Mrs. C.?" Juniper asked.

Abigail glanced up at Olive long enough to send her a look that was both accusing and grateful before she turned back to the girl.

"Let's count, shall we?"

★   ★   ★

Olive had watched and waited, biding her time throughout the weekend to find the chance to talk with Margery about Miss Browne's recommendation, but it wasn't until after everyone had retired that she herded Margery into the kitchen.

"That was a good idea you had to set Hugh up with Mrs. Wilkins," Margery said, settling at the table and lighting a cigarette. "Although I'm not sure he has any gardening skills."

"I doubt if that matters with Mrs. Wilkins. She's very like her husband was—good at giving orders."

Olive put the kettle on and pulled out the breakfast tray as she gathered her nerve to say what she needed to.

"And you were right about Abigail," Margery said. "Juniper may finish that sleeveless jumper after all."

With two points in her favor, Olive turned to face Margery.

"About the meeting with Miss Browne on Friday."

"Yes, sorry," Margery said. "How did it go? Juniper's a champion speller."

"Perhaps," Olive said, "but she has gaps in her arithmetic. Large gaps. And in the autumn, she must take the eleven-plus, and that decides whether she goes to a good grammar school or not. All sections must be passed. Miss Browne thinks she should move back a year now in order to catch up."

"Well, I suppose if Miss Browne thinks it best."

"But is it?" Olive asked. "She's only just settled in."

"She's only just started," Margery said. "How can it matter if she moves back a class now?"

"I'm not certain putting Juniper back a year is the best thing." Olive threw the teaspoons onto the tray, turned her back on Margery, and measured the dry porridge out by teacupfuls, her hand shaking. "It would be a shame to force her to sit through summer term and the entire next school year in a lower class when she knows so much."

"Except arithmetic," Margery pointed out. "You said if she fails that section, that's the entire eleven-plus failed. And then where would she be?"

"She could catch up without being put back. We could give her the lessons she needs here. It would be extra help."

"Isn't that what putting her back would be—extra help?"

"At what cost?" Olive said, the cups and saucers clattering as she set them on the tray. "I know she's barely started school, but she's already made friends. How many of those can she lose? Minnie sailed away, and now she'd have to say goodbye to Linda and Patsy too."

"Who is Minnie?" Margery asked.

"You know years don't mix," Olive said, pressing her point. "If she's moved now, she'll have to start all over at making friends. Again. And she'll be an eleven-year-old in a class of nine-year-olds."

"That's a bit extreme, isn't it?" Margery huffed. "We don't always get what we want in life."

"Always?" Olive shot back. "What about never? When has anything ever gone her way?"

"Juniper needs to do well at school," Margery said, jabbing her finger on the table. "Surely you can see that? I'm her guardian, Olive—I'm responsible for her. She'll need to pass this exam, do well at a good grammar school and then go to university. She'll need to make her way in the world."

"She needs love" was Olive's retort. "She needs to feel safe and that she belongs. She deserves to be happy."

Margery narrowed her eyes at Olive, who refused to look away. There was a crackling silence.

"Fine," Margery said, biting off the word. "Fine. If you think you know more than the teacher, then you go ahead and leave her in the class and see what comes of it."

Having thrown down the gauntlet, Margery sat back in her chair, took a drag on her cigarette, and blew out a stream of smoke toward the ceiling. Olive turned back to the hob. The kettle boiled, and she filled the bottle, screwed the top on, and walked out.

Juniper's room lay in darkness. Olive pushed the door open, and the lamp behind her sent a shaft of light in, like a searchlight that led the way to the girl's bed. Olive could see she was still awake.

"Sorry to be late with this," she said, slipping the bottle under the covers. "Dr. Atterbury said you feel the cold in your legs more than most of us. That's something you must always be careful of."

"Yes," Juniper replied. "Miss Olive, will I have to start in the lower class tomorrow?"

Olive squeezed her hand. "No, you will not," she said firmly. "We're going to sort something out—you just see if we don't. Now, good night."

Upstairs in her own room, Olive took out a sheet of writing paper and her fountain pen. She paused for a moment, then began: "Dear Miss Browne."

★ ★ ★

Olive sent the letter off with Juniper on Monday morning and got on with her day of washing, ironing, and changing linens.

In the afternoon, she was in Hugh's room when she heard the kitchen door to the yard bang, followed by the sound of Juniper coming through to the entry. Olive checked her watch and realized it was later than she had thought. She returned to the ground floor and saw the bathroom door closed and heard the tap running.

"Juniper?" she asked, knocking. "Everything all right?"

"Miss Olive?" The voice was tentative and nasal. "Do you have any cotton wool or something that wouldn't matter if—"

Olive burst into the bathroom to find Juniper leaning over the sink, blood dripping from her nose. Olive grabbed a towel from the shelf and ran to her.

"There now, there now," she said, trying to get hold of her own emotions, "you're all right."

"Yes," Juniper said with confidence, "I'm all right."

Olive looked closer and saw that the blood was not streaming. It was the water the girl had splashed on her face that ran pinkish red into the sink. Olive's tripping heartbeat slowed a bit, and she could breathe again.

"What's happened?" Olive asked, wetting the towel and daubing at Juniper's nose. Then, she noticed scratches on the girl's arms and the dirt streaked on her dress.

"Oh, well, you see—" Juniper started.

"Did someone do this to you?"

"No, no one. I mean, that is—"

A knock came at the kitchen door to the yard.

"You go on, Miss Olive," Juniper said, leaning against the sink and taking the towel. "Really."

Olive frowned. "Stay here," she said. "I'll be back."

Olive opened the door to Billy Grunyon, who looked as if he'd been through the wars. She took in the scratches on his arm and saw what appeared to be a black eye blooming.

"You?" she shouted. "Billy, what have you done?"

Billy took a step back. "What have *I* done?"

"It was you, wasn't it? You did this to Juniper."

"I *what*?" Billy looked aghast. "Look, Miss Olive—"

She shook a finger in his face. "Don't you try—"

"It was Billy who rescued me."

Olive spun round. Juniper had pushed open the kitchen door and now came all the way in. "I fell, and Billy pulled me up again."

The images that sprang into Olive's mind, one after another, did nothing to quell her anger and retroactive fear.

"How did you fall? Where?"

Juniper squirmed, shifting her weight and leaning against the doorpost. "You see, I thought I'd walk by the seafront on my way back from school, and when I got to the Parade, I decided to walk along on the other side of the railing."

"The other side?" Olive repeated. "There's no path the other side."

"Yes," Juniper agreed. "And—I lost my balance."

"Miss Hetty shouted," Billy said.

"I bumped my nose on the railing and slid down the bank toward the beach—"

"—I saw her go down and ran over, but she'd already come to a stop. In the gorse."

Thus, the scratches.

"You could've hurt yourself much worse," Olive said, her relief catching in her throat.

"Yes, ma'am," Juniper said in a small, contrite voice. "But, Billy pulled me out of the gorse and got me up to the Parade and found one of my sticks that I'd lost hold of. I'm afraid I hit him in the eye on the way up. Sorry, Billy."

The boy shrugged.

"It seems, Billy," Olive said, putting a hand on the kitchen dresser to steady herself, "you were in the right place at the right time."

"Yeah, well," the boy replied.

"Thank you," Juniper said.

Billy's chest swelled. "Yer all right."

There was the sound of the front door opening and Hugh's voice along with another—a woman's. It sounded familiar, but before Olive could identify it, Hugh looked in the kitchen door. He started when he saw Juniper.

"I'm fine, Mr. Hugh," Juniper said. "Really I am."

"That's good to know," Hugh replied, and turned his attention. "Olive, there's a visitor to see Margery. I've put her in the lounge. It's Mrs. Pagett."

CHAPTER 12

"Mrs. Pagett?"

Olive looked at Juniper. Her nose was swollen and dotted with spots of drying blood. The scratches on her arms called attention to themselves, and there was no disguising the dirt on her dress. Her eyes were as wide as saucers.

"Yes, right, well, then," Olive said, shifting her mind into high gear. She took a tea cloth, wet it at the tap, and handed it to Juniper. "See how much of that dirt you can get off your dress. Billy, bring in the grocery delivery. Hugh, put the kettle on. I'll be right back."

Sweeping loose strands of hair off her forehead, Olive took a deep breath and walked out of the kitchen, across the entry, and into the lounge where their visitor waited, handbag looped over her wrist, leather satchel tucked under an arm.

"Mrs. Pagett," Olive said with a smile. "How lovely to see you. And what a surprise."

"It is our way, Miss Kersey," the woman replied. "We want to see a child's actual environment, nothing put on for show. How is Juniper?"

"Juniper is well, very well. I'm sorry Margery isn't here. Shall I ring her at the shop and have her come round? Or would you like to go there?" Would there be any chance she would?

"No, there's no need for that. We can leave Miss Paxton for today. I would like to see Juniper, of course."

"Of course," Olive said. "Why don't you sit down and I'll bring tea in. And Juniper. Won't be a minute."

Olive backed out of the lounge, grabbed her handbag off the telephone table, and swept into the kitchen. Billy waited near the door to the yard; Hugh stood against the sink, with the kettle hissing on the hob; and Juniper sat in a chair, scrubbing at her dress with the tea towel. She was managing to remove a good bit of the dirt, leaving behind a wide swath of damp.

"Here you go, Billy," Olive said, handing him a penny.

For a moment, the boy stared at the coin in his open palm, a frown on his face. Then he thrust his hand out. "No, Miss Olive, that's not my usual tip. You can't give me money for pulling Juniper out of the gorse. I did that because . . . because . . ."

"Because he's my friend," Juniper said.

Olive looked from one to the other and took back the penny. "A farthing it is, then."

"Thanks, Miss Olive. I'll be off now—deliveries. See ya, Juniper."

"See you in class, Billy," Juniper called.

"Hugh," Olive said, "will you join us for tea?"

"No, I don't think I should."

"I don't see why not," Olive said with some defiance.

"I'm not certain I'd pass muster," he said and held out his hands. His palms were caked with dirt, there was a fair amount under his nails, too. Looking closer, Olive could see it dusted in his hair.

"Mrs. Wilkins already got you stuck in?" she asked.

"Those broad beans won't plant themselves, you know," he replied.

"I suppose it's just the two of us, then," Olive said to Juniper.

They walked into the lounge, Juniper first with Olive behind, carrying the tea tray. Mrs. Pagett took one look at the girl and gasped. "Gracious!"

"Hello, Mrs. Pagett," Juniper said cheerfully. "I had a fall."

Olive set the tea tray down on the table. "Shall we sit?" she asked with aplomb.

Mrs. Pagett lowered herself to the edge of the sofa and leaned forward.

"My dear girl, that's dreadful. However did it happen?" She cast a suspicious look at Olive, who avoided it and concentrated on pouring out the tea.

"Just a mishap on her way home from school," Olive said, handing Juniper her glass of Ribena. She held a plate out to the woman. "Biscuit? I'm sorry I've not baked today."

Mrs. Pagett took a biscuit, poured milk in her tea, and stirred, all the while her brow furrowed. Olive offered Juniper a biscuit and took one for herself.

"Miss Kersey, I realize this was something of a surprise to Miss Paxton—to learn she had a ward—but I felt that she had understood the gravity of the situation and the need for extreme sensitivity when it comes to caring for a polio child who is unable to care for herself."

"In hospital," Juniper said, "we would sometimes have our sticks kicked out from under us."

Mrs. Pagett's jaw dropped. "I've never heard of such a thing."

"They told us we needed to know how to take care of ourselves. I've looked worse."

"Worse?"

"These are just a few scratches," Olive jumped in, and Juniper, her mouth full of biscuit, nodded. "You caught us before Juniper had the opportunity to wash up."

Mrs. Pagett took the notebook and fountain pen from her handbag. She unscrewed the top of the pen and began writing, the pen scratching across the paper. Once, she paused, the pen nib hovering in a menacing way, then resumed until she'd filled half a page. Olive's heart thumped in her chest. Was Juniper not allowed to be a child? Would Olive be found negligent?

Juniper swallowed her biscuit and said, "Mrs. Pagett, I can use the lavatory all by myself now. Can we show her, Miss Olive?"

"Yes, we'll take a look when we've finished here," Olive said, grateful for the distraction.

"Mr. Casper and I worked on it together," Juniper said. "I drew the picture, and he built it."

Olive explained who Casper was, and then, during the next few minutes, she and Juniper played tag team relaying the highlights of school and home since the girl's arrival barely more than a week earlier. When they'd finished their tea, Juniper led Mrs. Pagett to the bathroom, but a second before they got there, Olive slipped in ahead to grab the bloodstained towel from the edge of the tub and hold it behind her back.

"This is fine work," Mrs. Pagett said, admiring the railings on either side of the toilet.

"Mr. Casper and I are designing something to make it easier for me in the bath," Juniper said. "It may involve a pulley."

"Juniper is full of ideas and draws them out. Why don't you show Mrs. Pagett?"

Juniper fetched her sketchbook and brought it back to the bathroom, where Mrs. Pagett flipped through a few pages, murmuring, "Oh, I see," and "This one is lovely."

Olive craned her neck to see the lovely one. It was a drawing looking out the front window and across the green to the empty bench that faced the sea.

"Well, I must be off." Mrs. Pagett gathered her things from the lounge, and the three of them stood in the entry. "I will make note of Juniper's accident in her file, but I hope such an incident will not be repeated. And your lodgers, Miss Kersey—I've met Mr. Hodgson now, but I would like to meet the other one too. A widow, I believe? To form a complete picture of Juniper's life."

"Mrs. Claypool is out at the moment," Olive said, hoping Abigail wouldn't surprise them by coming downstairs. "So, another time."

"Yes, another time," Mrs. Pagett said, "you can depend on it."

Olive shut the door behind the woman, leaned against it, and sighed.

"I'd say we dodged a bullet there."

"She liked my drawings," Juniper pointed out.

"She did, but still, we must be careful. It's Mrs. Pagett who has the final say round here, you know."

"I thought that was Miss Margery."

Olive laughed. "There are some things not even Miss Margery is in control of." She touched Juniper's cheek. "Did that really happen at the hospital—your sticks being kicked away?"

"Yes," Juniper said. "'All part of the service,' one of the orderlies said."

Olive reluctantly admitted it might've done the girl good, but still, she didn't like it. "Now, let's tend to your injuries. I'll meet you in the bathroom."

Juniper went off, and Olive returned to the lounge to collect the tea tray. She glanced out the front window and did a double take— Mrs. Pagett was standing in front of her car, talking with Constance Binny.

Binny, Olive cursed under her breath. Nothing good could come of that. Had she heard Hetty's version of Juniper's accident and was now adding her own embellishments? Olive watched, helpless to intervene, until the two women parted and Mrs. Pagett left.

Olive returned the tray to the kitchen and went back to find Juniper leaning against the railing by the lav.

"I have sand in my shoes," she said.

There was no "just kick them off" about it, because calipers and shoes were all a piece. Olive dug out an old bed linen from the rag pile, laid it on the tiled floor, and pulled off the calipers. Then, Juniper sat up and watched as Olive turned the apparatus upside down. Sand sifted out. The girl stripped off her socks, and out came more sand.

"Looks as if you're going to need a bath."

Juniper looked horrified. "I just had my bath last night."

"So you did. Well, then, a fair amount of washing up."

As they went about it, Juniper said, "Instead of a pulley for the tub, I think a bath chair might work. If I had bars overhead and a seat that was even with the top of the tub, I could pull myself right over to it. Oh, Miss Olive, there's a note from Miss Browne. It's in my school bag."

Along with more sand, Olive discovered. She took the bag out to the yard, and shook it upside down, returning with the teacher's reply to her letter.

Dear Miss Kersey,

Thank you for your note conveying Miss Paxton's wish that Juniper remain where she is and that there will be a concerted effort to remediate the wide gaps in her arithmetic skills. Although I am concerned about the arrangement for Juniper, I am delighted to keep her in my class as she is such a lovely girl. As you have requested, I will gather arithmetic books from each year for your use. Please do let me know if Miss Paxton has any questions. The best of luck.

★ ★ ★

Margery, almost late for the evening meal, came dashing in through the kitchen and would've kept going, but Olive stopped her and explained Juniper's adventure and Mrs. Pagett's visit. Margery listened and frowned and tapped her fingers on the back of a chair, and then asked, "But she's all right?" When Olive assured her Juniper was not only fine but seemed to have enjoyed herself, Margery said, "We can't keep her in cotton wool, can we?" Olive agreed, greatly relieved. She turned to take the cottage pie out of the oven, when there came a thump, followed by scuffling and low voices. Margery hurried out to the entry. Olive set the steaming dish on the table and followed to find Hugh kneeling at the bottom of the stairs with a limp Abigail in his arms. Her eyes fluttered as she came to. Margery hovered nearby, and Juniper stood a few steps away, leaning against the wall.

"What is it?" Olive asked.

"Would you like to go back to your room, Abigail?" Hugh asked. "I can take you up."

"No, please," Abigail said, pale but with a firm voice. Hugh helped her to her feet, and she patted his arm. "I'd prefer to stay down here. I'm so very sorry."

"Shall I go to my room?" Juniper asked.

"Certainly not," Abigail said, reaching out to the girl, stopping just short of touching her. "You pay no mind to my foolishness. It's only that . . . I came over a bit lightheaded."

"Why don't we go in the lounge?" Margery asked, waving her arm like a traffic cop. "I think you could just do with a brandy, yes?"

She took hold of Abigail and led her in, Juniper following. Hugh hung back, retreating into the kitchen with Olive.

"She took one look at Juniper and her injuries," he said in a low voice, "and said, 'Oh, you're alive!' or something like that, and then fainted. Was she thinking . . . did she lose a child?"

"Must've done," Olive said, "although she's never said."

They joined the others in the lounge, where Abigail clung to her brandy.

Margery eyed Juniper. "Look at you, now," she said. "Is it sore—your nose?"

"Oh no," Juniper said. "I mean, only a bit. It's fine, really. Are you a gardener now, Mr. Hugh?"

There's a good skill to learn, Olive thought—deflection.

"It seems I am," he replied. "Thanks, Olive, for thinking of me."

"I hope Mrs. Wilkins doesn't wear you out," Olive said.

"I'm no stranger to the soil," Hugh said in a grandiose voice.

Margery laughed. "That was the title of one of your Dig for Victory films during the war, wasn't it?" she asked. "*Don't Be a Stranger to the Soil—Grow Your Own Veg.*"

"Brilliant, wasn't it?" Hugh said. "I'm sure I single-handedly kept the British people from starvation."

"Well, now," Olive said, "let's go through to dinner."

As the food was dished out, Juniper asked, "Will we have spaghetti again one day, Miss Olive? It was very good."

Cottage pie seemed prosaic after the jolly meal of spaghetti à la Bolognese. For that, they had tucked tea cloths into their collars and made a general mess of getting the dangling strands of noodles from plate to mouth. The results were orange lips, a lot of laughter, and more laundry.

"Of course we'll have it again," Olive said.

Over dessert—tinned apricots and custard—Juniper said, "It's half term week after next, and Linda in my class invited me over one day. May I go, Miss Olive?"

There was the suggestion of a pause—of knives and forks suspended in midair. Olive raised her eyebrows, and Juniper shifted her gaze.

"May I go, Miss Margery?"

"Let me see," Margery said. "Linda's mum is . . ."

"Casper's wife, Betty," Olive filled in.

"Yes, that's right, Casper's wife. If Linda's mum says it's all right, I don't see why not."

Immediately after the evening meal, Abigail excused herself. Olive followed her out to the entry, and the woman paused on the bottom stair.

"I'm so dreadfully sorry about earlier," she said in a low voice.

"Not to worry," Olive said, and decided to take a chance. "Memories can come back to us at the strangest times, can't they? Is that what it was—a memory?"

"It startled me, that's all—seeing Juniper like that." Abigail looked off into the middle distance. "You think you're leaving them for only a moment, but you never really know, do you?"

She didn't wait for an answer, but continued up to her room.

★ ★ ★

There was no further exchange between Olive and Margery about arithmetic. Olive collected the books from school midday Tuesday and left them on the dresser in the kitchen, and there they sat when, on her way out the door Wednesday morning, Margery caught sight of them.

"Well," she said as she left, "after all, you did win that prize for doing your sums."

Yes, sums—but Olive had had a quick look through the books and realized that although she could add and subtract in pounds, shillings, and pence, these were only basic skills. There was long division and multiplying decimals and trying to understand if a train left the station at nine o'clock, going forty-two miles per hour, and another train left a different station at . . . Olive would have to learn before she could teach Juniper.

After finishing the breakfast dishes and her cleaning, Olive sat down at the kitchen table with *Constance Spry* and was reading up on cakes when Hugh popped in.

"Mrs. Wilkins asked me to collect a box of plants from the post office—begonias for the shady terrace. I'll nip over now."

"Right," Olive said.

He hesitated, threw a look over his shoulder, and added, "Sorry, Olive—I've just seen Miss Binny heading in this direction."

Olive sighed and rose to put the kettle on. "I don't suppose you want to put off the begonias until after coffee?"

"I would if I could—really."

She clicked her tongue. "Pull the other one, why don't you? Go on, then."

But when the knock came, Hugh said, "Let me get that for you." Olive followed him out, where he opened the front door with a flourish.

"Miss Binny," he said. "Lovely to see you. I'm sorry I can't stay, but I have a small errand to run for Mrs. Wilkins."

Binny stepped in and nodded. "Hello, Olive dear. Perfectly understandable, Mr. Hodgson, and let me say I wish you luck with Nancy Wilkins and her garden." The pheasant tail trembled. "The woman wins a first for her broad beans one year, and she thinks she owns the world."

"Yes, well," Hugh said, and with that he was gone.

"Why don't you go through to the lounge, Miss Binny," Olive said, "and I'll be right in with coffee."

When she returned with the tray, Binny had settled in one of the upholstered chairs. "Your Mrs. Claypool will join us?" she asked.

"Mrs. Claypool is in her room," Olive said. "She may not be ready to come downstairs."

"Not to worry," Binny said, "I'll wait while you go and ask her."

Binny was like a dog with a bone, and it was better that Abigail got it over with. Olive went upstairs and knocked lightly. The voice on the wireless lowered, and Abigail opened the door.

"I'm so sorry to disturb you," Olive explained in a whispered rush. "Constance Binny has stopped in for coffee. She was a friend of my mother's and still likes to keep up with . . . things. She wants to meet you if you wouldn't mind joining us. But it's fine if you're about to go out or something." Anything, Olive wanted to say. Flee.

A resolute look came over Abigail's face—a firm brow and mouth. "I will join you," she said. "And thank you for your kindness, Olive, and your persistence."

In the lounge, Olive poured the coffee and offered slices of currant cake.

"You're very welcome to Southwold, Mrs. Claypool," Binny said. "You are from London and a war widow, I hear. Terribly sad business, wasn't it? So much loss. And no children to speak of?"

Abigail froze, cup halfway to her lips and a blank expression on her face.

"Miss Binny has a nephew in London who works at the *Daily Sketch*," Olive said. It was like waving a shiny object in front of the woman, and it worked.

"Norman—my nephew—is a newspaperman," Binny said, lighting up. "And such a memory for facts! Why, I daresay he can recall every single person who has gone up before the Old Bailey since 1938 and what each person's offense was. What he doesn't know, he can find out. Yes, a world of knowledge at his fingertips. Although, I will admit that occasionally he can be a bit of a crusader for . . . questionable causes."

"Norman and Donald were good friends, weren't they?" Olive asked.

"Indeed they were, poor dear Donald," Binny said, and then leaned over the coffee table toward Abigail, as if offering confidence. "Donald was Olive's brother—killed at Dunkirk. Such a fine man. Donald and Norman were close, and Norman took it quite hard when Donald died."

Over the years, Olive had occasion to wonder just how close the friendship had been between the two young men. Norman had spent the spring and summer of 1939 with Binny, and he and Donald had been inseparable until Donald had signed up. Norman's poor eyesight made him unfit for the service, and so he had fought the war on the London home front. Olive had seen him only a handful of times over the years, but she felt certain that Binny, who had no inkling of Donald's preferences, hadn't a clue about Norman's either. Otherwise, he would not sit atop that pedestal where she'd placed him. Olive had never asked Norman and had no idea how she would go about it.

Binny's conversation then went off in a different direction, critiquing the poor job that was done cutting the grass on the Common. Abigail's attention seemed to have drifted off, and Olive glanced at the time, barely refraining from drumming her fingers on her saucer. She reminded herself of what Mrs. Wilkins had said—about Binny being not only alone but also lonely. Perhaps if she kept repeating it, she wouldn't lose patience with the woman so quickly.

When coffee drew to a close, Binny departed, promising to pass on Olive's regards to Norman. Abigail retreated to her room without a word, and Olive finished her housework, sat down to a plate of cheese and crackers and apple slices, and then readied herself for the afternoon.

CHAPTER 13

Olive stood next to Charlie Salt in front of the Hillman. "I'll be driving on an actual road today? Are you sure that's safe?" she asked.

"I wouldn't advise it if I didn't think you were ready, Miss Kersey. I know just the place."

They drove out of town and through the countryside to a quiet road with branches of beech arching overhead, the new leaves infusing the light with a fresh, bright-green quality. On either side ran low walls smothered in ivy. Salt pulled into a passing place, and Olive took over the driver's position. Immediately, she found that the road was not entirely deserted, and the first two times a car passed going the other way, she trembled slightly, but after that, she kept steady. Until, that is, they neared a place where the road curved sharply to the right. Olive heard the high whine of an engine—like a bumblebee caught in a tin—and the next moment, a motorbike appeared, turning wide into their lane and heading straight for them.

Charlie Salt shouted something, and Olive jerked the wheel to the left, abandoned the clutch and remembered only to slam on the brake. They left the roadway and came to an abrupt stop that threw them forward, but not so far that Olive bumped her head on the windscreen.

The engine shuddered and died while the motorbike, without pause, continued on its way, the whine receding to nothing.

Salt grabbed Olive's arm. "Are you all right? Miss Kersey?"

Olive had difficulty pulling her hands off the steering wheel, and even greater difficulty catching her breath. The entire episode couldn't've lasted more than a few seconds, but it felt like an eternity.

"Yes, I'm fine," she said. "What did I do wrong?"

"You did nothing wrong," Salt said with some heat. "The fault lies with that yob—" he looked back at the empty road "—not caring a whit for anyone but himself."

"I crashed your car," Olive said, the full realization hitting her.

"We weren't going fast enough to call it a crash," Salt said. "The important thing is that you are unhurt."

"And you?"

"I'm fine."

"But not the car," Olive said. She got out and put her hand on the car's bonnet to steady her shaking legs before making her way to the front. The road banked slightly at the turn, and there was an opening in the wall where a sheep track led off. Why couldn't she have turned hard enough to go down that way? Instead, she'd run right into the ivy-covered stone wall. Or, at least, the left headlamp had, and a protruding stone had cracked the glass. Salt got out and joined her.

"I'm so sorry," Olive said, her face flushed with humiliation. "I will pay for the damage, Mr. Salt."

"You will not," he declared. "This was not your fault. You took quick, decisive action that otherwise might've turned out worse. Well done, you."

Was he joking? Olive frowned at Salt, looking for a sign of jest or derision or . . . but, apart from his face as red as hers felt, he seemed sincere.

"Look now," he said, "what we need is a cup of tea, don't you think? A chance to quiet our nerves. There's a pub nearby. What do you say?"

His calm was contagious. Olive took hold of herself and looked up and down the empty road. "Shall I drive?" she asked.

Salt gave her a nod. "Yes, I think that would be best."

She reversed, turned onto the road, and drove for the three-minute, mishap-free journey. They arrived at the pub just as it was opening for the afternoon, and took tea in a corner near the cold fireplace.

Salt added two spoonfuls of sugar to his tea and stirred. "You did well under pressure, Miss Kersey."

"Did I? I'm not sure it feels that way. A cracked headlamp." She found she was more annoyed than upset—and then a thought came to her. "But perhaps this wasn't as bad as that fellow you told me about—the one who ruined the gearbox entirely. Was he a student of yours too, Mr. Salt?"

Salt set his teacup down and looked up at her. "No, Miss Kersey. Actually, I am that fellow."

"You?"

"I was fourteen and had never driven, but decided to try my hand at an old Morris lorry we had in the barn. I did quite a number on it. My dad wasn't best pleased."

Olive attempted to stifle her giggles with little success, and Salt grinned as he watched her. At last when she'd got hold of herself, she said, "Sorry."

He kept his eyes on her. "Never apologize for that smile."

Time stopped in a way Olive hadn't felt for such a long time. Her smile faded and then reappeared. Salt looked abashed at his own words, and then they both jumped when the pub door opened, and two men walked in and up to the bar.

Olive tucked the moment away to be examined later at greater length. "Do you have many other students?" she asked.

"You're my first and, currently, my only student."

"Am I?" Olive asked. "Well, I never would've guessed it. You're a good instructor."

"It's something I've always enjoyed. Before the war, I fancied myself becoming a teacher—conjugating Latin verbs for a classroom full of boys, that sort of thing."

"Did the war change that?"

"The war changed a great many things," he said.

She agreed. "I dreamed of opening a tearoom. I still enjoy trying my hand at baking. But you have become a teacher, after all," she pointed out.

"Of sorts," he said. "Last year, when I decided to open a driving school, I told my cousin Harold, who owns the garage, that I wouldn't shirk my duties as a mechanic and that I could do both jobs. Harold agreed. He's a good sort. He knew how much it meant to me, running my own business." Salt shook his head. "Seems a bit late to start a new life, doesn't it?"

"No, not too late," Olive said, frowning. "We can't think that way or . . . what's the point?"

★   ★   ★

At Mersea House, Salt walked Olive up to the door, and when she went for the key in her handbag, he cleared his throat and said, "Miss Kersey."

"Hiya, Miss Olive," Billy Grunyon called from the corner of the house. "You're just in time for your grocery order."

"I'll be right in, Billy." Olive turned. "Yes, Mr. Salt, you were going to say something?"

Margery opened the front door.

"I thought I heard voices," she said.

"What are you doing here?" Olive asked.

"It's Wednesday—my half day," Margery replied. "Good afternoon, Mr. Salt. Tea?"

"No, thank you, Miss Paxton," he said. "We have just finished a pot. And may I report that Miss Kersey is doing a fine job on her driving lessons."

"Is she?" Margery asked, smiling at Olive.

"Well, good afternoon, ladies."

"Until next week," Olive called after Salt as he left. She followed Margery in through to the kitchen and opened the door for Billy.

"Good afternoon, Miss Margery," the boy said, hauling the basket in from his bicycle.

The three of them unloaded the delivery, Billy taking back what was due at his next stop.

"A tin of pineapple—is this for us?" Margery asked.

"Yes," Olive said, and took it from her.

"Is it for a salad?"

"No, not for a salad. Where is Juniper?"

"Studying spelling words, I'd say," Billy said. He accepted a far-thing from Olive and took the basket out to his bicycle, adding as he pedaled off, "Miss Browne says we've had it too easy, and instead of ten, she's giving us fifteen words on Friday."

With Billy gone, Margery sat at the table, casually examining the groceries. "Mr. Salt is being awfully solicitous, isn't he?"

Olive, her head in the pantry, whipped round. "What's that supposed to mean?"

Margery shrugged. "You know—attentive?"

Olive took the jar of glacé cherries out of Margery's hand and pointed it at her. "Well, if he's being solicitous, it's because you're paying him to be."

"Is that so?" Margery said. "Well, in that case, I'll stop paying him."

"What?"

"You heard me—I'll cancel the lessons, and then we'll see if he's been solicitous because he was being paid or if there's another reason."

"You can't do that," Olive exclaimed. "This is his chance to make a new life for himself, to prove that he can be his own person, run his own business. If you cancel now, how will that look—his first student firing the teacher?"

"All right, all right," Margery said. "If you insist."

Olive huffed with indignation. Then, there was a knock at the front door. She handed Margery the glacé cherries and went out to answer.

It was Charlie Salt.

"Oh, hello."

"Sorry, there's just this one other thing," he said. "I had hoped to take the opportunity to ask you . . ."

Behind her, in the entry, Olive heard the swoosh of the swing door to the kitchen being pushed open. She stepped out and pulled the front door closed behind her.

"Yes?"

"Well, Miss Kersey"—Salt cleared his throat—"there's one of those grand old country houses not far from here, and it'll be open to the public on Sunday afternoon, and the gardens should be looking fine, and I wondered if you would like to come out with me for a visit?"

"Is this for a driving lesson?" Olive asked.

Salt blustered and shook his head and said, "No, no, it isn't a lesson. I only thought—"

"If that's the case, shouldn't you call me Olive?"

He laughed and took a deep breath. "Will you come out with me on Sunday afternoon, Olive?"

She smiled. "Yes, I will, Charlie, thank you."

They stood a moment without speaking, and then they both spoke at once, both stopped and started again, and finally arrangements were made. Charlie left, and Olive went back indoors in time to see the kitchen door swing closed and to see the back of Hugh disappearing into his room upstairs.

★   ★   ★

Not quite knowing how to go about catching Juniper up in arithmetic, Olive decided it would be best to start at the beginning. It was Saturday before they got to it. She sat the girl down at the dining table after breakfast with the first year's text, a lesson book, and a pencil.

"I thought you could try working the problems at the end of each chapter."

Juniper paged through the book. "But Miss Olive, these are easy sums."

"Yes, but it's a review. We'll get to the difficult part soon enough—we just aren't sure yet where that is. Now, you get started, and I'll come back round and check your work."

Determined not to hover, Olive left her to it and went upstairs. She came down later, when what she had deemed a sufficient time had passed, and put her head in the dining room. Juniper sat at the table, pencil to her lip and staring off into space.

"All right?" she asked.

"I have numbers swimming before my eyes," Juniper said.

Olive looked over the work—she'd done three pages of practice sums with single digits. It wasn't terribly thrilling, but her answers were correct. It was a starting point.

"Can you manage two more pages?" Olive asked. "Then come and find me."

"Right."

Olive went to the kitchen and made rock buns, setting them on the baking sheet just as the girl came in, pushing the door open with one stick.

"I've finished."

There was a knock at the front door. Olive looked down at her flour-covered hands.

"I'll answer," Juniper said, and slipped out.

Olive hurried through getting the rock buns in the oven and washing her hands. She could hear Juniper talking and a man answering, and just as Olive untied her pinny, the girl came back in.

"It's a man to see Miss Margery. I've put him in the lounge."

"Have you now?" Olive said. "You didn't happen to ask his name?"

"His name is Mr. Markham."

The gentleman stood at the fireplace. He was well dressed for a Saturday, and his gleaming dark hair was swept back, showing silver at the temples. He smiled when Olive walked in.

"Hello," he said, "I'm Geoff Markham."

"Hello, good morning," Olive said returning his smile, "I'm Olive Kersey." Who was this man? He didn't look like a laborer or a salesman. Had Margery found a new lodger and forgotten to mention it? "You're looking for Margery? She's at the shop."

"Of course," he said under his breath, "that damned shop."

Olive kept the smile up. "Have you come about a room?"

The man looked at her blankly. "A room?"

"We are a boardinghouse."

"Yes, of course you are," he said, laughing. "Sorry, I forgot that. No, I haven't come about a room."

Before Olive could ask for another clue, Hugh came down the stairs in rather a hurry and stood behind Juniper to look into the lounge. When he saw the man, he said, "Markham."

"Hodgson," the man replied, lifting his chin in greeting, "so this is where you washed up."

"BBC let you loose, did they?" Hugh replied, a coolness to his voice.

"Oh, you know, I wanted to see if this place was all it's cracked up to be."

Olive's gaze flitted from Hugh to the guest. *London.*

"Would you like coffee, Mr. Markham?" she asked.

"I'd love coffee, thanks."

"Hugh, you'll stay?" Olive said—a statement more than a question.

There was a moment's hesitation, and then Hugh said, "I wouldn't miss it," and went into the lounge behind Juniper.

The rock buns were finished baking by the time the coffee was ready, but they were too hot to serve, and so Olive returned to the lounge a few minutes later with coffee and shortbread. Juniper sat in her chair, and the two men across from each other.

". . . and he's gone now too," Markham was telling Hugh. "Went off to Australia to start his own magazine. Good luck to him. Oh, thanks," he said as Olive poured the coffee and handed him a cup. He added milk and sugar, then sat back. "Tell me, Olive, how do you know Margery?"

Olive and Margery's lifelong friendship, with its ups and downs and interrupted by more than fifteen years of silence, had re-formed so quickly that Olive didn't know where to begin.

"We've known each other since we were girls," Olive said.

Markham clasped his hands together, elbows on his knees, and leaned forward. "Good, that's good, then you can tell me—how is she? Is she doing all right? I thought she only needed a short rest, you know. I never thought she'd be gone this long. I can't imagine what she's finding to do with herself here."

Olive handed Juniper a glass of milk and held out the plate of shortbread to her as she answered. "Margery hasn't rested since she's been back, but she's quite happy. And you, Mr. Markham, how do you know Margery?"

"Please call me Geoff. We've known each other years. Worked together at the Ministry of Information during the war and after that for the BBC along with Hodgson and a few others. Then suddenly Margery decides to leave. I knew you were gone, Hodgson, but I didn't know you had followed her here," Markham said. "It was the BBC's loss, your rather abrupt departure—you, the one who introduced television programming to the masses."

Hugh colored at what had sounded to Olive like a compliment. "No need to exaggerate," he said.

"We don't have a television," Juniper said, "but we have a wireless."

Markham smiled at the girl. "You don't need a television with the seaside at your doorstep. You must enjoy it—good fun for children."

"I haven't been in the sea yet," Juniper said, "but we're going to sort something out."

He glanced down at her calipers. "Yes, of course. Sorry. So, Juniper, is Olive your mum?"

"No," Olive said, "Juniper is Margery's ward."

Geoff blinked at Juniper, his smile fading a bit. "Her ward?"

"Yes, sir," Juniper said. "I arrived a fortnight ago, didn't I, Miss Olive?"

Hugh leaned back in his chair. "Now that I think about it, Markham," he said, "Juniper is about the same age as your second oldest, isn't she?"

The man ignored Hugh, and instead looked round the lounge. "So, this is the place Margery's uncle left her?"

"Uncle Milkey," Olive said. "Yes. The house and the shop."

"Charming," Markham said. "Although small towns have their drawbacks, I suppose. Everyone knows everyone else's business. Must feel a bit constraining at times, wouldn't you say, Hodgson?"

They were like boys with peashooters, but Olive zeroed in on one clear truth.

"How many children do you have, Mr. Markham?" she asked, keeping her voice light, conversational.

He froze like a rabbit caught in the light of a torch. "Four," he said weakly.

"Have you left them behind with their mother in London to come to the seaside for the day?" she continued. "You should've brought your family along. Perhaps another time."

Out the corner of her eye, she saw the smile on Hugh's face. Markham drained his cup and stood.

"Well, thanks for the coffee, Olive. It was good to meet you—and you, Juniper. Hodgson, my regards to Sid—if you chance to see him." Olive cut her eyes at Hugh, who appeared impassive. "Perhaps I'll look in on Margery at the shop."

"It's just on the High Street," Olive said as she followed him to the entry. She opened the front door wide and added, "Paxton's Goods."

He nodded and said goodbye, but he'd gone only a few steps when he stopped and turned to her.

"The girl—is she . . . all right?"

"Yes, she's all right. But if you're asking why she wears calipers, it's because of polio, Mr. Markham. When she was four."

He shook his head. "Dreadful. I remember how frightened we were every summer during those years. My wife would—"

He flinched, as if catching himself. But too late.

"Goodbye, Mr. Markham," Olive said firmly. "Have a pleasant journey back to London."

She stepped inside as a frantic rapping came at the kitchen door to the yard, and Olive went through the kitchen to answer.

"Hiya, Miss Olive," Billy said, out of breath. "There's a Punch and Judy man at the pier—I just saw him setting up and thought maybe Juniper would want to see it."

"Punch and Judy!" Juniper exclaimed from the doorway. "May I, Miss Olive?"

Olive gave Billy a stern look.

"I won't let her fall into the gorse," he said, "I swear. We'll go down the Parade like normal people."

"I promise," Juniper said.

Olive sighed. "Wear your coat."

She watched them leave, the boy on his two feet and the girl swinging along on her sticks. Whether Billy walked slower or Juniper hurried up, their strides matched as they headed for the seafront. Olive returned to the kitchen, where Hugh leaned against the sink.

"He's married?" Olive asked.

"Yes," Hugh replied.

"And Margery was . . . his bit on the side?"

"It was more than that," Hugh said. "It went on for years. The wife and children live in Staffordshire. They rarely came up to London and never to the flat. But in the end, it was Margery who broke it off when she came back here. Has she never mentioned him?"

"No one ever tells me anything!" Olive shouted. "And why not? Am I not to be trusted? Do you all believe I would tell Binny what I hear so that the news would spread far and wide? That doesn't show a lot of faith in me, does it?"

"You know what it was with me," Hugh said. "As for Margery—I think she wanted to put it all behind her."

Olive fumed. She brushed Hugh aside, took the loaf and cut four slices, then fetched ham from the fridge and chopped it.

"Lunch already?" Hugh asked.

"I thought I might take sandwiches to Margery and Young Trotter. God knows what they normally eat for lunch."

"Olive," Hugh said, "Markham acted as if he'd never heard of you, but that isn't true. Margery mentioned you often. You, Uncle Milkey, this town, the sea. It isn't as if she forgot the place. Markham hears what he wants to hear."

★ ★ ★

Just before lunch on a Saturday, and the shop wasn't terribly busy—perhaps they were all out watching Punch and Judy.

"Hiya, Olive," Malc said when he finished up with a customer. "Shopping?"

"No, I've brought sandwiches for your and Margery's lunches."

"Oh, ta—all I've got is a cheese roll Dad put together, and he usually forgets the cheese."

"Where is she?"

Malc looked behind him to the opening that led to the office and storeroom. "In there. She had a visitor a few minutes ago, but he's gone."

Olive tapped once on the closed office door and then walked in. Margery sat hunched over her desk, smoking. She looked smaller somehow, and washed of color. When Olive came in, she barely raised an eyebrow.

"All right?" Olive asked.

"Yeah, fine," Margery replied.

When nothing more was forthcoming, Olive said, "I brought you and Malc sandwiches—here's yours."

She laid it on the corner of the desk, and Margery stared at it. "Look, Olive—"

"Why don't I put the kettle on?" Olive asked. First, she peered into the pot, found it empty, and spooned the tea in. Then, she filled kettle at the sink in the washroom and lit the spirit lamp, which looked as if it had resided on the corner table in the office for at least thirty years. The renovation of Uncle Milkey's shop had not extended this far.

"So," Olive said, moving a stack of files from the chair against the wall and sitting.

"So," Margery said. "Hugh has filled you in, no doubt?"

"He's told me more than you have—but that wouldn't be difficult, would it? Because you've not said a word."

"I wanted to explain—I did—but I'm not terribly proud of myself."

"What does that matter?" Olive demanded.

"You're the reason I came back, you know," Margery said.

"I—what?"

"You and Uncle Milkey." She looked round. "I love this place, always have. I remembered him saying, '*It'll all be yours one day, and never you mind anyone who tells you that you can't run a business, because*

I know you can.' But the war came and I wanted to see London, to be in the middle of things." She shook her head. "That day you and I met again—was it only two months ago?—I had come back to settle the estate—to sell this shop and the house. I swear I had. I suppose I didn't feel as if I were worthy of Milkey's confidence."

"He would've disagreed."

"True. I went looking for you that day, but you weren't at home. Then later, I saw you on your walk up the Parade—that stride I never could keep up with—and seeing you brought back that feeling we had all those years ago, that the world was our oyster. For the first time in I can't remember how long, I felt hopeful about my life."

Olive's anger dissolved because Margery's words were her own thoughts and feelings. The kettle boiled, and Olive poured up the tea.

"He . . . Geoff . . . does seem charming," she said, her back to Margery, but with a look over her shoulder.

"He's got charm in spades, that one." Margery stubbed out her cigarette and poured milk into their cups. "You know, looking back, I can see how it began with him, but I can't for the life of me explain how I let it go on for so long. Thank God I'm over it now."

"Doesn't sound as if he is," Olive said.

"He's a sore loser."

"He wants you to move back to London, doesn't he?"

"But I won't." Margery opened the paper wrapping on the sandwich. She took half and pushed the rest over. "Here. No sense you missing your lunch to come on a rescue mission."

They ate in silence. Then, because Olive sensed a crack in the shell, she pushed further.

"Did you live with him?"

"Yes. In his London flat. Twice I moved out, but it never lasted for more than a few months. He was going to divorce her, you see— or she was going to divorce him. The story changed from time to time. Hugh and Sid bolstered me up through the worst times. I don't know what I would've done without them."

"You could've come to me."

"I'd forgotten, and that was my fault." Margery picked a crust off her sandwich and ate it. "What do you think would've happened if I'd stayed and married George and you'd married Stan?"

A memory blew into Olive's mind, tattered and worn from years of handling it. Late at night, she and Stan lay on the sofa in the lounge of the house on Field Stile Road, trying their best to be quiet with her parents upstairs asleep. But the scene was like a snapshot. Olive found she could no longer remember how his skin felt against hers or hear his whispered promises.

"Stan died," Olive said. "If you and George had married, would you have had Juniper? But your child wouldn't have been Juniper, would she? Juniper wouldn't exist." The thought made Olive queasy. "No, it's no good trying to imagine what-ifs."

CHAPTER 14

Olive met Juniper and Billy returning to Mersea House, and the rest of the way they regaled her with a retelling of the Punch and Judy show.

"And Punch with his baton!"

"But he always missed the crocodile!"

"The dog was real, and he sat right on the edge of the stage, put his paws on Judy, and they danced!"

"We had ice cream from Miss Hetty," Juniper said.

"She didn't just give them to you, did she?" Olive asked.

"Oh no, I paid," the girl said, "because I had my sixpence from Miss Margery."

"I'm paying next time," Billy said.

"How about lunch to follow up your ice cream?" Olive asked as she opened the kitchen door. She sat them down at the table and gave them tomato soup and bread and butter.

After, Olive sent Billy away with four rock buns wrapped in a tea cloth with strict orders to hand the packet over directly to his mother. The house grew quiet in the afternoon—Hugh was off at the matinee, and Juniper had got through two pages of double-digit sums and was taking a rest in her room. Olive went to the kitchen and put the kettle on, and just as it came to a boil, Abigail looked in.

"Tea?" Olive asked.

"Yes, thanks."

Olive added another spoonful of tea leaves to the pot and poured it up. "Shall we take it into the lounge?"

Abigail glanced round the kitchen. "How about in here? If I wouldn't be in your way?"

"Certainly not—have a sit."

Olive busied herself with cups and saucer, and milk and sugar, all the while hardly breathing lest she frighten Abigail away or give her second thoughts, because—well, because Abigail had something to say.

The tea brewing, Olive sat across from the woman.

"There was a Punch and Judy man at the pier today," she said.

"Yes, I saw him when I was out. I saw Juniper and . . ."

"Billy."

"Billy," Abigail repeated. "He's the boy who delivers the groceries."

"He is."

"I had two daughters," Abigail said. "Charlotte was nearly eleven, and Doreen was six."

There it is now, Olive thought. Abigail rested her hands in her lap and kept her eyes down.

"My husband died in '42," she continued, her tone measured. "We did all right, the girls and I, because we had each other, but then one morning before school, I left them. The twenty-eighth of October 1944. Do you remember when the V-2 rockets started up and how you never heard them coming. I heard when it hit, though—I was in the next street over and I felt the ground shake, and I ran home. But home wasn't there. Instead, there was an enormous pit in the ground." Abigail looked up, her eyes hollow and bewildered. "I'd only gone out for a pint of milk."

Olive reached across the table, touched her arm, and felt her tremble. "How dreadful. You don't have to say anything more."

It was as if once started, she needed to finish. "I'm sorry I acted the way I did when I saw Juniper after her fall, but you see, they never found the girls. That is, they never . . . and there are still times when I think, what if they got out? What if they survived—injured, but alive? And for that second, I mistook Juniper for . . . she doesn't look anything like Charlotte—it's only her age. It was wrong of me to faint and scare everyone."

"Abigail, you've had such a terrible burden to bear," Olive said.

"But I didn't bear it, did I?" Abigail asked with bitterness.

The swing door opened a few inches. One of Juniper's sticks led the way, followed by the girl herself.

"Hello, Mrs. C.," she said.

Abigail smiled. "Hello, Juniper. Are you coming in for your tea? Don't let me get in the way."

"Stay," Olive said, and poured out their tea. "After all, we have rock buns."

And with that they moved into safe territory.

★　★　★

On Sunday morning, Hugh caught Olive before she left for church.

"Anything more from Margery?" he asked.

"About Geoff?" Olive asked. "No. She was awfully quiet at breakfast."

"You both were," Hugh said. "It took me pulling that shilling from an empty teacup to get a reaction from either of you."

"You're a good showman," Olive said. "I wonder you don't have your own booth at the pier along with the Punch and Judy man." She pinned her hat on and, without looking at Hugh, said, "She won't go back to him, will she?"

"I can't see it," Hugh replied. "She's truly made up her mind this time."

Olive put a large pan with two trussed chickens surrounded by potatoes and carrots into the oven and then hurried off to church. When she returned an hour later, she was met with the fragrance of roasting poultry and the sight of Margery bringing the coffee tray into the kitchen.

"I'd offer you a cup," she said, "but it's quite cold." As she unloaded the cups and saucers, she added, "You should've invited Mr. Salt for Sunday dinner."

"Maybe next week," Olive said. Or maybe never—rather depended on how their afternoon went.

"That's a lovely frock you have on," Margery said. "Will you wear it for your outing?"

It wasn't a lovely frock, and Margery knew it—it was one of Olive's oldest dresses, and that was saying a great deal.

"No, I have something else."

After their Sunday lunch, Margery and Hugh shooed Olive away from washing up, and so she went upstairs to fuss about her appearance. She returned in the purple-plaid day dress she'd got from Mrs. Tees—her first chance to wear it—and with her hair down. She was reaching for her old Norfolk jacket as Margery pushed the swing door open and saw her.

"You mustn't cover up your dress with that," she said.

Olive clutched the brown-and-yellow plaid jacket to her chest. "It isn't terribly warm today, and I don't have a cardigan that suits."

"Give me a minute." Margery disappeared into her bedroom and returned in only a moment. "Try this."

She held out a swing jacket, the soft pleats at the back giving the sense of movement even when still. Olive slipped it on and stood on tiptoe in front of the mirror above the fireplace in the lounge, trying to get a good look at herself. *Not too shabby,* she decided.

"You won't stand watching as we leave, will you?" she asked Margery. "I'm not sixteen."

"No, of course I won't. Hugh and I will huddle in the kitchen and wait until we hear the car doors close, then we'll run out and wave."

Fortunately, no one was about when Charlie Salt arrived. Olive opened the door when he was only halfway up the walk, and he stopped and looked at her. She blushed and he smiled, and they were on their way.

★   ★   ★

The skies were overcast on their journey north, but Olive barely noticed because there was enough sunshine inside the car. She would make certain never to repeat that to anyone, because it sounded daft—it sounded as if she were a starry-eyed young girl and out on her own with a boy for the first time. Still, she couldn't help noticing that Charlie acted fairly lighthearted himself. They seemed to have a great deal to talk about, although later, Olive could barely remember what was said. She decided that Charlie's serious nature was for professional purposes only—as a teacher he would remain sober, but outside of that he was amiable, soft, encouraging, and funny.

"You could have a good ramble across Suffolk without too much difficulty, couldn't you?" he asked as they motored up a road that cut through fields of green. "Nothing much to climb."

"True. You'd be hard-pressed to find a hill more than four hundred feet or so high," Olive said. "And for that you'd need to go east, to the other side of Halesworth and into mid-Suffolk."

"Mountains aren't all they're cracked up to be," Charlie said. "I find there's something quite beautiful about the flat land and sky coming straight down to it."

They could see their destination before they arrived—an expansive Georgian edifice that had replaced a Tudor building that had replaced a priory knocked down during Dissolution of the Monasteries. The house sat on one of those rare Suffolk hills at the end of a drive that wended its way up from the road. They reached the gates at the bottom of the drive and found a fellow sitting in a wooden chair, leaning against the lodge and reading the newspaper. He turned out to be the earl whose family had owned the place for the past few hundred years. They paid him a pound for entry. "There's tea in the ballroom, if you like," he said. "Two bob each. My wife baked the cakes. Enjoy."

★ ★ ★

They had just finished the long gallery, admiring family portraits that began in the 1700s with a traitor to the crown during the Jacobite Risings. As they made their way through the centuries, Charlie had commented on the men's wigs and the little spaniels at their mistresses' feet, and Olive had pointed out the fashion of skirts that ballooned, deflated, and puffed up again. When they'd reached the painting of the most recent earl—the fellow they'd met at the gate—most people took the stairs to view the bedrooms, but through a window Olive and Charlie could see the sun had pierced the clouds. Out they went.

After a stroll between a tall yew hedge on one side and billowing garden beds on the other, they came to a bench set in a niche in the hedge. It was positioned to take in the long view of the grass lawn flanked by two avenues of trees that led the eye to a statue in the far distance. They sat.

"I want to explain something," Charlie said, patting the palms of his hands on his knees.

"All right," Olive replied.

"I was married."

Olive waited, but when he didn't continue, she said, "And now you aren't."

"I am divorced." Charlie paused and watched her for a moment, as if he thought she might flee at this pronouncement. "We were married just before I shipped out at the beginning of the war, and divorced not long after I demobbed in January '46. Not a great deal to commend me, is it?"

"We're too old not to have a past, Charlie."

"You aren't old," he said.

"That's kind of you to say, although sometimes it seems an awfully long time since I was young. But what I mean is, if you and your wife weren't suited or events and such intervened, it might've been for the best. There's no shame in it."

Charlie inclined his head as if to agree—or not.

"I stayed on in Southampton," he said, "working. But when I learned Harold was looking for help, I jumped at the chance to leave the place."

It was Olive's turn. "I've never lived anywhere else and never married," she said, "although there was someone a long time ago. He died early in the war, and then so did my brother, and my parents needed me and . . . well, that's been my life. Not much to it."

"I doubt that," Charlie said.

They gazed down the avenue, and Charlie squinted at the statue in the distance.

"I think it might be Nelson," he said. "Bicorn hat, isn't it? And I can see only the one arm."

"Very well could be," Olive said. "Wasn't he from Norfolk? Good thing your ships in the war were a far cry from the *Victory*."

Charlie looked off to the left at an enormous purple beech, its branches layered to the ground like a petticoat.

"We began with leftovers from the first war, but the navy ended up a modern-day wonder. Although, I'm sure it's changed even more since I walked off my last frigate and back into my civilian life. Such as it was." After a moment, he glanced at her out the corner of his eye. "There's something about spending so much time at sea," he said. "It was years before I could walk in a straight line again."

Olive smiled. There—they'd peeled off the top layer, and although there might be more to discover, this had been enough for one afternoon. She slipped her arm through his and returned her attention to the borders. Charlie covered her hand and did likewise.

★   ★   ★

"Will you come in?" Olive asked as Charlie pulled the car up to the curb in front of Mersea House. It was near seven o'clock. "There's only a cold supper, but you're very welcome to join us."

"I will," Charlie said with conviction, as if answering a challenge. "Thank you."

Olive half expected Margery, Hugh, Abigail, and Juniper to be waiting in the entry for them. They weren't, but both the kitchen and dining room doors stood open, and so they were easy to locate by their voices and the clattering of dishes and chinking of cutlery.

"There's cress," Margery shouted from the kitchen, "but what if it's meant for tomorrow?"

"I took a look." Abigail's voice came from the dining room. "I'm not sure it would go another day."

Juniper came out of the kitchen wearing Olive's pinny, which hung down almost to her ankles. "Hello, Miss Olive. Hello, Mr. Charlie."

Margery followed her out. "There you are. How was the afternoon?"

"Lovely," Olive said. "Charlie's joining us for supper."

"Good. Olive, is there piccalilli?"

"Of course there is," Olive replied.

"Yes, Hugh," Margery called out, "there is piccalilli."

"Well, if there is, she's hidden it well," Hugh replied. He appeared from the dining room. "Oh, Olive, you've returned. Thank God. Mr. Salt, I presume? Good to meet you, sir."

Behind Hugh came another man. He looked to be in his fifties, no taller than Olive, with short black hair and a wiry build. He grinned at her, and well-used smile lines round his mouth deepened.

"Olive, Charlie," Hugh said, "this is Sid Davies, just down from London for a brief visit."

Charlie and Sid shook hands, and Olive said, "I'm happy to meet you, Sid."

"And I, you," Sid replied. "Margery's always talked a great deal about you. Now, Hugh as well."

"You've arrived in the nick of time," Margery said to Olive. "Could you check and see we're eating what we should?"

The gathering in the entry broke apart. Juniper escorted Charlie to the dining room, Abigail set another place, and Olive and Margery got the food on the table—cold chicken and ham and cress salad.

"Miss Olive," Juniper said, "did you drive to the country house?"

"No, I'll leave the long journeys until after I have my driving license," she replied.

"Mr. Charlie is going to teach me to drive," Juniper explained to Sid. "When I'm old enough. I'll have a car with hand controls, you see."

"You're a girl of many talents," Sid replied.

"Mr. Sid can draw," Juniper told Olive.

Sid shrugged. "Scribbles—storyboards for television programs."

"And some fine watercolors," Hugh added.

"Now, you, Juniper," Sid said, "you have an eye for composition."

"Thank you," the girl replied. "What is that?"

"It's knowing where to put things in your picture."

"Like your sketch looking out the front window to the bench," Abigail said.

"You could do anything with your talent," Sid said. "You could be an architect or an engineer—of course, those take a fair bit of arithmetic too."

Juniper's face, elated at the beginning, fell by the end. "I'm behind in my arithmetic," she said.

"Are you?" Sid asked with a glance at Hugh, who must've been his source. "Doesn't mean you can't catch up."

When the meal was finished, Margery murmured to Juniper, "Bath night—I'll go start the water."

The others carried the dishes to the kitchen—Juniper with the cutlery clanking in the pocket of Olive's apron. It made for quite a crowd, and so Olive said, "Why don't I take care of the washing up later?"

"In that case," Hugh said, "pub anyone?"

The only taker was Sid.

"You aren't going back to London tonight, are you?" Olive asked him.

"No, I've got a room at the Swan. I'll be working with Hugh in Mrs. Wilkins' garden tomorrow."

"Good. We'll see you again."

The two men left, Abigail went to her room, and Margery popped back in.

"Right, you," she said to Juniper, "I've the tub filling."

"I'm coming too," Olive said, but Margery waved her away.

"We can manage, can't we?"

Juniper didn't look entirely convinced, but Margery herded her out the door.

Olive and Charlie stood in the kitchen alone.

"That was a quick clear-out," she said.

Charlie glanced over his shoulder to the door. "I suppose you're needed."

"I rather think I am," Olive said. Neither of them moved. "I had such a lovely afternoon."

"The best I can remember," Charlie said.

"You aren't prone to exaggeration, are you?"

"Never." He drew close, his fingertips brushing her arm. "I'm a bit rusty with this part."

He leaned in and kissed her. His lips were warm and dry and the kiss was nice, but brief. Then they kissed again, and Olive stopped analyzing the moment, because something stirred in her, radiating warmth through her body.

Charlie cupped her face in his hand and she slid her arms round his waist.

"I'll see you Wednesday," he whispered.

"Yes," Olive replied. What was Wednesday? "Yes, driving." She walked him to the door.

"Reverse parallel parking," Charlie said. "And crossing road junctions."

"Junctions. Parking. Right. Good night."

After he'd gone, Olive leaned against the door. The house was quiet, nearly empty, but nonetheless, there was a sense of hope within. Sid had come to visit Hugh. Abigail now entered into conversations. Margery had sent Geoff Markham packing, and, although Olive was new to the subject, she believed this to be a good move. The vacant places in Olive's heart had begun to be filled. There was Charlie and, of course, Juniper. Olive's reverie broke at the sound of a large splash from the bathroom.

She knocked first, then went in. "How goes it?" she asked. Juniper sat in the tub, her hair dripping, and Margery, standing next to the tub, looked about as wet.

Margery pointed at Olive. "You'd best stand clear in that frock."

"Better yet," Olive said. She unbuttoned her dress, pulled it and her petticoat off, and hung them on the door. Slipping off her shoes, she stood in her bra and knickers and said, "Now, is your hair washed yet?"

CHAPTER 15

A week later, the Tuesday of Easter half-term break, Juniper spent the afternoon at Linda's. During those few hours Olive couldn't stop herself from imagining the worst. Linda and Juniper wouldn't get along. There would be some sort of mishap. Perhaps Betty, Linda's mother, wouldn't understand that although Juniper had particular needs, she should be treated as any other eleven-year-old. But her anxiety was for naught. Just after teatime, Casper brought the girl back in good spirits.

"Miss Olive, look what Mr. Casper gave me." Juniper leaned against the telephone table and plunged her hand into the cloth bag slung across her shoulder, and brought out a square metal tape measure. "I'm to make measurements—length and width and height—and draw pictures for a bath bench."

"Thanks, Casper," Olive said.

"Happy to help," he said, and turned to Juniper. "Now, Missy, you have any trouble with the multiplying and such, we'll work it through next time."

The idea had occurred to Olive after watching Juniper plod through pages and pages of arithmetic problems. Put her sums into action and the girl might be motivated. Olive had enlisted Casper in her plan.

She mentioned the scheme to Margery too, and Wednesday morning before she left for the shop, Margery had looked in the bedroom as Olive helped Juniper into her calipers for the day.

"Would you like to come into the shop this morning? See how we do things?"

Juniper's eyes widened as if she couldn't believe her luck. "Yes, please. Billy's coming over—may I invite him?"

"Why not?" Margery turned to Olive, "Driving lesson this afternoon?"

Both Charlie and Olive had made it clear to Margery that driving lessons were all business, and something quite apart from—or at least vaguely apart from—any personal relationship that flourished. Margery had made it clear she wasn't worried, but she had asked for a report of the Sunday afternoon outing. Olive had told her that although Charlie seemed reserved, he was kind, sincere, and had a good sense of humor. Also . . .

"He's divorced," Olive had said.

"Is he? Well, better that than the alternative," Margery had replied.

Olive hadn't pointed out that the alternative in most people's minds would've been "never married," not "married and carrying on with another woman." Olive suspected Geoff Markham still lurked in Margery's mind.

★   ★   ★

Juniper and Billy went off to the shop midmorning Wednesday. Olive gave it an hour before she followed, and walked in to see a woman with a shopping basket on her arm standing at the counter. "I'm afraid it's too high for me to reach," she said. "Shouldn't we ask Young Trotter?"

"No need for that, ma'am—I'll fetch it for you." Billy Grunyon popped out from behind the counter, wearing a green apron with "Paxton's Goods" stitched across the front. "'Morning, Miss Olive," he said, "be with you in a moment." Bemused, Olive stood near a display table of toasters and watched. Billy fetched the ladder standing in the corner, positioned it against the shelving, and bounded up to the top in order to reach the pudding bowls. "Is it the blue one?" he called over his shoulder.

"Yes, that's the one." The woman caught sight of Olive, and said, "They're a bit young to be working, don't you think?"

The woman shifted, and Olive saw Juniper propped up on a stool behind the counter, also wearing a Paxton's apron along with a wide smile. Her eyes were hot with excitement as she gave Olive a little wave.

For a moment, the present-day scene faded, and Olive saw herself along with Margery on a rainy Saturday afternoon. They couldn't've been more than six or seven, and had set up their own miniature shop in the back corner of Paxton's Goods. Under the watchful eye of Uncle Milkey, they displayed their wares on an upturned crate— odds and ends scrounged from the damaged goods shelf in the store-room. They'd made a couple of sales to sympathetic customers, which resulted in a farthing or two before they tired of the game, after which they had taken themselves off to the sweets shop.

Now, Olive glanced round for Margery or Malc, but they were nowhere in sight.

Billy returned with the bowl, tore off a length of brown paper, and began wrapping. Juniper tapped her pencil on each of the other five items on the counter and then bowed her head over a notepad in concentration.

At last she looked up at the woman. "That will be four pounds, twelve shillings, and seven pence, please."

Billy glanced over Juniper's shoulder, reached over, and pointed at one line of numbers. The girl looked again, her eyes boring into the paper. She crossed off the sum and started over in an unhurried way, eventually saying, "Oh, sorry, it's four pounds, thirteen and nine, please."

"Here you are," the woman said, handing over a five-pound note.

Juniper took it, placed the note on the counter, and opened the till. She gave Billy a sideways glance and then stared at the coins for a moment before gingerly selecting a handful and passing them over.

"Six and three is your change, ma'am," she said. "There you are."

The woman turned a skeptical eye on the money in her palm and muttered calculations of her own, but at last said, "Yes, and so it is," and with a "good day" left.

"Well, you two," Olive began, but another customer came in. The woman glanced at the children and then scanned the shop, her eyes finally falling on the only other adult in sight.

"Good morning, Olive."

"Good morning, Mrs. Dyrham," she replied.

"Good morning, Mrs. Dyrham," Billy said. "What can we get for you?"

Where were they—Margery and Malc? Olive looked beyond the counter, through the opening to the storeroom and office, but she saw no movement. When Mrs. Dyrham finished her transaction, Olive would go and find them, but the woman walked out the door at the same time that Mrs. Pagett walked in.

"Hello, Mrs. Pagett," Juniper said. "Can we help you find something?"

Mrs. Pagett stood stock-still. "Find something? Are you . . . working?"

Enough of this. Olive rushed out from behind the table of toasters.

"Good morning, Mrs. Pagett."

"Miss Kersey. Is this your idea, or is it Miss Paxton's?" Mrs. Pagett looked round. "Where is she?"

"At the bank," Juniper offered.

Olive, as surprised as Mrs. Pagett, asked, "Where is Mr. Malc?"

"He's off on a ramble, working on one of his maps," Juniper said. Billy remained silent, his gaze shifting back and forth between the adults.

"Well," Mrs. Pagett said, eyeing Olive, "I suppose if you are overseeing this—"

"Miss Olive just arrived," Juniper said with pride. Olive cringed. "We've been all on our own, but we were fine, because Billy could get things customers wanted, and they could pay me."

Mrs. Pagett's face turned to stone. "The children's committee does not condone child labor." She reached into her handbag, drew out the notebook, and unscrewed her fountain pen.

"It isn't work," Billy piped up. "It's doing sums with money. It's arithmetic practice for Juniper."

"That's right," Juniper said. "I'm behind from being in hospital and moving to all the different homes. We have to sit the eleven-plus in the autumn, don't we, Billy?" She didn't wait for an answer. "This is schoolwork, Mrs. Pagett. See?" She held out her notepad with its columns of pounds, shillings, and pence.

Mrs. Pagett leaned forward and peered at the paper, then straightened and began making notes. The shop door opened, and Margery strode in.

"Oh, Mrs. Pagett," she said, and stopped. She glanced at the children, and then hurried on with a firm voice. "Good morning. Lovely of you to visit. I do hope you're being seen to."

★ ★ ★

"It was only a bit of fun for them," Margery said to Olive, who had followed her into the office after Mrs. Pagett had gone and the children had been sent away. "You remember."

"Uncle Milkey was here to keep an eye on us," Olive said. "We didn't have the run of the place."

"I was only across the road at the bank," Margery said. "I could see the shop from the window."

"You couldn't see Mrs. Pagett walk in, could you? That took you by surprise."

Margery sniffed. "I don't understand why she was so agitated. And didn't they do a fine job?"

"That's beside the point," Olive said. "Mrs. Pagett made notes."

"Let her make all the notes she likes," Margery said. "I'm the one responsible for Juniper."

Although annoyed with Margery for leaving the children to run the shop, if pushed, Olive would have admitted the experience seemed to spark an enthusiasm in Juniper for adding and subtracting money. If that got them through even one phase of her arithmetic catch-up, then all the better. Still, Juniper remained quiet and thoughtful through lunch, as if she sensed a disagreement about the shop adventure.

After lunch, when Olive pulled out the flour, sugar, eggs, and butter, the girl perked up.

"Are you baking a cake?" she asked with reverence. "May I help?"

"Yes, a cake and yes, you may."

They read the directions together, and Juniper weighed out the ingredients. If she caught wind of the fact this was another arithmetic lesson, it didn't appear to matter.

Olive lined the bottom of the cake tin with sugar and slices of pineapple from the tin she'd tucked away in the pantry, then she directed Juniper to add the glacé cherries. "Be sure to count how many you've used," Olive said.

After the cake had been put in to bake, Olive pointed to the jar. "Now, turn the rest of them out and count. Then, tell me how much of the jar is on the cake and how much is left."

Juniper sighed.

Olive went up to her room, and when she returned, she found Juniper still keeping the kitchen vigil. When at last the cake was done, they turned it out onto a plate, and the girl took a deep breath.

"It smells lovely," Juniper said.

"We'll have it for tea when I come back from my driving lesson."

"Will Mr. Charlie come for tea?"

"Perhaps."

"Is it a special tea?"

"No," Olive said. "I only wanted to try a new recipe and see what everyone thinks. You may not like it at all."

"I can't imagine not liking cake."

When the knock came after lunch, Juniper answered.

"Hello, Mr. Charlie," she said. The girl moved back and pushed the door open wider with one of her sticks. "Miss Olive, Mr. Charlie is here."

Olive came up behind her. "So I see."

"Good afternoon," Charlie said. He took off his hat, held his clipboard to his chest, and looked just as a driving instructor should, although with the addition of a twinkle in his eye.

"Mr. Charlie," Juniper said, "there's cake for tea—Miss Olive made a special cake. No, not special, but a new recipe. You're invited. Isn't he?"

"Yes, of course he is," Olive said. "But we both baked the cake—you were in charge of the recipe, remember?"

"Will you stay for tea, Mr. Charlie?"

"I don't know as I can resist cake."

"That's what I think too," Juniper said. "Come and have a look."

She led them into the kitchen, and there on the table was a single-layer affair, browned from the syrupy sugar coating, with rings of pineapple baked right into it, and studded with glacé cherries. Olive put her hands on her hips and frowned at the offering.

"An upside-down cake," she said. "It's American, according to Constance Spry."

"I put the cherries on," Juniper said, "eight of them. There were twelve cherries left and that's the same as three-fifths of the jar, so I used two-fifths. It's more arithmetic, but I don't seem to mind if it has to do with cake or building something."

"Well, Miss Juniper, I look forward to tasting it," Charlie said. "And now, Miss Olive, those traffic junctions await. Shall we away?"

Once outside with the door closed, Olive said, "There were thirteen cherries left, but I ate one when she wasn't looking." She shook her head. "Fractions."

$\star$ $\star$ $\star$

Working at the shop had been thrilling, but the next most exciting event of the half-term holiday was Juniper's first time in the sea. Charlie said the trip—no more than a few hundred steps from Mersea House—took the planning of one of Churchill's campaigns. Olive thought it took at least as much equipment—a windbreak, blankets, towels, shovels and pails, sandwiches, a thermos of tea, a wheelchair borrowed from Mrs. Tees's treasure-trove of jumble sale items because Juniper couldn't wear her metal calipers into the sea, and a chair with short legs Charlie found at the garage for Juniper to sit in on the beach.

The adult-sized wheelchair swamped Juniper, but she didn't appear to care, and chatted with Billy as he pushed her along the Parade. They left the wheelchair at the top of the steps, and Charlie carried her down to the beach.

The sun made a good show of it and the wind remained moderate, making for near-perfect conditions. And so the afternoon went— two dips in the sea, and between those a sandcastle built, sandwiches eaten, and hot chocolate drunk down. Billy was the ideal companion for Juniper. He acted as her tour guide and stayed by her side when Charlie carried both girl and chair into the surf. Billy also relayed the news with great enthusiasm that an unexploded bomb from the war had been found recently on the beach only a few miles up the coast near Lowestoft and that the army had been called in.

"They took it away and exploded it. Wish I could've seen it," Billy said wistfully. "That would've been brilliant."

On their return to Mersea House in the late afternoon, the boy left to take the wheelchair back to Mrs. Tees. Juniper waited in the bathroom for Olive, who said goodbye to Charlie in the kitchen.

"Thank you for today," Olive said. "It's meant so much to Juniper. And to me."

"I enjoyed myself," Charlie said, reaching for her, his arms circling her waist.

"And thanks to Harold for letting you off for the day."

"I'm sure he's left me a bit to do," Charlie said. "At least I'll sweep up."

Olive moved closer and felt a crunching of grit underfoot. "As will I."

★   ★   ★

In the late afternoon of the last Thursday in May, Mrs. Wilkins came to the door of Mersea House.

"I'd like to have a word with Hugh," she said in an enigmatic fashion.

"Certainly," Olive replied, leading the woman to the lounge. "Can I get you tea?"

"That would be lovely."

Olive tapped on Hugh's door and said, "It's Mrs. Wilkins. For you."

Hugh came out, and his eyes darted down the stairs and back to Olive. "About her garden?"

Olive shrugged. What else could it be? Olive thought about this as she made the tea and took it into the lounge—only two cups and saucers on the tray and a plate of seedcake. Mrs. Wilkins didn't invite her to stay, and so Olive closed the lounge door behind her and went off to the kitchen to worry.

Sid had become a regular visitor to Southwold over the few weeks since he first appeared. Every Saturday, he would get a room at the Swan and eat meals with them at Mersea House. He insisted on giving them a few shillings for his food, although both Olive and Margery protested. On Monday morning, he and Hugh went off to work in Mrs. Wilkins's garden, and Monday evening, Sid returned to London. Olive found him a delightful man—funny, smart, and quick— and she enjoyed his company, the more so because Hugh seemed so much brighter since Sid had come back into his life. They'd done nothing that Olive thought anyone could complain about.

They were certainly better behaved than Olive and Charlie, who had taken to going out for an evening walk two or three times a week. They would follow Olive's usual route, but pause along the quiet footpath that had once been Southwold's railway line or stop behind Hetty's tea hut after it had closed in the evenings.

The evening before, they had been in each other's arms when three boys on bicycles shot past them along the Parade. They broke apart, and Olive leaned back against the hut, letting Charlie play with the buttons on her dress.

"We've no privacy," Olive said. It was a mutual complaint whether they were in the lounge at Mersea House, at the pub, or here, behind Hetty's.

★ ★ ★

Now, Olive heard Mrs. Wilkins and Hugh burst into laughter in the lounge. She dunked a biscuit into her tea and wondered what was the topic of conversation between those two. Surely they wouldn't be in such good spirits if it had anything to do with Binny's penchant for gossip? Over coffee, Binny had quizzed Olive about Sid and continued to try to winkle out information concerning Abigail. Olive was not forthcoming, but Binny was undeterred—it seemed the less Binny got, the more she asked.

Juniper came in from school and went off to her room, and after that, Billy arrived with the grocery order. When he'd gone, Olive remained at the kitchen table, listening to the rise and fall of voices in the lounge. At last, Hugh and Mrs. Wilkins emerged, talking about ordering bulbs for the fall planting.

Olive saw her out because she was the housekeeper, and that was her job.

Mrs. Wilkins thanked her and paused on the doorstep. "Olive, I want you to come for coffee one morning when there's no surgery."

"I'd love to," Olive replied, after which Mrs. Wilkins went on her way.

Hugh had returned to the lounge and went to the door.

"Nice visit?" she asked.

"Yes, it was."

"Everything all right?"

Hugh poured gin into two glasses and opened a bottle of tonic. "I think so," he said. "Yes, I believe it is." He saw Olive's look. "I'm not being secretive—that is, I am, I suppose, but only for the moment. I want to see how things settle out; then I promise you'll hear the details." He handed her a drink. "Cheers."

Nothing was said of Mrs. Wilkins's visit during dinner. Instead, Margery told them the about her first Chamber of Commerce meeting in Ipswich and how one of the businessmen had spotted her when she walked in, gestured her over, and said that instead of tea, he'd like coffee, one sugar and no milk. She'd replied that she'd like coffee, too, but would prefer hers with milk and no sugar and could he remember that, or should she write it down for him?

★　★　★

It wasn't until the following Monday at dinner that Margery mentioned she'd booked all three of the empty rooms at Mersea House for the upcoming June bank holiday weekend.

For a moment, no one said anything. Olive, for one, was too stunned to find her voice. When it did come out, she squawked. "You what? *This* holiday weekend? The one only five days away?"

"Don't you remember we said we'd give it a try—taking in holiday lodgers?"

"I thought you meant August," Olive said.

"Yes, August," Margery said, her face red. "Of course. But this is only three days and will be good practice for that, won't it?"

The week ahead, which had appeared to Olive like the glassy surface of a calm, empty sea, populated itself so quickly with planning and cleaning and shopping and baking, it took her breath away.

"Who is coming? What are you charging? Will they expect meals?"

"Steady on," Margery said, and Olive glared at her. "They'll be no trouble at all. There's an older gentleman, and two ladies—sisters, and a family."

"We don't have family accommodations," Olive pointed out.

"There are only three of them," Margery said. "The parents and a small child. They said they would bring a cot."

"I'll help," Juniper said. "I could set up the breakfast tray for you before I go to bed."

"Anything extra you need from the shops," Abigail said, "I'll nip out and get."

"I'll do the hoovering," Hugh said.

Sid lifted his hands, palms up. "I'm sorry I've no talent to offer."

"Apart from your sparkling personality," Hugh said.

"Hmm." Margery tapped a finger on her chin. "You could do the washing up over the weekend."

"Oh no, Margery," Olive said, "I'm leaving that for you."

CHAPTER 16

"Mr. Wiggan," Olive said to the man on the doorstep. "How lovely to meet you. Please do come in."

Olive expected their paying guests for the holiday weekend to arrive Saturday morning, but here was the first one at Friday teatime.

"I'm early," the man barked. He was an elderly gentleman, not tall, and slightly hunched over. He wore a dapper linen suit and carried a small case in one hand and a cane with a brass top in the other. He looked at Olive from under a beetle brow, and she saw sharp eyes. "If you aren't ready for me, I'll have a walkabout"—he waved his cane in the general direction of town—"and return later."

"Not at all," Olive said, "you're very welcome. I can show you to your room now. Shall I take your case?"

"No, thank you. I can manage." He hooked his cane on the arm carrying his bag and took hold of the railing, and she led him upstairs to the empty room on the first floor. "Mr. Hodgson is across from you, Mrs. Claypool next to you, and the bathroom is just there. Come down to the lounge for tea if you like—it'll be ready in ten minutes."

Mr. Wiggan was down in nine minutes, as he pointed out to Abigail when Olive introduced him. "I'd rather be early than late," he said.

Olive set the tea tray down and next introduced him to Juniper—she was on her chair at the front window. "And you, young lady," he said to her, tapping his cane on the floor a few times. "I see we have something in common."

"Yes, sir," Juniper replied.

Olive handed Juniper her glass of Ribena and poured out three cups of tea. "Sugar, Mr. Wiggan?"

"One, please, Miss Kersey, thank you." He took a shortbread finger along with it.

With everyone served, Olive sat down with her own cup.

"You're the housekeeper here, Miss Kersey?" Mr. Wiggan asked.

"I am."

"And you sit down with the lodgers and have your tea—your meals as well, I suppose?"

Cautious, Olive answered in a mild tone, "Yes, Mr. Wiggan, I do."

"Good!" The man thumped his cane on the floor for emphasis, and teacups rattled in their saucers. "Good! I don't take with this division of the classes—never did. Can't tell you how many times my father got after me for helping our cook out when she was shorthanded. But the truth is, I'd just as soon do for myself. Helps me keep my wits about me, you know?"

"Yes, of course, and what a fine attitude you have." Although Olive thought she might change her mind if she walked into the kitchen the next morning to find Mr. Wiggan stirring the pot of porridge. Wearing a pinny. She swallowed a snort. "Have you been to Southwold before?"

"Passed through once about thirty years ago. Always meant to return, and now here I am." He turned his beetle brow to Abigail. "Are you a permanent lodger, Mrs. Claypool?"

"Yes," Abigail replied. "I live here."

Mr. Wiggan glanced round the lounge and then out the window. "A good choice, I'm sure. There's a sense about the place—a homely feeling. It's peaceful and calm. Just what a body needs."

★ ★ ★

By midday Saturday, Mersea House was anything but peaceful and calm. The sisters arrived just after breakfast. Flinty and Pats Harkins—they were near to each other in age, Pats the elder, Flinty the younger—and perhaps a few years older than Olive. That put them in their early forties. At first glance, they could've been twins. They both carried rucksacks and wore sturdy trousers and blouses in muted greens and browns, reminding Olive of grown-up Girl Guides, lacking only sashes studded with badges.

"We're walkers, you see," Flinty said as they followed Olive up to the second floor. "We're very much interested in East Suffolk at the moment, perhaps as far inland as, say—what was it, Pats?"

"We'd prefer to stay this side of Henham," Pats replied, "and concentrate on the coast as far down as Aldeburgh. Get a good idea of the place, you know? Have you lived here long, Olive? I'm not sure we're up on where to cross the Blyth. Is it ferry or bridge?"

They continued to quiz Olive as they unpacked their kit. She broke away at last to answer the front door, leaving the sisters in a hot debate about whether they would need the canvas tarpaulin that afternoon.

The young family on the doorstep stood among bags, baskets, and a fold-up cot. Olive didn't see a car and wondered if they'd carried it all on the bus. If so, what would the little girl have toted? She looked barely four years old and clutched by the foot a worn, brown teddy dressed in a red waistcoat, the top of his head brushing the ground.

"Mr. and Mrs. Larcher?" Olive asked.

"Yes," the man said, although he looked taken aback at the question.

"You're very welcome to Mersea House. I'm Olive Kersey. Come in."

They picked up their paraphernalia and entered, but stopped barely inside, making it difficult for Olive to close the door. "Sorry," she said, "could you go a bit further?"

They gave a few more inches, moving as a single unit.

"There, now," Olive said. She leaned over the little girl. "Hello, there. What's your name?"

"I'm Poppy," the girl said.

"She's Poppy," Mrs. Larcher said, laying hands on her daughter's shoulders.

"Hello, Poppy," Olive said.

Poppy held up her bear. "This is Gerald."

"Hello, Gerald," Olive said. "Delighted to meet you."

Poppy giggled, and her mother's grip tightened.

"I hope you enjoy your holiday," Olive said. "Now, let me tell you about the house." The lounge, the dining room, the stairs—everywhere Olive gestured, their eyes followed as if watching a fly buzzing round. When she finished, she led them up to the second floor, where the Harkins sisters still chatted away in their own room. Behind Olive, on the landing, the Larchers remained silent.

"Here you are," Olive said, walking in and across to the window. "The evening meal is at six." Their accommodations, which she had thought spacious, now seemed quite close. "I do hope you won't be too crowded in here."

Mr. and Mrs. Larcher looked round the room, strangers in a strange land. Poppy, having been lifted onto the bed first thing, had promptly fallen asleep, arms wrapped round her teddy.

Olive excused herself and left. Pats caught her on the landing.

"I say, Olive, there wouldn't be a few sandwiches going, would there? That we could take away with us? I do think we should start just as soon as we possibly can, you see. New horizons and all that."

"Yes," Olive said, "certainly. Stop by the kitchen on your way out."

"Jolly good."

Olive assigned Hugh to make the sandwiches, and good thing he worked quickly, because the Harkinses soon appeared. Olive introduced him as the women stuffed the food into their rucksacks.

"You run the picture palace!" Pats exclaimed. "We never have time for the pictures, do we, Flinty?"

"What are you showing this evening, Mr. Hodgson?" Flinty asked.

"*The Incredible Shrinking Man*," Hugh replied.

"Oh, Pats," Flinty said. "*The Incredible Shrinking Man*."

"Don't get carried away, Flinty," her sister warned her.

"Perhaps we'll see you there?" Hugh said. "Holiday weekend, after all."

"Well, depends on how we get along today, doesn't it?" Pats replied. She opened a ragged map with corners worn through to small holes. "Now, Olive, we've found no good walking maps of the area, and so we'll be working from this. I hope you can help us."

"I can certainly point you in the right direction," Olive said. "We have someone in town who is quite keen on drawing his own maps of all the footpaths around Southwold. I'd say if you stopped by to have a chat with him, he'd be more than happy to help you plan your route."

The Harkinses went on their way with directions—to Paxton's Goods, where they would find Young Trotter, a budding cartographer. Next, Mr. and Mrs. Larcher came down the stairs carrying the blanket off their bed and towels meant for their baths. Poppy trailed behind with Gerald.

"We're going out to the beach," Mr. Larcher stated.

Dressed in the clothes they arrived in, apparently.

"If you don't mind," Olive said, "I'd prefer you leave the blanket and towels here—I'm happy to provide others that you can take." Olive reached over and tugged on the items before Mr. Larcher would release them. "There now, would you like to wait in the lounge? I won't be a minute."

When she returned from the linen cupboard, Olive saw Poppy had detached herself from her parents who were looking out the front window. She was dragging Gerald across the entry and through the open door into the dining room, where Juniper stood at the table with her sketchbook.

Olive introduced the girls.

"Hello, Poppy," Juniper said. "I'm named after a tree, and you're named after a flower. I like your bear."

"This is Gerald," Poppy said. "What's that?" The little girl pointed at one of Juniper's sticks.

"That's my stick."

"Why?" Poppy asked.

Juniper nodded to her feet. "See, my legs don't work right, and so I use these sticks to help me walk."

"What's that?" Poppy asked, pointing to the pencil in Juniper's hand.

"That's my pencil. I was drawing a picture," Juniper replied.

"Why?" Poppy asked.

"Because I like to. Do you want to see? Look, here's our front door, and this one is the fireplace in the lounge, and this one is a dog I saw out on the green."

Olive looked closer—the dog was the first live figure she had seen Juniper attempt, and it was quite good. She could almost see the tail wagging.

Poppy held her teddy up by its foot. "Make a picture of Gerald."

"All right," Juniper said.

"Poppy!" Mr. Larcher called from the lounge. "Poppy?"

"She's in here," Olive said, looking out the dining-room doorway. "She's here with Juniper.

Mr. and Mrs. Larcher rushed across the entry and into the dining room, where they stopped, frozen. Olive introduced Juniper, and the couple looked her up and down, their eyes growing wide. Mr. Larcher leaned over and said, "Poppy, come here."

Mrs. Larcher leaned over, too, and held out her hand. "Come away, Poppy love. Come to Mummy."

Poppy went to her mother, who snatched her up with such force that the little girl cried out.

"Hush," Mrs. Larcher said, "you're all right now."

The family was out the front door and on their way, with Olive staring after them in disbelief. She glanced at Juniper, who leaned against the dining table, toying with her pencil. No words came to Olive—no appropriate words that she could say aloud.

Instead, she offered, "Poppy seems nice."

"Yes," Juniper replied.

"Did you meet Miss Flinty and Miss Pats?" Juniper nodded. "They'll be great fun, won't they?" Olive was trying too hard, she knew it. "And Mr. Wiggan is interesting—rather gruff, but kind, I think."

"He asked me what he should do first this morning," Juniper said, "and I told him he should sit on the bench. Here he is." She turned the page of her sketchbook, and Olive saw the bench along the Parade and the back of a stooped figure looking out to sea.

"It's lovely," Olive said. She put her hand on Juniper's shoulder. "We've quite an assortment of lodgers for the weekend, don't we? I suppose you never can tell what people will be like."

Juniper leaned against Olive. "They're frightened of me—Mr. and Mrs. Larcher."

"Nonsense," Olive said with heat, and then sighed. "No, you're right. They seem the sort of people that frighten easily."

"Sister Freddie said that there will always be people like that—people who believe they can catch polio from me. She said those people have small minds that won't let the light in."

At the same time she was awash with gratitude for Sister Freddie, Olive trembled with rage. An eleven-year-old girl shouldn't have to be practical about such matters. Olive would tell the Larchers to leave. She would go upstairs and throw their belongings out the window of their second-story room and watch them drop onto the green below. She would throw them out the window too, if she could. Not Poppy, of course. Poor little girl.

The wave of anger passed through her, and Olive knew she wouldn't tell the Larchers to leave—however much she wanted to—if only for their little girl's sake.

"Poppy liked you," Olive said.

Juniper smiled. "I'm going to draw her a picture of Gerald."

★   ★   ★

They were twelve round the table for the evening meal Saturday, counting Sid, and it gave Olive a taste of what it would be like to have a full house. Conversation was constant—sometimes the entire table joined in on one subject, but often two or three conversations were going at once, voices rising higher to be heard. Much of the talk came from the Harkinses, who thanked Olive for sending them to Malc, and said he'd been such a help to them that they had invited him to the cinema that night as a gesture of thanks.

"And also, I'm not sure I didn't see a spark or two fly between Flinty and Malc," the elder Miss Harkins said.

"Oh, Pats," Flinty said, her face turning pink, "don't be silly. He was only being kind."

"Malc is a treasure," Margery said. "I don't know what I'd do without him in the shop—so don't you two try to pinch him."

"Good thing tomorrow's Sunday and your shop's closed," Pats said. "He's going out with us to Dunwich Heath. We'll need more sandwiches, Olive."

Margery turned a thin smile on the small family. "Now Mr. and Mrs. Larcher, how was your day?"

"It's our first time to glimpse the sea," Mr. Larcher said. "It's quite large. Rather overwhelming."

"Well, there's no getting away from it, is there?" Margery asked. "After all, we do live on an island."

Mrs. Larcher frowned as if to disagree—or perhaps in the full realization of the truth of the statement.

Poppy, having her meal while sitting on her mother's lap, said, "Mummy, I want to play in the water tomorrow."

Mrs. Larcher appeared taken aback at this request, and Olive thought, *I wouldn't count on it, Poppy.*

After the meal, Sid stayed, Hugh left, and Malc called for the sisters. Mr. Wiggan and Abigail sat down to a chess game, and Juniper settled in her chair and opened *Black Beauty*. The Larchers disappeared, but it was only to put Poppy to bed, and then they came back downstairs and stood in the entry, looking lost.

"Come into the lounge," Margery said to them. "Shall we switch on the wireless?"

Juniper looked up at the Larchers when they entered and smiled. Mrs. Larcher smiled back—or at least, her mouth twitched in a way that might've meant to be a smile. Then the couple gave Olive a wary look and sank onto one end of the sofa.

The family had returned from the beach late that afternoon, sunburned, exhausted, and with Poppy thrown over her father's shoulder like a rag doll. Olive had followed them up the stairs. In a calm and even manner, she had told them that she was happy to have them at Mersea House, but, "We cannot tolerate mistreatment of other lodgers or our own family because of any misperceptions you hold, and so I want to clear this up. Many years ago, Juniper contracted polio." Mrs. Larcher's hand flew to her mouth as if to stifle a gasp. "Her legs were affected, but otherwise she is a bright and sociable girl, as you can see, and she makes her way through the world with good spirits. Do you have any questions for me?"

The Larchers, momentarily struck dumb, recovered when Mr. Larcher cleared his throat and said, "I don't see how you're allowed to take in lodgers when you have disease in the house."

Olive had steadied herself and, in a steely voice, said, "No one in Mersea House has a disease unless it's the disease of ignorance. But if you persist in believing something that isn't true, perhaps you would prefer to leave early. I'm sure we can provide a partial refund."

"What, are you turning us out?"

"Do you want to be turned out?" Olive had snapped, and Mr. Larcher had drawn back. "If not, then we will muddle through the rest of the holiday weekend as best we can. But if I even suspect you are ill-treating Juniper, I'll pack your bags for you."

Not long after, Margery had returned from the shop through the kitchen. "What a day! Drink?" she asked.

"Wait." Olive had set the lid on the potatoes and then explained about the Larchers and how they'd treated Juniper, watching Margery's color rise as she did.

"We'll chuck them out now," Margery had said. "I don't mind."

"No, I've put them on notice," Olive said. "Should I have talked with you first?"

"You did right," Margery had told her. "But, I'd say the Larchers had better beware—I've seen that look in your eye before."

★   ★   ★

Now, Olive left the others in the lounge and began gathering the dinner dishes. Sid joined her, and she washed while he dried.

"Thanks, Olive," he said, slipping each plate behind the railing on the dresser, "thanks for how welcome you've made Hugh. I didn't want him to leave London. I tried to talk him out of it, but it was one of his fits of chivalry, thinking he needed to protect me. I was that worried about him, but now, I see how relaxed and happy he is."

"He has been relaxed since he arrived," Olive said, "but the happy part came when you showed up."

After the dishes, they set the breakfast tray, and then Margery put her head in the door.

"Everyone's gone to bed," she told them. "Sid, I'll walk you back to the hotel and we can have a drink. Olive, want to come along?"

There was a tapping at the kitchen door to the yard, and Olive opened it to Charlie.

"Or maybe not," Margery said. "Sid?"

"Ready," Sid replied. "Charlie, how are you?"

"Good, and you?" Charlie said. "You're around tomorrow?"

"I wouldn't miss Sunday dinner with this crowd for love or money."

Margery and Sid left, and when the door closed, Olive rested her head on Charlie's chest as he held her close and kissed her hair.

After a moment, she sighed. "C'mon." She took his hand and they walked across the entry and into the empty lounge, where she drew the curtains. There was something she'd been meaning to explain to Charlie, but had yet to find the moment and didn't really know the words to use.

"About Sid," Olive said, moving to the drinks cabinet. Charlie sat in one of the upholstered chairs and looked attentive. "Sid is Hugh's friend."

Was the distinction clear enough? It wasn't the same as saying "Sid is a friend of Hugh's," but would Charlie hear the difference? Olive wanted him to understand but didn't believe she should offer further explanation and wasn't sure, in any case, how she would.

"Ah," Charlie said. "I see."

Olive considered this. "You knew, didn't you?"

"I had a fair idea," Charlie said, "but it makes no difference to me. I like the two of them."

"You'd've liked Donald too," Olive said.

Charlie gave a nod. "I'm sure of it. Now, how was your day?"

She surveyed the bottles in the cabinet. "Brandy?" she asked.

"That bad?"

She poured them drinks and took his to him, leaning over for a long kiss before she gave him his glass. Then, she sat in the other chair with the small lamp table between them. They had learned that was the best arrangement when others were nearby.

Olive described their boarders in objective terms, but Charlie's question— "What about these Larchers?"—told her she may not have sounded as unbiased as she thought.

And so she explained the rest.

"How is Juniper?"

"She's taking it better than I am."

★   ★   ★

Monday morning the sun rose fiercely bright. It was the last day of the long weekend, and with it came the frantic need to have as much fun as possible. Malc and the sisters left early. By midmorning the High Street surged with day-trippers, and the beach was heaving. The Punch and Judy man had a constant crowd round him, and a long line stretched out from Hetty's tea hut. Olive avoided it all by walking along the smaller lanes in town until she reached a stretch of modest cottages with washing hanging out the windows and a low front wall of brick in need of repointing.

She went up the front walk of one cottage and rattled the flap on the letter box to knock. From within, there was the sound of rushing water being shut off, a squeal, and then footsteps. The door opened, and there was Billy Grunyon.

"Miss Olive!"

"Hello, Billy. Is your mum about?"

"No, she's cleaning the surgery this morning."

"Look, I wonder—"

Olive's voice was drowned out by Billy's sister, Sammie, who was just over a year old and careering straight toward them. She held her arms up to her brother, opening and closing her hands, and chanting, "Biddy! Biddy! Biddy! Biddy!"

"All right, you," Billy said. He picked her up and rested her on his hip. "What was that, Miss Olive?"

"Biddy! Biddy!" Sammie shouted in her brother's face.

"Yeah, yeah. Whoo!" He made a face and flapped his free hand in the air. "Time for a fresh nappy, I'd say. Will you come in, Miss Olive?"

"No, Billy, thanks. Tell your mum I have a day's work for her tomorrow if she's interested. She's welcome to bring Sammie along. The place needs a good cleaning after the holiday weekend."

"Will you take in temporary lodgers again, Miss Olive? Because if you do, someone as bad as those Larchers could book in."

"Juniper told you?"

"She didn't complain and she would never say, but it hurt her feelings." Billy scowled. "If you get another lot like that, you let me know, and I'll sort them out."

"Thanks, Billy—I'll keep that in mind."

Olive made her way back to Mersea House by wading through the throng down the High Street toward the sea, freshly angry about the Larchers and at the same time grateful for Billy's loyalty. She paid no attention to the crowd until she came to the Parade and almost walked into a threesome—Hugh, Sid, and Miss Binny.

"Olive, dear," Binny said, taking her arm to stop her escape, "Look now, I've just this minute met Mr. Davies. You've not said a word about taking in another lodger."

"Hello, Miss Binny," Olive said. She cast a glance at Hugh and Sid, whose smiles appeared strained. "Mr. Davies isn't a lodger; he's a friend from London who worked with Margery."

"And now a regular visitor to our little town?" Binny said. "We must seem quite dull in comparison to London, Mr. Davies. But are you not staying at Mersea House?"

"I have a room at the Swan," Sid told her.

"I don't know what you find to occupy yourself. Look at Mr. Hodgson here—managing the cinema doesn't fill his days, and so now he must toil away in Nancy Wilkins's garden. Such an enormous undertaking." She shook her head sadly.

"Mrs. Wilkins has a fine garden," Sid said with a note of defiance. "As it happens, I'm lending Hugh a hand there the days I'm here." Olive saw Binny's eyes brighten.

"Are you now?" she asked in a speculative tone. "You and Mr. Hodgson at Beech View? Aren't you very good friends to be able to work side by side in the garden."

"Well, Miss Binny," Olive said, "we won't keep you from enjoying your afternoon. Good day." She took hold of Hugh and Sid each by an elbow and moved them along, leaving Binny where she stood.

"She's a collector, isn't she?" Sid asked. "Collecting any interesting little pebble she finds and putting it in her pocket to bring out another day."

"Yes," Olive said. "And I'd say those pockets are quite heavy by now. Sorry," she said, dropping her grip on their arms, "I didn't mean to commandeer you. Are you off somewhere?"

"Mrs. Wilkins's, as it happens," Hugh said. "Something about a late sowing of peas."

Olive watched as they made their way along East Street, and then shifted her gaze up the Parade to make sure that Binny had continued on her way.

Olive squinted and blinked. Binny had turned off, and her attention was caught by another sight. Near Hetty's tea hut, Olive saw two people getting up from a bench and walking away. One of them was Margery, and the other looked very much like Geoff Markham.

CHAPTER 17

The weekend lodgers had gone by teatime Monday, but Olive had spoken to each before they left.

"I hope you enjoyed your return to Southwold, Mr. Wiggan," she said. Several times throughout his stay, Olive had looked out the front window and across the green to see the man sitting on the bench facing the sea. Other than that, he and Abigail had played chess, their conversation minimal but easy.

Now, the man stood with his bag in the entry, tapping his cane on the floor as others might mindlessly tap their fingers.

"Restorative," Mr. Wiggan said. "What is it about the sea, Miss Kersey? I daresay you may see me again sometime. And if I do return, I hope there will be another Bakewell tart going."

"I'm sure there will be," Olive replied. "Goodbye. All the best."

"Goodbye, young Juniper," Mr. Wiggan said, peering into the dining room, where Juniper stood with her sketchbook.

"Goodbye, Mr. Wiggan."

The Larchers came down next, at a slow pace, because Poppy had resisted being carried. Olive needed to separate them—parents from child—because she wanted Juniper to have the opportunity to say goodbye to the little girl. That opportunity arose when the sisters came down directly behind the family.

"Pats." Olive put a hand up to stop her. "Earlier, I was trying to explain to Mr. and Mrs. Larcher just where Dunwich Heath is from here, and I made a terrible mess of it. I'm certain you and Flinty can do a better job. It's such an interesting spot, and I believe Mrs. Larcher expressed an interest in butterflies, and so they may want to visit on some other holiday. Here, why don't you walk them out to the green and explain it. I'll keep an eye on Poppy." She took the little girl's hand and gave the parents a smile.

The sisters needed no encouragement to talk about their ramblings, and the Larchers let themselves be herded out the door and to the middle of South Green, where—accompanied by broad gestures—the story began.

Poppy had spotted Juniper and gone into the dining room, and the two girls stood at the table as the little one exclaimed, "Gerald!" not at the bear she had hold of, but at Juniper's sketchbook.

It was Gerald, quite recognizable in pencil. Poppy held up her bear so he could see.

"You did a fine job on it," Olive said, and turned to Hugh, who had just come downstairs. "Look."

"Well done, Juniper," he said.

Juniper smiled. "Poppy, do you want to take the picture of Gerald with you?" She glanced at Olive. "Would that be all right?"

"I don't see why not." But she thought the Larchers might not be so accepting of the gift. As Juniper tore the drawing out of the book, Olive stepped into the entry and looked out the front door to check the progress of the proceedings on the green. It looked as if the story of the Harkinses' ramble had wrapped up. "I tell you what," she said, hurrying back to the girls, "let's fold up the picture and slip it into the pocket of Gerald's waistcoat. That way, it will be in a safe place."

"Is it a secret?" Poppy asked.

"If you like," Olive replied. She could hear voices in the entry and gave Hugh a pleading look. "Could you . . .?"

Hugh met the Larchers at the front door, stopping their forward movement. "On your way? Do you have a long journey? Would you like a hand carrying your bags out—I'd be happy to help."

While the blockade held, Olive folded the drawing and tucked it into the bear's pocket. "There!" she whispered, and Poppy giggled, put her finger to her mouth, and said, "Shh!"

"Poppy!" Mrs. Larcher called.

"Here she is," Olive said, bringing the girl out and nodding for Juniper to follow. "We were saying goodbye."

The Larchers' eyes darted from their Poppy to Juniper and back, but they didn't complain, which Olive took as progress, whether it was or not.

The family left with its secret cargo in Gerald's waistcoat, the sisters went to the lounge, and Olive turned to Hugh.

"I'm a subversive," she said.

"You are indeed," Hugh replied. "And all the better for it."

★   ★   ★

"You're saying he came all this way to eat fish and chips?" Olive asked when she confronted Margery in the kitchen before the evening meal.

"Isn't that what everyone does on a bank holiday weekend?" Margery replied, examining the cutlery on the tray. "It doesn't mean anything. It's only that last time he was here, he didn't see much of the place—"

"Or of you," Olive interjected.

"—and he thought he'd take a look round. That's all. End of story."

"Is it?"

"You haven't seen much of Charlie these last few days."

Olive hadn't seen anything of him. "You recall I did have a few things to attend to," she said, rolling the meat croquettes between her hands. "And they were busy at the garage at all hours—punctures, burst radiators, petrol. They even had to open on Sunday."

"I didn't expect a great deal of business at the shop this morning," Margery said. "I thought we'd sell a few pails and shovels, but it seemed everyone had shopping to do—it was like Paddington Station in there. And I do know how busy you were. You did a smash-up job. Won't it be nice to get back to normal—just the handful of us. Nothing much going on except your driving lesson on Wednesday."

Olive had only one lesson left, and then she could take her test and be allowed to drive. She wasn't much bothered about whether or not she took the test, but she wouldn't quibble with having had the lessons—they had meant the world to her.

"Drink?" Margery asked. Olive followed her out to the lounge, where they joined the rest of the household. With the weekend lodgers gone and Sid back to London, the house seemed oddly empty. Not in a permanent way, but as if it were only pausing between breaths.

"They weren't that bad, were they—the holiday guests?" Margery asked. When no one answered, she added, "Young Trotter and the sisters are planning an extensive walking tour come his summer holidays."

"I enjoyed chess with Mr. Wiggan," Abigail said. "Did you know he owned a company that manufactured typewriters? I told him I'd worked as a typist before I married, and I'm sure it was on one of his machines."

No one mentioned the Larchers.

Olive rose to see to the evening meal just as the telephone rang. It was Mrs. Wilkins, asking her to coffee. Would Thursday be convenient? It was the receptionist's morning off.

Olive accepted, hoping she didn't sound too eager. She'd never seen Beech View, but had recalled Mrs. Wilkins occasionally looking in on Daisy during her final months. And Olive didn't forget the woman's recent visit to Mersea House to talk with Hugh.

Olive mentioned the invitation over dinner, hoping Hugh might give her a bit of background information, but his only comment was to ask if she'd check on the broad beans.

★　★　★

Lorna came to clean the next morning, knocking at the kitchen door to the yard. Billy's mother was a slip of a thing, with pale skin and black hair and a fleeting smile.

"You didn't bring Sammie?" Olive asked, stepping aside to let her in.

"Oh bless, Olive," Lorna said, "but Mrs. Rattray next door took her in. Leaves me both my hands and my head free."

Olive waved at the mountain of bed linens to be washed. "I'm happy to have you here—you see what we're up against."

"But now with your two-tub electric washer, life must be easier," Lorna said, dropping her bag in a chair at the table.

"Yes, of all of Margery's modernizing, it's what I appreciate the most." Although, if pushed, she would admit to a growing fondness for the Hoover. "How are you doing, Lorna? How are things at home?"

It's a euphemism, isn't it? Olive thought. But naturally Lorna understood and replied with candor.

"The brewery has taken Pauley back on and that's good, because Sammie's got another tooth coming in, and she can be a bit fussy and get on his nerves. It isn't really his fault—the bouts he has. It's his leg. If Pauley's leg is bothering him, then nothing seems to go right."

Olive said nothing about this all-encompassing excuse for Lorna's husband's behavior. Olive's mother had used the same sort of excuse for her father—war injuries—and it hadn't washed then either.

★ ★ ★

Thursday morning Olive walked over to Marlborough Road and down to Beech View, which sat surrounded by a high hedge. Olive held up at the drive to take in the scene: a detached Victorian brick house with, according to Hugh, variously themed, abundantly planted areas—a rose garden, a shrubbery, a perennial border, a vinery, and a folly surrounded by topiary figures losing their shape. This in addition to the all-important veg garden, starring the broad beans.

Mrs. Wilkins spotted Olive coming up the drive, greeted her, and took her in the house. They passed through a sitting room and a study with an enormous desk neatly stacked with old books, and a globe on a stand next to it, and then through open French doors and out onto the stone terrace that ran the length of the house in back.

"We'll have our coffee en plein air, why don't we," Mrs. Wilkins said. "We shouldn't miss out on such lovely weather." She gestured to the table already set. "There's Madeira cake from Dawson's, but probably not as good as yours. I remember Daisy mentioning your baking skills, and that was lovely seedcake I had at Mersea House. So sit."

Coffee taken outdoors took on another dimension, Olive thought as she breathed in the aroma wafting up from her cup, just as chips eaten outdoors at the seafront tasted better than anything cooked at home.

"I miss seeing your husband strolling up and down the High Street," Olive said. "The Major and Margery's uncle Milkey were good friends, weren't they?"

"Oh, thick as thieves, those two. It was good for the Major to have someone closer to his age—he was a bit older than I, if you recall."

Olive did recall. "He was a lovely man," she said. "Do you have family here? Is that how you ended up in Southwold?"

"Dear me, no," Mrs. Wilkins said. "And that's for the best. His people couldn't believe he would look twice at a woman who had lost her youth and made one too many bad choices and had nowhere to go and no one to care what happened to her. The Major's people are in Wiltshire, and mine, if there's anything left of them, are in East London, and so we chose someplace entirely different. We had many good years together here. The Major worked on the history of his grandfather's regiment during the Crimean War, and Dr. Atterbury took me on."

"I remember when you started," Olive said. "It wasn't long after my father died. Mrs. Atterbury had her hands full as nurse and running the office—you were desperately needed."

"It's as close to the medical profession as I need to be, although there was a time when I rather fancied growing up to be a modern-day Florence Nightingale. We should all be happy that inclination passed. But it has recently come to me that I could do more."

"At the surgery?"

"No, no." Mrs. Wilkins set her cup down. "You see, it was the Major's birthday in March—he would've been eighty-seven. I was having a drink in his honor, and it's as if I could hear him say, '*Right, Nancy, time to get back into it, don't you think?*' 'Life' is what he meant— being involved in the world round me. He was right, of course. He was always one to know that even the smallest action can make a difference. Next thing I knew, you came into the surgery with Juniper, and I mentioned the garden, and you suggested Hugh."

"I'm glad that's worked out for you both," Olive said.

They fell into a silence, both gazing out across the garden. Just below the terrace, the bees worked their way round the catmint; their humming sounded like monks chanting, and it so relaxed Olive that she closed her eyes.

"I've asked Sid to stay here at Beech View," Mrs. Wilkins said, and that woke Olive up. "When he's in town at the weekends. When I met him and understood what was between them, I realized, here's a place to begin, with a bit of human compassion. After all, what's the point of these empty rooms? There's no sense in him putting up at the Swan, and if he stayed at Mersea House, you and I both know there would be talk."

And we know where it would begin.

"He accepted, but he said he wanted to pay me," the woman continued. "I told him I'd take it out in garden work."

Olive smiled. "You're very good to do that."

"It'll give the two of them some time together."

Olive wondered if Mrs. Wilkins might not give her and Charlie a room occasionally so that they could have some time together. The thought made her blush, but not with embarrassment.

"How's your Juniper?" Mrs. Wilkins asked.

"She's happy," Olive said, not bothering to correct the woman. "She's settled in and doing well at school—even catching up in arithmetic. And she has friends."

"I've seen her and Billy Grunyon about town. Funny," Mrs. Wilkins said, "you'd look at Billy and think about his situation, and you would never believe he's such a carer—looking out for his mum and his sister. He hasn't had it easy, and neither has Juniper, so perhaps that's their bond. Not as strong as hers with you, of course. You are exactly what she's needed."

Don't say it, Olive thought. *Don't jinx it.*

Mrs. Wilkins veered off in another direction. "I'm undertaking a new project. Come and see."

Olive followed her over to the former stables and opened half the wooden door. Along the walls were rusted bits of machinery, and in the middle hunkered a large form under a canvas tarpaulin. Mrs. Wilkins flung back the cover, and underneath was a two-seater MG that had seen better days—its tires were flat, the leather seats grimy, and rust had bloomed where the green paint had flaked off.

"I'm going to have the old girl restored," Mrs. Wilkins said. "The Major loved this car, but he wasn't able to drive the last few years of his life, and so here it sat. She patted a fender. "I've found a garage over in Reydon that will do the job."

"Reydon?" Olive asked.

"Yes. And once she's ready"—Mrs. Wilkins drew herself up to her full height—"I'm going to learn to drive it. As it turns out, the fellow who owns the garage has a cousin who is a driving instructor."

"Charlie?" Olive asked her.

"Olive?"

They hadn't heard him come up the drive, but when Olive turned, there was Mr. Salt, wearing his best suit and holding his clipboard.

"And here he is now," Mrs. Wilkins said. "I believe you two know each other."

"Yes, we do," Olive said, smiling at Charlie. "Mr. Salt was my driving instructor, and I can recommend him highly."

"Thank you, Miss Kersey," Charlie said with a red face and half a wink.

"Do you know, this is what I like about living here," Mrs. Wilkins said. "The way our paths cross and recross. Well, what do you think of the car, Mr. Salt? Can your cousin bring her back to good driving condition?"

Charlie lifted the bonnet for a closer inspection, and the metal creaked and groaned. He threw the rest of the tarp off and made a circuit of the car, bending over and peering into the floorboard on the driver's side. A mouse popped out of the glove box and scurried off on its own business.

"I'd say Harold will do a fine job, Mrs. Wilkins, and when he's finished, we can begin your lessons."

"Outstanding," Mrs. Wilkins said. "Mr. Salt, would you like coffee?"

"Yes, thank you."

"Olive, why don't you show the gentleman the broad beans while I brew up a fresh pot?"

Olive had seen no sign of broad beans, but she had noticed the brick wall and thought it likely they lay in that direction. She took Charlie's hand and led him off, fighting back an over-enthusiastic honeysuckle at the arched gate to the veg garden.

"Did you arrange this?" Charlie asked.

"No," Olive said, laughing. "I had no idea. I've never spoken to Mrs. Wilkins much. I know her because she's the receptionist for Dr. Atterbury, and she was kind to my mum. Her husband, the Major, died two years ago, and it appears that she is ready to spread her wings." Olive stopped in front of the broad beans. "It's a happy surprise for you, isn't it?"

"It's very good news," Charlie said, "but seeing you is the happy surprise."

★   ★   ★

Olive left Beech View feeling as if she'd just met her fairy godmother.

Over coffee and after Charlie and Mrs. Wilkins had gone into more detail about driving, the woman had said, "Wouldn't it be fun to have one of those enormous garden teas here this summer—just as they do at Buckingham Palace? We'll do it for charity. We'll ask for a shilling or two to start a bursary fund to help students with grammar school fees. I suppose we'd better wait until August when Hugh and Sid have got the place into proper shape, although I wonder will there be any roses left. Well, can't worry about that now." She had turned to Olive. "Could I hire you to make the cakes?"

The morning had ended with still a great many details to be decided about the tea, and as Olive and Charlie walked out to the drive, she thought aloud.

"How many cakes will we need? I suppose that depends on the number of people Mrs. Wilkins invites and how many slices each person would eat? I wonder how many cakes I could make in one day?"

"I know someone who could do the sums for you," Charlie said. They stopped at the Hillman. "I'll give you a lift back."

"No, it's all right, I'll walk." She leaned against the car. "Isn't it odd how you know someone for years, but just in one way. I knew Mrs. Wilkins as the receptionist at Dr. Atterbury's surgery, and she's always been very nice, but I had no idea what an interesting woman she was." She took his hand. "You'll enjoy giving driving lessons in the Major's car, won't you?"

"It'll be a treat." Charlie set his clipboard on top of the car, propped an elbow on top to keep it there, and kept hold of Olive's hand, toying with her fingers. "My Wednesday afternoons are reserved for driving lessons, even though you're finished with yours and Mrs. Wilkins isn't ready to begin. So that means I find myself at loose ends next week."

Olive considered this. "Good," she said. "Why don't we go on a picnic? And you can choose the place. All the scouting you've done to prepare for driving lessons, you probably know just the spot."

Charlie watched her for a moment before giving her a brief kiss and whispering, "Picnic it is."

Olive watched him drive off and then put herself into gear walking back to Mersea House. With her mind full of cakes and picnics and whatever else, it was a short journey, and Olive was surprised to find herself arrived home and startled to have the door opened for her by Hugh.

"Back from your coffee with Mrs. Wilkins?" he asked.

"Were you on the lookout for me?"

"No, I only happened to . . . yes, I was. What do you think of her idea?"

"About Sid? I think it's marvelous." Olive's brow furrowed. "Would you move there too?"

"I don't think so—how could I leave here?"

"Good," Olive said, giving him a kiss on the cheek. "What does Sid have to say about it all?"

"He's for it. He enjoys his days here. I believe he may fall in love with the place and want to chuck it all in London. Move here and become a landscape gardener." Hugh grinned. "At least he would have time for his painting. There's a man who lives not far from here who runs an art school, and he's a gardener too—has quite a show of iris, apparently. Next free day when Sid is here, we'll go and visit. He might be a good influence."

Hugh's eagerness took ten years off his age.

"Did you mention Charlie to Mrs. Wilkins?" Olive asked.

"The MG," Hugh said, nodding. "That came about rather by accident. I was looking for a scythe in the stables and peeked under the tarpaulin. I asked about the car and said wouldn't it look grand restored. She seemed interested, and so I told her about Charlie's cousin's garage. Then, I had to explain who Charlie was, and by the end of the conversation you'd've thought she'd had the plan in her head all along. Did she, do you think, or was it all off the cuff?"

"I'm learning that with Nancy Wilkins you might never know."

★　★　★

"Do you always work on a Saturday, Mrs. Pagett?" Olive asked as she ushered the woman into the lounge.

"We carry out our visits all days and hours, Miss Kersey," the woman replied. "Within limits, of course."

Olive wasn't quite sure she believed Mrs. Pagett had limits. It was as if she had made Juniper her special project. She was becoming a bit of a pest.

"So you won't be knocking on the door at ten o'clock one evening?" Olive asked, but accompanied the question with a smile, and the woman responded likewise.

"You do seem to have a great number of people coming and going," Mrs. Pagett said.

True. The moment Mrs. Pagett had arrived, Abigail had returned from a walk. Next, Old Trotter had delivered two cartons of new bath towels and bed linens from the shop. He had stopped long enough to be introduced to Mrs. Pagett and comment on what a fine girl Juniper was. Lastly, Hugh had passed through, saying a quick hello and goodbye before leaving early for the matinee.

"Is that a problem?" Olive asked. "That we have a busy household?" She asked partly because she wanted to know and partly because the statement annoyed her.

"No, certainly not, as long as Juniper's needs are being met and she is not being exposed to unsavory elements."

Olive didn't like the term "unsavory elements"—it smacked of Binny—and came up with a reply or two that fortunately didn't come out of her mouth. Instead, she said, "Our lives are full of many interesting people, and I, for one, am delighted that's the case. All the better to prepare Juniper for her life ahead."

There was a commotion from the kitchen, and Juniper and Billy came spilling out into the entry, discussing boats. Both children stopped in the door of the lounge.

"Hello, Mrs. Pagett," Juniper said. "This is my friend Billy."

"Hello, ma'am," Billy replied, easing back out of the doorway. "Sorry to disturb you, Miss Olive."

"You're not disturbing us," Olive said. "Why don't the two of you come in and sit. I'll bring out drinks for you."

Quick as she could, Olive was into the kitchen, mixing two glasses of Ribena, and then back to the lounge. Not quick enough, because she walked in to hear Juniper say, "We took the rowboat ferry across the river and back again."

"You went all the way to Blackshore Quay?" The question came out of Olive before she could stop it.

"It's all right—we didn't walk back," Billy said. "Mr. Richards was down at the quay and gave us a lift." He turned to Mrs. Pagett. "He's the fishmonger."

"We sat on the back end of his lorry," Juniper said and, at seeing the wide eyes of both Mrs. Pagett and Olive, added, "I held on."

Out came the notebook and fountain pen. As she unscrewed the top and began writing, Mrs. Pagett said, "A rowboat—you could've fallen out and drowned."

"I'm a good swimmer," Juniper said. "I learned to swim in hospital—it was part of my physiotherapy. You don't need working legs to swim, and my arms are strong."

"I don't know how to swim," Billy said.

"But you're very good at climbing the rocks at the beach," Juniper said.

Olive quickly changed the subject.

CHAPTER 18

"If she has a complaint, Mrs. Pagett should come to the shop and talk with me," Margery said. "I'm the one responsible for Juniper."

"She's tried that already, hasn't she?" Olive said.

They were in the lounge Sunday afternoon—Margery, seated and flipping through the new issue of *Picturegoer* while Olive stood looking out the window, across the green, and to the bench facing the sea where Charlie and Juniper sat talking. He had come to Sunday dinner, and when it was time for pudding, he had quizzed Juniper on how she would divide six slices of apple tart among the seven of them.

Juniper had pressed her lips together as she contemplated yet another problem of fractions.

"I don't think Mr. Hugh will want a slice of apple tart," she said at last. "And so that would make six of us."

"Hang on," Hugh said.

Sid laughed. "Oh, you've got that wrong, Juniper."

Look at us, Olive had thought, what an odd lot we are—an odd, lovely lot. If I could draw, I would draw this picture. As it was, all she could do was keep it in her heart.

And now this picture too, the one she saw from the window—Charlie and Juniper on the bench.

"Coffee." Sid came through to the lounge with the tray. "Where's Abigail? I promised her a chess game."

"I'll go fetch those two," Olive said, nodding out to the bench.

When she reached them, Charlie was pointing out to a ship on the horizon and saying something about Norway.

"Miss Olive!" Juniper exclaimed. "Mr. Charlie was on a ship during the war. He ran the engine room—that makes the entire ship go, doesn't it?"

"I believe it does," Olive said.

"Oh now," Charlie began, but Juniper cut in.

"And he knows a song about being a sailor, but he wouldn't sing it for me."

"Probably just as well. Ready to go in?"

Juniper extended her legs and locked the caliper joints at her knees, then Olive and Charlie each put a hand under one of her elbows and helped her stand. The girl looked up at one and then the other. "Thank you."

The three of them walked across the green, and as they drew close to Mersea House, Olive could see Margery standing in the front window, watching them. Was she smiling? Olive couldn't tell.

★ ★ ★

Olive had packed surreptitiously for the picnic Wednesday, waiting until everyone was either out of the house or otherwise occupied and keeping the basket and the two blankets in the pantry. She clicked her tongue at her own silliness.

In case they weren't back in time, she had asked Abigail to keep an eye out for Juniper coming home from school.

"I'll make sure to be around where she can see me," Abigail said, and then a knock came at the door. "Enjoy your afternoon."

Charlie wore a jacket, but no tie, and took his hat off when Olive opened the door.

"Do you want to come in?" she asked.

"No, not if you're ready. Let's be on our way." He looked into the blue sky. "Good day for it."

"Those going on a picnic must be prepared for any sort of weather," she replied. She picked up her cardigan along with the blankets, and Charlie carried the basket.

"Would you care to take the wheel, Miss Kersey?"

"Seeing as how it's Wednesday afternoon, I will, Mr. Salt."

Olive drove out of town in the direction Charlie indicated—west, into the country, and along roads familiar to Olive from her recent lessons. Charlie complimented her on her careful crossing of the A12, but other than his directions, they were quiet, wending their way down one lane and then another. Finally, they bumped along a sheep track and came to a stop—"just here"—in the shade of a broad oak tree at the edge of a field where the land in front of them gradually fell away, and the only sign of civilization was, in the far distance, the spire of a church steeple.

"Sun or shade?" Charlie asked.

"We're spoilt for choice," Olive answered. "How about sun—and a bit of shade?"

They spread one of the blankets and settled themselves. Charlie made a show of looking through what Olive had packed—cold chicken, bread, strawberries, two bottles of beer, and two slices of apple tart—but neither of them had food on their minds. Olive leaned over, making a show of looking into the basket, and then turned her face up to Charlie and kissed him. His arm went round her waist, and they forgot about the picnic for a while.

Later, when a breeze nipped their bare skin, Olive pulled the second blanket over them and they dozed, waking to the afternoon sun in their eyes. Charlie sat up.

"Ready for that chicken?" Olive asked.

"I shouldn't eat with my shirt open," Charlie said, doing up the buttons.

"You might do up your trousers too." Olive sat up and pushed her hair off her face. They heard the faint sound of a tractor in the distance, and it seemed to be growing louder. "I suppose I should dress too."

After they'd eaten and rested and packed up, Charlie held the car door open for her as a look of concern scudded across his face.

"I don't want you to think I had this planned," he said, his hand hanging onto the top of the car door. "That is, it wasn't the only reason to come out for the afternoon. Not that it hasn't been on my mind." She giggled and he looked chagrined.

"And mine," Olive said.

Charlie lifted her chin with a finger and then kissed her throat down to the top button of her dress. He sighed and stepped back.

Olive kept her window down on the drive back, letting the wind hit her in the face and feeling that odd sort of languid contentment mixed with possibility and energy. When they arrived at Mersea House, Charlie carried in the blankets and basket, then left. Olive returned to the kitchen and was unpacking the leftovers when Hugh popped in.

"Here you are," he said. "The place seemed empty without you. Abigail and Juniper walked down to Hetty's and should be back any minute. How was the picnic?"

"Lovely," she said. "Tea?"

"I tell you what," Hugh said, "why don't I put the kettle on, and you can go upstairs and pick the grass out of your hair."

Her hand flew to her braid. She didn't look at Hugh but said, "Yes, right, I'll just—" and she was gone, flying up to her room.

★   ★   ★

It was a peaceful Friday morning when the knock came. *Ah, Binny.* Olive hadn't seen the woman in a fortnight. She'd timed her visit perfectly—the currant cake had just cooled enough to be sliced.

No Binny on the doorstep. Instead, it was a man she knew but had not seen for a while. He was no taller than Olive and wore round glasses that echoed the shape of his face. He had a slightly perplexed air about him, which you wouldn't expect from a newspaperman. He had a high forehead, reminiscent of Binny, but the fellow couldn't be blamed for that, as his mother had been her sister.

"Norman, how lovely to see you," Olive said, opening the door wide. "Do come in. It's been ages, hasn't it?"

"A good few years, Olive," he said, looking about the entry. "I'm sorry about your mum. Aunt Connie told me, of course—and about how Margery had returned and how she's put poor dear Olive to work here, slaving away for God knows what reason at the beck and call of paying guests."

Norman had assumed Binny's tone, and it made Olive laugh.

"And there's a young girl—she had polio?" Norman asked.

"Yes, Juniper is Margery's ward. She's the daughter of George Wyckes—did you know him?—and his wife. She's a wonderful girl." Olive started to close the door, but paused at the last moment, stepped out, and looked round the green in case Norman had been followed.

"Aunt Connie is with Mrs. Tees this morning," Norman said.

"Good," she murmured. "Will you have coffee? Go into the lounge, and I'll bring the tray out." When she returned a few minutes later with cups, saucers, and cake, Norman was leafing through *Picturegoer*.

"I forgot to ask, hot or cold milk?"

"Cold milk is fine," he said. "Thanks."

Olive settled on the sofa across from him. "The coffee won't be long."

Hugh came down the stairs at that moment, and Olive called to him. "Here's Hugh Hodgson," she said to Norman. "He's one of those paying guests who orders me about."

Hugh stopped in the doorway, but Olive smiled and waved and said, "Come in and have coffee with us. This is Miss Binny's nephew, Norman Tyne. Norman's down from London—he works for the *Daily Sketch*."

The men exchanged pleasantries, and Hugh sat on the sofa with Olive.

"So, Norman," she said, "what has brought you to Southwold?"

"Aunt Connie," Norman said, "but you could probably guess that. She's been asking me to look into the background of your lodgers."

Hugh didn't move, but it was as if Olive could feel him withdraw.

"And not only your lodgers but your friends too," Norman said. "Sid Davies, for one." He looked from Olive to Hugh and back again. "I thought I should give you fair warning."

"A shot across the bow, is it?" Hugh said with scorn. "Using your aunt as an excuse for an exposé?"

Norman's round eyes narrowed to slits behind his glasses. "The *Sketch* is hardly muckraking journalism."

It was as if Hugh hadn't heard him. "Haven't you ruined enough lives?"

"I think you misunderstand me."

"No, I understand your kind all too well," Hugh said.

Olive leapt up. "Hugh, would you help me in the kitchen, please?" He didn't move. She gave him a light kick in the shin, and he shot her a hard look. "Please, Hugh—now." He dragged himself off the sofa, and she put a hand on his back to get him moving. Turning to Norman as they left, she said, "Just fetching the coffee."

The door to the kitchen had barely swung shut when Hugh spun round to Olive.

"I won't put you through this, Olive—I'll leave."

"You won't," Olive said.

"You don't understand this kind of journalist—the lengths they'll go to. It's sensationalist dirt they're after, and they don't care who they hurt."

"Hugh, I don't think he—"

"I can see he takes after his aunt."

"He doesn't!" Olive said. "Now be quiet for a moment and listen to me. Norman spent some time here before the war, and he and Donald were good friends. I think they were . . . you know."

Hugh didn't look entirely happy, but he appeared less angry. "Are you sure?"

"Yes. Fairly sure."

"Then why is he talking like that?"

"Well, we haven't given him much of a chance to explain, have we?"

"No," Hugh said. "I suppose not."

They marched back into the lounge, Olive carrying the coffee and an extra cup and saucer. As she poured, Hugh sat, cleared his throat, and said to Norman, "Sorry about that."

Norman grinned as he took his coffee. "Apology accepted. Thanks, Olive."

Once they had cake and coffee, Olive asked, "Now, what's this all about?"

"Aunt Connie has given me a few names and wants to know if any of them has been in trouble with the police—as if I can snap my fingers and come up with a complete life history for a person in an hour or that I have all day to look through back issues of the paper."

"What have you told her?" Hugh asked.

"I've told her nothing," Norman said, lifting his cup, "and I intend to keep it that way."

"Good," Olive said. "It's one thing picking up gossip in town and passing it along, but why is she going to such extremes?"

"It could just be news in town is a bit thin lately, and she doesn't know what to do with herself—my mum used to say Aunt Connie was born a nosey parker. But I think she misses your mum, or 'poor dear Daisy,' as she would say. And in some misguided loyalty, she believes she now needs to keep an eye on you. 'Poor dear Olive.'"

"So, it's all down to me," Olive said.

"I don't think she has enough to keep herself busy." He took his glasses off and polished them with the end of his tie. "By the way, Hugh, I recognized Sid's name because we did an article on BBC children's television programming. He's working on an action-adventure idea that involves spaceships and marionettes?"

"Yes," Hugh said, reaching for another slice of currant cake and sitting back with great ease. "He's quite keen on it. Again, about before—sorry."

"It's fine, really." Norman looked round the room. "I don't think I was ever in Milkey's house. How's Margery?"

"She's joined the Chamber of Commerce and is working herself silly," Olive said. "She loves it."

When the coffee pot had emptied and the cake plate held nothing but crumbs. Norman rose to leave. He and Hugh parted warmly, and Olive followed Norman out.

"Let me know if Aunt Connie tries to cause any trouble," Norman said. "I'm not sure what I could do about it, of course—the woman has a mind of her own."

"I'm happy you stopped in regardless of the reason," Olive said.

Norman glanced round the green and, it seemed, beyond. "I have good memories of this place."

"I remember that spring and summer before the war," Olive said. "You and Donald knocking about town."

"Yes, our salad days." Norman looked out between the buildings to the patch of sea. "Seems a long time ago."

"I still miss him," Olive said.

"So do I."

★   ★   ★

Billy was late with the groceries Saturday, and it was with a harried look he lugged the basket in, set it on the table, and began unloading. Olive helped and when they'd finished, he ran the back of his hand over his forehead.

"Everything all right?" Olive asked.

"Oh yeah, fine," Billy said. "I'm sorry to be a bit behind, but Ma needed me first."

Olive didn't go further, because Charlie appeared at the door to the yard.

"Hello," she said.

"Hiya, Mr. Charlie," Billy said as he repacked the items for his next delivery.

"How are you, Billy?" Charlie said with a nod, and then to Olive, "I thought I'd just put my head in. I was nearby, arranging with Old Trotter to move the MG over to the garage tomorrow afternoon."

"Sunday?" Olive asked.

"Harold's only just today cleared out enough space to work on it, and thought it best to get stuck in."

Billy had replaced the basket on his bicycle and sat astride it, about to ride away. "An MG?" he asked.

"Mrs. Wilkins's husband's car," Charlie told him. "Been sitting in her stable with no attention paid to it, and she's asked my cousin to restore it."

"I didn't know the Major had an MG," Billy said as if he should've been informed.

"He stopped driving it years ago," Olive said.

"Blimey, I'd love to see it," Billy said.

"It's practically in bits," Charlie said.

"Is it?" Billy asked. He sighed.

Charlie looked at Olive, who offered a tiny shrug. "I tell you what," Charlie said to Billy, "why don't you come along tomorrow and watch us move it?"

The boy's eyes grew wide. "Could I? I mean, I wouldn't . . . it would be . . ." A dark cloud passed over his face. "Nah, I can't. Sunday afternoon."

"Your mother won't allow it?" Charlie asked.

"It's my pa," he muttered.

"Billy," Olive said, "why don't I go over and ask your father if you can go?"

An air of hope seemed to swirl round Billy. "Would you, Miss Olive?"

The kitchen swing door opened a couple of inches, and one of Juniper's sticks appeared, then the girl herself pushed it open the rest of the way.

"Are you late delivering, Billy?" she asked.

"Juniper," he said, his voice rising with excitement, "tomorrow afternoon, we're going to Mrs. Wilkins's to watch Mr. Charlie move the Major's MG to the garage. You're going too, aren't you? Won't that be brilliant?"

"Yes, brilliant," Juniper said. "Am I going?" she asked Olive.

"Perhaps we all should. I'll telephone Mrs. Wilkins, and then I'll go have a talk with your father, Billy."

Billy threw his shoulders back. "Do you want me to go with you?"

"No, you finish your deliveries."

As Charlie and Olive walked through town together, he asked, "What about Billy's dad?"

"Pauley?"

"Pauley. Will there be a problem? Why don't I go to the door with you?"

"I'll be all right," Olive said.

Still, Charlie lingered at the corner of Billy's road until Olive turned up the Grunyon's front walk. Olive waved and watched him leave before going to the door and rattling the flap on the letter box.

She heard Pauley shout, "Door!" and in a moment Lorna answered, looking startled.

"Hello, Lorna, I want to have a word with Pauley."

Lorna threw a look over her shoulder, as here came her husband. She stepped back and he filled the doorway, looking down on Olive.

"Hello, Pauley."

"Olive," he replied. "The boy giving you trouble?"

"Billy's no trouble at all," she said. "Listen, do you remember the MG the Major used to drive round town?"

Pauley looked puzzled. "Green two-seater?"

"Tomorrow afternoon, it's being hauled off from Mrs. Wilkins's to a garage in Reydon to be restored, and Juniper and I are going to watch."

"Juniper. Billy's always on about her," Pauley said. "She's yours— your girl? Did I know that?"

"She lives at Mersea House," Olive said. "I've invited Billy to watch the car being moved."

"Tomorrow's Sunday," Pauley growled.

"Yes, so it is."

"He can't. The boy's got jobs round here on a Sunday."

Olive locked eyes with the man. "I want Billy to be there."

Pauley frowned at Olive. He screwed his mouth up to one side, took a deep breath, and blew it out. "Yeah, well, all right, I s'ppose."

★　★　★

Mrs. Wilkins stood on the drive at Beech View to greet Olive, Juniper, and Billy on Sunday afternoon. She led them to the stables, where the doors stood open and the car uncovered. Billy let out a low whistle as he circled the thing. Harold and Charlie arrived wearing coveralls and flat caps, which they doffed to the ladies, and next, Old Trotter rumbled up in his van. The men, with Billy eager to lend a hand, got to work.

The women stayed on the terrace, watching the show and discussing Mrs. Wilkins's broad beans, which looked on track to win another first at the local show next month. "Of course, you never know until the last moment, do you?" Mrs. Wilkins said.

Meanwhile, Juniper sat with her sketchbook at the end of the terrace closest to the stables, in order to record the event. The MG made it up a ramp and into the van without too many pieces falling off, and after that, the three men and the boy squashed themselves into the front and drove away. Mrs. Wilkins put the kettle on.

"It was kind of you to bring a cake with you," Mrs. Wilkins said when she returned with the pot and they sat admiring the Victoria sponge on the table.

"It's to say thank you for letting us turn the afternoon into entertainment," Olive said. "Also, I thought you should taste my sandwich sponge to make sure it's suitable for the garden tea."

"I'm certain it will be," Mrs. Wilkins said. "Well, why don't we tuck in? It's a large cake, and I'm sure there will be plenty left for the men when they arrive back."

Not an hour later, here they came. Mrs. Wilkins invited them to sit, and Charlie and Harold, who had left their coveralls behind, did so. Old Trotter said he would prefer to take his tea near the van, as he was still dressed in his working togs and a bit oily. Mrs. Wilkins asked him up onto the terrace, saying that although she wasn't a communist, she had a great deal of respect for the worker, and he deserved to be treated well. Old Trotter's brow furrowed at the word *communist*, but he complied. Billy didn't care how he was dressed as long as he could eat cake. He sat on the stone terrace next to Juniper's chair with his legs dangling over the edge. And so, not long after Mrs. Wilkins brought out a fresh pot of tea, the large Victoria sponge had vanished.

At the end of the afternoon, they bade Mrs. Wilkins goodbye, and Charlie said, "Well, Miss Juniper, Miss Olive—may I walk you home?"

"Yes, you may, Mr. Charlie," Juniper said. "Billy, are you coming?"

"Nah, I've chores," he said. "Thanks for talking with Pa, Miss Olive."

"My pleasure, Billy."

Billy struck off, and Olive, Charlie, and Juniper made their way to the pier and then turned down the Parade, stopping along the railing to look at two ships on the horizon. The Sunday crowd had dwindled, but Olive noticed a woman sitting on the bench near Hetty's, watching them. When Juniper set off again, they let her get ahead and then Charlie followed, but the woman gestured Olive over.

"I just want to tell you how lovely it is, seeing the three of you out and about," the woman said with a smile. "You see, my brother is a polio—came down with it when he was a baby—and all the years he was growing up, my mum wanted to hide him away, saying he needed to be protected. I wish she'd've let him be a child the way you and your husband are with your daughter."

Olive swallowed. "I suppose it's difficult sometimes to know whether it's enough freedom or too much," she said. "Have a good afternoon."

Charlie was waiting for her only a few steps ahead. Olive's face was hot when she reached him, and she didn't look up. "It was easier than trying to explain," she said quietly, and hurried after Juniper.

★   ★   ★

Charlie stayed for the cold Sunday evening supper, and later, after the house was quiet, he sat across from Olive in the kitchen.

"It was a good day," he said.

"Yes."

He set his forearms on the table and clasped his hands. Olive sat across from him. He studied her face for a moment and then said,

"There are people who think that if you were in the services during the war, you should have something to show for it."

"You mean an injury?"

"An injury. A medal. Both, if possible. Being a war hero matters to some people."

"I don't see how it's necessary," Olive said. "You put yourself in harm's way just as every other sailor did."

"But I had nothing to show for it."

"You have that burn on your back," Olive said. She'd seen it.

Charlie dismissed that with a single shake. "Carelessness—backing into a hot pipe in the engine room. Hardly counts."

"Who thinks you should've been injured?"

"My former wife."

"She said that to you?"

"She didn't have to put it into words." Charlie looked down at his hands. "We'd barely met when we were married, and I left only a few days later. People were doing mad things at the beginning of the war, weren't they? And there I was, gone the entire time, and all she had from me were letters. And my pay. When I returned, what did I have to show for myself? In the meantime, she'd met a real war hero who had saved his commanding officer from being buried under rubble in some action in Italy. He had both an injury and a medal to prove it. A finer man you'll never meet."

"You met him?"

"No. Her words. We divorced three months after I was demobbed, and they moved God knows where. I stayed in Southampton and worked on the docks because it seemed my navy pay hadn't been enough to keep her housed and fed, and there were debts that needed settling."

"You had to settle them?" Olive asked.

"Who else was there? It took a few years, then I heard from Harold, and I moved up here. It's only, I thought I should tell you the rest of the story."

Olive took his hands. "Remind me to thank Harold."

Later, in bed, Olive couldn't sleep and so replayed the conversation in her head. Why had Charlie chosen that moment to tell her more about his past? The woman on the Parade had seen them and believed Olive was Charlie's wife and Juniper their daughter. Had he seen how much Olive wanted it to be true? But Juniper was Margery's ward, and she and Charlie weren't married, and perhaps he didn't want people to think they were. That would teach her to hope.

CHAPTER 19

When the knock came Tuesday morning, Olive was prepared for Binny, who was overdue a visit—the percolator sat ready next to the hob and a plate of shortbread on the table—but when she answered the door, it was to Charlie.

He smiled at her, and any of the worries left roosting in her mind from two nights before flew away.

"I hope you don't mind," he said. "I just delivered a repaired car over near the church and thought as I was so near . . ." He shook his head. "It was the best excuse I could come up with—I really only wanted to see you."

Olive leaned over the doorstep and kissed him. "Come in. Coffee?"

They sat at the kitchen table, and Charlie gave her a rundown on the MG and how he'd decided Mrs. Wilkins needed the same sort of introductory lesson to the automobile as Olive had, so that's where he'd be next Wednesday afternoon—at Beech View with the Hillman.

Movement caught Olive's attention, and both she and Charlie turned to watch the swing door creep open, until there was Hugh standing in his sock feet with his shoes in his hand.

"Ah, good, just as I thought." He came into the kitchen and leaned against the doorpost to slip his shoes back on. "How are you, Charlie? Don't mind me. I heard a knock at the door a bit ago and thought—"

"You thought it was Miss Binny, and you were going to sneak out the front door, but then you heard Charlie's voice?" Olive asked.

Hugh colored. "I'm sure you're as relieved as I am that it wasn't Miss Binny."

"Is it a gardening day?" Charlie asked.

"That damned pond," Hugh said. "I'm beginning to think it's a figment of Mrs. Wilkins's imagination. I'm off now—you two, carry on."

Hugh left, but then so did Charlie, back to the garage.

Olive walked him to the front door. "Thanks for stopping."

"My pleasure," Charlie said. "Maybe a walk after dinner this evening?"

They agreed on it, and Olive saw him off. Before she went in again, she looked round the green, but it was empty of Constance Binny.

★ ★ ★

After dinner, when the washing up was finished, Olive met Charlie at the Harbour Inn at Blackshore Quay. They had a drink and then began walking without any obvious direction, but ended up at Harold's garage and, more specifically, at Charlie's cottage.

"I should walk you back," Charlie said.

"You don't want me to see inside?" Olive asked.

"It isn't much," he said, but when she was quiet he unlocked the door and pushed it open for her.

It was much as Olive had expected from the outside—a shed converted to a one-room dwelling, plus a bathroom. It was neat as a pin.

Charlie frowned at his surroundings.

"Margery would be happy to see you have an electric kettle," Olive said, standing in the middle of the room and pointing to the corner table. "That's quite modern. She's always threatening to bring one home to Mersea House. Well, now I've walked you home, I should be getting back."

"Would you like a coffee?" Charlie asked.

Olive considered coffee. "Yes, thanks." She went to the bookshelf under the window. "You've a fine collection of Zane Grey."

"Found them in a charity shop." Charlie switched the kettle on and then came over to where she stood, lifted her braid, and kissed her neck. When he slipped his hands round her waist, she leaned back against him, her head on his shoulder, and they stayed that way until the kettle switched off.

Charlie cleared his throat and set about spooning the Nescafé into the mugs and pouring the water. There was only one chair, and he shifted a stack of newspapers and brushed the seat off. "There you go."

Olive walked past the chair to the bed and sat down. It squeaked. She bounced up and down lightly and looked up at Charlie. "I think I'm fine here."

★   ★   ★

"I'll walk you back," Charlie said, reaching for his trousers.

Olive buttoned her dress. "I've already walked you back here. We could walk each other back and forth all night long. There's no need—it isn't far."

He walked her halfway—to the end of the bridge over Buss Creek—and they stepped off the path and away from the road.

"You never had your coffee," Charlie said.

"We forgot that, didn't we? Coffee next time. This evening, you were what I needed."

★   ★   ★

Olive had spent most of Thursday afternoon with Abigail and Mrs. Tees in the storage room off the church hall, sorting clothes and household goods for the jumble sale, but she left the other women working to be home for Juniper at the end of the school day. She was halfway down Queen Street when someone called her name, and she turned back to see Geoff Markham hurrying toward her.

He reached her, breathless, and said, "Sorry, Olive—hope I didn't startle you." He smiled, smoothed his hair back on the side, and straightened his tie.

"Hello, Mr. Markham," Olive said. "Are you looking for Margery? Thursday isn't her half day, so she'll be at the shop."

"Yes," he said, looking over his shoulder as if to verify that, "but it's you I wanted to have a word with. Do you have a few minutes? Shall we go for a drink somewhere?"

"I need to be at Mersea House—Juniper will be home from school soon. Would you take a cup of tea?"

"Yes, I'd love one."

Olive turned and continued walking. "Have you already been to see Margery?"

"No," Markham said as she unlocked the door. "No, I've come here today to talk with you, Olive. I hope you don't mind, but it's because you know Margery better than anyone, and you'll understand."

They stood in the entry, Markham watching her expectantly. Olive thought about this. *"You know her better than anyone"* was a far cry from his first visit, when he hadn't a clue who Olive was.

"Why don't you sit in the lounge and I'll bring the tea through," she said, and went off without waiting for an answer, going through the motions in the kitchen and then sitting at the table and keeping her mind in neutral until the kettle boiled.

"Here we are," she said, carrying the tray back in. Markham had been standing at the mantel but came over and took the tray from her and set it on the table. Olive wished Hugh were there, but he was at Mrs. Wilkins's, still searching for the pond at the bottom of the garden. Olive told herself perhaps it was better to face Markham on her own.

She poured out the tea, and they settled across from each other with their cups. Olive waited.

"I want you to know I take all the blame," Markham said. "None of it is Margery's fault. This . . . separation, I mean. But it's been torture because we understand each other. I know this"—he waved vaguely—"is a lovely place. Of course it is. And I don't mean to say anything against it, but you can see that she isn't suited to this sort of life. Small town, small minds, you know."

Small minds when it came to infidelity—is that what he meant? Olive offered a smile—not one of her usual smiles, but pleasant enough—and didn't speak. Markham apparently didn't care for the silence, and so he continued in the same disjointed fashion.

"She misses London, I know she does. The arrangement was mutual—that is, I mean, you know, work and . . . living. She was her own woman there, I can tell you. People here don't want a woman running a business, do they? But in London, it's nothing. If she wanted to own a shop, I'm sure I could arrange it. And vibrant, well, really the city is lit up all hours. Margery loves to go out of an evening, hates to just lie about. You can see it, can't you, Olive? You know her, and you can see she isn't happy. I only want the best for her."

Olive had an image of Sunday afternoons at Mersea House with Margery stretched out on the sofa, napping and only rousing herself when tea was brought in. She thought of how her eyes shone when she was at the shop and chatting up customers. At the lively conversations they had enjoyed over the evening meals. How, even though she'd only just met Mrs. Wilkins, Margery had plans to ask the woman to organize a gathering of secretaries and receptionists—a social club of sorts. How late one evening sitting in the kitchen with Olive, Margery had said, "He was a brilliant man, my uncle Milkey—how else could he know I would be so happy doing this?"

It's as if Markham were talking about someone Olive had never met. Or had Margery hidden her unhappiness that well? Olive knew that Margery had been shaken when Markham showed up, but she'd recovered. Would she really consider going back to London?

"The girl would be no trouble, of course," Markham said, and Olive snapped to attention. "London's a grand place for a girl to live. Or perhaps she could go away to a good grammar school, somewhere they would be able to, you know, look after her."

It was as if a curtain she'd kept closed had suddenly been flung open, and Olive knew with certainty that if Margery left Southwold, she would take Juniper. After all, she was responsible for the girl.

There was a noise in the kitchen, and Juniper herself came out through the swing door and saw them in the lounge.

"Hello, Mr. Markham."

Markham rose and spoke in a rush. "Hello, Juniper, how are you doing? Say, have you ever been to London? You'd love it—I'm sure you'd love to live there. It's a grand place." And then, under his breath, Olive heard him mutter, "Damn. No lift in the building."

Olive shot out of her chair. "Would you like your Ribena in the kitchen?" she asked Juniper. "Billy will be here before long, and you can help him with the groceries. Why don't you go on in, and I'll be along."

Once Juniper had gone back into the kitchen, Olive turned to Markham, and her voice cut the air like a knife. "Well, Mr. Markham, I need to get on with my afternoon, and I have the evening meal to prepare. Safe journey back to London."

She walked out to the entry and opened the front door. After a slight pause, Markham came out of the lounge, looking a bit at sea.

"Yes, well, all right, then," he said. "I only wanted to . . . thank you for the tea."

He had stepped out and looked ready to say something else, but Olive closed the door in his face and went to the kitchen.

"How was school?" she asked, going straight for the bottle of Ribena, her hands shaking as she mixed two glasses.

Juniper wrinkled her nose. "When school is finished, will I have to drink warm milk every day?"

"You need to drink milk, but it won't be warm," Olive said. There seemed to be no happy medium for the schoolchildren's daily third of a pint. The bottles sat warming half the day before they were drunk. Even in winter, when the bottles had to be thawed by the heater, the result was often the same.

"Why does Mr. Markham want me to go to London?" Juniper asked.

Olive set the plate of biscuits that she had meant to take into the lounge on the kitchen table, and replied in a casual tone that, she hoped, disguised her fear. "He lives there, and I suppose he thinks everyone should."

"If I went to London to live, would you go too?"

"No, I live here."

"Then I don't want to go," Juniper stated.

Olive told herself not to ask, but the question came out of its own accord.

"What if Miss Margery went to live in London?"

Juniper thought for a moment. "We could go and visit her."

★   ★   ★

Olive observed Margery during drinks in the lounge that evening. She watched for signs that she'd had an encounter with Geoff Markham—frustration, annoyance, longing. Margery showed none of that but instead told them—her, Hugh, and Abigail—that Mrs. Wilkins thought a social club for secretaries and receptionists was a brilliant idea. Margery outlined their plans, but her voice was drowned out by Olive's internal argument about whether to say anything about Markham's visit.

As Hugh was leaving for the cinema, Olive caught him.

"I want to have a word with you."

He stopped and waited.

"Not here," Olive told him, and then called toward the dining room, "I'm just stepping out for a moment."

She walked out the door with Hugh and down to the corner, where she finally felt out of everyone's earshot, and told him about Markham.

"Can he not give it up?" Hugh asked, his face like thunder. "He's in his own world if he thinks he could sway you."

"I ought to tell her he was here," Olive said. "Oughtn't I?"

Hugh conceded she did. "She should see this as further evidence she's done the right thing."

Hugh left, and Olive walked back to Mersea House to find that Margery had started in on the washing up. Olive began drying plates before she said, "Geoff Markham was here this afternoon."

"Here?" Margery asked. She seemed surprised, but not alarmed. "I didn't see him."

"He came to see me," Olive said. "To lay out his case for you returning to London."

Margery brushed this off. "He made a wasted journey. Pay him no mind—I certainly don't, and you shouldn't either. How is Juniper doing on her sums?"

★ ★ ★

The following Monday, Mrs. Pagett telephoned.

"I rang Miss Paxton at the shop, but a man answered"—for one moment of panic, Olive thought Geoff Markham was there—"Trotter, he said his name was. He told me Miss Paxton was too busy to take a call, and so I turn to you, Miss Kersey."

"Yes, Mrs. Pagett, how can I help?"

"I've been told that you may have another lodger."

"We had lodgers for the bank-holiday weekend," Olive said. "And we may do again in August, but they're temporary."

"You don't have another gentleman at Mersea House—a Mr. Sid Davies?"

And how had this news traveled from Southwold all the way to Mrs. Pagett, children's officer from the local authority?

"Mr. Davies does not live at Mersea House, Mrs. Pagett," Olive said coolly. "Who told you he did?"

The woman stumbled. "I'm not sure . . . you can understand the reason . . . it is in the girl's best interest—"

"It's in Juniper's best interest to be in a loving, stable home. Temporary lodgers may come and go, but we have formed a solid and supportive family. Of sorts."

"Of sorts, yes," the woman agreed. "We fully support your efforts, but this appears to be an unusual situation, and we must be vigilant in rooting out any issues that appear to hinder the girl's living circumstances in this situation."

That sentence circled in on itself and made no sense. Olive wondered if Mrs. Pagett had taken training to sound so officious.

"Mr. Davies is a friend of Miss Paxton's from London. He currently visits on weekends and works as a gardener." A giggle almost overtook her as she imagined Sid's face if he heard he'd been labeled as a gardener. "For the receptionist of our doctor."

"And he doesn't lodge with you?"

"I don't see that it makes any difference where he lodges," Olive said with some heat.

"The receptionist's name, Miss Kersey?"

"Mrs. Nancy Wilkins, Beech View."

Over the telephone line all the way from Ipswich, Olive heard the sound of Mrs. Pagett unscrewing her fountain pen. After the woman thanked her, the conversation ended, and Olive put the phone down, then picked it up again, and rang the surgery. Mrs. Wilkins answered.

First, Olive explained who Mrs. Pagett was and her role and perceived power in Juniper's living arrangements. "Now, because of Miss Binny, I believe she's got wind of Hugh and Sid. I put her off, telling her Sid worked for you at the weekends. She wanted your name—I thought I should warn you." Olive sighed. "I shouldn't've been so shirty with her."

"Thank you for letting me know," Mrs. Wilkins said. "If Mrs. Pagett rings, I'll take care of my end of things. I suppose in a way she's paid to be a nosey parker."

"Yes, but Binny's snooping is done of her own free will."

"Connie will not win, Olive. You and I will see to that."

★   ★   ★

Abandoning her washday activities, Olive marched out the door of Mersea House and down the road, with no cold north wind in her face to cool off her anger. Instead, the sky was dull gray and the air still on a quiet day in town, with only local people going about their business. Olive nodded to one or two but didn't stop until she came to a row of cottages on Victoria Street and pulled up at the middle one, where Constance Binny, her sister, and her brother had all been brought up by their father. Her siblings had left home after they had finished school, but Constance had stayed. Only a year later, her father had died suddenly, leaving her settled in as queen of her domain, living off a small income from her mother's side of the family.

Olive rapped on the door and waited, half expecting no answer because wouldn't Binny be out on her usual rounds? Perhaps Olive would need to search for the woman at Hetty's tea hut or at Dawson the baker's or wherever she gathered her news. But then, she heard footsteps approaching.

"Oh," Binny said when she saw Olive on her doorstep. "What a lovely surprise, Olive. I've only just . . ."

Even in the dim light of the entry, the sight shocked Olive. Had she ever seen Binny at home? The pheasant-tail hat was missing, and so nothing covered the gray hair that was pulled back into a lackluster bun at her neck. Also, she was minus a shawl or two. But it was more than that—gone, too, was her usual assured tell-me-all-you-know attitude, and as a result she presented a rather pitiful figure.

Olive did not let that sway her. "Hello, Miss Binny. I have something I want to discuss with you. I won't stay long."

"Yes, of course. Do come in."

Binny led them to the tiny sitting room thick with Victorian furniture and heavy brocade curtains. They sat.

"Coffee?" Binny asked tentatively.

"No thank you. Did Norman tell you he stopped to see me when he was here recently?"

"Norman," Binny said, and shook her head, and Olive imagined the pheasant tail quivering. "I'm afraid my nephew has . . . why would he . . . well, it isn't for me to say, but what he's told me . . ."

Had Norman told her he was homosexual?

"It was lovely to see him," Olive said. "I know you're proud of him." When there was no reply, she added, "Not only for his professional accomplishments, but because he's a good and kind person. Just as Donald was."

Binny's face contorted in a way that suggested some inner battle.

"Norman and Donald—my two boys," the woman said. "I don't know how I can face anyone in this town."

Anger flooded into Olive. "It's nothing to do with you—can't you see that?" Binny flinched, and Olive struck again. "Have you been talking with Mrs. Pagett about Hugh?"

Binny's eyes filled with tears. "The way Norman spoke to me. 'You mustn't do this,' he said." She sniffed. "I'm sure I don't know what he means. I never meant to harm anyone."

"You want the best for Norman, don't you? For him to be happy?"

"It's my dearest wish," Binny said.

"Can you not wish that for others too? For me? You cared about my mother. Think, Miss Binny. Wouldn't she be happy knowing I've found a place to live with people I care about and that a child has found a home where she is loved and cared for by everyone in the house? Would you jeopardize that?"

"I have only your best interests at heart," Binny insisted. "Poor dear Daisy."

Yes, Poor Dear Daisy. Poor Dear Olive. Poor Dear Norman. The visit ended when Binny said she had an appointment with Dr. Atterbury. Olive left unsatisfied with the outcome of their conversation, but at least she could take a bit of pleasure in the picture of Binny walking into the doctor's surgery and being faced with Mrs. Wilkins.

CHAPTER 20

Later that evening in the kitchen, Olive set up for breakfast while she gave Margery a cursory version of what had occurred.

Margery frowned at the burning end of her cigarette. "I don't know how you put up with her," she said. "It was someone like Binny that caused Hugh to leave London. This fellow who deservedly got sacked from his job, tried to get his own back, and called in 'suspicious immoral activities' on Hugh. What a silly thing to make a crime, as if we don't have enough of real criminals in the world. Hugh thought it best to get away—keep the spotlight off Sid. He gave up everything and came here. What's the point of any of Binny's talk—does she even know?"

Olive didn't think Binny ever looked far enough ahead to have an intention, but that didn't mean her thoughtless words couldn't do their damage.

"A part of me felt sorry for her," Olive said. "She lives only through the lives of others."

Margery flicked ash into her empty coffee cup and leaned forward. "We could give her something else to talk about. We could start a rumor that I'm the illegitimate daughter of the Spanish mistress of Prince Albert."

Olive measured the dry porridge into the pot and smiled at the memory. "You would try that again?" she asked. "It didn't wash when you were ten years old. I doubt if it would catch on now."

"Seemed like a rip-roaring tale at the time," Margery said.

"Uncle Milkey didn't think so."

"Bless him. Do you remember my punishment? He had me write out a detailed time line of Queen Victoria's reign. To this day, I know more about the nineteenth century than I do the last war."

★   ★   ★

Tuesday afternoon, Juniper came in the kitchen door from the yard, with her face flushed. Olive reached over and felt her forehead.

"Next Thursday is the last day of school and the prize giving," the girl said, leaning against the sink and washing her hands. "It's in the school hall, and there's tea after."

So no fever, only excitement. Olive buttered a slice of bread and set it on the table. Already the end of July, she thought, and in another month, Mrs. Pagett's trial placement of Juniper at Mersea House would end. As legal guardian, Margery didn't believe Juniper could be taken away, but if that was the case, why was Mrs. Pagett still around?

Juniper plopped down in a chair, released the locks at her knees, and shifted her legs under the table. "All the parents are invited." She looked up. "Will you be there?"

"Of course I'll be there," Olive said, "how could I miss it? Isn't there someone else you want to ask too?"

Juniper pulled the jar of strawberry jam close and spread a thick layer on the bread. "Would Mr. Charlie come?"

More than anything in the world at that moment, Olive wanted to say yes, they would both be there along with the other parents. If only it were that easy.

"We can ask him," she replied, "and I'm sure he'd love to go, but he may not be able to leave work. What about Miss Margery?"

"Oh yes," Juniper said, "let's ask her."

Juniper tucked in, and soon the bread was gone, and a red ring had appeared round the girl's mouth. She licked a finger and said, "Mr. Charlie said he lives at the garage."

"Yes, he does."

"It doesn't seem like a very pleasant place to live."

"Well, he doesn't actually sleep in one of the cars. He has a little cottage just beside it."

"Is it a big cottage? Could it fit other people too?"

Olive sat down across from Juniper, set her elbows on the table, and looked at the girl. "It's quite a small place—only the one room."

"If you and Mr. Charlie got married, would he move here and live with us?"

"What's brought this on?" Olive asked.

Juniper grinned. "I saw you kissing."

Olive meant to look stern, but instead she laughed. "Been peeking round corners, have you?"

★   ★   ★

Not unexpectedly, Mrs. Pagett appeared at Mersea House on Wednesday afternoon.

"Miss Paxton—" Olive began.

"Yes, yes, Miss Paxton is at the shop. I've already stopped to have a word with her, but I'm perfectly aware of your . . . influence in this situation, Miss Kersey, and so here I am. Now, I'm sure you understand why I am concerned about Juniper's welfare."

They were standing in the entry, and so Olive gestured to the lounge and followed Mrs. Pagett in.

"You're concerned because it's an important issue," Olive said. "To Juniper, of course, but for you too, Mrs. Pagett, in your position." It was a suspicion that had been growing in Olive's mind.

Mrs. Pagett placed her handbag and satchel on the sofa but did not sit. Instead, she walked over to the mantel. Olive stood behind the sofa.

"It is an important issue, Miss Kersey, and I don't mind admitting it. You see, there is so much I can do to improve how we look after our children in care, but—and I'm sure you'll agree with me here—a woman's voice isn't always heard."

Olive felt a pang of shame. As her ire toward Mrs. Pagett grew in relation to her worry about losing Juniper, it had never occurred to her the woman's officious manner might cover a concern greater than a single child. But as that thought settled in her mind, here came her heart at a gallop, catching up with her brain. This single case of a child in care, Juniper, mattered more than Mrs. Pagett's promotion.

"I must keep my record without blemish," the woman continued. "It's the only way they'll listen to me."

"I don't see how Juniper's placement could threaten that," Olive said.

"Oh, I believe you do," Mrs. Pagett said. "It's your paying guests."

Olive bristled. "We may have an unconventional family arrangement here—"

"Unconventional, yes, with this odd collection of people under one roof, but I couldn't call it a family."

Olive bit back her answer as she heard Hugh on the stairs—no creeping round without his shoes this time, but firm footfalls. He came to the door, and when she saw the grim look on his face, Olive realized he'd been listening in.

"Come in, Hugh," Olive said.

He did so, but not far. Two steps behind him was Abigail, who stopped in the doorway.

"I'm not disturbing?" she asked.

"No, of course you aren't," Olive said, "come in. Mrs. Pagett, I don't believe you've met Mrs. Claypool on your other visits." She made the introductions. Everyone remained in place, scattered about the lounge like misaligned chess pieces.

"Well, Mrs. Pagett," Olive said as a prompt, "as you were saying?"

The woman put her chin in the air. "This will come out, Miss Kersey—there's no way it can't. A house harboring anyone breaking the law is not a fit home for a child."

It was as if Olive felt a tremor underfoot—as if the world shifted, and instead of knocking her down, she found a new way to stand. She whirled round and said, "Hugh, have you robbed a bank?"

For a moment, Hugh looked too startled to answer. His eyes darted to Mrs. Pagett and returned to Olive. He gave a mild chuckle. "No, I have not."

"Have you knocked down an old woman in the street and stolen her handbag?" Olive demanded.

"No, I have not. Olive, you don't have to—"

"Well, Mrs. Pagett," Olive said, "I'm not at all certain to what you refer."

"It isn't Hugh she's talking about—it's me."

They all turned to Abigail, who stood framed by the doorway with a light behind that made her look like a saint in a stained glass window.

"Isn't that right, Mrs. Pagett?" Abigail continued, "because I have a criminal record, don't I? Suicide—that is, the failed attempt."

Olive went to her. "Abigail—"

Abigail put her hand on Olive's arm. "It's all right." Her voice was calm, and her eyes were shining. "I threw myself off Tower Bridge, Mrs. Pagett, after my daughters were killed in London in '44. I had no reason to go on, no one to make me see that my life was worth living. But I didn't die—someone saw me, and I was fished out of the water and had to go up before the magistrate, who thought he was being kind when he leveled only a small fine and let me go free. But I wasn't free, of course, not in my mind. For years, I hid myself away until a few months ago. When I moved here, I found no one would let me wallow in my self-pity"—she turned to Olive with a smile—"although they were quite nice at chivvying me along. And little by little I stopped judging myself. So, Mrs. Pagett, will you now punish Juniper and everyone at Mersea House for my action all those years ago?"

There was movement behind Abigail as the swing door to the kitchen was pushed opened. A stick protruded, and Juniper followed.

Her large chestnut eyes took in the scene, but if she was surprised, she didn't show it.

"I'm home from school," she said.

Olive slipped past Abigail. "So you are. Good day?"

"Yes," Juniper said. "Hello, Mrs. Pagett. I haven't been in a row-boat today."

Olive gave Juniper a quick hug. "Wash up, and I'll see what I can find for you to eat."

"All right." Juniper went straight to her bathroom.

Mrs. Pagett came out to the entry. "Mrs. Claypool," she began, and then faltered. "Miss Kersey, Mr. Hodgson. We all want the best for Juniper. It isn't that I don't see that this is a loving home, and if it were up to me . . . but in order to do further good, I must put aside my own opinions and toe the line."

"Must you?" Olive asked.

Mrs. Pagett sighed. "Miss Paxton mentioned London. That could solve everything. Of course it would be her decision to take the girl with her—after all, she is responsible. Well, I'll be on my way now."

Olive fumbled through a goodbye and, once Mrs. Pagett had gone, gave Abigail's arm a squeeze.

Hugh came out, and the three of them stood in the entry. "You didn't need to do that," he said to Abigail.

"Do you know," Abigail said, "that's the first time I've ever told anyone. No, Hugh, I've been hiding for far too long. I have a voice and I should use it. Olive, is Margery really thinking of moving back to London?"

Hugh looked as if he were about to speak, but said nothing. Olive searched for an answer but instead came up with more questions and so only shrugged.

"I don't know," Olive said, and she left them and walked to the bathroom. It was quiet within. Juniper had left the door partly open, and Olive called, "All right in there?"

The tap came on and over the sound of the water, Juniper said, "Yes. I'll be right out."

★   ★   ★

The evening meal was a dull affair. Olive avoided drinks with Margery by remaining in the kitchen, fussing with piping the potatoes on the cottage pie. At the dining table, it was Abigail and Hugh who carried what little conversation there was.

After the meal, Hugh left for the cinema, Margery claimed she had work to do at the shop—something about inventory—and Juniper went to her room with a book. Abigail helped Olive with washing up and kept up a mostly one-sided conversation about Juniper's knitting project and how the sleeveless jumper was almost ready for finishing off.

"Thank you," Olive said when the dishes were done.

"You won't lose her, Olive," Abigail said.

"She isn't mine to lose or keep, is she?" Olive reflected. "And neither is Mersea House." She shook out the tea cloth and hung it to dry. "I'll just turn out Juniper's light, and then I'm going out for a bit. Would you mind listening in case she needs anything?"

"I'd be happy to."

Olive had telephoned the garage and asked Charlie if he'd like a walk. Now, setting out to meet him at the Harbour Inn, she went first to the seafront and stood at the railing, filling her lungs with briny air, watching the waves roll in, and the eastern sky darken from washed-out blue to navy. Then as she turned south, down to Ferry Road, along the harbor and Blackshore Quay, her usual stride slowed because her mind was a muddle.

Charlie waited outside for her. He smiled, kissed her forehead, and rubbed his hands on her arms. "A bit cool without your jacket?"

So, they went indoors, and Olive sat in a far corner of the empty room while Charlie went up to the bar and brought back a pint for him and a gin and tonic for her.

"Now, what's this all about?" he asked.

It poured out of her without restraint—Miss Binny, Hugh and Sid, Abigail, Mrs. Pagett, Margery and Geoff Markham. Juniper. London.

Charlie's face became careworn as Olive talked, as if absorbing her woes. At last, he reached across the table to clasp her hands.

"Would she do that?" he asked of Margery.

"I don't know. She swears she won't, but she mentioned it to Mrs. Pagett, and that must be something. There. That's the end."

"What can I do?" he asked.

Olive, her mind now empty of thought except for Margery's next move, said, "Oh, I don't think there's anything you can do."

Charlie frowned. "Yes, that about sums it up, doesn't it? Nothing I can do."

"You listened—that's a great help. And I'm not complaining about you; I'm complaining about Margery."

"Still," Charlie persisted, "you're right. I've got to be a disappointment. Me a mechanic, living in a shed—nothing to offer."

"A disappointment?" Olive repeated. "Are you confusing me with your former wife?"

"No," Charlie said in a rush. "God, no, it's only that—"

"Do you believe I think you have less worth because you . . . what? Don't have a Victoria Cross?"

Charlie withdrew his hands.

"Perhaps I was getting ahead of myself," he said quietly.

"Neither of us was getting ahead of ourselves. At least I didn't think we were. I felt that we . . ." *How did the conversation get here?* Olive thought with despair. Or had she come with this in her head all along? She looked round the room, still nearly empty, and felt confined. "I have to go."

She rose and left without seeing if he followed, but Charlie was on her heels.

"Olive." She stopped and turned. "Look at how I live," he said. "It may seem all right now, but who is to say if that's true?"

"I would be the one to say," Olive shot back.

A man came out of the pub, and they didn't speak until he'd passed them and walked down the quay.

"You deserve more," Charlie said.

"What do you think I'm demanding?" she asked. "I know how hard you work—how well you've done at making your way after starting with less than nothing. That's not in question. All I ask is a willing heart. And I felt that in you. What's the good of backing away from something precious because you're afraid you might spoil it? Or, maybe it isn't so precious to you after all, and you've only been looking for an excuse."

"You can't believe that," Charlie said.

"Well, it's one or the other, isn't it?"

She turned and walked off, setting her usual pace and without stopping to think or speak or almost breathe until she arrived at Mersea House, where she went into the kitchen and set up for breakfast.

★ ★ ★

The next morning, Margery had gone before Olive came downstairs, the only signs of her an empty cup with the dregs of tea and the fading aroma of toast. At least she'd eaten, Olive thought, remembering times when Margery thought she could live on cigarettes.

Olive made her best effort to appear cheerful over breakfast.

"Spelling test tomorrow?" she asked Juniper.

"The last one," Juniper said. "Miss Browne says that someone has perfect marks in spelling tests this year. Linda thinks it's her friend Patsy, but I think it's Billy. Trouble is, he can't remember if he got any wrong or not this year, so he'll have to wait for the prize giving."

"Well, then, next week I'll be there to hear if he's won," Olive said.

Juniper paused in her chewing and then continued.

Olive had a smile at the ready for Hugh and Abigail too. The approach had always worked for her as a shield, regardless of how she felt. She had learned to employ it during those last months of her father's illness, when his usual bad temper had escalated and people she met in the street would ask after him.

It was a relief to be alone in the kitchen, but when she contemplated her day, Olive could cast it in no other light than bleak. As bleak as it had been in March when her choices were so slim that she had seriously considered becoming Binny's companion. No, worse now, because she had seen possibilities and had begun to hope.

Margery could go or stay. Olive hoped she stayed—they'd lost each other once, and Olive didn't want it to happen again. But if Margery did decide Geoff Markham was worth moving back to London for, might she consider leaving Juniper behind? The girl had just found a home, and if Margery were responsible for her—as she declared regularly—then she would know how important that was. If Juniper stayed, what might the arrangements be? Olive's heart wanted the girl well and truly to be her daughter, not just a child whose care she oversaw, but that wasn't in the cards. Imagine Mrs. Pagett approving Mersea House as Juniper's residence, as well as her adoption by an unmarried woman. *Because—face reality, Olive,—that's what you are: a spinster.*

Just what had occurred between Charlie and her the previous evening, Olive still couldn't sort out. She went through their conversation with care, trying to find the point at which talking had become arguing, but she could see neither cause nor reason. Olive's heart was in peril, and she couldn't see a way out.

Juniper came in after school while Olive was paging through *Constance Spry* without really seeing the words.

"Would you like something to eat?" Olive asked.

"No, thank you. I think I'll go to my room and rest."

Olive looked into her eyes. "Are you feeling all right?"

"Yes," Juniper said. She kissed Olive on the cheek and went out.

Not long after, Olive was upstairs when the phone rang, and Hugh called up that he would answer. When she came down, he gave her the news that Margery wouldn't be back for dinner as she'd too much to do at the shop. Then, there was a knock at the kitchen door to the yard, and Olive went to let Billy in with the grocery order, but it wasn't Billy.

"Hi, Miss Olive—I've your order here."

It was Lonnie, the fifteen-year-old nephew of Mr. Farnham, the grocer. Lonnie usually worked in the stockroom, but now here he was with Billy's bicycle and the basket full of groceries.

"Come in," she said, holding the door open. "Whatever are you doing delivering?"

"Billy couldn't make it, so I'm filling in," he said. He set the basket on the table. "I hope you know what you've ordered, because I sure don't."

Billy always knew what she'd ordered and only rarely got something wrong. Olive rather enjoyed chatting with him about what she would do with the groceries.

"Is Billy ill?"

"Dunno, but if he is, I hope he's well tomorrow. He's better at this than I am."

Olive picked out her order from the list she'd made that morning, and Lonnie went on his way, leaving her staring at the odd assortment of items before her. What had she been thinking when she'd phoned this in? What was the jar of capers meant to be for? Had she not asked for mince from Bass the butcher, or ham or a chicken? She hoped no one would object to scrambled eggs for their evening meal.

Olive sensed a storm building, but when she went to the window in the lounge, she saw no clouds gathering on the horizon and realized that feeling of the air round her growing heavy and squeezing her was all in her mind.

After dinner, Hugh left for the cinema. Olive needed a walk and went to Abigail. It was a bright spot in the day, knowing that Abigail no longer had qualms about keeping an eye on Juniper.

They both went to the girl's room and found her at the dressing table with her sketchpad, looking at the ceramic jungle animals that Margery had left for her.

"I'm going to draw the elephant," she said.

"You could fill in his missing trunk, if you like," Olive said. "I'm going out for a bit, but Mrs. C. is here, and I'll be back before your bedtime. All right?"

"Yes," Juniper said. "I'll be all right."

*   *   *

Olive needed the walk, but once out the door, she considered other options. She could go to Margery, so that they could talk, really talk about everything, but instead, her feet took her down Marlborough Street, and she ended up at Beech View. It was only after Mrs. Wilkins didn't answer the bell, Olive remembered it was Dr. Atterbury's evening surgery.

That sent her to Paxton's Goods after all. It was closed, of course. Malc was gone home and the blinds had been drawn, but Olive found a gap and peered through into the darkness to see tables laden with the ghosts of toasters and hair dryers and the specter of thermoses lined up on a high shelf. Behind the counter, through an opening to the back, Olive saw a thin band of light and knew that Margery was in the office. She raised her hand to knock, but then dropped it again.

A walk it was—out by the water tower, along Blackshore Quay, up Ferry Road—and with every step she had a clearer head and a harder heart. When her mother had died, Olive had been ready for whatever would come, and she would be ready again. Perhaps, when Margery moved to London, she would keep the boardinghouse running, and Olive could continue to manage it, living alone in her room at the top of the stairs. Perhaps Margery might occasionally bring Juniper down from London for a visit. These were solid, practical plans with no unnecessary sentiment, and she would hold true to them.

When Olive reached South Green, she couldn't understand why, if her heart was so hard, her face was covered with tears. She stopped to dry her eyes and blow her nose and then continued across the green, but her steps slowed as she detected a figure standing in the shadow of Mersea House. It was Charlie Salt.

Chapter 21

"Abigail said you'd gone out for a walk," Charlie said, "but she didn't know which direction, and I knew I'd never catch you, so I thought I'd better wait." He let out a nervous laugh, much as he had the day he'd asked her out. "That sounds daft, doesn't it?"

Olive kept her distance—an arm's length, at least.

"Hello," she said, and nodded to the car parked at the curb. "I see you drove the Hillman." That sounded a bit daft too, but she didn't know where else to begin.

"I'm a fool."

He said it with such conviction that Olive wanted to disagree, but she held back until she knew for certain which way the wind blew.

"I don't know what I was thinking last evening," he said, shaking his head as if the words were still rattling round inside. "There you were in distress, and I took it to mean I wasn't living up to who I should be. That I was letting you down by not being able to sweep you off and . . ."

"Sweep me off?" Olive said, and she smiled, and then blushed at the look of longing he gave her. "No, Charlie, it wasn't only you—it was me. I wasn't thinking clearly, and so I couldn't explain myself. All the wrong words came out, and I couldn't stop them."

"I love you, Olive."

She didn't breathe for a moment, just let the words encircle her like a light, warm blanket.

"I love you," he said again, "and I know we'll make it because it won't be me alone—it'll be the two of us in it together."

He was closer now—quite close. She felt his warmth. "I love you, too, Charlie. But, what if we were three from the very start?"

Charlie's eyes widened, and Olive laughed. "I mean Juniper. What if we could adopt her?"

"It sounds as if you've been reading my mind," Charlie said, and even in the dark, she could see that sparkle in his eyes. "The three of us. Will you marry me? What do you say, Miss Olive—shall we make a go of it?"

She put her hands on his chest. "You're the only one for me, Charlie Salt."

His arms went round her waist and they kissed, and Olive didn't care who saw. Finally, she looked up at him.

"I don't know if it's possible," she said. "About Juniper. So we shouldn't say anything yet. But come in, and we can at least tell her good night together."

They found Abigail knitting in the lounge.

"Is Margery back?" Olive asked.

"No, but Miss Binny was here."

"Binny—in the evening?" Olive asked.

"She arrived not long after you'd gone. I told her you were out, and she decided to wait. She left just before Charlie arrived."

"Whatever did she want?" Olive asked.

"I'm not sure," Abigail said, "but I kept the lounge door closed in case it was something Juniper didn't need to hear."

"That was good thinking."

"While she was here, she talked about her nephew, Norman, and said what a fine man he was. She mentioned your brother and said the same. Then, she said Nancy Wilkins had been to see her."

"Did she? Well, we'll have to thank Mrs. Wilkins for that." She turned to Charlie. "Sit down, and I'll see if Juniper wants to come out and sit with us a few minutes. I could make cocoa."

Olive knocked on Juniper's door. "I hope I haven't been too long," she said as she walked in. The room was empty. Olive's eyes went from bed to chair. "Juniper?" she asked, as if she thought the girl might come out of the wardrobe. She stepped out and looked in the bathroom. Empty.

Puzzled, she opened the door to Margery's room, too, and then went back into Juniper's room. Only then did her puzzlement begin to change into something else. No, wait—the kitchen.

She pushed the swing door open. No one there. She spun round to the lounge, holding onto the doorpost for support and trying to quell the rising fear.

"She isn't here."

Both Charlie and Abigail leapt up off their chairs.

"She is here," Abigail said. "I looked in after you left, before Miss Binny arrived. She's here in her bedroom, reading."

"Perhaps she went out to her bench," Olive said. It was dark— why would she go out there?

"I'll take a look," Charlie said. The women watched from the doorway as he trotted out and back in less than a minute, shaking his head.

The three of them remained calm, although Olive felt stretched to a snapping point. "The yard," she said, and started into the kitchen, but didn't make it far, because on the table was a note—a page torn from a lined lesson book, folded over, and addressed to "Miss Olive."

Dear Miss Olive,

Thank you very much for helping me with my sums and for letting Billy be my friend and for being such a very fine cook. I do not want to move to London, and I think that must be a problem. If I cannot live at Mersea House, I will go back to the home in Newmarket, even though my friend Minnie won't be there because she has gone to Canada. I know the way and I have my money from Miss Margery. I will write to you when I arrive. Please tell Mr. Charlie I will miss him. Tell Mr. Hugh and Mrs. C. I will miss them. I will miss you most of all.

Love,
Juniper

Abigail sank into a chair and covered her mouth. "I did this," she mumbled. "It's my fault."

The word *again* hung in the air.

Olive kept standing, the note clutched to her chest. She wanted very much to fall to pieces, but she couldn't allow it. Nor could she let Abigail continue with her thoughts.

"It isn't your fault, Abigail," Olive said. "She probably slipped out while Binny was here. Geoff Markham asked her if she wanted to live in London, and then she heard Mrs. Pagett mention London too. Did she think we didn't want her here?" Olive's voice quavered.

"She wouldn't think that," Charlie said. "She knows you love her. Children, they get the wrong end of the stick sometimes, and they think everything's their fault. Come on. We'll find her. She can't have gone far."

"How long has she been gone?" Olive asked. "Do we know?"

"I was waiting for you about fifteen minutes," Charlie said. "If Juniper left while Miss Binny was here, she's had thirty minutes? Three quarters of an hour? How far could she get in that amount of time?"

"It's like one of her arithmetic problems," Olive said. "Right, I'm going to get Margery—she's still at the shop."

"I'll take a look at the Parade," Charlie said.

"Why don't you stay here until I get back?" Olive asked.

"I don't need minding," Abigail said. "I'm all right—you worry about Juniper."

"It isn't that," Olive said in a rush, although, of course, it had been partly that. "Margery will blame herself, and she'll need someone here. Also, the two of you can watch out for Juniper to come home."

Charlie made for the seafront, and Olive ran to the shop and rapped so hard on the door, she feared her fist might go through the glass. The slit of light in the back widened, and Margery came out, and even in the dim interior Olive could see she was angry. Until she recognized the after-hours visitor.

The locks slid back, and Margery opened the door.

"What is it?"

"Juniper's gone—you've got to come back with me."

Margery asked nothing further. She dashed back to the office, shut the light off, and came out with keys in hand. She locked the door and they started back, running down the pavement as Olive told the story.

"She's taken her money," Olive concluded, "but you gave her only sixpence a week, so she can't have more than a few shillings—where will that get her?"

"Oh dear," Margery said. "I'm afraid she has more than a few shillings."

"Margery!" Olive said with exasperation. "How much did you give her?"

"Just a ten-shilling note here or there. I still put money in her post-office account."

"Good thing the last bus left hours ago," Olive said, "or she could've paid for her journey just about anywhere."

"Stop!" Margery said as they reached Market Place. She put a hand to her chest, breathing heavily. "The place on the beach the other side of the pier. I showed it to her—told her it was our favorite place. She may have gone there. I'll go look and catch you up."

"No," Olive said. "I'm coming with you."

They ran the short distance and stopped, both panting. There was still enough light in the sky to see that the patch of beach on the other side of the pier was empty.

"We always climbed down the rocks," Olive said, squinting at the shadows under the pier. "Juniper couldn't manage that."

"Yes, but remember further up it's not such a drop. She could've got down that way."

"But she isn't here. Come on—we can find Charlie as we go back."

They walked now, their eyes scanning the gorse, the beach, the stretch of houses across from the seafront, and as they searched, Olive asked, "Is that what you want? To go live with Geoff Markham and take Juniper with you?"

"No, I do not want to go back to him, and I don't want to live in London. I mentioned London to Mrs. Pagett to distract her. But Olive, there is something I want to say."

"Abigail thinks it's her fault that Juniper is gone," Olive said and retold Abigail 's story.

"That's awful for her," Margery said.

They made it back to Mersea House without meeting Charlie, but the front door flew open and there he was.

"Anything?" Olive asked.

"I came back and telephoned Casper, and he asked his daughter Linda, but she hasn't seen her. Then I tried Mrs. Wilkins. She said when she returned from the evening surgery, she found the crusts of a jam sandwich on her front step. Thought a fox had been through the bins."

"Ah!" Olive cried.

"Beech View is a big enough garden to hide in," Charlie said. "She's probably fallen asleep under a hedge. I'm going over to search. I phoned the police, and they'll send a constable out to help."

What seemed like good news took a turn for the worse in Olive's mind. Her stomach tied in a knot, and she felt as if she were choking from the inside.

"There's a pond at the bottom of the garden," she said. "It's all grown over. Hugh and Sid have been trying to find it."

Charlie grabbed her hand. "If it's hidden, it's probably long filled in with soil and leaves. There won't be any water to cause a problem. Do you have a torch?"

Olive dashed off and came back with two.

"We'll have blankets and the like ready," Margery said, "for when you bring her back."

Olive and Charlie got in the Hillman, and Charlie drove off. They'd barely got to Market Place when Olive put a hand on his arm.

"Billy," she said. "Billy may know something. I'll get out here, and you go on to Mrs. Wilkins. We'll meet you there."

Charlie left her, and Olive hurried to the Grunyons' cottage.

CHAPTER 22

S he rattled the flap on the letter box, and when there was no immediate answer, rapped hard on the door. She heard a bellowing from within, and then Billy opened the door. The smell of drink lay heavy in the air, and beyond, sprawled on the sofa, was Billy's father.

"I'm sorry to disturb you, Pauley," she called over Billy's shoulder. "I need Billy's help."

"You come back in here, boy," Pauley shouted.

Olive looked at Billy. "Are you all right?" she asked.

"Yeah, fine," Billy said in a low voice. "It's just . . . Ma's out with Sammie, and I'm keeping an eye on him. He'll fall off to sleep any time now."

In Olive's mind, there was no competition whatsoever between Pauley, drunk and needing to be watched, and Juniper missing.

"Billy, Juniper's gone."

"Gone?" he asked, his face a puzzle. "Has that woman taken her?"

"No, she's gone away on her own. Did she say anything to you about doing this?"

Billy's face lost all color. "No, Miss Olive, I swear she never said nothing. Where is she? Where's she gone?"

"I don't know. It can't be far, and we're all out looking for her. Will you come?"

"Let's go."

Billy was out the door when Pauley tried to scramble up from the sofa as he bellowed, "Where do you think you're going?"

"Pa, Miss Olive needs me."

"You're not at the beck and call of the women in this town. Get back in here."

Olive put her hand up to stop Billy, and then she marched into the sitting room and looked down at Pauley, who had given up trying to stand.

"This is important," she said in a reasonable tone. "I need Billy's help."

The man roared something unintelligible. Olive leaned over and put her face in front of his.

"Pauley," she shouted, "look at me. Look at me!"

Whether it was the volume, her tone, or both, something worked, because she saw Pauley's eyes focus on her face.

"Olive?"

"I need Billy to help me find my girl. She's lost, and I can't wait until Lorna comes back. Right? Billy is coming with me."

"Yeah, yeah, all right," Pauley mumbled. "Billy, you go find Olive's girl, and then you come straight back." His head flopped back on the sofa, and with that, he was asleep.

"Thanks, Miss Olive," Billy said when they were outside and the door closed. "It's just one of his spells, that's all."

"I know," Olive said, putting an arm round Billy's shoulder. They hurried down to the corner just as the Hillman turned toward them. Charlie stopped and opened the door.

"Nothing yet," he said, "but Casper is there too, and so I came to find you two."

Olive got in the front, and Billy jumped in the back. "Any ideas, Billy?" Olive asked. "Where should we look? She can't have left town. The buses have long finished for the day."

Billy frowned as he considered the question. "The rowboat ferry's stopped too—and anyway, where would she be if she took it, but in Walberswick, and that isn't away."

"Mrs. Wilkins was working this evening, but Juniper may have been by her house. Mr. Casper and the police are searching her garden."

Even saying the words frightened Olive, and by the look in his eyes, they did Billy too.

"She likes to go down to the beach," he said.

"We've checked along the Parade."

"The place the other side of the pier," Billy said, and with more confidence he added, "Yeah, that's it. She showed it to me, said you and Miss Margery went there. A good place to have a think, she said."

"We've looked there too."

"But we should look again. Maybe it's the last place she's gone to, not the first."

"Right," Charlie said. "The pier."

★　★　★

The tide was coming in. Following the irregular coastline, it hurried further up the beach in one place and lagged behind in another. Charlie and Olive flashed their torches in the gorse on the way up the Parade, and Billy called, "Juniper! Juniper!" over the sound of the waves. On the other side of the pier, they stopped. There had been a stretch of shingle beach when Olive and Margery had stopped to look, but now, even without shining their torches down, it was easy to see that there was little land left.

"Juniper!" they called over and over, sounding like the ringing of the bells in the church tower, crossing over each other. Charlie put a hand on Olive's shoulder, and they fell silent until Billy cupped his hands round his mouth and shouted her name one more time.

There came a weak response. "Billy!"

Olive couldn't tell where it came from. She ran her torchlight back and forth across the sand, and Charlie did likewise while Billy called, "Where are you?"

"Here!" came the answer just as the beams of both lights showed a small figure leaning against one of the pilings, her fabric bag slung across her shoulder and her hair hanging lifeless. The sight of her pierced Olive's heart.

Charlie said, "I'll find a place to get down," and he ran up the north end of the Parade, his torch beam on the beach below.

"Are you all right?" Olive called.

"Yes, I'm fine," Juniper called back. A wave came in, running up along the sand and over her shoes.

"I'm coming down, Juniper!" Billy shouted.

"No, Billy," Olive said, catching at his arm.

But Charlie ran up and said, "The sea is already to the wall further up. He's right, we'll have to go down here." He waved down to Juniper. "On our way!"

"Wait!" Juniper shouted. "Look, there!"

She pointed to the beach a few yards in front of her, the last bit of sand and shingle unclaimed by the sea. A wave rushed up covering the spot, but then pulled itself away, and then they saw a dark object. Torchlight revealed it to be a rusty metal cylinder, half-buried, but wholly menacing.

"Cor blimey," Billy whispered. "Is it? Is it a bomb?"

"It may be," Charlie said, "but we aren't going to investigate now. Here we go."

Charlie sat on top of the seawall and let himself down onto the rocks. Billy followed.

"I'm coming too," Olive said, but Charlie handed her his torch.

"Stay there and light our way," he said. "It'll keep our hands free."

Olive's entire body shook, and the torch beams danced as she guided their steps down the rocks. It was a drop of only about ten feet and Olive had scrambled up and down it her whole life, but now it seemed as if Charlie and Billy were descending Mount Everest.

Landing on the beach, the two edged their way round to Juniper. Charlie picked her up under her arms and Billy took her sticks. Then, up they went through a series of handoffs. Charlie would climb onto rock and then turn and lift Juniper to a place she could stand and cling to a surface. Billy followed and kept his hand on her back for support. It seemed to take forever, but at last Olive could reach down and grab hold as Charlie lifted her onto the Parade and into Olive's arms. Charlie put a hand out to Billy and pulled him up onto the path. The boy looked back down to the cylinder on the beach, and Charlie leaned over, his hands on his knees and breathing hard.

Olive could feel Juniper tremble. "You're cold and wet," she said, "and we can't have that. We'll get you to the doctor."

Charlie carried Juniper in his arms to the Hillman.

"Billy," Olive said, "run ahead to Mersea House. Margery has blankets ready. Tell her to ring Dr. Atterbury and say we're going to the surgery."

The boy tore off, taking the most direct route. Olive climbed into the back seat of the car, and Charlie handed Juniper in, and they were off.

With her calipers still locked, Juniper lay on her back, her head in the crook of Olive's arm. With her free hand, Olive pushed up Juniper's dress and fumbled with the buckles at the girl's waist.

"We'll get this off you."

Juniper's teeth chattered. "I'm sorry, Miss Olive."

"It doesn't matter, love—nothing matters except you're safe."

"I missed the last bus," Juniper said, "and then I went to Mrs. Wilkins, and she wasn't home. I didn't know what to do, and I wanted to have a think. That's why I was at the pier. It's a good place to have a think unless the tide is coming in."

When they arrived only a minute or two later, the front door of Mersea House stood open, the light pouring out. Olive could see Margery on the telephone. Abigail came to the car and helped remove Juniper's calipers and then covered both the girl and Olive in blankets, and Olive kept Juniper close against her own body for more warmth. Billy got in the front seat, and as Charlie drove off, the boy turned and got up on his knees to lean over the seat with another blanket.

"Here, Juniper, put this one over your head."

"Thank you, Billy," Juniper said.

"Don't climb all over the place while the car's in motion," Charlie said. "It isn't safe."

"Yes, sir." Billy sat down again.

Charlie gave him a quick look and then said, "It was Billy who knew where you were, Juniper. It's all to him we found you. Good work, son."

Billy smiled. "Thank you, sir."

"You saved me, Billy," Juniper said.

"Why didn't you say anything to me?" he asked.

"I was going to tell you after school, but your mum came early and took you out," Juniper said. "I wrote you and put the note in the old inkwell at your desk. You can read it tomorrow."

The boy was quiet, and then he looked over his shoulder and said, "You know, Juniper, you could be in the newspaper about finding that bomb."

Dr. Atterbury and his wife, the nurse, lived only next door to the surgery, and so were waiting for them. Olive went into the examination room with Juniper, and soon Mrs. Atterbury appeared with two hot-water bottles, which she tucked inside the blankets wrapped round Juniper's legs and feet.

Olive sat nearby while the doctor carried out his examination and asked Juniper questions.

"It's a bomb, you say?" Dr. Atterbury said, taking the thermometer out of Juniper's mouth.

She nodded. Color had come back to her cheeks and with it, her spirit.

"Billy says so. The army will have to come and explode it. He says he hopes they don't take it off someplace else, because it would be great fun to watch."

"And where have your calipers got to?" the doctor asked.

"We've got them," Olive said. "I'm afraid the shoes are ruined, but we can replace those, can't we?"

"You might as well replace the entire contraption," Dr. Atterbury said. "You've a growing girl here, and as I recall, those have been extended just as far as they can go. I'll put an order in, but you'll have to go into Ipswich for them to be fitted."

"I've never been to Ipswich," Juniper said as if it might be a great adventure awaiting.

When he'd finished, the doctor said, "Look now, you appear to be none the worse for wear. Do you feel warm? I'd say you could go to bed just as you are and wait until tomorrow for a bath. A day off school and you'll be fine. I know Miss Olive will keep an eye on you. Next time you want to go exploring, tell her first."

"Yes, sir. May I go home now?"

★ ★ ★

The waiting room looked as busy as a regular afternoon surgery, with half the town waiting to see the doctor, instead of it being—Olive checked the time—half past ten in the evening. Mrs. Wilkins sat behind her desk, and Margery, Abigail, and Billy in chairs lined against the wall. Charlie and Hugh stood in one corner, with Casper and the police constable near the door. All eyes were on the doctor.

"She's fine," he proclaimed. The room sighed with relief, and then the crowd broke up.

Mrs. Wilkins switched off the lamp at her desk, a true signal the surgery was about to close. Although others began filing out, Billy lingered.

"I'd best be home," he said.

"Will your dad be awake?" Olive asked.

"He could be." He looked none too happy about it.

"I'll go back with you and explain," Olive said.

Billy looked hopeful until Charlie said, "No, don't. We'll get Juniper settled in her bed, and then I'll have a talk with Billy's dad."

At this, Billy frowned. "Mr. Charlie, sir, it might not—"

"It's all right," Margery said. "I'll do it. Pauley will listen to me, just as he listens to Olive."

Olive smiled. "Yes, he will."

Charlie carried Juniper out to the Hillman and put her in Olive's lap in the front seat, still wrapped in blankets.

"Am I too big to be on your lap?" Juniper asked.

"You are not," Olive said. "At least, not for tonight."

On the brief journey to Mersea House, Juniper snuggled her head under Olive's chin and closed her eyes.

"Why is that?" Charlie asked. "That Billy's dad listens to you and Margery?"

"That story goes back a long way," Olive said. "Pauley was in our year at school, you see. Late one evening when we were fourteen, Margery and I had spent too much time talking to a couple of young fishermen at the harbor. We were running up Ferry Road to get home when we heard a shout and looked over just in time to see Pauley fall face-first into the model-yacht pond that's there just off the road. Too much cider, apparently. It can't be that deep, but he was flailing round like crazy. We ran over and dragged him out. He said he thought he was dying, that he'd seen his life flash before him, and we had saved him and he'd be forever in our debt. Margery and I made a bit of a thing of it for a while, but then ordering him round got tiresome, and so we let it go. But he's always remembered."

★   ★   ★

At home again, Juniper lay in bed with the lamp on as Olive emptied the contents of the girl's fabric bag. First, she pulled out the two small, framed photos—George and Holly Wyckes.

"Why didn't I notice these gone when I looked in here for you?" she asked herself.

Juniper's latest sketchbook—she seemed to go through them quickly—was damp. Olive opened the cover and unpeeled the first page from the inside. It was a drawing of Mersea House with the impression of someone standing in the window.

"Oh, it's lovely," Olive said. "Who's that?"

Juniper giggled. "I need more practice with people. It's you."

The drawing swam in Olive's vision. "Oh," she managed to say, "but the seawater's got to it."

"Never mind," Juniper said. "I can do a new one tomorrow."

Olive kissed her forehead. "I'll look in on you before I go up to bed."

In the lounge, Hugh was waiting with a large brandy for her. After a drink, she sank down on the sofa next to Charlie.

"Dear God," she said.

"The misadventures of youth," Hugh said. "Abigail and Margery have filled me in."

"She had it mostly well planned, taking that jam sandwich with her," Abigail said.

"She won't need to run away again," Margery said.

Olive sat up. "Margery." She took another drink. "I want to talk with you about Juniper."

Charlie took Olive's hand. "We both do," he said.

"Good thing," Margery said, raising her glass to them, "because I want to talk with the two of you. But we can leave it for tomorrow, can't we?"

The others finished off their drinks and said good night, leaving Charlie and Olive.

"I'll go in and sit with her until she's asleep," Olive said. "Will you wait?"

"No, you go on, and I'll see you tomorrow."

They stood in a tight embrace, silent. After a moment, Charlie leaned his head back and looked at her.

"It's quite interesting having an eleven-year-old daughter."

"You just wait until she's fourteen," Olive said.

Charlie left and Olive went back to the Juniper's room. She was barely awake. Olive switched off the lamp, bent over her, and said, "I'll stay until you fall asleep—how's that?"

The girl raised up and put her arms around Olive's neck. "Good night."

★ ★ ★

"Olive. Olive."

Olive opened her eyes to Margery holding a cup of tea, whispering in her face, and shaking her shoulder lightly. She looked round and found herself still in the armchair in Juniper's room, her shoes kicked off and a kink in her neck. Daylight streamed in through the window.

"What time is it?" she whispered back when she saw Juniper was still asleep.

"Eight," Margery replied. "Come into the kitchen. I've started breakfast, and the tea is ready."

Olive got herself out of the chair and hurried out the door. "I'm behind my time," she said. "You should've come to wake me earlier. I don't know how I slept there all night."

"Here," Margery said, "take your tea upstairs and get yourself sorted."

"But the breakfast," Olive protested.

"I know how to cook porridge," Margery said.

"Yes, all right," Olive said, but as she took the stairs, she added, "you won't put any piccalilli in it, will you?"

Margery grinned. "I was ahead of my time all those years ago. Not even your Constance Spry has thought of that yet, has she?"

★ ★ ★

The entire town knew what had happened even, it seemed, before breakfast. Dawson sent over a half-dozen butter buns. Casper came early to see if he could fit an old pair of his daughter's shoes onto Juniper's calipers and to begin work on the pipes—the first step in adapting the tub. Margery stayed, letting Young Trotter open the shop. Billy appeared before school, out of breath, pushing an empty wheelchair in front of him.

"I went and woke up Mrs. Tees early and explained," he said, taking the slice of toast offered. "Now, I can push you round in it, Juniper, until you've got your calipers back."

"What a fine idea, Billy," Olive said. She had been about to telephone Mrs. Tees after breakfast herself. Olive liked the way the boy thought.

"Billy," called Hugh as the boy left, "*Earth vs. the Flying Saucers* on the Saturday matinee—you and Juniper are my guests."

"Flying saucers," Billy whispered in reverence. "Thanks, Mr. Hugh."

Charlie arrived after breakfast. Harold's wife was so overwhelmed with joy at the news he and Olive would be married—and moved by the tale of Juniper's rescue—that she insisted her husband give his cousin the day off.

"May I have a word with you two before I go to the shop?" Margery asked Charlie and Olive. She led them to the lounge and closed the door.

"Margery," Olive started first. "Charlie and I are going to be married."

"Congratulations," Margery said, and gave Olive a kiss on the cheek. "I hope you don't think that comes as a surprise? Anyone could look at the three of you and know."

"The three of us?"

"That you're already a family," Margery said.

"But she's your ward," Olive said, as if arguing with herself.

"And I love her, I truly do," Margery said. "I love her because George was her father and because she's a remarkable girl. But I don't love her as a mother should. Not as you do."

A sob caught in Olive's throat. Charlie put his arm round her shoulders, and she got hold of herself and said, "I don't know how it is, but from the moment we opened the door and I saw her for the first time, I felt as if I'd always loved her."

"Stop," Margery said, wiping a tear off her own cheek with the back of her hand. "I hope you'll remember that the first time she comes in after her curfew. And you too, Dad." She patted Charlie's arm. "I'm off now before Malc creates havoc in the shop." And she was gone.

"Malc couldn't create havoc if he tried," Olive said, pulling her handkerchief out of her pocket.

"You realize," Charlie said, "we've another person's approval to gain before we're at the finish line."

"As far as Juniper's concerned, I believe you and I crossed that finish line long ago. But let's go tell her and see."

Juniper was at the kitchen table, drying cutlery, and Charlie and Olive sat down with her. The girl's big chestnut eyes grew wide as they made their offer.

"It's what I wanted most in the world," she said. "I've never wished for something that's come true before, but now this has." She thought for a moment. "Maybe I should wish that I pass my eleven-plus."

"Hard study will get you that one, love," Charlie said. "And you've already proved it'll be no trouble, because you've caught up with your arithmetic. Now, I'm going over to Casper's. He's taken your calipers, and we'll see if we can get them in working order for a bit longer, until you get your new ones."

Olive carried on with her housework as if the world hadn't changed, although Hugh, returning with an armful of dahlias from Mrs. Wilkins, did catch her in the lounge, with the volume on the wireless turned up and doing a dance with the Hoover as her partner.

Abigail kept an eye out for first the morning post, then the afternoon post, saying she was expecting a letter. Juniper spent the day drawing and reading and waiting for Billy, who turned up as soon as he could after school to take her out.

"You won't go too fast when you push Juniper, will you?" Olive asked as she tucked a blanket over the girl's legs.

"Oh no, Miss Olive, not too fast."

Billy made a show of a stately departure as they set out for a stroll down the Parade as far as the pier, to check on the bomb.

As they left, Olive heard Juniper say, "Guess what, Billy? I was right."

★ ★ ★

It was only at teatime that the day took a downturn when Geoff Markham showed up.

"Mr. Markham," Olive said with little enthusiasm when she opened the door. "Margery is—"

"Yes, yes, at the shop," he said.

"But please do come in." She led him to the lounge. "You know Hugh, of course, and this is Abigail Claypool, and this is Charlie Salt."

"Yes, hello, pleased to meet you," Markham said, sounding anything but.

"How do you do?" Charlie said.

"Markham," Hugh said with a nod.

"Pleasant journey?" Abigail asked.

"Yes, thank you."

"What can we do for you, Mr. Markham?" Olive asked.

"Well, I had hoped to . . . it's a surprise to see . . ." Markham bumbled through a few more starts before giving up.

"Margery isn't going back to London," Olive said.

At once Markham smiled, regaining his confidence. "Well, I know Margery too well to believe that. She's certainly not said as much to me, and until I hear her speak the words, I must disagree."

"Margery isn't going back to London."

Markham spun on the spot. Margery stood in the doorway to the lounge.

"There, I said it myself—and with witnesses. Do you believe me now?"

Markham's face fell. "But Margery . . ."

"I'm not going, Geoff." Margery used the sort of voice she had always reserved for people who were, as she would say, thick as two short planks. Olive thought Markham had better watch out.

"But Margery, I've done it. I've got the divorce—it's nearly ready to sign off on."

"Well, bully for you."

At that moment, there was a commotion in the kitchen. The swing door opened, and out came Juniper in the wheelchair being pushed by Billy. They were talking about the army on the beach, the crowd that had gathered, and how long the queue was at Hetty's tea hut. They stopped short when they saw the gathering in the lounge.

Markham looked at the new arrivals and gave a knowing nod. "It's the girl, isn't it, Margery?" He went out to the entry and dropped to his knees beside the wheelchair.

"Juniper, don't you want move to London, and Miss Margery and I become your parents?"

"No thank you, sir," Juniper said. "I live here. Miss Olive and Mr. Charlie are going to be my mum and dad."

"Are they?" He looked round the room, his eyes wide with astonishment.

"Tea?" Olive asked the room.

Markham stayed for tea, which Olive, for one, had not expected. He said little but listened to the conversation as if he'd only that moment noticed there were other people in the world.

Olive had just gone to the kitchen for a second pot of tea and the spare seedcake when Mrs. Wilkins stopped in with Miss Binny in tow. Today, the pheasant tail appeared in no mood to bob a greeting and sat stoic and silent atop the hat.

"Come in," Olive said, "both of you."

"Well, and here's a happy household," Mrs. Wilkins said when Olive led them into the lounge. "You're looking quite yourself, Juniper."

"Thank you, Mrs. Wilkins."

Hugh jumped up and brought in two dining chairs. Everyone settled, and several conversations broke out.

Mrs. Wilkins turned to Olive. "I've come to have a word about the August garden tea," she said. "I've asked Connie to help, you see. I thought she might collect the shilling at the gate."

"Remember, Nancy, I haven't said yes," Binny declared. "I won't be dragooned. It isn't the sort of activity I'm terribly accustomed to."

"What?" Mrs. Wilkins asked, "talking to people?"

"You see," Binny said to Olive, "that's just the sort of thing I mean."

At that moment, Abigail said something, and Binny turned away. Mrs. Wilkins leaned in to Olive. "She'll come round."

Margery stood. "I'd best get back to the shop before closing. Lovely to see you, Geoff. I'm sure Hugh will show you out."

"Margery," Abigail said.

"Yes, thank you for that reminder, Abigail—I'd almost forgot. Olive, I just wanted to say that we have a new lodger."

"For the August holidays?" Olive asked.

"No, a permanent lodger," Margery said.

Abigail smiled. "It's Mr. Wiggan."

"Oh, how lovely," Olive said.

"He told me he didn't want to wait another thirty years before he visited again," Abigail said. "But don't worry, he isn't arriving until tomorrow."

Margery had yet to leave when Charlie and Casper arrived with Juniper's calipers. Olive went off to the kitchen, and Charlie followed her.

"I hope they aren't all staying to dinner," Olive said, halfway wishing they would. "I forgot to put in a grocery order this morning. I may have to send you out for fish and chips."

"I doubt anyone would begrudge you a night off cooking," Charlie said. He put his hands on her hips.

Olive rested her arms on his shoulders. "How will you feel about living at the top of the house?"

"Come to think of it, I've never seen your room." Charlie pulled her close. "I don't suppose we could go up now and have a look—do you think anyone would notice?"

Olive heard a knock at the front door but decided she'd rather stay where she was. In a moment, the swing door pushed open, and Margery looked in.

"Olive, Mr. Wiggan has arrived."

ACKNOWLEDGMENTS

Thanks to all who saw the potential in this story for their guidance, suggestions, and assistance, especially my agent, Christina Hogrebe of the Jane Rotrosen Agency. At Alcove Press, thanks goes to my editor, Tara Gavin, and to Melissa Rechter, Madeline Rathle, and Rebecca Nelson, who helped shepherd this book to publication. I appreciate my writing group—Kara Pomeroy, Louise Creighton, Sarah Niebuhr Rubin, Tracey Hatton, and Meghana Padakandla—more than they probably know. Loving thanks to family and friends who always ask, "How's the book going?" and then nod as if they understand the gibberish that comes out of my mouth.

I was inspired by the stories of the many people who survived polio and shared their own memories in A Summer Plague: Polio and Its Survivors (Tony Gould) and Paralysed with Fear: The Story of Polio (Gareth Williams). Children's Homes: A History of Institutional Care for Britain's Young (Peter Higginbotham) provided invaluable background information. It's all stellar material, and any mistakes about the homes, adaptive equipment, and the aftereffects of polio are my own.

Southwold is a real place, but this is a work of fiction—historical fiction, at that—and so I have taken certain liberties about the town. Still, you may recognize the Parade when you visit.